Border Brothers

MARGARET COOK

PUBLISHING

Published in 2017 by MKRY Publishing

ISBN Paperback: 978-0-9931698-4-7
Ebook: 978-0-9931698-5-4

A CIP catalogue copy of this book can be found
in the British Library.

Published with the help of Indie Authors World

IndieAuthors
World

Dedication

To all my teachers at Edinburgh Medical School in the sixties who taught the practice of compassionate medicine.

Also available by this author

A Bit On The Side

Acknowledgements

I would like to thank Dr Brian Moffat for the work he and his Group 'SHARP' have done in excavating and researching the Soutra site; I have used some of the medical details in this book. I am grateful to Kim and Sinclair of Indie Authors World for making this publication possible; to my editor Julie Fergusson for her patience and thoroughness; and to Steven Parry Donald for the photographs. Lastly, thanks to my husband Robin Howie for walking with me over the Soutra site, Lindean Gorge and surrounding landmarks.

Historical Note

The book is based on the story of Soltre Augustinian Abbey Hospital (now known as Soutra) on Fala Moor in the Scottish Borders.

With an international reputation for medical excellence, the Abbey came to a sudden, catastrophic downfall in mid-fifteenth century when a rogue Master was accused of various vague misdemeanours. Such behaviour, not unusual in senior churchmen of the time, seems an inadequate reason for such a comprehensive dismantling of the entire establishment.

Researching the surrounding events, it seemed to me as if much history had been expunged from the record, and the real story had been buried. 'Border Brothers' is my fictional reconstruction of Soltre's end.

Prologue

1455

To most of the folk who were drawn to Edinburgh's Newbygging Street market on that murky November morning, the day was special, a holiday. It was a release from the daily grind of work and with a free spectacle besides: a witch to be denounced by the Church, cast into the hands of the secular, then burned at the stake. There would be a bit of ceremony before the climax, some solemn processing, chanting and lamenting, but the fate of the victim was sealed. There was no possibility of reprieve; the conflagration would go ahead. The event had been widely broadcast by announcements from pulpits throughout Lothian and by notices in church porches, where the few who could read passed the message on to those who could not.

From an early hour people made their way down the cobbled lanes and wynds that gave onto the muddy marketplace, well wrapped against the penetrating cold, some even supplied with sacks of provisions. The best view and the greatest share of warmth were up for grabs, so a long wait was a fair price to pay. The marketplace, which had seen a few hangings in the past but seldom a burning, was sheltered from the worst of the wintry blasts by encircling stone-built houses and by the castle rock rearing up on the windward side, looming over the town at its feet.

As they chatted and waited, the faces of the assembled crowd were drawn to the far end of the marketplace where stood a freshly prepared pile of wood and peat faggots around a stake. Built high so that even those at the back could get a good view, the size of the pile ensured a good, long spectacle. To one side was heaped spare fuel, some wood, tar and more faggots. The job of the executioner was to ensure no part of the charred corpse remained to provide any collectors with relics or totems. Such items could become the focus for myths, miracles and cults, and could cause no end of trouble for the establishment. But most folk simply relished the drama. The height of the flames, the intensity of the heat, the noise of the crackling fire as it licked and consumed the accused and, above all, the writhing and shrieking of the witch herself would provide topics of discussion for weeks to come. In time, a raft of myths and legends, super-natural happenings, wraiths, omens and sinister spectral sounds would emerge, to weave into the fabric of the tale.

To one side of the stake, at a sufficient distance, a stand of wooden benches with an overhead shelter had been erected for the officiating clerics to sit. For the present, it was empty. The morning hours passed, and the marketplace became so full that people were forced to stand in the narrow side streets. Those who lived in houses facing onto the square leaned from upper windows, and many had invited parties of friends and neigh-bours in to share the view. The excitement built up to an atmos-phere of tense expectation.

Suddenly a bell sounded, echoing, repeated, ominous, while a frisson of murmuring arose from the crowd. Then a muffled roar grew as a drummer came into view, beating hollow units of time as he marched down Tollbooth Crescent onto the market square, followed by a young cleric bearing aloft the Inquis-itorial banner. A line of stately, black, slow-stepping figures appeared, guarded on each side by rows of soldiers. The digni-fied churchmen processed down the street to take their places in the stand according to rank. When they were all in place, the soldiers arranged themselves as a barrier between the crowd and the pyre, with much metallic clanking and imperious shoving. Others remained on guard around the clerics' stand. A nervous silence fell.

The rattle of chains was only momentarily audible before the crowd exploded, jumping in excitement and elation.

'Burn the witch!'

'Away with her!'

'Foul fiend of Hell!'

'Satan's whore!'

Only those at the front could see the terrified elderly woman, dragged along between the soldiers, dressed in filthy rags that barely covered her, bruises and sores visible on her legs, her hair long and greasy. The executioner, a large figure in black, wearing a hood covering most of his face, assisted the accused up the steps placed at the back of the stake. He then lashed the visibly shaking figure with ropes to the stake, where she stood with eyes closed and head bowed, hair hanging in clumps, the image of abject despair.

A stern-faced cleric stood up in the stand and held up an authoritative hand. Those at the front of the crowd turned and frantically hushed the craning heads at the back. Obedience was swift and silence quickly fell. Disjointed words wafting on the wind were all most of the crowd could catch: 'Sorceress... practitioner of witchcraft and the black arts... pernicious... dissolute... temptress... wanton... idolatress... consorter with devils... succubus... heretic...' The last was the most damning accusation, for it cut off all hope of salvation. The cleric then made a gesture of dramatic rejection and grief, which was the moment for the fire to be lit. The people immediately began to chant and shout, gradually working themselves into a frenzy of fury and hate, matching the billowing smoke and the spiteful crackle of the first flames. It was as well that the victim could no longer see the mass hatred in those eyes, as the smoke engulfed her in advance of the fire, for who would be able to bear such concentrated venom?

At this moment of heightened expectation and visceral blood-lust, no one noticed an old, bearded Grey Friar making his way through the throng to the very back of the crowd. He was furtive yet purposeful, his objective a woman standing with a boy of about ten or eleven, presumably her son. They were huddled together, trying to avoid notice, but noticeably haggard and tearful amid the holiday atmosphere. The Grey Friar's approach provoked a reaction of terror in the pair; the boy thrust the woman behind and faced the friar with a defiant expression. But they were caught between the milling crowds and a stone wall and there was nowhere to flee.

The friar opened his arms in a calming gesture, though his face expressed urgency. He came close so that only they could hear his hurried whisper.

'You must come away. Now. You are in danger – you especially, mistress. You must put your trust in me. Come, now, I beg you.'

'Why should we trust you?' challenged the lad, gulping down his nerves. 'Where will you take us?'

The woman, who had been weeping into her shawl, raised drowning, desperate eyes.

'I promised her I would stay to the end. I promised. I won't go. Not till it's over.'

'My daughter. It is over. She is dead.'

They looked at him, disbelieving.

'It is true. I was with her this morning, hearing her confession. I paid the executioner to shorten her anguish, to strangle her as the smoke arose and before the flames got to her. And I waited to see it done. God bless her soul and God forgive me.'

'Oh, thank God for that small mercy,' said the woman, and, turning to the flaming pyre, choked out, 'Mother, rest at last in peace.' She made the sign of the cross and dipped her head.

'Amen,' said the friar, casting uneasy looks around, for they were attracting some attention. 'Now let's go, for every minute counts. You may trust me, for I am in as much danger as you. The Inquisition is here, and as soon as all is over in this place, they will come looking for you.'

As the lad hesitated, the friar brusquely indicated the poverty of his garb, his stout stick and dilapidated shoes.

'Look at me, son. I am an outcast too.'

The woman showed herself willing to be shepherded, convinced by the frank manner of the friar. As they worked their way towards a narrow wynd, he drew another grey cloak from under his own and swiftly covered the woman, lifting the hood over her shawl.

'This will give you some measure of disguise. Keep the hood well over your face.'

Once away from the marketplace, the streets were unusually empty and the friar took the lead, looking around him at every twist, turn and corner. They made good speed, keeping to narrow alleys and following a tortuous route to the town boundary. Even then the pace did not slacken. The friar explained that he was heading for a hamlet to the west where he was known and where he could claim shelter and some food. They should put as many miles as possible between themselves and the authorities in Edinburgh, he said. Only then would he explain how he hoped to serve them. He would not allow them to walk on the main roads, but took them through woods, across country, along cattle tracks and through shallow streams. Every so often, he would stop and look behind.

'I'm sure we are not being followed,' he said eventually. 'We can rest awhile; it has been rough and hasty going.'

'We are not going in the direction of home,' said the lad challengingly.

'No. That is the first place they will look for you.'

'Why now? Why didn't they take us before? And what have we done to offend them?'

'My son, the Inquisition is involved. They are obsessed; they slaver for victims. Anyone who associated with a condemned heretic, who was sympathetic to her, or even took a cure from her, is tainted with heresy in their eyes.'

'Mother has not given her cures to anyone for years, not since... But why are you endangering yourself, helping us?' asked the woman.

'I am already cast adrift,' said the friar with a wry smile. 'Simply by shriving your unfortunate mother, hearing her confession, I am condemned as impure. An associate of undesirables. They could, if they chose, accuse me of heresy too. But I have long been under suspicion simply by keeping strictly to my vow of poverty. The Church establishment is deeply hostile to that practice.'

He laboriously got up on his feet, easing his stiff limbs. 'Come. I think we should be on our way. We'll talk further when we rest tonight.'

Some hours later, with the dark hindering their progress and their pace slowed to a weary stumble, the friar indicated a small homestead ahead: a few humble, flimsy cottages with byres attached. The travellers were kindly received and accommodated in an outhouse, with bannocks, cheese, ale and, best of all, some hot porridge. The shelter, hay and proximity of a couple of cows provided warmth and a sense of comfort.

The woman, who had been nibbling and drinking sparsely, deep in thought, said, 'Father, you said you heard my mother's confession. Does that mean that she will go to heaven?' She looked at him imploringly.

'Daughter, I am sure of it. She was a good woman and did not deserve such a way of dying.'

'How do you know she was a good woman?'

'I knew her a long time ago. She was very special, the best, caring and loving to all around her. I knew you too, mistress, as a young girl. And I knew this young man's father. I was at Soltre with him for many years. If I had not known who you all were, I should have recognized him, for the likeness is astonishing.'

The woman looked at him wonderingly for a few moments.

'You knew my father?' asked the boy.

The friar nodded sadly. 'Yes, I knew and loved him as a son. That is why I am here. I will take you to a place where you are outwith the punitive reach of the Church, and where there are kin, close kin, to receive and love you for his sake. And on the way, I will tell you the story of who he was and his part in Soltre's downfall. But it is late and we have an early start. Enough of revelations and emotions for one day. We should get some sleep.'

Part 1

Chapter 1

1423

The day they brought the injured boy to Soltre was stormy, blustery and raw, but no more so than usual on those bitterly cold moors that formed a border between England and Scotland. There was no special climatic omen to which people could look back, pretending they always knew there was something unearthly and portentous about his coming. There was nothing of the harbinger about this thirteen-year-old lad, wounded in combat and likely to die before achieving mature masculinity, as were so many in those brutal, lawless lands.

In the top room of the abbey gatehouse, the watchman, whose sole job was to look out for all arrivals from the road, had wearied of his game of chuckie stanes. His heated stone had long given up every shred of warmth. Sighing massively with tedium, he reckoned his shift must surely be nearly over; it must be time to look forward to a warming meal of broth and bread in the kitchen, a mug of ale and a good sleep in the hay back in the servants' quarters. He would be glad, in a few days' time, to change his duties for a stint in the stables. Right now he could do with some animal warmth and company. He was weary of solitude and idleness; with darkness falling, few would be out on the roads. If there were any at this time of day, they would certainly stop over at Soltre, the only hostelry for miles on this major thoroughfare.

Walt heaved himself out of his chilly inertia and back to his post at the window. Peering northward into the swirling and keening gloom, no shadows impinged on his vision. He was not imaginative or unduly sensitive, not prone, like some, to see wraiths and spectres, ghaists and bogles in the swirling mists.

He turned his gaze southward. Paused. Peered. Was there or was there not...? He squinted and focused. Yes, there was a party coming. His sharp ears could even make out the measured walking pace of horses, muffled by the fog. Lucky he had got up when he did, for the brothers were strong on hospitality, and if he did not give due warning he might be punished for his neglect. Leaning out of the window, he hollered, 'Party coming!' then leapt to the door of the tower room and repeated the message in a booming voice, which bounced and echoed off the spiral staircase walls. There came the instant sound of movement from below, lights flared and a chain of voices like dominoes spread the message to all corners. Someone called up, 'How many? On foot?' Back at the window it was clear now that there were some five or six mounted – well mounted – and a litter. That meant either a high-born lady or a sick person. Behind by a short distance was a small train of probably sumpter mules and attendants.

'Mounted party, six and a litter, and baggage,' he yelled mightily to the window below and again down the spiral stairs. Where all had been silent, now all was bustle and lights. He heard the sound of footsteps on the spiral stairs. In came two servants, James from the infirmary and Dick from the travellers' hostel. They leaned out the window and tried to see the approaching strangers.

'Your eyes are keen, pal,' said James.

'My eyes are taught by hours sitting here in the dark,' Walt grumbled.

They heard the creaking and rattling noise of the mighty gates opening, and saw the gloom dispelled by crackling torches as a welcoming party of assorted servants and two brothers assembled far below. 'Let's get down there. Good on you for spotting them. See you later, pal.' They were off, chasing down the stairs with youthful agility, pausing to give the relief watchman space to trudge up past them.

After handing over to the relief, Walt lumbered clumsily down the stairs, stretching his limbs, stiff with cold. He looked heavenwards with a conspiratorial air, grateful that some higher guardian had nudged him in time, and sketched out a cross sign on forehead, shoulders and chest. Sending thanks both for something of interest to liven up the end of his shift, and for saving him from being caught daydreaming. The courtyard – the abbey garth – was alive with activity centred on the travellers, who were, judging by their garments, noble and on military business. Walt recognised the Douglas insignia.

'Holy Mary,' he muttered. 'Real high heid yins.' Himself insignificant and off-duty, he stood staring at the horses – fine beasts, up to the hocks in splattered mud – and hoping for a glimpse of a classy lady stepping down from the litter, a rare enough spectacle for the likes of him. But then he noticed the unmistakably huge, burly figure of Brother Peter, the infirmarer, attending on the person within and judged it was probably a person ailing, most likely injured and therefore a man. He was also aware that the kitchens would be running full tilt to supply the travellers' empty stomachs, and that he had better stake his own claim as soon as he could. Moreover, everyone seemed to be busily scurrying to and fro, and while idling he was in some danger of being sent on an errand; impossible to refuse, for in this world the needs of guests came before all else. Walt at that moment put his own comfort well before either kindness or curiosity, and he hastened away into the shadows, feigning a preoccupied air and avoiding authority, in the direction of the kitchens.

If he had stopped a little longer, he would have seen a young man being assisted from the litter, politely refusing to be carried into the hospital. Wrapped in an assortment of furs and cloaks, little could be descried of his person. After he had been tactfully helped towards the infirmary doors, the crowds soon melted away, the horses led off to their stable comforts and the men conducted to the best of the travellers' rooms in the guest hostel, where they could freshen up before tasting the finest meat and wine Soltre could provide. Which, as the Douglas men knew, was as fine as any in the land.

After centuries of practise at providing sustenance to all road users on this major highway, the brothers were masters at identifying the precise position on the social scale of their guests. They were accustomed to entertaining royalty and all lesser shades of societal brilliance. Many times they'd had whole armies camped on the doorstep, expecting provender as well as pastoral care. Long years ago they had tried to escape from the world, in keeping with the teaching of their founder, St Augustine, but the world kept coming to them and making its urgent demands. This late arrival had them all on their toes, for a Douglas contingent was second only to royalty itself, a mighty clan, dominating the western marches and scarcely answerable to even the king and his regent. But Brother Peter's immediate concerns were for the ailing boy committed to his care, whose appearance, even when still covered with rich cloaks, gave cause for concern.

'What is your name, young sir?' he asked with due deference, while ushering the boy between the pillars towards the enormous fire in the infirmary hall, as gentle as a woman, despite his size. The briefest of gestures and nods produced an army of underlings who stoked up the fire, turned down the covers of a nearby bed and, best of all, produced a goblet of warm, herby wine.

'I'm Fergus MacBeath,' said the boy. If Peter was surprised, he did not show it. The Highland name carried by a youngster in typical squire's garb was incongruous, but reinforced by the saffron colour of his silk shirt, a hallmark of Highland aristocracy. Fergus sank with an involuntary sigh of relief into the chair offered, now with his cloaks peeled away. He accepted the wine with a shaky hand and drank deeply. Peter hovered, a still, authoritative presence. Sending the servant away with the empty wine cup, he squatted on a stool, half facing the boy so as not to be too intimidating.

'In what way can I serve you, Master MacBeath?' he enquired. 'Your lord, Sir Colin Douglas, mentioned an injury in the chest? Some weeks old? Do you have pain anywhere? May we take a look, if you are ready?' He observed the slender, coltish body and limbs, the straight, sandy red hair, the grey eyes; the whole person nearer boy than man. With practised deftness and motherly confidence, Brother Peter assisted the weary boy onto the nearby couch, gently unbuckling and removing his outer garments down to the fine linen underclothing, which he left, knowing the exquisite shyness of teenage lads. Between them they uncovered the left side of Fergus's chest. While performing this tender service, Peter had been making a professional inventory of signs and observations: evidence of recent weight loss; a mild feel of fever on the skin of the neck; a faster pulse rate than normal; a withdrawn expression which suggested a degree of pain unacknowledged; blue, cold fingertips. The boy was shivering in spite of the fire. Lastly, a musty smell assaulted his nostrils, and Fergus's too, for he turned his head away, wrinkling his nose in fastidious disgust.

Heavily soiled dressings, encrusted with yellow-brown material, were bandaged in place over the chest wall and under the left armpit. Two servants hovering in the shadows came forward with implements and warm water, ready to assist in removing these. Underneath became visible a diagonal scar, partially healed, which ran down the chest wall for about a handspan, overlying the ribs which were faintly visible under the skin. Two thirds of the way down, the skin was red and inflamed where the scar had not healed. A small aperture with swollen lips oozed yellowish matter, the source of the noisome odour. Peter perched on his stool and observed for a few minutes. He gently pressed the surrounding skin, curiously soggy to the touch, and murmured instructions to a servant to prepare some warm salty water and soaked sphagnum moss dressing. Meanwhile, he probed for the story, but the boy was too weary to tell him much. After washing the wound and applying the green fragrant moss, he gave Fergus another cup, which had appeared as if by magic.

'This is wine with some medicine in it, young master. It will give you the best sleep you've ever had. We'll talk more in the morning. With your leave, I'll get the story from your young lord?'

Fergus nodded assent, dutifully drank the potion and sank back thankfully on the couch.

After giving the servants some instructions, Peter left the hall and crossed the expanse of garth, wrapping his heavy black cowl around him and flipping up his hood, for the night was raw with penetrating cold even within the shelter of the immense abbey buildings. He strode over to the guest hostel, where he was reasonably sure Sir Colin would still be found. Brother Peter guessed Sir Colin and his entourage liked their wine and victuals and would not leave the table for some time yet. And indeed, inside the hall the group were already relaxed and merry, guffawing and chaffing and toasting one another. As Peter approached, one of the company stopped short in the middle of a scurrilous tale, but he merely smiled and signalled to a servant for a cup of wine for himself. At the head of the table Peter espied Sir Colin Douglas, one of the sons of that great dynasty; a young man of sinewy, athletic build, short dark hair and rather scanty beard. He would be in his twenties, but carried himself with the assurance and arrogance of the well born and well connected. His face was narrow; a bit mean and sly, Peter thought.

Peter drew up a seat with an expression of cheerful courtesy. 'May I take a quick drink with you, Sir Colin? I won't disturb your relaxation after your arduous travels for more than a few moments.' Sir Colin moved a little to allow the canon a place to sit, though he did not look overly delighted. Peter continued, 'Your young friend Master Fergus is exhausted and cannot give me a coherent story of his injury. Otherwise I would not dream of troubling you tonight. Can you tell me how he came by it?'

His guest sighed, then drawled with ill-concealed boredom, 'He was wounded in a skirmish. A lance in the side, just a flesh wound, nothing serious we thought at the time.'

'Did he have no armour on?'

Sir Colin gestured at his empty cup. Brother Peter signalled to a servant who came in haste to fill it.

'Actually, no. Fergus has only been my squire for about half a year. He's of exceedingly good family, you know, though unfortunately… ill gotten. His problem is he can't sit a horse well. It's not a skill Highlanders hold much store by. Anyway, we had to give him a rush course in riding and fighting astride, and he learned fast enough. But my father wanted us patrolling the marches, for there are always English ruffians who need to be shown their place. So we took ourselves off, and Fergus came, but too soon for him to be able to manage armour on horseback. That takes years of practice. Apart from a bascinet and shield he only had leather. And because he couldn't restrain his mount and stay well back as I told him, he was in the thick of it, wounded and unhorsed in his very first fight. Just as well he had no armour or he would never have risen again. He has guts. He told me the wound was not serious.'

Sir Colin paused to drink. 'Did he have no medical attention at the time?' asked Peter.

'No. There was not much bleeding. He's from a medical family himself.'

'I recognised the surname.'

'So we thought he'd physic himself. He said little more about it till about a month ago. Said the wound wasn't healing. I thought he was being a milksop, didn't pay any attention. I thought he couldn't stand the pace. We live quite rough in the field.'

Peter nodded politely, gazing at the depredations the hungry gathering had made in the feast set before them.

'When we came to Langholm Priory, moving north, Fergus asked the monks there for advice. They made a fuss, said he should come here for the best medical attention. But he said he couldn't ride this far. The monks lent us this litter for him and it really slowed us up. Took us two whole days. He really would have been better mounted.'

Peter knew how uncomfortable travel in a litter was, and no longer wondered at his patient's extreme exhaustion. Two days from Langholm was a fast pace even for riders. He could imagine the suffering Fergus had endured in the jolting vehicle, and with unsympathetic company.

'So what's to do? Can you fix him?'

Peter paused, thinking how best to put his patient's case.

'You must leave him with us. He's sicker than he looks. He has been too plucky, he should have asked for help sooner. There has to be a reason why his wound is not healing. I don't know why yet. It may take a few days to find out; it may take a lot longer. We may never find out.'

'He's in danger then?'

'Maybe. He may have some grumbling illness that under-mines his capacity to heal. We don't know. He has fever and a dirty wound, and these need urgent attention.'

Sir Colin actually looked relieved, no doubt pleased to shuffle off his responsibility. 'We'll be away the morn in that case. No sense in biding here to see if he can come on in a day or two from what you say. Many thanks, brother. Tell him I'll drop by before we're off tomorrow.'

Brother Peter arose, aware that he had been dismissed by this stripling lordling. He took himself off to his own more modest supper, before attending compline in the abbey church.

Chapter 2

By the next morning Fergus was looking more like a survivor, Peter was pleased to see. He was well rested.

'I haven't slept like that in weeks,' he told Peter with a faint grin. 'The last two days have been murder. I hope to never, ever be inside a litter again. I'd rather have walked here.'

When he heard he was to stay in the care of the infirmary staff, his relief was touchingly visible.

'What did you give me in that wine last night?' he asked. 'If it's not a professional secret.'

'Not at all. It is a mixture of opium poppy, black henbane and hemlock.'

'Heavens! No wonder I slept. Is that not a dangerous brew?'

'Yes, in the wrong doses and careless hands. You know something of herbs, Master Fergus?'

'Yes, my people are physicians in the Western Isles.'

'But you have chosen a knightly career instead?'

'I thought I'd give it a try. Now I'm not so sure.' He gave a shy smile and briefly made eye contact.

Probing, Peter said, 'You may get your enthusiasm back once you are on your feet again.'

'Mmm. It's possible.'

At that moment, the tranquil atmosphere in the infirmary hall was disturbed by a loud voice, banging doors and clattering spurs. Sir Colin Douglas, followed by his gang of attendants, strode in, brushing aside the protests of the servants. With brash bonhomie, he greeted Fergus.

'Well, lad, aren't you the lucky one. We've to take to horse again in these vile conditions while you sit in state by the fire.'

Fergus had begun to struggle to his feet, but Peter gently restrained him, hand on shoulder.

'As you see, I'm under orders,' said Fergus. 'Do you go immediately?'

'Yes, we've a few groaning heads and livers here that need shaking up after last night's hospitality. Master Infirmarer, are the roads to the west any better than those we travelled yesterday?'

'A great deal worse, my lord, once you get beyond the lands of Soltre. We maintain our own roads, but not those beyond our boundaries.'

Sir Colin's face was scornful. 'Who ever thought of building an inn and hospital on this wild and sodden moor? Our horses struggled on this boggy terrain. One is lame and will have to be left.' He turned to Fergus. 'By the by, your lady mother is in residence not far from here. Galagate, I believe. Maybe she'll visit you. That would be a reason to delay us, eh lads?'

He chortled, turning with a knowing air to his followers, who dutifully laughed and nudged each other.

Fergus's face closed and became set. There was an awkward pause. Then, with dignity, Fergus lifted his chin and repeated, with coldly emphasised politeness, 'Where do you go from here, my lord? To Neidpath Castle?'

'Yes, there today, then on to Thrieve to report to my father. You'll send your duty to him, of course?'

'Yes, of course, if you please. And my regrets for my inadequacies.' Fergus glanced up briefly, shooting a hostile look through his sandy eyelashes.

After the midday dinner, Peter and the medicus, Brother Malcolm, usually met to discuss matters relating to their patients. Malcolm had not been seen since the previous evening, having been called to the aid of a young village woman having a catastrophic post-partum haemorrhage. Then Peter saw him striding across the garth. He looked composed enough, but Peter knew the likelihood of a good outcome was low.

'How are they?' he asked, examining his friend's demeanour.

'The child is fine. Mother is still alive, mirabile dictu. But very weak. This is when I get so frustrated; if she were a farmer with an injury we could have her in the infirmary and give her constant care. But... Well, you know the rest. I'll mention her to Father John, but you know he won't step too far out of line with Church policy. It was ergot that finally stopped her bleeding. And I gather I've missed some excitement. You've had a contingent of the Douglases here!'

'Yes, bringing an injured squire. I need to discuss him with you. There's a problem, it's not straightforward.'

Peter loved a challenge and was already devising ways to address the impasse of the unhealed wound. As they sauntered through the cloisters, deep in conversation, they were joined by the magister of Soltre, Father John, whom they greeted reverently. It was unusual for them to see him around at this time of day, for his duties were onerous and extensive, keeping him office-bound more than he liked. He wore the same black wool tunic, scapular and cowl as the other brothers on ordinary occasions, and was not imposing in his physique, as Peter was, but John had considerable presence.

'We were just heading for our daily medical communion in the parlour, father,' Peter decorously joked.

'Indeed, I knew exactly where to find you,' said John affably, walking between the two men with a hand lightly resting on the shoulder of each. 'I come to join you, if I may. We have a very interesting and unusual visitor, I hear, in the infirmary. I'd like to know the background, for I may be called upon to talk on his behalf with kin and others. Maybe you could brief me.'

They turned into the parlour, a room slightly less austere than the rest, with wooden chairs facing a small fire. Over the fireplace hung a large plain cross. Father John settled himself, then the other two respectfully sat down.

'Firstly, let me tell you the news from my outside informants,' said Father John. 'There have been no new reports of the Great Pestilence since those few in Leith last week. I fear they were dealt with as ruthlessly as ever. And no reports of lepers on the roads.'

'Since you raise the topic of patients to whom we do not allow admittance, father, may I again raise the subject of women?' asked Malcolm. He briefly told the story of the young mother and her dire complication of childbirth.

'Malcolm, it grieves me sorely, and I respect your compassion. But you know my hands are tied. We do not admit cases of pestilence and leprosy because we cannot help them, and they would do immense harm within our community. And with regard to women, the thinking of the Church is still that they are a source of sin and potential harm to the community here.'

'The belief that if women get into trouble in childbirth it is due to sin on their part, and they must thole the consequences, that is not, should not, be modern thinking,' replied Malcolm. Peter shifted uneasily; one did not normally speak to the father so brusquely. But Father John listened quietly. 'After all,' continued Malcolm, 'the equivalent for men is getting wounded in battle, and no one would suggest that that is due to their own wickedness. Our reputation here at Soltre was built on our treatment of the wounded in the ancient battles between England and Scotland.

'The Pestilence gave us proof that sickness is not due to sin! When it first struck in the south some seventy years since, it was called the English Pestilence, and we said they had brought it on themselves – until it came north and struck us here! The obvious passage of that disease by proximity and contact, its random affecting of whole populations, indiscriminate between rich and poor, high and low, priest and peasant, was a revelation, changing our ideas of the cause of sickness. And we must extend this change to our attitude to women.'

Father John listened attentively, but looked uncomfortable. 'You are right, Malcolm, I know. I agree, fully. But official doctrine is slow to change. It does not like to admit it has been wrong. As you know, we have recently agreed that for you to treat women outside the abbey is acceptable, and even to have them join the queues in the morning clinics in the garth is allowable. But even that could easily be challenged by our bishop. We are protected here by our long reputation for excellence, as you know. We even have renown overseas, as both of us know from our university days.

'But Bishop Wardlaw's own University of St Andrews still teaches the old doctrine: that sickness is due to sin and due repentance is the surest way to cure. And he won't change until the Vatican does.

'Meanwhile, I believe with my whole heart that Soltre is a great force for good in a wicked world, and I will not take any steps that might undermine it. We shall proceed step by step, Malcolm.' He paused and lifted both hands in a supplicatory gesture. 'I do believe that the solution lies ultimately with women themselves. They need education. This needs to start at village level. There are prejudices to be overcome, not least among the parish priests. Educated women nowadays often go into nunneries, where they are not often motivated to help their own secular sisters. Our influence could best be used in getting girls to attend schools. It would be a start. I'll put it on the agenda for chapter meeting today, Malcolm.'

Father John looked at Peter. 'Let's talk about this newcomer, the wounded squire. There must be some strange history here, if he's a Highlander?'

'Yes,' said Peter. 'The young squire to Sir Colin Douglas, who arrived last night, is a member of the Highland clan MacBeath. It is the famous name of an extraordinary medical family. MacBeaths have been doctors to Scottish kings and royalty ever since Robert the Bruce. They have also been close to the Lords of the Isles; maybe still are.'

Brother Malcolm sat forward with raised eyebrows.

'Now I know, from what he said, that this young man, Fergus, is indeed a member of that family,' continued Peter. 'But I also picked up, from something his lord dropped, that he is... a natural son. There was also a snide allusion, very cruelly made in front of the boy, that his mother is a flibbertigibbet. I do not yet know how this illegitimate youth, himself seemingly a sensitive and intelligent twig of a cultured, clever family, comes to be cavorting about the countryside, armed to the teeth and looking for trouble, with thugs of the Douglas persuasion. I do believe he is now questioning it himself.'

Father John raised his hands in mock horror and put his finger to his lips in gentle admonition at the unflattering allusion to the Douglas clan.

Peter grinned and ducked his head in apology. 'He was injured at the first clash of arms they encountered, predictably. He was hopelessly unprepared. He may be an expendable embarrassment to someone, I suppose. Certainly to the Douglases, who could not offload him quickly enough and make their escape.

'But more important is what we can do for him. He seems a good, reverent Catholic, has been confessed and absolved. He has a suppurating wound in the chest, grumbling on and now causing his general health to decline. I need to ask my colleague here to review and apply his greater experience to the matter.'

John nodded, absorbing the details of the human problem. He turned to Malcolm with a gesture, inviting him to share his thoughts.

'I know the name MacBeath very well indeed,' Malcolm responded. 'Any medical man in Christendom would know it. They are a truly astonishing family, with undoubted skills and wisdom. Many tales and myths abound, but there is no doubt about their gifts in healing. Nor do they hold on to their knowledge jealously; they have enquiring minds and travel abroad to exchange views and cross-fertilize, as it were. They are indeed attendants on the Lords MacDonald of the Hebridean islands. I believe the head of the family MacBeath dwells on the small island of Islay, where the Lords have their headquarters. Being so close and so indispensible to the country's elite has been their talisman, keeping them above political brawls, drawing them into that circle by marrying above their station. Are you certain this lad is of their ilk, Peter?'

'Yes, and he showed knowledgeable interest in the medicines I gave him,' Peter rejoined. 'Why should he be in company with the Douglas warlords, do you suppose?'

'The Highland clans' reputation for ferocity and fighting is, after all, what they are chiefly known for,' said Father John. 'It is not surprising if this young blade has inherited a taste for blood. It does not preclude a taste for other, better things. Highlanders, like the Irish, are great storytellers; they love music and poetry, books, education. I've met some of them in France. All this sounds astonishing to those who only think of them as brawny, hairy, half-naked warriors.

'I shall visit the lad if he's well enough. Peter, I'll task you with finding out more about the background. He may be MacBeath on his mother's or his father's side. Find out who the parents are. There must be some of his clan who are concerned about him, else he would not have been placed as a squire so prestigiously. Quite apart from his own welfare, there may be good contacts to be made out of this stranger who has come for our help. I'll go to him now.'

The magister arose, the others too, and all bowed politely as Father John smiled benignly and glided purposefully away.

Malcolm instantly relaxed and slouched down into his chair. He turned his toes up to the fire. 'I must catch up on sleep,' he said, rubbing his eyes. 'But first I must arrange for some sea kelp for my poor wee mother. And come see this young lad of yours. Did you hear father's words? He's looking for the next medicus while I'm still in my prime! And I sense there's something of an omen here – the MacBeath family is one that is steeped in the old Celtic traditions of matriarchy. They have female doctors and are experts in childbirth. They are more objective than our Church allows us to be, more in line with oriental practice. Maybe this youngster will be the link I'm looking for. Don't you think this is an answer to our prayers?'

'Maybe,' said Peter. 'But we have to save him first. Let's go now and look at this intractable wound.'

Chapter 3

I n spite of the best efforts of the team to sanitise the foully leaking wound, Fergus became weaker by the day. Those days slid by as beads on a rosary, days became weeks and still no change occurred for the better. He was a model and obedient patient, but apathetic and weary. He ate little. Malcolm was convinced that there was deep contamination in the wound, but probing with metal instruments caused pain and no benefit. Peter experimented with hollow plant stems and eventually devised a tube out of a folded rush leaf, inserted it into the aperture and instilled salt water, washing out pus and debris. They gave the lad small doses of medicated wine to dull the pain. This seemed the best plan so far, so Peter instructed one of his most trusted servants, Thomas, to perform lavage of the wound every four hours. With such regular sedation and the effects of the illness, they had found out no more about Fergus's background. He was withdrawn and unwilling to talk. Peter wondered if the boy had something dreadful on his conscience.

One evening at compline, Peter was standing in his usual place in the choir stalls with the other canons. The service was being led by Prior Richard, John's deputy, whose chanting voice was quavering and insecure. At the end of a hard day, Peter's responses were muted, his bowed attitude of devotion more to do with weariness than piety. In the winter, with the long hours of darkness, bedtime was early. With luck, four hours sleep, thought Peter, before the call to matins at midnight. He had missed his siesta as usual, too preoccupied with important things to do for other people. From this mixture of personal musings, and as he intoned by rote, '*In nomine Patris, et Filii, et Spiritus Sancti*,' Peter was somewhat guiltily distracted by a tug on his sleeve. He had a fleeting impression he was being reprimanded for not concentrating on the psalms and prayers, then realised he had been hovering in that noisy anteroom between waking and sleeping. The senior infirmary servant, Thomas, was beckoning, his eyes large as saucers. Peter, whose place was at the end of the row for just such an eventuality, slid from the pew and padded out after him.

Thomas led the way along the east cloister. The wind howled, so they hurried on without pausing to speak until they reached the shelter of the infirmary hall some distance beyond.

'Fergus?' asked Peter. Thomas nodded. At the boy's bedside, Peter found him looking surprised and a bit alarmed at this late visit. The wound was uncovered, for Thomas had been engaged in the last lavage of the day. He pointed to the aperture, bringing a crusie lamp near the boy's chest. Peter knelt down to peer closely. Squinting, he could just see a tiny fragment of off-white cloth protruding from the gaping mouth of the wound. Peter looked up at his colleague with a gleeful grin.

'As we thought!' he said. 'Now. Warm water, tweezers, basin, my lad. He's had some sedation? Good.' Once equipped, Peter sat on his stool and with the utmost patience and steady-handed delicacy, withdrew a piece of sodden, brown-stained linen about the size of a thumbnail from the wound. After close inspection and a little further pressing and probing of the aperture, he showed it with triumph to Thomas and to Fergus.

'That, my lads, is why this wound has not healed. The body is wise in its ways. Won't heal where there is foreign stuff lurking inside.'

'Is that a bit of my shirt? And will I get better now?' Fergus asked, showing more animation than for many days past.

'Well, yes, if that's all that's in there. But it's my guess there's more to come. More may make its way to the surface, or we may have to help it. It's good news; we have some answers and a direction to go in. Brother Malcolm and I will get our heads together tomorrow, as soon as there's good light.'

They thought the wound probably contained more torn linen and other matter, carried in by the point of the lance. They planned a small operation to open up the soft tissues and clean out any foreign matter, so that healing could proceed unimpeded. It was a bold decision, for the lad's condition was sadly weakened. Fergus seemed quite enthusiastic, a contrast to his former state of languid and depressed acceptance.

Preparations went ahead, all the infirmary staff abustle. Operations were not all that uncommon, though usually they were amputations, needed to save life. This time there was an atmosphere of excited optimism. Malcolm and Peter conferred over the wound site, discussing where the incision should begin and end, the direction of the weapon and the extent it would have reached under the skin. Fergus was given a richer mixture than usual of the herby wine. The dose was judged with an eye to his weakened state but also to the necessity of sparing him the stress of agony. Peter applied a local anaesthetic unguent made from pig lard and poplar buds with extracts of mandrake and nightshade.

While Malcolm held the now drowsy boy steady on his right side, Peter approached with rolled up sleeves, carefully washed hands and a surgeon's lancet, which he made sure Fergus could not see. After bowing his head for a moment in prayer, he carefully incised over the insensitive scar tissue, trying to open up the track of the lance. Malcolm leaned over, following the procedure, ready with advice. Working swiftly and deftly, Peter probed the tissues; not difficult as the boy was so thin. In no time he had extracted some more shreds of stained linen, some yellow threads of silk, and even a fragment of discoloured leather.

'Make absolutely sure there's nothing left,' Malcolm instructed. Fergus was still and uncomplaining, breathing steadily. Peter ran his fingers inside and outside the wound, and felt nothing out of the ordinary. He washed the site with warm water and sat back. He put gentle pressure on with a mossy sponge to stop the bleeding. He dabbed on a weak solution of ergot.

'Come and see. What do you think about closing up?'

Malcolm beckoned Thomas to take over as support, then came round to Peter's side.

'Looks good and clean. Also shallow. I think the best is not to close up; leave it uncovered, except when he's sleeping. Just a light covering at night so we can see if the exuding stops, whether anything else emerges, and check daily on healing.'

Fergus slept almost twice around the clock after his operation, under the watchful care of Thomas, James and others. The first thing he announced on waking was that he was starving. 'I can't remember when I last ate,' he said, puzzled. There was a new animation about him that delighted those around, including some of the other patients, who, unbeknown to him, had followed his progress with the keen interest of the old for the young. After his immediate needs had been attended to, Fergus was eager to get out of bed.

But getting up was not as straightforward as Fergus had expected. Even with the support of James and Thomas, he found his legs did not obey him, and his head went peculiar. He subsided, alarmed. 'Will I ever be able to walk again?' was his first reaction.

Peter smiled. 'Yes. And run, ride, swim and get up to mischief. It takes time. You've been bed-bound for several weeks.'

Both Peter and Malcolm, accustomed to the unpredictability of illness, were astounded at the transformation in Fergus. It was as if he had been resurrected from the dead, thought Peter, somewhat irreverently. His youthful spirit had been revived along with his improving health. The healing of the wound progressed by visible daily changes, needing no further intervention other than letting the air get to it. Fergus wore a loose linen shirt over his breeches, and gradually increased the amount of steps he took, first assisted, then alone. He felt as weak as water but his appetite was gargantuan. The perimeter of his world for some weeks past had been the fire on one side and a pillar on the other. The infirmary hall was divided by these massive columns in order to give the patients some measure of privacy. Only now did Fergus register that there were several other inmates in there, beside himself.

The splendid news of the young lad's progress spread rapidly around the gossip trail that linked the community at Soltre. Everyone was agog for news of him, partly because of his exotic origin in the Highlands, partly because of his link with the feared and revered Douglas clan, but mostly because of his youth. And as Fergus's own horizons widened and he came into contact with more people, all agreed that he was a lovely lad, polite, cheerful and comely – and most grateful for his salvation from an early grave. 'Let's hope Soltre hasn't put him together again only for him to rush off and break his head and bones in battle,' they agreed in the kitchens, where concocting recuperative recipes for the lad's restored appetite was just about keeping one cook in full-time occupation.

So far, no enquiry had been made about Fergus from the outside world. Peter was at last able to ask about his background with a view to contacting his family. Fergus, previously so withdrawn as to give the impression he was fey and not of this world at all, was willing to talk about himself with openness and frankness.

He explained that his MacBeath family had come originally from Ireland, sailing to Scotland in the train of an aristocratic bride destined for Angus Og MacDonald, Lord of the Isles, in the time of King Robert the Bruce. The MacBeaths' legendary medical skills were engaged by Lord MacDonald and then by the Bruce himself. Since then, all the kings of Scotland had appointed MacBeaths as their doctors. The present King, James I, held captive by the English since 1406, still had his MacBeath medical adviser with him, and so did his regent in Scotland, the powerful Robert, Duke of Albany.

Fergus's own mother, Catriona, was a MacBeath from Islay, where her father still attended the Lords of the Isles as physician-in-chief. Auburn-haired and bewitchingly beautiful, from an early age she had been intended for a prestigious marriage, to extend the family influence. To this end, she was conducted into society as much as possible. On one of her debutante trips, the blossoming Catriona thwarted all her family's intentions and formed a liaison with a fairly insignificant and not very wealthy knight, Sir Roger de Vere. The love match between them, being sealed by pregnancy, could go no further since Sir Roger already had a spouse and a daughter. The MacBeaths were sufficiently elevated in society for the situation to be retrieved. Baby Fergus was born in Islay and brought up by his grandparents there, where he kept the family name and grew in its rich soil of learning. Catriona left the island and continued her courtly life undaunted, soon making a suitably prestigious match with Sir Donald Dampierre, one of the king's legal advisers. Sir Roger de Vere was very attached to his love child, having no other sons, and visited him several times in his boyhood.

On one of his visits to Islay, Sir Roger found Fergus restless within the small insular community and wanting to spread his wings. Fergus had always been a willing scholar, accompanying his grandfather on medical visits and learning well the family herb-craft. He played well on the clarsach and could tell stories with panache. He was more of a bookish boy than a daredevil, though he liked sailing the wicker-and-skin coracles of the Isles, scrambling, wrestling and other boyish pursuits. So his island family were aghast when they discovered Sir Roger offering to place the lad as knight's squire in some highly placed family on the mainland; and horrified to learn that Fergus was keen on the idea. All that was really needed was for someone to take the lad on a trip abroad, to France maybe, where he could satisfy his adolescent yearning for adventure. But nobody thought of it, and the rash experiment was underway before Fergus began to realise just what he had undertaken.

The Douglas contingent thought of nothing but hunting, hawking and warfare. And wenching, of course. There was no conversation late into the night, there were no books, no poetry, no music. Fergus had prudently left his clarsach at home. As it was, his lack of horsemanship was a serious shortcoming. He had leapt on and off Highland garrons throughout his life, but the swift destriers and massive warhorses he now encountered were something different. He had been promised some hunting experience, for that was how most young knights learned to control their horses so skilfully, but he was starting later than the others, who had been riding and hunting from a very early age.

The thing that irked him most was his lack of status in Douglas eyes. He had been warned that he must earn his spurs, and expected to do so, but the reality was different. He had none of the skills needed to excel amongst the Douglases and was rated even lower than the other squires. And he was a virgin. They mocked him for that, but Sir Colin and the others took steps to rectify it. Fergus's first sexual experience was with a servant girl, a rite of passage that was conducted with his new companions in attendance, shouting encouragement, so it was lucky for him he did not fail. 'I had seen sheep and cattle do it often enough, so more or less knew what to do,' he admitted to Peter.

And worst of all, he had seen that the Douglas contingent with whom he rode were not honourable men in any way. He had expected to find them among the law-givers and maintainers of society, but it seemed that they mostly indulged their appetite for fighting and violence in many forms.

He had a brief moment of glory, when he was among the frontline men in the border attack on a group of English soldiery, but he was not supposed to be in front, and everyone knew that it was lack of skill rather than sheer reckless courage that caused his injury. He knew that one put a brave face on such things. But as his health and strength sapped away, he felt his status slipping further and further, till he was treated by his companions with mocking disdain. Whereas previously they had politely glossed over his irregular parentage, now they alluded to it slyly and often. It became a standing joke, and snide remarks about his mother's concupiscence too. This was gall and wormwood, and scarcely to be born. Fergus did not know how to handle it at all.

This story did not come out all at once, or indeed in quite so much detail, but was told by degrees. Brother Peter, who had seen much of the world's vanities, silently filled in one or two details, and was sympathetic.

'You won't go back with the Douglases, I presume?'

'No.'

The gist of the story was relayed to Father John, who had visited Fergus more than once in his decline. The brothers busied themselves writing letters on his behalf. However, no relatives of either the de Vere or the MacBeath families appeared in the following days. All the same, Fergus seemed full of a sense of carefree joy at this time, revelling in being the centre of attention and delighted with his restored sense of self-worth as well as well-being.

He had never questioned the religious faith that was a part of his life, but it had not been especially important to him. Some of his kin were bishops in the Isles and in Wester Ross, but he had not thought of the Church as a way of life for himself. But now?

Were the fates sending him a message? And were his soaring spirits an indication that he had made friends with his destiny?

'Where exactly is Soltre?' Fergus asked Peter. 'Are we really high up on the moors here?'

'Yes, it is built in the wild, but it is also on the main highway from England,' Peter said. 'On an ancient road heading due north for Edinburgh and Stirling. Any traveller caught out in bad weather up here would struggle to survive without this haven. Soltre was founded as an Augustinian abbey nearly three hundred years ago, and has seen plenty passers-by in that time, armies headed by kings included, armies stretching twenty miles from vanguard to tail. In those ancient wars, the canons did not take sides, and helped all who were in need. That is why we have so much expertise here in dealing with wounds like yours. And there have never been acts of depredation on Soltre, which is remarkable. Other abbeys not far away – Kelso, Melrose, Jedburgh – have all suffered assault in wartime. A retiring and defeated army often practices a scorched-earth policy, though sometimes holy places are spared. Soldiers are aware of being close to death and have heightened reverence for that reason.

'Nowadays the traffic is mostly non-military: people on state business, messengers, pilgrims, tradespeople. We are besieged every day by country people who come seeking our help. They come with anything from farming accidents to toothache. Chest complaints, joint pains, wame-ill, falling ill, fevers, scrofula, scurvy, colic, stone, worms. You name it. We can't always cure, but we can usually alleviate. Most of these are Soltre's own as they work on abbey lands.'

'Heavens!' said Fergus, impressed. 'I'd be interested to see what medicines you use for all those diseases.'

'When you are feeling a little stronger, you can certainly come and give a hand with our morning clinics.'

'Do you use bloodletting in fevers?'

'Not very often. But we do bleed the young canons regularly. Sometimes there are problems that arise between young monks closeted together in a community like this. They get urges that seem to be beyond their control. There can be disruption, passions aroused, quarrels, emotions. Bloodletting acts as a mild sedative.'

'I've never heard of that before,' said Fergus. 'Though my doctor relations do agree that bloodletting is often used lazily, just because it's expected. My family believes that nature is a great healer, and should be helped rather than hindered. They use the power of touch – you know, the laying on of hands. It seems to convey great benefits, though not everyone has the power.'

Peter was more and more impressed with the young man, his interest in matters medical and his compassion.

Chapter 4

Fergus, whose recuperation had been slower than he wished, was eager to explore the abbey and its surroundings. Peter decided he should ride a mule to spare his still-limited strength after some weeks, indeed months, of confinement. As they set off, Peter on foot, Fergus joked that he was glad none of the Douglas set could see him thus modestly mounted; knights were forbidden to ride mules. After viewing the various parts of the abbey, the trio emerged onto the quiet moorland. The sun beamed down from a clear, eggshell-blue April sky, and high above them a skylark fluted ecstatically. The mule's feet stepped delicately in the spongy, straw-coloured grass. They moved slowly along the rim of the moor, where it fell steeply away towards the north, to a plain of green and fertile farmland speckled by settlements and darker green woodland. There was a delicate scent of mingled gorse, pine, wet earth and thyme. In the distance, some twenty miles away, Fergus could see the shining waters of the Firth of Forth, and beyond that to the coast of Fife, with small hamlets at the water's edge, fine details visible through the pure air, clean after rain. Further still, he could see peaks of high mountains, still snow-capped, etched against the skyline. Over to the right, where the Forth flowed on to meet the sea, were the dark, pyramid shapes of the Bass Rock, Traprain Law and Berwick Law. Not that he knew the names of those striking landmarks, but Peter pointed them out. It was an awesome, breathtaking view. 'It's not often so clear as today,' said Peter. 'Usually there is a blanket of mist over the horizon. Drink your fill while you may.'

'It's one of the most beautiful views I've ever seen,' Fergus declared, deeply moved. It was like love at first sight; a fateful, defining moment. Just as Peter and John had hoped it would be.

'I'm glad to see water again, brother. I feel something's missing when I can't see the sea.'

'See how green the land is down there compared to the moorland up here. Most of the good farmland you see belongs to Soltre, and we rely on it for our produce. Up here on the moor, things grow more sparsely. Carts bring stuff up the hill every day for our needs, including imports from the coast there, providing our spices and ingredients for medicines. We get the first edge of the cruel wintry blasts up here, and the deepest snows, and the roads around are impassable, sometimes for weeks. We try to plan ahead and have our cellars well stocked. There have been winters when we have gone on half rations; the brothers first of course.'

'Do you grow your own medical plants and herbs?'

'Yes, some grow in the abbey garden. There's a small plot of bitter vetch that we grow in case of shortages in wintertime. The tubers can be chewed to ward off pangs of hunger. Many of our most important plants grow wild in a secret location, a deep gorge nearby, called Lindean. We must make sure that no sheep or other grazing animals can get in there.'

'I recognize a few things around here growing wild. I saw stonecrop on that wall back there. There's viper's bugloss, clover, tormentil. Shepherd's purse, St John's wort, heather and gorse. We get lots of that at home. We have stacks of wetland plants like yellow iris, willowherbs, rushes, marsh marigold.'

'And all those can be used for medicines,' said Peter, eyeing him thoughtfully.

'I'd love to see this Lindean gorge. Will I be allowed to go there?'

'Yes, of course, but maybe not now. You've done enough for one day. Let's head back.'

Chapter 5

In the cold, Spartan halls and stairways of Galagate Castle in the Scottish Borders, certain rooms were always comfortable, abundantly provided with fires, rich tapestries and elegant furnishings to obstruct any impertinent draughts, and strewn with thick, colourful rugs to protect delicate pink feet from the rough stone floor. These apartments belonged to the Lady Catriona Dampierre, now in the middle of her latest pregnancy. In spite of enforced immobility and aches in her belly and back, she was not prone to mope and complain, but set about ordering her minions to provide her with comfort.

Beside a blazing fire, a tub of water steamed invitingly. Set near the fire was a couch covered with furs, on which the lady lay on her side in superbly abandoned nakedness, clutching a mantle to her belly and breasts while her maid massaged her back. With her eyes closed and an expression of rapt concentration, she directed the therapy.

'Mmm, lower down now. To the right, more, more. Moira, I'm afraid your hands are too small and rough. Mary, you've got nice big hands, you wouldn't mind taking over for a bit? What an angel. I'm sorry to make you do something so beneath you, but I know you don't mind. Ahh, now that's more like it. Moira, check that water. Is it getting too cold? Fetch some more hot, will you? I'm so sore this morning, I can hardly move. I wish this brat would come soon.'

'You know your time is many months off yet, my lady. Perhaps it was not wise to walk out so far yesterday,' said Mary.

'Oh, I must get out, I'm so bored. I think each time gets worse. Anyway, I rode back.'

'I was horrified. You rode astride, too. You'd better not let Sir Donald hear that. I would get the blame for sure.'

'My dear, sweet Mary, it was a dumpy pony, most comfortable and sedate. Anyway, you know I would protect you from the wrath of Donald.'

'Not if you or the infant came to harm. I would be tossed away like an old shoe.'

With the departure of Moira for more hot water, Mary, Catriona's companion, became more at ease. Although she was titled Lady Mary Cathcart, she was a penniless widow and always addressed her ladyship formally unless they were completely alone.

'Mary, your massaging is doing wonders, but I long, I yearn, for a man's hands on my body. Why is it when one is so grotesque, so misshapen, the lust is as demanding as ever? I do look forward to having my body to myself again. I'm a selfish creature, Mary, and I don't really like this business of whelping. Donald will be home next week, but he treats me like fine china, and never gives me a good romp when I'm breeding. And what other man will help me out when I look like this?'

She sat up, and stretched like a cat, remarkably lithe. Her breasts hung in their fullness like autumn fruit, the nipples mahogany and enormous. Her belly was only just beginning to show a rounded shape, revealed as the silk cover slipped to the floor. Her skin glowed, her profuse auburn hair hung in free-flowing, curly disarray over her shoulders and back. She sat with legs apart, looked down with a complacent and uninhibited pride that belied her words, lifting her breasts with her hands, gently rubbing the nipples to a state of erectness. Her lips pouted.

'I even long for the baby to hang on my breasts, for that blissful sensation…'

She glanced up slyly through her eyelashes, expecting signs of prudishness from Mary, but that lady turned away to tidy some of the clutter of clothes and expensive gewgaws that invariably surrounded Catriona. There came a sharp knock on the door.

'Here's your water, my dear, do cover yourself.' Mary took the wrappers and covered the shoulders, the magnificent breasts and shapely body. A manservant had brought the water up the stairs, but it was Moira who struggled across the floor with the buckets and poured the heated water into the bathtub. Catriona stood up and, with a graceful shrug, even before the male servant had fully closed the door, cast off the silk mantle again, tested the water with a toe and allowed the ladies to help her in. She rocked sensually from side to side, letting the water lap over her shoulders and breasts, looking down admiringly at her fecund self.

When the leisurely ablutions were complete, and Catriona had been adorned with her loose-fitting morning gown, Moira set about brushing the unruly hair. Catriona was compliant under this domestic routine, enjoying the soothing sensation of the brush strokes. She smiled and held her head back, wriggling her shoulders and occasionally peering critically in a filigree hand mirror, a richly worked present from the orient.

'Don't hurry, my sweet, there's all the day to be got through. I like to savour these bodily attentions as long as I can. Mary, can you order some refreshments, my love? This imp within needs to be fed every hour, it seems. Must be a lad, and he'll be a demanding one, I don't doubt.'

Mary returned a few minutes later with a servant in tow, bringing milk and almonds, crowdie and dried fruits. With a small gesture she indicated for Moira to finish Catriona's hair and then remove herself to the far end of the chamber. Catriona looked enquiringly up at Mary, who was allowed some leeway of authority but which she used tactfully and sparingly. Mary bent and whispered in her ear,

'Sir Roger is here, Kitty. He has some news and wishes to speak with you rather urgently.'

Catriona was transformed. She clasped her hands aloft in triumph, laughing in astonishment at her luck, pulled Mary's face down and kissed her on the mouth.

'There, you prudish old dear, there's my prayer answered. Sir Roger will do anything I want. Fetch him up this minute. Take away the food. No, leave it here, but bring some more hearty stuff that he will like – wine, meat, all that. How welcome he is, always coming when he's needed.'

Mary's suggestion that Catriona should put on some more formal garment was brushed aside with a sardonic look. Moira was ordered out with an imperious gesture and Mary was commanded to collect Sir Roger with all possible haste. Down in the hall, divested of his spurs and outer clothing, Sir Roger looked too sombre for his role as illicit lover. Tall, broad-shouldered, travel-stained and stern-faced, he followed Mary silently up the narrow winding stairs to the chamber where she only lingered long enough to hear Catriona's rapturous welcome.

Mary did not care to speculate about what was going on behind the closed door. Catriona was spectacularly robust and healthy, and presumably the child in the womb would not be as vulnerable now as in the earliest weeks. Most women of privilege did virtually nothing through their time, though the peasant women got on with their tough lives, like breeding cattle. She told Moira to leave the wine and cold meats at the door to the boudoir and to retire to an anteroom, within earshot should she be needed.

Meanwhile, inside the boudoir, Catriona's delight fell like a dead weight between them as she took in her lover's distracted and serious air. His embrace was brief and he rapidly and firmly extricated himself. Drawing a tapestried chair close up beside her he sat down heavily. She drew back, big-eyed and pale, not knowing what to expect.

'My dearest love, I'm afraid I come with disturbing news. It's about Fergus.'

Catriona did not want to hear bad news about her firstborn son, and her immediate reaction was irritation. She wanted some physical comfort before all else. Who was he to disrupt... Then some maternal pangs broke through, but not too many. She had been separated from Fergus since birth, had severed the ties as much as she could. Her brow clouded; she waited.

'He's very ill. He may die.' He looked at her. There was not much reaction. She looked down, ashamed of the thought that might surface, that perhaps this was an outcome to be desired.

'As you know, he has been patrolling the marches with the younger Douglas set. He was wounded in some foray. He's been taken in by the abbey-hospital at Soltre. They have had him in their care since the end of last year, all through the winter months. Now Spring is here and he is still ailing. If they can't save him, I don't know who can. I've only just heard of this, from the earl himself. They've not been in a great rush to let me know. Perhaps they waited for better news.'

'Have you been to see him?'

'No. I'm on my way now, in some haste. But I thought you should know too. Better have some preparation for what sounds like the inevitable, my love.' As he leaned forward to give her a fatherly kiss on the forehead, she realised that his eyes were moist, and felt ashamed that her own emotions were so little touched.

Forcing herself to seem caring, she said, 'You have been closer to him than I have, Roger. You are at least able to acknowledge him openly. I have ever been forced to ignore him. My lord has been generous and I do not wish to remind him of my former life. I can't go to him, of course. My state forbids it even if prudence did not. But you will send me what news there is of him, won't you?'

She knew that Sir Roger adored his son, his only one, as men do love their sons. Catriona watched his distraction, his unusual imperviousness to her charms. He had often talked of his love child, thinking she would like to hear about him. And he was his only son, whereas Catriona had four others besides and a daughter, born respectably in wedlock, as if she had wanted to obliterate the aberration of her untamed youth. In truth, she was jealous; jealous of Roger's affection directed elsewhere, and perhaps simply of the strength of his feeling. She had never felt like that. His dark eyes were seeking hers, looking for an empathy she could not produce, even now, when the lad was in mortal danger.

After an awkward pause, he said, 'Well, my love. I'd better be on my way. Sorry to be the bearer of solemn news. Look after yourself. No, dearest, I really should be gone. Heaven knows I may already be too late.' He drew himself away from her fondling hands and clinging arms, her pouts and sighs, and walked to the door. He did not look back, not really trusting himself. Pausing with his back to her, he said in muffled tones, 'Take care of yourself, Kitty.'

Sitting in an anteroom, working on some fine needlework, Mary heard the unmistakable sound of Sir Roger's boots clattering down the stairs and was surprised at the haste. She put her materials aside. He had taken no refreshments, she thought, hearing him pulling on jingling spurs and outer garments down in the hall and ordering his horse to be brought. She went to the closed boudoir door, paused to listen, and then knocked. She went in, expecting her skills to be taxed to the uttermost in calming her lady's ecstasies, and to be obliged to listen to a more detailed account of the visit than she would have wished. But there were no effusions; indeed, the lady sat still, looking downcast and glum.

'My dear Kitty, are you well?' Mary bustled forward, all anxiety and concern. But this was one of the rare occasions when she seriously misjudged the climate. Catriona's green eyes pierced her, the brow clouded with rage, the expression malignant.

'Who said you may enter?'

'My lady, I'm sorry, I heard... I thought you were alone...'

Catriona's reined-in wrath exploded. 'What right do you have to think anything, you sly vixen? Creeping in like that, you poxy cat. Get out, get out, get out!' And she reinforced her command by slinging the nearest thing that came to hand at Mary's hastily retreating back. It was the filigree mirror, which smashed in smithereens against the door.

Chapter 6

When Peter and Fergus, on his mule, turned back towards Soltre, Fergus was able to appreciate the immensity of the ancient stone buildings that made up the abbey, with the tower of the Church of the Holy Trinity standing up proud in its midst. As they wended their way between the buildings, they saw that a small party had arrived in the garth. A bustle of attendants and horses were there, a knightly figure, a squire and, unexpectedly, Father John in person.

Peter was immediately alert, scanning the scene and piecing together the unfolding story. Suddenly there was a cry from Fergus. 'It's Papa – look, it's my Pa!' Trying to kick his lazy mule forward with his weakened legs, he lost patience and scrambled out of the saddle, stumbling and nearly falling; heedless of Peter's sharp exclamation, 'Take care, son.'

Fergus ran, as he had not run for many a month, into his father's astonished arms.

'Good God, son, is it really you? I thought you were bedbound. They told me you were at death's door.' Sir Roger was unashamedly emotional, as all around witnessed. After the first bear hug he held his son at arm's length. 'I can't tell you... how wonderful... my prayers... answered.' Struggling to control his voice, he let the tears run.

Fergus was just as emotional, burying his face in his father's chest, unable to do more than hold him and mumble, 'So good to see you, Pa, so good,' while trying to wipe his eyes. Peter slowly advanced towards them, bringing the mule. He was conscious of painfully mixed feelings: warmed and pleased that Fergus had someone who cared so much about him, yet also displaced in his bonding with the lad. It was the nearest he would ever come to a paternal relationship, and he was aware of the sin of envy. He made a mental note to include it in his next confession.

Sir Roger was saying, 'You have lost weight, my boy, I can see that. Let me look at you. You must tell me everything. But God be praised. And who do I thank here for your recovery? And did I really see you riding on a mule?'

At last Peter and John could move in and be thanked, and the party moved inside for refreshments. Peter continued to feel troubled; he did not think he could bear to lose this young fellow for whom he had a wealth of affection. More practically, he had an eye to Fergus's immediate welfare, for he had only just risen from a sickbed, was still very weak and had had an eventful morning. Peter noted after a while that the lad was looking a bit pale, and directed him to go and take a rest. Father and son were clearly reluctant to part so soon, and so Sir Roger was invited to stay in the guest quarters for a day or two. Fergus was escorted to his bed, and mused about how biddable he had become before falling into a deep slumber for several hours.

Later, Father John and Peter shared their concerns.

'Sir Roger's not comfortable in these surroundings, being a man of the courtly world, I suppose. He's asked for a thanksgiving Mass to be said, and has promised us a generous donation. But he clearly wants to take his son away soon.'

Peter replied firmly, 'He most definitely can't do that. Fergus can't travel for a good while yet.'

'I got the distinct impression that Sir Roger expects the lad to be dashing off to join the Douglases again as soon as he regains his strength.'

'And he'll be disappointed. Fergus has told me it was all a great mistake. He had become bored and restless at home and let himself be persuaded that this was the life for him. He's got far too much going on in his head to be satisfied with a world of armoured clashes. Horrifying to think what nearly happened. What a waste!'

Father John glanced at Peter, aware of his strong feelings for the lad. 'How long do you think we can insist on detaining him for his health's sake?'

'Oh, I can make the most of that. He truly needs at least a month. I won't keep him against his will, of course, but I feel he is genuinely drawn to our way of life. If that is indeed the case, the longer he stays the more likely he is to commit.'

Father John put his hand on his colleague's shoulder. 'It is as well that our order does not exclude an illegitimate person from taking holy orders, as some do. I can put him in your hands with complete confidence, my dear friend.'

'I'm sure Sir Roger is a fine and good man, but one would hardly expect him to have a son of Fergus's intelligence and perceptiveness. I wonder what the mother is like?'

'I don't expect we'll ever know.'

Chapter 7

Sir Roger left the following day on the pretext of informing Catriona that their son was safe. Fergus found, after the initial reunion, that he was relieved to see his father go. He now associated Sir Roger with the disastrous Douglas experiment, and there had been hints about Fergus resuming his activities with the clan.

Fergus's recovery proceeded without hitch, and he was soon exploring the abbey's various departments, the kitchens, work-shops, stables, the church, the scriptorium and the library. Father John gave him free rein and encouraged his curiosity. Fergus's chief interest was in people: the brothers, the employees and the patients. His home base was the pharmacy, where he would pester Peter with questions and explore the spices stored in pots, jars and barrels, and the herbs, grasses, reeds and leaves hung up to dry. He was soon helping Malcolm with the regular bleeding sessions of the younger canons. He found that they rather enjoyed the special treatment awarded after the bleeding session: a couple of days off duties, sleeping without interruption in small cells attached to the infirmary and receiving richer food than usual.

'Does the bleeding do what it's meant to do?' he asked. One of the canons, not at all shy, said, 'Oh, it doesn't stop us having wicked thoughts, but it makes us feel more guilty about having them. And we do enjoy these days of being pampered.'

Fergus learned about the senior canons from gossiping with these new friends. Father John in particular was held in high regard. His career was an amazing success story: having been low-born, but gifted academically, he was sent to two universities in France and Spain and won his present position on merit alone. He was gifted with the common touch, said the young canons, and would play them at bowls and football as well as teaching them Latin. Brother Malcolm was an aristocrat, a Maxwell, and could have won any prestigious bishopric he desired, but he was devoted to his work at Soltre. And as for Peter, well, everyone loved him; he never spared himself, he was a saint in the making.

One recent arrival at the hospital was a young farm worker called Callum, returning to Lanark after a pilgrimage to Santiago de Compostela in the north of Spain. His feet had become so badly inflamed and ulcerated that he had been hardly able to walk at all. His route through the Borders had ground to a halt near Kelso; luckily he had found help at the abbey there, and his transport to Soltre was arranged. Fergus saw him arrive and befriended him, helping to settle him and running errands for the infirmary staff as they worked out his treatment. He was fascinated by the young man's story.

Peter found him one morning drinking in the traveller's tale while he prepared unguents of primrose leaves for the injured feet.

'We need to replenish the stock of these leaves very soon,' he said to Fergus. 'Would you like to come to Lindean Gorge and give me a hand to gather some? I think you're well able to scramble up and down the steep sides by now. We could go today, it's good gathering weather. We'll take a sack of lunch with us. Pity you can't come too, Callum, but these feet will heal up quickly, you'll see.'

Lindean Gorge lay about a mile east of Soltre's boundary wall. They strode over the rolling dun moors, among the grazing sheep, following a well-worn footpath which led to a gate in a double wattle fence – put there, Peter said, to stop the sheep wandering into Lindean. Passing through this, they quite suddenly found themselves at the lip of a steep-sided, grassy gorge, hidden until the moment it yawned at their feet. Far below, a sparkling burn rushed between rocks, swirled into a pool, then meandered away round a bend in the valley. The green grass of the opposite bank was darkened in swathes where streamlets fell from the upper marshy bogs, with cascades of tiny yellow primrose faces marking the wet slopes. 'That's what we're after,' said Peter. 'We might collect some violets too. The cooks use those in convalescent food.'

Scrambling down the slippery slopes, Fergus looked longingly at the water coursing over the pebbles to the brook and the pond. He tested it with his hand.

'Too cold for a dip,' said Peter.

'Some of the old Celtic saints used to immerse themselves, fully clothed up to the neck, to pray,' said Fergus. 'They did it for penance, even in winter.'

Peter stopped in his tracks. 'Did they really do that? That is astonishing, because we have the same story here! A monk called Drythelm, hundreds of years ago, would stand up to his neck in the icy winter waters of the Tweed. And Saint Cuthbert, who is highly revered around here, did the same. They did it to mortify the flesh. I wonder if they got the idea from the island saints, or the other way about. Or did they just happen upon the same idea?'

Fergus thought about this. 'If I leap into freezing water on a wintry morning, I do it for the excitement of the thing. Once you're in there and swimming, you feel great, living life to the full. Pleasure and pain are not so far apart. Bad things seem good when you look back on them. And sometimes you have to put up with nasty stuff to achieve good things.'

'Rather like Callum and his travel-worn feet,' said Peter. Chatting amiably, they busied themselves gathering the leaves, leaving the fragrant flowers untouched. After a couple of hours they sat in the sun to enjoy hearty chunks of bread and cheese with a treat thrown in – a few raisins and almonds. They drank water scooped up from the stream.

After lunch, Peter was showing Fergus juniper bushes, mosses, ferns, wild garlic and foxglove as they continued their gathering. A sudden sound made them look across the gorge. One of the abbey servants was skidding and scampering with great agility down the slope, shouting to get their attention. Right at the top they could see another servant holding two horses.

'Well, Dick, what is it?' asked Peter, going to meet the young man. After a brief discussion, Peter waved Fergus over and said, 'It's you that's needed, my son. You've a visitor just arrived. A lady!'

Fergus was puzzled. Surely no one would have come all the way from Islay?

'It seems she was impatient to see you, so they've sent a horse to take you back. Dick, maybe you can take some of these sacks back? We've done a good job here. Almost more than we can carry.'

In the guest rooms at Soltre, Catriona and her entourage were installed, the lady herself in a chair by the blazing fire, wrapped in rugs with her bare feet on a low stool. Moira, the servant, was on her knees, massaging her ladyship's feet while Lady Mary, still in her riding habit, attended with wine and sweetmeats.

'Mary, do stop hovering. Sit down and have something yourself to eat and drink. I wonder how long we'll have to wait. The boy's health must be much improved if he's out in the fields working.'

'When he comes, do you want me to go away or stay with you?'

'Oh, stay. I'll be glad of your opinion.'

'Opinion on what, exactly? You haven't told me why you had to come in person to see him. Even you wouldn't undertake such a journey in your state of health without a very compelling reason.'

'Now, don't nag. At least I humoured you and used a side-saddle. That's enough,' she said to Moira, roughly kicking away her hands. 'Cover my feet and go away.' Once the door was closed behind the girl, she said, 'Sir Roger and I differ on the matter of Fergus. He is committed to seeing his son in the military. Like father, like son. Nothing's decided between them yet but Roger fears there may be bad blood with the Douglases if he doesn't send him back.'

'And you don't want him to follow a military career?'

Catriona sighed. 'You'll think I'm heartless. Well, you're right. I just want him to sink into obscurity. If he'd succumbed to his wounds, as seemed likely for a time, that might have been a good outcome for me. If he's out in the battlefield doing heroic things, he'll be talked about – and linked with me. He might even end up as a favourite in high places. I'll always be aware of my changeling brat out there in the world. My lord husband is insanely jealous. When Fergus was hidden in Islay he could be forgotten. I'd hoped he would become physician to some Highland laird. When he and Roger cooked up this plan to send him off on Border actions I was appalled. But the deed was done and I had no influence.'

'And so what do you plan to do?'

'I got the impression from Roger that Fergus has gone off the idea of the Douglas jaunt. He was hoping that once his strength was restored, he'd want to go around cracking heads and causing mayhem, but he doubts Fergus's enthusiasm, and from what I've heard, so do I. The boy is not cut out for soldiering.'

'Would you want him to be an Augustinian?'

Catriona's face lit up. 'It would be such a perfect solution – as if it's been preordained. What better position for a MacBeath than one of the most prestigious hospitals in the country? And he can bury himself here, do the most wonderful things and yet it'd be as if he were dead to the world! As a priest he would have no separate identity. The fame, if there was any, would come to Soltre, not to him. And I needn't have a guilty conscience, hoping he'll meet his end in a military campaign.'

Mary was saved from replying by the sound of footsteps leaping up the stairs and went to investigate. She found Fergus freshening up in a small vestibule. She introduced herself courteously as Lady Mary Cathcart and ushered him into the room to meet his mother – for the first time since his birth. Mary's first impression was very favourable: a slender lad, not yet grown into manly proportions, tall and with good bearing. He was courteous, glowed with the health of outdoor activity, and carried his dun working clothes with confidence. He was not at all abashed but smiled and bowed and took his mother's hand.

'My lady mother!' His tone was polite but restrained. 'I am very honoured that you should come to visit me, and at such a time. I do apologise for my clothing, but they said it was urgent. How was your journey?'

Catriona was giving him a thorough inspection, as Mary could see. 'We managed. Well, son, you look better than I had anticipated. Were you as ill as they said?'

'Yes, I believe so, and I have the scar to prove it.' Mary had moved over to the window seat with her needlework, and Fergus sat on the chair near Catriona.

'Oh, do let me see it!'

Fergus looked astonished and his cheeks flushed. 'Hardly a pleasant sight, my lady.' But he lifted his shirt and showed the livid, puckered scar across his chest. 'Did you think I was faking it?' He grinned boyishly. She smiled back. Mary, watching from a distance, could see the family likeness, especially the flaming hair colour. If Catriona wanted to disown such a son, she herself would have him any day and be immensely proud.

'You seem to be happy and useful here,' said Catriona. 'Do you really want to be rejoining with the Douglas clan, as your father wants?'

Fergus paused, surprised at such an abrupt question. Mary watched closely from her perch. 'My father and I have not discussed it in any detail. Everyone seems to think decisions should not be made until I have recovered fully.'

'You look in excellent health to me!'

'Indeed, the brothers have done an almost miraculous job on me. I had lost a good deal of weight, and that is not fully restored.'

'And would the acquisition of a bit more muscle help you to make up your mind as to your future?' The tone was acerbic, but Fergus looked completely cool.

'My lady mother, you have not hitherto been involved in any discussions about my future. I should take into account my father's wishes, up to a point. My family back in Islay have a still greater claim and an interest in what I decide. They were opposed to the Douglas scheme and it is possible I should have given them greater heed. Since the important members of my family have differing views, I can resolve them best by making up my own mind.'

Mary was transfixed; her hands stilled, wondering how Catriona would respond. She was impressed. A thirteen-year-old lad, and he was not cowed by this most dictatorial lady.

'You're a child, and must do as you are told.'

'I have shown myself willing to listen to those who have any authority over me.' His grey eyes flashed with brief defiance. In the room, all was quiet for nearly a minute. Mary bowed her head over her work while still paying close attention. Catriona had been firmly snubbed, and yet with such measured coolness! Maybe in her son she had met her match.

'Why did you not pursue a military career in the army of the Lord of the Isles?'

'My father had influence, or family connections, with the Douglases. He considered the independence of the MacDonalds potentially dangerous.'

'Does it not occur to you that there is a higher reason you ended up here? That you have been led here since you so perversely turned your back on your destiny?'

Fergus looked uncomfortable. 'To me it feels like an accident that I ended up here – but with a better outcome than I deserve.'

Catriona turned sharply towards Mary. 'Mary, dear, we have been quite thoughtless. Could you go and order some ale for Fergus?'

When they were left alone, she said, 'I think your injury was intended by some spiritual guardian, rescuing you from a life of fighting and putting you into better hands. You should learn to recognize portents. You were born in a leap month in the old Celtic lunisolar calendar, which is not a lucky event. Being under that influence goes with a short life, in which men do not see their sons grow beyond infancy.'

'Are you then trying to persuade me that a retired and celibate lifestyle would protect me from this malign influence?'

Catriona looked into his eyes. 'It is something you should take into account when you are making your decision.'

Mary entered the room with the ale and handed it to Fergus. He swallowed it rapidly and stood up, preparing to leave, but Catriona stood up too and grasped his arm.

'If your father should make difficulties for you, or if the Douglas men insist you fulfil your pledge, let me know. Mary will give you directions as to making contact. Our family and its connections are not ones to be trifled with. Your father, dear man though he is, does not carry much influence. They might thumb their noses at him. But they would not offend me.'

She turned away without any show of maternal fondness at parting. Fergus thought of the insulting way in which Sir Colin and the rest had spoken of his mother, and doubted her influence carried as much weight as she believed. As he left, Mary hastened out after him, saying quietly, 'Your mother is impressed with you, Fergus, though she may not show it. Look, here is a kerchief with her crest on it. If you should need one of us urgently, send this to me at Galagate Castle. I hope we meet again. God go with you!'

The things they'd discussed birled in his mind as he went to help with storing the primrose leaves. He felt outraged that his mother had marched in out of the blue and tried to influence his future life. She had her own reasons for wanting him to remain at Soltre; it was plain that she was not remotely interested in his welfare.

One thing was certain: he wanted no more of the Douglas way of life, stirring up disorder for its own sake, wreaking havoc and attacking people who were alien and helpless. His father had seriously misled him, probably wanting Fergus to become a source of pride for his own image. Fergus now knew that his father might have some unpleasantness with the Douglas clan if he did not return to their ranks. But should that be allowed to influence what he did? He would have loved the guidance of his wise grandparents, which would be given for the best of reasons – for love of him and not for any selfish agenda of their own.

Later in bed, in his little cell in the guest house, he dreamed he was rocking on the ocean about a mile off the coast in a light coracle; on one side was his mother in a huge birlinn, savagely trying to pull him over with a hook, and on the other side was his grim-faced father, trying to do the same with a jousting lance. As he tried to evade them both and struggle to shore, his grandparents and the brothers waved and called to him urgently.

Waking with a start, as if he had fallen, he knew what he should do. He loved the brothers of Soltre and everything about the abbey and its activities, and he was aware also that they wanted him here, too. He was honoured, but he did not want to be a pawn, pushed around at someone else's will. He thought, as sleep crept up to overcome him again, that he would talk to Callum in the morning. What a stroke of genius! Within seconds he was deeply asleep.

Chapter 8

Fergus sat beside Callum's bed in the infirmary. Callum's feet were exposed to the air in the daytime, a good healing influence, and he would be having a short walk later, trying to harden up the feet for the remainder of his walk home to Lanark, some fifty miles away. He was a tall, rangy young man with a pockmarked face, supposedly nineteen but looking much older. He came from a small farm, run by his brother, and his family had endured a run of serious bad luck, including the deaths of both his parents. It was for this reason that Callum had undertaken the pilgrimage.

'Will your fortunes change now, once you return?' asked Fergus. Callum was in no doubt that they would. Fergus half admired his certainty, but was not sure.

'Did you feel you had a calling to go to Spain?'

'I did, for sure. I was aye dreaming aboot it. There had been some fechting near us, and oor ferm was wrecked, one of the bands burned everything behind them. We were starving. My parents died that year. My brother and I had nae food for days at a time. Our priest was a guid man, he went begging for us. When I told him about my unco wild dreams about travelling in furrin lands, actually fleeing ower them, he said it could be a message and that I should heed it.'

'But if you had nothing, no money or means, how could you go travelling?' 'You can ayeways walk!' said Callum. 'My priest gave me letters to use on the way. Letters to other priests and abbeys and holy places. I canna read, but they seemed to dae the trick.

Many places took me in and gave me food and shelter. Other times I slept rough, in woods and byres and barns. I snecked some food when I could, and did penance later.'

'But how did you know which route to take?'

'I got to meet someone who had done the pilgrimage, and he learned me the way from his minding. I had to mind all the places before I left hame, especially where I could get a passage ower the sea. I got lost a few times. The pilgrimage letter worked like magic. Not many people refused it. Once you are on the actual pilgrim route, it's easier, people look out for ye. At one of the hostels they gave me this.' He showed Fergus a perfectly formed scallop shell in the palm of his hand. 'It's like a haly check. Even helps you to heaven if you should dee!'

'How long did the journey take?'

'I'm not too sure; three years I think.' Fergus was so fascinated he almost forgot that he had come to discuss his own problems. No wonder Callum was treated with almost reverential respect, even by the brothers.

'I think you have something on your mind, Master Fergus. Tell me aboot it.'

'I made a mistake, going with a fighting troop, mainly attacking the English along the Border, but they were thieving and rustling as well. I had thought they were good men, but they were probably just like those who wasted your farm. I got injured and brought here.' Fergus paused. 'Do you think this was some intervention – from on high? My father, who is a knight, will want me to return to that way of life. But nothing would make me. My mother wants me to stay here. Become a priest and a canon. And a doctor too, for that runs in the family and I do know a lot about it. I'm angry that *she* has told me to do what I want to do; she doesn't care at all about me. Can she be right?'

To his amazement, Callum grinned widely, almost laughing. He reached forward and grasped Fergus by the shoulders. 'Oh, man!' he said. 'The answer's so easy. O' course you were sent here. You belong. What would I gie to hae your gift? To spend a life here amang these people, aeways doing their best for ithers? Makin' sick people better.' He shook his head. 'Dinna let your disagreeance mislead ye. That's the de'il trying to distrack ye.'

'What do you think about family curses?' asked Fergus. Callum had never heard of such things, so Fergus told the story his mother had related.

'I dinna ken. I guess your mother was just trying to find ways to persuade you. Maybe she even made it up!' Fergus laughed. Callum had astonishing wisdom.

'I think you are a lucky chiel,' Callum continued. 'I've never felt sae cantie as here. It has a guid, holy feel. And the food! I'll never get such guid fare ever again. Perhaps I might come back. Do you think they'd find me work here? But I don't hope for that, I'll be needed back hame.'

Chapter 9

One morning, a few days later, Fergus found Callum up and about, walking round in a new pair of shoes that the tanneries workshop had made for him, commissioned by Peter.

'Look at these, Fergus. A pair of shoes as I've never had afore. Ah'm dumfoonered! They'll walk me back home in a trice!'

'They look right dandie Callum! When are you planning to go?'

'As soon as Brother Peter gives me leave. With these shoes I could a'maist go straight away.'

Peter appeared from the shadows. 'You'll need a couple of days to work these shoes in. The leather is firm, but it'll soon soften up. Why don't the pair of you go for a walk this afternoon? Maybe no more than a mile the first day. We don't want any more blisters. Your feet need to be hardened up, even though they've healed.'

Fergus could contain himself no longer. 'I've got such an idea! Why don't I come with you when you set off? I should love to do it. We are both recuperating. You'd have company and it's safer travelling with someone. Do say yes!' He looked bright-eyed and pleadingly at both men.

Brother Peter seemed astonished, but Callum just grinned and nodded. 'I had thought of it, Master Fergus, but didn't like to propone it. I would be richt glad o' your company.' He gave the young man a friendly punch on the shoulder.

Peter looked at both of them, not wanting to dampen their delight. 'Well, now, let's think this through. What would you do after getting to Lanark, Fergus? Would you be coming back here? If so, you'd need to do that on your own. Could be a challenge.'

But for once the two young men seemed oblivious of Peter's presence and words, so wrapped up were they in their new plan.

They took Peter's advice and set off for a stroll and test run of Callum's new shoes, laughing and high-spirited, chaffing each other good-naturedly as young lads will do. However, they got no further than the far side of the abbey garth before one of the servants came running in hot pursuit, shouting, 'Master Fergus! You've got a visitor!'

Fergus's heart sank. He knew it would be his father, and he had a premonition of difficulties. What a shame he and Callum had not already sped off on their journey.

'I'm sorry, Callum, I'll have to go. I think it's my father, and he'll want to change my plans. But I won't change my mind. I'll come and find you later.' They grasped hands and gripped each other by the shoulder, grinned and parted.

Fergus followed the servant to the guest wing, the same room where he had met his mother, and entered. His father was pacing to and fro, and stopped in the middle of the room. Fergus greeted him affectionately enough, but there was awkwardness on both sides.

'Well, my lad, it's time you took up with your friends again; they are nearby and anxious for you to join up and be off. If you can be ready today, that would be desirable.' This was said with strained heartiness, as Fergus could easily detect, and he was taken aback by the abruptness of it. He had expected some interval for debate. He stood for a moment, thinking of his best form of response.

'Come now, you haven't lost heart for the manly way of life, have you? I think you've had time enough to regain your strength. Look at you – you've grown since I was last here. You have become a man instead of a boy!' Fergus knew this was true. 'Let us be about a man's business then. I have a horse for you. Come, I'll help you gather your belongings…' Sir Roger moved as if to usher Fergus toward the door, and the young man realised that he needed to steel himself and stand very firm.

'Father, I am sorry, I am not ready to go – not today nor indeed any day. I thought you and I would have time to discuss this, so that you would know how we stand before summoning me to take to horse.' He stood and faced his father, quailing inwardly at the now scowling face. 'I made a mistake before. I thought I was joining something altogether different. I thought I was joining a band of guardsmen, of custodians of society, men of humanity who would see that justice was enforced in a community, where the good people would be helped and only the lawbreakers would be punished. But if there was a pretence of that, it was very thin and soon cast aside. They were hooligans, frankly, as I picked up in their conversation, even before we took to the field. Their treatment of women was outrageous, and when we got to the English border they were nothing more than raiders and cattle rustlers. There was no way I could protest, and I did things of which I am now most heartily ashamed. There was violence and even killing, poor people's property wrecked and their fields and crops burned. Apart from being wrong, it showed me clearly what I do not want to do. My wound saved me from compromising my sense of right any more than I had already done. I shall not under any circumstances go back to that way of life.' He stood upright and gazed at Sir Roger, meeting his eyes.

His father's expression was of mingled astonishment and anger, and possibly a hint of desperation. 'What namby-pamby talk is this? You must have known that the military way of life was going to be rough. You've been listening to too much pious talk in this place. Fighting men's behaviour can't be regulated by strict decorum and chivalry. They learn to be tough the hard way. All this you did with Sir Colin Douglas was mere preparation for the real thing. Boys hardly older than you have led armies, you know. I can't have a son of mine turning into a milksop.'

'No doubt we need fighting men, though as far as I've seen, both here and in the Isles, they seem to damage more than they protect. I want to do something different with my life.'

'And that is?'

'My calling is most definitely to medicine and the healing arts. I should have known before, but I was a child and wanted a taste of excitement.'

'But you are now committed to the Douglas clan. You can't just walk away from your contract with them.'

'I made no such contract.'

'As your parent, I made it for you. And you cannot abandon such people as they are without repercussions. They will pursue you and take you by force if necessary. And if they have to do that, it will not be pleasant for you.'

'Then I must ask by what right you committed me to them without explaining all this. You gave me to understand that I was going for a trial period only. My trial has failed and I am astonished they still want me. I didn't cover myself with glory. But more than this, if you knew how tyrannical they are then why did you hand me over in the first place?'

'I thought you had the makings of a man and could cope with it.'

'I don't think it is manly to go out bristling with armour and weapons to terrify poor folk, women and children, ride rough-shod through their fields and homes, and to steal their livestock.'

'I expect there was good reason. Such riff-raff need a lesson at times. But enough of talk. Let's leave this place, its atmosphere oppresses me. If I get you away from here, you'll see sense.'

'I am not going anywhere with you, father. You have been wrong, even more so than I thought. I have my own plans. You and Mother have both tried to bend my will to yours, in different ways. I am not beholden to either of you.' Sir Roger's jaw dropped and a look of horror came into his eyes.

'Your mother has been here?'

'Indeed she has. She wants me to become a canon, here at Soltre.'

'The Devil she does! Look, son, even if you stay here, you will not escape them. Your friends here at the abbey may be at risk. The Douglases' vengeance can be terrible, even for a small slight. Sir Colin especially is renowned for that. And if I don't hand you over, I and my family will come to grief at their hands, as like as not.'

Fergus could see his father was becoming more and more agitated. 'I am sorry to put you in danger,' he said. 'But the more I hear, the more I wonder that you started all this off in the first place. I am not going to regulate what I do through fear of them or anyone else. Besides, surely you exaggerate. They would not threaten such a holy place as this, which has the protection of Church and state – and of almighty God himself!'

Sir Roger stood for a moment, white-faced and undecided, then shot his son a look of concentrated malevolence before striding in haste to the door, violently wrenching it open and leaving it to slam after him. Fergus could hear him roaring for his squire.

Outside in the garth, the morning's batch of sick people was dwindling. They and the brothers in attendance looked up, startled, as they heard the knight bellowing for his attendant. The squire had been walking the two horses around, refusing any offers to take them to the stable while he waited. He hastened to his master, leading the horses; then the two men were in the saddle and cantering at speed to the gate, which was fortunately open, sparks flying up from the cobbles and onlookers hastily moving aside. The guards gazed, astonished, at the sight of the two men galloping away as if all the fiends of hell were after them.

Peter was absorbed in his work in the infirmary as well as his thoughts, and was unaware of Sir Roger's arrival. Malcolm found him in the pharmacy, pounding roots and leaves for ointments as if his life depended on it. He knew that Peter was troubled, and he had news that would trouble him further.

'Father John's lookouts have reported that Sir Colin Douglas and his band are not far away. Last seen at Hawick. John is surprised that Sir Roger hasn't come back yet; last time he was here he gave John to understand, quite clearly, that he expected to hand over his son to the Douglases. Indeed, the promised gift to Soltre will only be given when that is done. It would be easier for everyone if Sir Roger could be the means of persuading Sir Colin that Fergus is no longer his man. We have no authority to do it, and I doubt Fergus could stand up to them on his own. Has Fergus said anything to you, Peter, about his intentions?'

Peter put down his pestle and wiped his hands on a towel. 'No, nothing definite. And now he has got it into his head to accompany Callum back to Lanark. I think he wants to do his own small pilgrimage.'

Malcolm nodded, looking as if the idea pleased him.

'They are both overjoyed with the idea,' said Peter. 'But there are dangers. If the Douglases arrive here and he's away, we could perhaps persuade them that he's gone for good. But they could well intercept him on the journey and that quite probably would be an end of things. He'd be spirited away regardless of his wishes.' Peter's voice wavered, and Malcolm was aware of how emotional he felt. They had all become very fond of the young man.

'The Lanark plan has only just been thought up,' Peter continued, 'and I don't know what Fergus thinks of doing afterwards.

It's time to stop beating about the bush. Insofar as his father hasn't appeared, we are in loco parentis. We should make him a formal offer of training here for the priesthood, for abbey life and for the furtherance of his medical training. If he commits to his novitiate with us, Father John can arrange for a spell at St Andrews University and perhaps even for some experience abroad. More importantly, he would then be our responsibility, and we could protect him.'

'We should be aware,' said Malcolm, 'that we would then be putting ourselves in the firing line with the Douglases.'

'Indeed,' agreed Peter. 'But do you think the Douglases – and it is only the junior branch, remember – would visit violence on Soltre? If it comes to a confrontation, we need only remind them of their immortal souls.'

'We should also remember that Fergus is an intimate of the Lords MacDonald of the Isles, and the Douglases won't want to offend them too gratuitously,' mused Malcolm. 'Maybe we should suggest to John that a message should be sent urgently to the Lord MacDonald, putting him on the alert on the youngster's behalf, should it be needed.'

Peter had been pacing anxiously to and fro. 'I am certain we should do all we can to ensure his safety before he embarks on this journey to Lanark. If he is willing – and I think he is – to join us here as a novice, we need to know immediately. Can we take him through the initiation ceremony, as a matter of urgency? Then these marauders might think twice before they try to kidnap him. I am reasonably sure he will want to pay a visit to Islay at some stage. We should ensure that the protection of the Lords of the Isles is fully operational before he does so. Maybe they can even accompany him on the journey. I think, brother, that we should try and speak to Father John. Soon. Right now, in fact. If the Douglases are anywhere near, matters may come to a head quickly.'

Even as he spoke, they heard footsteps walking purposefully across the infirmary floor. A messenger knocked, opened the door and said, 'Brothers, excuse me, you are both wanted by the father – something has happened and he needs you urgently.'

Chapter 10

Malcolm and Peter hastened to Father John's office, where he was seated with Fergus and Callum. He briefed them about Sir Roger's visit that morning, and Fergus's courageous response.

He continued, 'We can expect some hostile response from Sir Colin Douglas, which I hope and expect will be limited to sabre-rattling and words. I do believe he is a wild one, even by that family's standards, and I have sent a message to his father, who is generally anxious to be on terms of civility with us and who reveres the Church, as he should. He will certainly be able to modify his son's activities if we can reach him soon.'

At that point, a messenger tapped on an interior door, entered and padded up to the father to murmur in his ear. John nodded and the messenger left.

'Interesting,' said John, glancing round. 'The lookouts say that Sir Roger is heading north at speed – the opposite direction to where Sir Colin and his contingent are, moving this way from Hawick. They may assume you are with your father, Fergus, knowing that two riders left here in haste. We know that they have their spies checking on what happens here; not as good as our scouts, but they pick up a lot. The Douglas party may continue north in pursuit – or they may stop here.'

Fergus was leaning forward, looking concerned. 'Father John, I do hope I have not brought trouble on you all here.'

'Whenever the junior Douglas contingent are involved – and even the older members at times – trouble is not far away. We need to be canny and manage them. We must wait until their intention is clear. If they speed past us on the way north, we then put you two on the road to Lanark. Suitably dressed down as pilgrims, you will not attract attention. That should give you good time to get on your way before they return here. By then, it may be that Douglas *père* will be in the vicinity, and we can do some diplomacy.' He turned to Callum. 'Now, my lad, I know you would like your friend to accompany you. But you should be aware that if he gets into trouble, you may be involved also. If you prefer, after all, to go your way alone, no one, including Fergus, will think the less of you.'

Fergus nodded his solemn agreement, looking at his friend.

Callum spoke in his slow brogue, 'I should like Master Fergus tae gang wi' me. We'll do well thegither. We'll hae the protection of my scallop shell and staff, and the letters you are going to gie me, father. I think in my company he will be well guised too.'

The young men grinned and nodded at each other and John looked approving. Peter kept a neutral expression, hiding his anxiety.

'Now, Fergus, these events have created a certain urgency about matters I had hoped we could take time to discuss.' He looked around. 'Could I ask that you all leave Fergus and myself for a short while? We shall need to reconvene afterwards. Shall I find you in the infirmary?'

When Father John and Fergus were left together, they sat for a moment with eyes locked. Then John spoke. 'Fergus, I speak for our entire community when I say that we hope you will join us on a permanent basis. It is clear that you are destined for a career in medicine; your family, your cultural background, your leanings and natural skills all indicate this. You are a person who will in time add considerably to the corpus of medical wisdom. We hope you will join us and become an Augustinian canon. It is this particular commitment that may need a little thought on your part. However, do not think that it would be an irreversible decision. We are not like these hordes of Midian who were your previous associates!'

Fergus found his eyes were moist and dropped his gaze briefly. 'Father, I am more honoured than I can say. It would be my dearest wish to spend my life here, helping people as you all do, for the whole tenor of the abbey is bent on this single purpose. I have shown I do not always make good choices. But at the least I can say this time I really do know what I would be taking on! As for taking holy orders, it is only this past few weeks that this has even occurred to me. I think the answer is yes, but I have to admit I can't be certain.'

'It is right that you have doubts and own up to them. It is a big step. And there is no reason you should be pushed into a decision. If, however, you were indeed an accepted novice, we could give you the novice's garb, which would be at once a disguise as well as protection on your journey. Might I ask if you can define what reservations you have about the priesthood?'

Fergus thought for a moment. 'I think it is the giving up of freedom that would be hardest. But whatever walk of life one is in, there has to be some such restriction.'

'Indeed. But as a student of medicine, you would be given a longer rein than most novices enjoy. And you understand, I am sure, that a long period of study and training would be expected. You would go, in a year or two, to university, including a spell in France or Spain or Italy, in all of which countries there are seats of learning with extra specialities. Then you would return here, and take your place as a senior brother – and a very honoured one.'

Fergus absolutely glowed at the prospect. But even as he savoured it, another thought struck him. 'I am aware that my father has not, as he promised, favoured Soltre with the generous gift of which he spoke immediately after my recovery. I regret that, deeply. I know that my family ought to support your generosity to me with some financial recompense. I do not know how my family back home in Islay is placed, but I am quite sure they will do what is right. Meanwhile…'

Father John interrupted gently. 'I will be quite honest with you. We value you sufficiently to make this investment in you without any outside help, so that will not be a condition of your accepting our offer. Needless to say, the abbey can always make use of the generous offerings that come our way, and if your family is willing and able to donate to us, we shall accept and be grateful. If not, then we shall work you all the harder!'

This was said with humour, and Fergus gave his boyish grin. 'Would it be possible to send a message to Lady Catriona Dampierre – my mother – before I set off with Callum?'

'Indeed we can do that. If you write it out now, it will be sent by mounted messenger and be there tonight.'

'Father, I am completely overwhelmed by your offer, and I am in no doubt now that I really, really want to accept – with all my thanks.'

'I am right glad to hear it. Not least, it gives us a claim on you and the right to protect you. Without any ceremony, we shall garb you as a novice and give you letters of commendation to all holy places on your route. On your return we can plan a programme of study. You will have the right to change your mind for many months, even years, so let your mind be at peace over that.'

Father John rose and gathered up the materials for Fergus to write his letter. He called for his scribe to send for Peter, Malcolm and Callum to return so that the practicalities of their journey could be discussed. As they waited, another message came in, informing them that Sir Colin and a small retinue of five men had galloped past without stopping, apparently in hot pursuit of Sir Roger. 'So far, so good,' murmured John.

'What would have happened if Sir Colin had stopped here?' asked Fergus as he wrote.

'We'd have had to let him in and have his confrontation. It would not have been pretty. But we'd have put you in your novice dress first. Even he would not offer disrespect to a member of the community of Soltre.'

Fergus stopped writing and played with his quill pen. Writing his letter had brought other thoughts crowding in, and he was troubled. 'Father, I do believe that I should meet Sir Colin in person and explain my reasons for not wanting to continue with him. I had thought that my father and I would do this together; but he seems to have abandoned me. If Sir Colin is going to continue making trouble, we should clear the matter up, man to man.'

'If Sir Colin was an honourable man, I would agree with you. But he is a vicious thug. He does not recognise good qualities like courage and rectitude, and he certainly does not value them. I cannot see any good coming of such a meeting, Fergus. You would be entering the lion's den.'

'Well, I have already done so and managed to come out alive. Father, the more I think about it, the more I realise I must do this. Already I seem to be at risk of dragging the whole of the abbey community, and Callum too, into my own personal aura of danger. I must sort it out. I would rather be dragged off with the Douglases than be the cause of any harm to you all.'

Father John stood up abruptly and began to pace around the room, a frown on his forehead. 'Do not have any illusions about good overcoming bad in a confrontation with Sir Colin,' he said. 'Biblical stories about David and Goliath are not things that happen in this wild region.' He came and sat down again, his fingers steepled. His normal calm and dignified mien was somewhat ruffled. 'If you are going to face this fiend, Fergus, be like a wise general in battle and choose the time and place of the engagement yourself. You must not go out to meet him. The best would be if he came here to you.'

A knock on the door indicated the arrival of the group from the infirmary. Without ceremony, Peter, entered and said, 'Father, may I have permission to speak? I am riven with anxiety about this plan to put these young men on the road tomorrow. They will both be at the mercy of the Douglas clan. Callum is not even quite ready for the road. I do beg you, may we rethink?'

Father John stood and drew his colleague to his chair. 'As always, you are right, brother. Things have, even in this short interval, moved on.' He explained the movement of the Douglases and Fergus's resolution to face Sir Colin. There was a pause while all eyes turned to Fergus, who had joined them at the table.

Fergus looked up at Peter. 'Do you remember our conversation in the Lindean Gorge, brother? That wonderful day. We talked of good things coming out of bad? I can see that nothing immediately good, and maybe the worst thing possible, might come of this meeting with Sir Colin. But I cannot make his badness an excuse; I must do the right thing and face the consequences. If I am forced to go with him, I shall do so under protest, and seek to extricate myself.'

Plans for the journey to Lanark were put on hold, although Father John dictated to his scribe the necessary supportive letters and certificates for the two young men. Fergus's letter to his mother was sent. John, Peter and Malcolm conferred again once the Fergus and the scribe had left the room.

'Fergus thinks his father may have headed to Haddington, where he has a castle in which his family reside,' said John. 'But why would he do that, if he is trying to escape the Douglas wrath? Besides, the scouts said his direction was more northerly, and his speed was reckless. He was a man in fear of his life.'

'How soon do you think Sir Colin will realise his mistake and return here to look for Fergus?' asked Peter.

'Probably within twenty-four hours,' replied John. 'These fellows don't hang about making polite conversation. And he will not be in the best of tempers. I am curious as to what Fergus said in his letter to his mother; I wonder if she would exert herself on his behalf. She has not done so hitherto. And I wonder if my message has caught up with Sir Archibald, Colin's father; or if my message to the Lord of the Isles has made any progress. We must just wait and see.'

John had told his colleagues of Fergus's response to his proposal. They all felt the dreadful irony of being accepted by this wonderfully promising young man, only to have him placed in mortal danger by the mindless actions of a spoiled sprig of over-indulged aristocracy.

'Should we all go to the church and pray?' asked Malcolm.

'Before we do that,' said Peter, 'can we plan a bit further? Tonight, Fergus must dress in his novice's gear, have his hair trimmed and a tonsure done, and sleep in the dormitory, don't you think? Get up at midnight for matins, at six bells for prime, then breakfast in the refectory. He will actually begin to feel like a novice.'

'Yes,' said John thoughtfully. 'He wanted to meet Sir Colin outside the gate, but I believe it would be better if we invite the contingent into the garth and have the encounter there. We shall be present in support. We should carry prayer books and have Brother James, the precentor, bring the processionary cross. Remind the rogue of the power of the Church over his immortal soul, and the risk of excommunication should he offer violence within the precincts. Everyone is alerted, and I have tripled the number of scouts and messengers on the ground, especially on the roads to the north. Come, let us go to the church.'

Chapter 11

The morning began for the abbey just like any other, except that there was a new novice in the dormitory who joined in the programme of activities, including rising for Mass at midnight.

There was an air of expectation afloat. Everyone was aware that Fergus was exotic and well connected, but had some shady aspects in his history too, and the rumours about some troublesome encounter that would take place at an unspecified time had leaked around the rumour network.

Things were not progressing at their usual measured pace. The senior brothers wore faces that looked worried rather than dutiful. Father John had even been seen hurrying at an early hour to the great gate to speak with the janitor, his black cowl flapping in the wind. Everyone knew that there had been an increase in the number of watchers in the tower and of mounted scouts in the surrounding countryside. The weather, having been settled and almost warm, had changed in the night to sultry and heavy, adding to the sense of tension. The sky was overcast, threatening rain or even storms.

Breakfast was in progress, with Brother William doing the reading in his soft, educated voice. One or two of the younger canons with sharp hearing lifted their heads and turned; then, like a wave, everyone heard the shouts from the gate, picked up by those close by and conveyed around the abbey grounds to the farthest corners. Normally, the brothers would wait until the reading finished, but today they had received instructions. All, including Brother William, rose and left the tables, the food, ale and reading unfinished.

They hurriedly donned their cowls, picked up their prayer books and moved in an orderly stream, fifty black-clad figures, along the passage and into the abbey garth, where they fanned out to face the great gate. Brother James, the precentor, appeared in his ceremonial robes, carrying the magnificently ornate processionary cross mounted on a staff. They could hear the commotion of many mounted riders outside, and raised angry voices, but the gates remained closed. Father John was talking to the guards and the janitor, as well as those in the lookout tower, who were shouting from the windows. Then he opened the small door in the gate and stepped outside.

Fergus had slept deeply until midnight Mass, but when that was over and they all returned to bed, he found himself wide awake. He had few illusions about the outcome of his intended encounter with Sir Colin Douglas, knowing all too well the aggression and assertiveness of warlords when their will was opposed. Was he himself not a Highlander? He was aware that this first night as an accepted member of the Soltre community, his first step towards a beckoning future, might be his only one. His new friend, Callum, to whom he had pledged his company on the last stage of his pilgrimage, would probably have to journey alone. He tried hard not to feel bitter, but was aware of mounting anger against his father, who had hitherto seemed to love him. That final look from Sir Roger, full of fear and loathing, had shaken him to the core.

But it was better not to dwell on that. He should plan his meeting with Sir Colin. How should he behave? What words should he choose? No plan came to him, no inspiration, no message from beyond. He hoped he would be strong, courageous, dignified, but he was aware that his continued resistance might mean that the fury of this lordling could fall on those around him, destructively and at random. And so, if it seemed the only way, he would ride away with the Douglases, and plan on the hoof what to do thereafter.

He rose again with the others at prime, afterwards following them to wash in the cold water of the conduit in the cloister, then to a breakfast of bread and ale in the refectory. With all the happenings of the previous day, the senior brothers had had no time to explain the daily routine, but he was aware of much of it and followed the herd. At that moment, he felt like praying – that this terrible obligation might be taken from him and that he could be allowed to follow this simple life without such infernal intrusions. Deep in thought as he was, he did not notice the messenger until he pushed a written note down beside his plate.

He nodded his thanks and quickly opened it. The clear hand-writing showed it came from the Lady Mary Cathcart, his mother's companion. The note said that his mother was happy to donate a goodly sum to the abbey at Soltre on his behalf, and would arrange it when the countryside seemed settled enough for a party to convey it in safety. Mary added that the Earl Archibald Douglas, Colin's father, was actually staying at Galagate Castle, but had heard that his son was behaving in a manner wildly out of control and would be travelling at speed to Soltre that morning. Her parting comment was thus: If he threatens you, hang on, Fergus! Help is at hand.

It was as if a cloud had moved and the sun shone through. Perhaps all was not lost, after all. As he read the note, the others had been getting up and scrambling for their gear, so he was last to leave the refectory. Entering the abbey garth, he was amazed to see the entire assembled company facing the gate, all carrying their prayer books, and the precentor standing prominently in all his ceremonial finery. He was aware of a moment of stage fright; he would have preferred no witnesses to what, after all, might have to be a dreadful retreat on his part.

Then Brother Peter was beside him. 'Father John is trying to calm the situation. Sir Colin is outside with a company of about twelve men – armed, of course. father has said that you are ready and willing to meet him. He's trying to limit the numbers who enter, hopefully leaving their arms outside.'

At that moment, the small door in the gate opened and John came through. He hurried over to Peter and Fergus. 'He was in a fury at first, but knows that you are here. He wanted you to go outside but I insisted he should come in. I have not managed to persuade him, however, to leave any of his cronies or their arms outside. We are opening the gate now, Fergus. Are you ready?'

As the three of them moved away from the gate into the centre of the garth, Fergus said, 'Father, brother, this is my meeting, my duty. Please let me stand alone.'

They fell back to stand with the ring of canons, just as Sir Colin on his horse, closely followed by his men, clattered and clanged into the garth. Sir Colin jerked his horse to a walk then, as he spied his quarry, pranced over. His horse still restive, he stared down haughtily at Fergus.

'So! At last! I wondered where you were hiding. They've dressed you up as a monk, I see. Fancy dress or no, it's time to get to horse.' He jerked his head and a squire rode up and leapt off a spirited black stallion, holding the reins towards Fergus, who ignored them.

'I told my father and now I tell you: I am not coming with you, now or ever.'

Colin let out a loud grunt of disgust. 'You have the guts to say so to my face at least. Your father fled – he's taken a ship to France. There's no one looking out for you now.' He made another jerk of his head and two burly riders slid out of their saddles and moved forward menacingly. Fergus felt his guts turn to water; he knew these two men to be ruthless. But he stood his ground without flinching, aware of a rising throaty growl from the abbey company, who all stepped forwards. Fergus could also see that the gate had been closed and the janitor's men stood in front of it.

'How many men does it take to capture one unarmed canon?' he asked with a joyless laugh. At that moment a figure came up and stood beside him. He looked round to see Callum standing there with his staff.

'What's this?' asked Colin in mock amazement. 'Your body-guard? What a weapon to make us all scared, eh, men?' There was a dutiful, half-hearted laugh. Fergus was becoming grad-ually aware of – what? Could it be reluctance, on the part of Colin's men? He knew the fear and reverence most folk had for the Church and its priests. Some of the riders were glancing at each other uneasily while the two threatening aggressors stood as if halted in their tracks. Fergus stood tall and spoke loudly so all could hear.

'This is Callum, who has walked to Spain and back, to follow the pilgrim's way from the Pyrenees to Santiago de Compostela. He undertook this act of faith to restore his family's fortunes; fortunes that had been wrecked and destroyed by men of war. Men like you and yours, Sir Colin.' Entering into the spirit of theatre, Callum produced his scallop shell from his pocket and held it aloft. There was a stirring among the mounted men.

'Oh, spare me the holy talk! Priests and pilgrims bleed like anyone else. They can fight too when it suits them. You can try to be a monk, but you're still coming with us. You are part of my army and only death will release you. You are alone in the world.'

No one moved. Fergus looked around the garth. 'I am hardly alone. I seem to have plenty of supporters here.'

Colin threw his head back and forced a guffaw. 'If they feel like fighting we shall make short work of them.' The uneasy body movements and glances among his men increased visibly.

'We are men of God here,' said Fergus, 'and fight the good fight with spiritual weapons.' As he spoke, a dark cloud drifted over the weak sun and a deep shadow fell. The mounted men looked upwards in fear.

'But sometimes He uses earthly means,' continued Fergus. 'I am protected by my Lord Alexander MacDonald of the Isles, as you should know. Your father, the Earl Archibald Douglas, is on the road this morning, not to help you but to protect me. Thus does our heavenly father look after his own.'

Fergus had been aware of lightning flashes on the horizon for some time, and now came a growl of thunder, enough to set the men and their horses shifting very anxiously indeed. One of the dismounted men, whom Fergus knew to be a younger Douglas brother, stepped over to Colin and spoke in a low voice. Colin made an impatient gesture, but at that moment there was an immense clap of thunder that stuttered and clattered and broke overhead as if huge stone boulders were being rolled across the sky. The sultry air was shifted by a sudden blast of icy wind that swept across the garth, sending garments flapping and horses prancing.

The disciplined troops were now becoming a shifting, almost mutinous rabble. At last, seeming to realise that he had lost the upper hand, Colin roared angrily, 'Come, men, to horse. Why are we wasting time here if my father's business is to hand? Let us leave these feeble men of words and find some action!' Barely audible with the thunder still crashing above, he turned, gesturing to the gates that the guards were now opening. Men heaved themselves back into their saddles while some of the others hastily made signs of the cross, and the company rode off in short order. Sir Colin and his two bullies were the last out, so anxious had his men been to escape.

They had gone, and the garth was suddenly still and silent, except for the creaking of the closing gate and the dying of the thunder. Fergus had almost expected they would turn and come back, roaring and cursing, but the silence continued as the cloud overhead drifted away and the weak sun re-emerged. Bemused and somewhat atremble, he turned to Callum, who was gazing at him intently.

'Oh, man!' said Fergus. 'Oh, man, you have wrought a miracle!' And he took his friend into his arms and hugged him to his breast.

'Oh no, freend, I havena!' said Callum with evident emotion. 'You were sae strang, they didna dare touch you. And then the heavenly signs – I have never seen warnings like that. Never ever. Did you see those sodgers? They couldna flee frae here quick enough! I'll remember this to my dying day.'

John and Peter were suddenly beside them, both congratulating Fergus, elated and looking at him with renewed respect. He embraced them too, and the precentor who came up to him, followed by a stream of delighted brothers, all wanting to smile and grip his hand. 'Thank you, thank you, friends, brothers all! Your wonderful support has won the day,' he repeated over and over, thinking back to the enraged roar that had come spontaneously from every throat.

Father John eventually held up his arms and all turned respectfully and silently to hear him. 'We have indeed witnessed a miracle here, and have much to be thankful for,' he said. 'Let us call this a feast day, to be celebrated in years to come. The day when pacific words have turned away wrath. Our High Mass today shall be a celebratory one, when we shall fall down on our knees and thank our Lord God who has delivered us from the forces of evil. Meanwhile, let us return to our tasks that were interrupted by the tribes of Midian. Tonight there will be a special feast for everyone.'

As everyone dutifully left the garth, John, Peter and Malcolm held back to discuss the events of the morning. Fergus was saying to Callum, 'It was definitely a turning point when you stepped forward. I was expecting those thugs to toss me onto the stallion. They'd have made short work of it. And he'd have probably tossed me off again. I know that horse, he strikes fear into everyone and only one of the squires can ride him. It seems to me that the main intention was to humiliate me and inflict punishment, perhaps injury too. None of Colin's actions are altogether rational.'

'How did you know that the Earl Douglas is heading here, Fergus? Or was that a bit of invention?' asked John.

'I had a note from my mother's companion, Lady Mary, this morning. The earl has been staying at Galagate Castle.'

'That and the obliging thunder sealed his climbdown,' said Malcolm. 'But my impression was that all his men were reluctant for any expression of violence.'

'Indeed,' said John. 'But it only needs one action to break through, and it can trigger an avalanche. Fergus, Callum, you both have my undying respect for how you have handled yourselves today.' He put an arm round the shoulder of each of them and turned towards the refectory. 'Come, I think I shall join you in a belated breakfast.'

The even tenor of the abbey's work and routine having been interrupted, most people had gone scurrying off to their duties. The novice master, Brother William, who had done the breakfast reading that morning, hovered in the refectory while Father John partook of some bread and ale with his protégés.

John said to Fergus, 'You should come to chapter meeting this morning, part of getting used to the new routine. I think Brother William wants to give you some instruction and a list of books to study, but perhaps now isn't the best time for that. Would you like to join Brother Peter in the garth with the morning's visiting patients? I expect that right now it may be better to be doing rather than thinking.'

Fergus, amazed at Father John's insight and kindness, nodded. 'I want to reiterate, father, how grateful I am for the support you have all given me this morning. With such friends, a man may indeed move mountains.'

'It was a particularly vicious and amoral young man you were facing this morning,' said John as they rose from the table. 'Even though you and I both know that those climatic disturbances were completely coincidental, I am glad that they thought it was divine displeasure. It will give you protection should you ever encounter them in the future.'

'I don't think Colin is very much in awe of the Church,' said Fergus. 'His men, and his brothers especially, have had to restrain him when he threatened priests and holy places. He is, though, most definitely in awe of his father – his earthly father.'

The three men parted then: Callum to go for a walk and continue to break in his shoes, the father to management business, and Fergus to join Peter and his helpers in the garth. The queue of waiting patients was smaller than usual.

'Quite a number were frightened away when the Douglas horsemen came storming up,' said Peter. 'And who can blame them? My son, I can't tell you how worried I was. Are you still planning to go off to Lanark with Callum? The scouts will tell us about the state of the surrounding countryside later today. Father John thinks that if Colin has had a dressing-down from his pa, tomorrow might well be a good time to go. You will understand, all the same, that I shall not feel at ease until you return.' He looked ruefully at Fergus who, still feeling emotional, gave him a hug.

Chapter 12

After the midday dinner, Fergus was glad to go with the other novices to have a siesta, suddenly feeling profoundly tired. While he was in the depths of sleep, another group of mounted visitors arrived at the abbey gate, peacefully this time, and was admitted. It was Lady Mary Cathcart with a small retinue. Father John was alerted and went in person to greet the lady in the visitors' parlour.

Lady Mary cut a very fine figure in her riding habit, as even Father John noticed. Apart from her abundant brown hair, which was tidied away in a snood, she could almost have passed for a lithe young man.

After the greeting, she said, 'I come from Lady Catriona Dampierre, who wishes to give a donation to the abbey on behalf of her natural son, Fergus MacBeath. She wished him to become a canon here, and he has taken steps to do so. She wanted to make a donation from her own wealth, which is mostly in the form of jewellery, and not trouble her husband in this matter, as you will understand, father.'

As she spoke, she took a wooden box out of the leather saddle-bag she had brought with her and opened it. Inside there lay a brightly shining gold torque, which Father John could see was exquisitely worked, probably very old indeed and very valuable. Mary continued, 'There is a note of its valuation. It's solid gold, of course. My lady does not want her husband to know about this transaction. But he has also, privately, given me to understand that he too will make a donation to Soltre, and I am not to let my lady know.'

Father John was accustomed to the ways of the noble classes, and made his thanks as he accepted the box. 'That must be a delicate position for you, is it not, my lady?'

She inclined her head and her worried expression was softened by a fleeting smile. 'Maybe. Donald Dampierre and I understand each other well. He is aware of her gift, but she is not aware of his. I must sometimes... conceal things.' She became serious and anxious again, then continued, 'My lady is eager to hear what happened here yesterday. We were concerned about the activities of that notorious scion, Sir Colin. He has been disrupting Borders communities, and has now got himself into very serious trouble.'

Father John described to her the encounter of that morning, while Mary listened intently. 'My lady will be delighted to hear this – she has her own reasons for not wanting young Fergus to follow his father's career. I don't know if you were aware that the Earl Archibald Douglas had come to this area expressly to curb his son's violent activities, but unfortunately came a little too late to stop the worst.' Suddenly she looked distressed and sat down.

'No harm was done here,' said Father John. 'Although things were in the balance for a time. What else has he done?'

'Oh, father, I am afraid it is very bad.' Mary covered her face with her hand. 'The only good thing is that the earl has had to take very extreme steps to contain Colin, and there will be a court case.' She appeared distressed, and Father John came and sat down near her in a calm, supportive manner.

'Fergus's father, Sir Roger, behaved very foolishly,' Mary said, shaking her head. 'There was no need to cut and run as he did. Colin is like a feral hunter and loves to inspire terror. When he heard that Roger had fled – seemingly heading for Leith, to take ship for France – Colin gave chase. He thought Fergus was with Sir Roger at first. But apparently, not far north of here, it had occurred to Roger that maybe his own family would be in danger and that Colin would wreak vengeance on them. So he sent his squire east towards Haddington, where his wife, Kathleen, and two daughters, Kate and Elspeth, live at the family home. He intended that they should leave home and hasten after him to the port at Leith, but he was intent upon saving his own skin and didn't go to them in person.

'Colin split from his retinue and went eastwards with a few men, thinking, I suppose, that they were pursuing Fergus, while the rest continued northwards after Roger.

'And then, at the de Vere home, Colin caught up with the poor squire, who was set upon and savagely beaten up. And the ladies – all three, mother and two daughters, the younger only eight – were grossly abused, raped.' Mary broke down in sobs and tears. 'The squire is in a bad way, and the younger daughter is unlikely to survive. Sir Colin has undoubtedly done such things before in war situations – still reprehensible, but accepted when it's wrought upon your enemies – but he cannot do such things to neighbouring noble families! There is an uproar, and Earl Douglas is trying to deal with the situation. He has demoted Colin and removed his retinue, all his income and privileges. But he must incarcerate the fellow to satisfy the family. Lady Kathleen is well connected. Sir Donald Dampierre, being on the King's Council, is involved up to the neck.'

Father John's face had become grave throughout this account. 'So Colin must have come here this morning after committing these savageries at Haddington?'

'I think it all happened yesterday. I don't know where he and his men spent the night. No one dares stand up to him except his father. It is all the more amazing that Fergus did so this morning.'

'And where is Colin now?'

'He has been taken in chains to Lauder Castle, where he will be held in a strong dungeon before being moved to prison in

Edinburgh to stand trial. Imagine! The son and heir of the Douglases. He will be disinherited, I'm sure. And the weird thing is,' said Mary with a sigh, patting at her eyes with a kerchief, 'I don't think Colin was unduly worried about losing Fergus as a squire. But when he got scent of Roger's fear and panic, it brought out the worst in him.'

'Fergus said that Colin wanted to humiliate him this morning,' mentioned Father John. 'Damage him, punish him, diminish him. Colin expected Fergus to be paralysed with terror. Those poor people in Haddington. Lady Mary, I believe we should not tell all this to young Fergus. The two young girls so dreadfully treated are his half-sisters. He has had enough on his plate lately and we should spare him this horror for as long as possible.'

'I had not thought of that – the close relationship to Fergus. I think of him as all MacBeath,' said Mary. 'And you are right, father. There is a strong rule in Highland culture that injuries and insults to close kin are to be revenged unto death. That obligation takes precedence above all else. Catriona has told me many stories about this.'

'Let us hope that the incarceration of the rogue and his trial is enough for the present. He will get a severe sentence too. A death sentence, unless the earl wields his influence. Fergus will doubtless hear of his crimes sooner or later. But the later the better. And what of Sir Roger? Was he intercepted too?'

'No, it seems he got away – without waiting for his family.'

'And there is another burden for Fergus to bear: that the father he idolised has proved to be so dastardly and cowardly.' John shook his head in sorrow. 'We must protect him from this news if we can.'

So Father John had a discreet word with Brother William, the novice master, and instructed him to keep the new novice, Brother Fergus, fully occupied, and to try to head off any conversational contact with the servants. It was only a temporary expedient, because plans were afoot for the journey with Callum to Lanark, and outside on the road, anything could happen. John decided he would take Callum into his confidence. He walked out into the cloister, where he spotted the young man sitting peacefully, watching the world go by. He explained to Callum the dreadful things perpetrated by Sir Colin, and the consequences. Callum paid silent and solemn attention. Then John explained how and why he wanted to keep Fergus unaware of the details, now and on the journey to Lanark, as far as it might be possible.

'You will be going westwards,' he said, 'and away from the focus of the terrible business. You will understand, Callum, that we want Fergus to settle down into his new life and not be disturbed by the passions, obligations or distractions of family life. I feel heartsore for those girls, the lady and the young squire, and shall remember them in my prayers, but it's up to others to repair the damage – insofar as it can be repaired. It's not Fergus's responsibility to feel guilt or take action. And it would be simpler to achieve all this if he never gets to hear about it.'

'Father, I will dae ma best,' said Callum, after thinking awhile. 'He has caused a grand stushie among the folk here. A' the crack is about whit happened this morn. Maistly about the dark cloud, the thunner and that sudden gust o' wind. A'body believes it was a heavenly ongaun, a sicht frae above. And if folk hear that Sir Colin Douglas has cam doon in the world, they will think it's his richt fairin for trying to do down the Lord's anointed. People are in awe of Fergus and I dinna think they'll be blethering about what Sir Colin did the nicht afore last; things he's been doing for months past onieways. They're calling Brother Fergus a saint for getting rid of a troublemaking, wicked man, who has caused muckle fashery to ordinary folk.'

Father John listened and watched Callum as he spoke. 'Do you think of your friend as the Lord's anointed, Callum?'

'Yes, father, I dae.'

Chapter 13

Two days later, the two pilgrims were to set off on the road for Lanark. They had planned their route with the help of Brother William, and both had memorised it. Peter had tried to avoid a farewell, feeling deeply emotional at parting with both of them, but they sought him out. He gave them his blessing and told Fergus he would not sleep until he returned. The ceremonial grand farewell at the gates was cheerful and warm: a few words of blessing from the father, hearty words of encouragement and good wishes and claps on the shoulder from the others. Then the two lads were away, striding down the road a little way before heading westwards over the moor.

Fergus was glad to be free of Brother William, who had been watching him like a hawk, keeping him to his studies of Latin, chants and prayers. 'I felt he was shielding me from something,' he said to Callum. 'Have you heard what happened after Colin left the abbey?

'I can tell you a bittie,' said Callum. 'His father, the earl, is fashed and has put him in lockfast. His band of soldiers is breaking up, and willna be disturbing the ordinary folks for the present. He has been behaving wild and snell, even more than these guys usually dae. Onyways, there are nae Douglas rochians aroond to thraiten us.'

'Who told you this?' asked Fergus.

'Ach, it's common clavers, the servants were fu' o' it, and the local people are makin' foy. That animal has been causing fashery ower a wide stretch of the countryside. They are also saying that you were sent specially to bring about his whummle, and the crack o' your meeting is causing a big stir – not just at Soltre but aroond the countryside too.'

'Did you hear what became of my father?' asked Fergus.

'No, I didna,' said Callum, glad he could answer honestly.

They talked about the reading at breakfast, which had been the story of St Paul's conversion on the road to Damascus.

'I wondered if Brother William was trying to draw a parable for us. Do you think he was saying that Sir Colin Douglas could have a road-to-Damascus transformation?'

Callum laughed so much at the idea that he stopped in his tracks.

'No, but seriously!' said Fergus. 'Saul was dreadfully violent, involved in capture and murder of early Christians. He seemed to think he was bumping off wicked people, so it was justified.'

'Hmm, well I dinna think Sir Colin even maks a fashion o' that,' said Callum. 'Dae ye ken that whaur I stay is nearaboot the Douglas family hame, and it could ha' been his gang that hashed my family fairm? He jest rides roughshod ower folk, thinks we're beneath him. Same as all the toffs.'

The sun climbed in the sky and after a couple of hours they stopped by a burn to drink some water and rest.

'D'ye think that Colin could hae a sudden change o' hairt like St Paul?' Callum asked, stretching back in the tussocks of grass.

'Some men who face torture or death for their crimes can suddenly become very pious. But Colin, I suspect, will get his knuckles rapped and soon be as bad as ever. Douglas sons and heirs are hard to destroy.'

After a pause, Callum said, shielding his eyes from the sun, 'D'ye think it happens the other way, ever? Good men suddenly turning into bad apples?'

Fergus looked down at him, grinning. 'I can't imagine it happening to men who are good through and through. I'm afraid your character is stuck for life, Callum.'

Chapter 14

Stories kept coming into the abbey from the outside world. The Armstrong family of Lady Kathleen de Vere were making their outrage known very thoroughly, and the Earl of Douglas was forced to make amends by whatever means he could. This meant that his son and heir must be seen to face the full force of the law. Usually, such a man could expect his powerful family to extricate him from the consequences of his behaviour. But not this time, it was rumoured, and the ordinary folk throughout the Borders rejoiced.

The young squire, also well connected and a member of the Kerr family, seemed to be rallying, though badly injured; he was to be brought to Soltre for treatment. The eight-year-old de Vere daughter was too ill to be moved and teetered at death's door. The fate of Sir Colin hung upon this outcome, for if she died he would be tried for murder. So the inhabitants of Soltre faced a moral dilemma, and not a few of the servants secretly hoped for her death. Prayers were said in the abbey church services, and perhaps those who hoped for a fatality confessed their unchari-table thoughts. No news had been circulated on the whereabouts of Sir Roger de Vere, whose name was held in odour almost as bad as Sir Colin's. He should be galloping back in a rage to take vengeance, but perhaps this was impossible for a man who had fled so ignominiously a day or two earlier.

Brother Peter found time to examine his feelings, about which he was sorely troubled. His affection for young Fergus was as powerful as any he had ever felt before, and its nature worried him. He had considered his warmth to be like that of a father for a son. There was nothing wrong in sublimating one's feelings in that way when one had taken a vow of celibacy. But his innate honesty forced him to explore whether or not there was any other aspect that he had pushed down into his subconscious. He thought of the young canons who frequently had problems with the vow of celibacy; sometimes this confusion was expressed in a love relationship that would only be appropriate between a man and a woman. It was not often that there were physical acts of love between them; none, at any rate, that came to light. It had been recognised for centuries that this was a potential source of temptation and sin wherever young men were closeted together, particularly in the more contemplative orders of monks.

In an abbey like Soltre, where service to the sick and to travellers was central, hard work alone kept them from too many wayward impulses. Bloodletting to minimise passions was performed regularly on all new novices and young canons four times a year; fewer than the usual practice elsewhere. Sometimes the bleeding sessions could be reduced or stopped. Very occasionally they were continued for many years. Some confessed that they felt temptation strongly and begged to continue. None of the senior canons were bled, having found other ways of regulating disorderly passions, or perhaps having grown out of them.

But now Peter wondered whether he should submit to bleeding sessions again. It would be humiliating, for it would be apparent to everyone that he felt himself in danger of falling into temptation. He did not think his feelings for Fergus were of a sexual nature, yet he knew well how easily one could deceive oneself. There was only one thing to be done, and that was to discuss the matter with Malcolm.

They met for a private chat in the parlour during the siesta time after midday dinner, about three days after the departure of the two pilgrims to Lanark. Peter did not feel much anxiety about laying bare his feelings, and he thought Malcolm might well have an idea of what was troubling him. He spoke about how emotional he had been when Fergus departed, that he had even shed tears in the privacy of the pharmacy. He knew deep down that Fergus would return; but if he did not, he hardly knew how he would bear it. He also talked about the emotional confusion he had felt when Fergus had greeted his natural father so ecstatically.

'Is this the affection of a man for the son he will never have?' he asked Malcolm, looking him in the eyes. 'Or is it an unnatural affection that needs to be nipped in the bud? I was thinking of getting myself bled.'

'What do you really think?' Malcolm asked. 'You are young enough to remember what sexual urges feel like.'

'I had a girlfriend or two,' said Peter, thinking back. 'The one I left to become a canon wanted me to marry her. I was fond of her, and yes, I recall the physical effect she had on me. But it wasn't strong or even very important. I never felt any attraction to the other novices when I was young, though I got my bleeding sessions. Maybe I am someone for whom sex is not important.'

'Do you daydream about Fergus in a sexual way? Do you want to touch him in an intimate manner?'

'No, not at all. I like it when he shows me affection, of course. I enjoy his company, I like working and talking with him. But I feel strongly protective of him, I want to shield him from – something, I'm not sure what. All these baneful influences in the outside world, certainly. And that is painful and I feel terrible anxiety if I don't know where he is. Like now.'

'Well that is wholly and completely parental,' said Malcolm. 'I have always thought that the two of you have a lovely relationship, born of similar minds and interests. It would be a terrible shame if it were spoiled because of fear of something that wasn't there. If you were to start on a bleeding programme, you would be committing to the idea that somehow this empathy between you was wrong. Fergus needs a father figure too. He's had an absentee father and mother, and now his natural father is so disgraced he may never be seen in Scotland again. I believe Fergus will look to you as a role model, and you should not let him down.'

They sat for a while in companionable silence. 'Do nothing for the present,' said Malcolm. 'It would be a cause of gossip if you did submit to bleeding. I don't want to see you humiliated by such silly chatter. Are you trying to punish yourself, give yourself a bit of chastisement for some imaginary sin?'

Peter laughed. 'As always, you are a fount of common sense. I have felt very happy in Fergus's company, but I shouldn't feel guilty about being happy. We shall go on as before, when he returns. How do you think he will cope with his new reputation as a miracle-working saint? Father says that Callum is convinced the thunder and lightning were portents, and many others are too.'

'Including the young novices who are completely awestruck by him. I think and hope he is too level-headed to be swept up in that way of thinking. Even so, events did work out in his favour, didn't they? Both the storm and then the earl being so close at hand.'

At that moment, there came a knock and the door creaked open slightly. Father John discreetly peered in. 'Ah! They said I'd find you here. May I come and talk to you both, or am I being a nuisance?' Both Brothers stood and made welcoming gestures.

'We were having a discussion, but that's sewn up now,' said Peter. 'Come and get some warmth from this fire, father. I'll just give it a prod.' He attacked the logs with a poker as Malcolm drew up a chair for John.

'I've got news. Some of it is good, probably, but I'm afraid some of it is bad. The child, the de Vere daughter, has died. God rest her innocent soul.' All three looked solemn and contemplative. 'This means we have a murder trial. It is politically most inconvenient for the Douglas family, to say the least. You know that the Earl of Douglas, having not always allied himself in the past with King James, has been in touch with him over the last year or two, in London? Now it seems there is every likelihood that the king will be released from bondage and come north – and that will happen very soon. Colin's wantonly vicious behaviour could not have come at a worse time for the family. However, they may redeem themselves by showing loyalty to the Crown at this delicate juncture.

'And there is a strong probability that the king will stay here on his journey north. We are the only sizeable place for travellers north of Durham, and it is likely that he will want to make a significant stay here, and possibly meet with some of the nobles, the Douglases included. And the Maxwells and the Kerrs, and hopefully the Duke of Albany. That could be a little tense and we shall have to be mediators. Scotland has been without her sovereign for eighteen long years, and the changed relationships may be stormy. The guardian, Albany, won't like giving up his power, and there will have to be an income found for the King as well as money for his ransom.' John was thinking on his feet, and it was clear that he relished the prospect of getting involved in high-level politics.

'When are we likely to know for certain of his coming?' asked Malcolm.

'Very soon, a matter of a week or two. I have been told he is making ready to travel north from London with his new queen. I must also go and apprise the cellarer and other key people.'

'When do we expect the young Kerr squire in the infirmary, father?' asked Peter.

'Today, I believe,' said John. Peter promptly rose, aware that he should make ready for an injured and sick young man – who would probably need as much care as Fergus had. The little party broke up, Malcolm and Peter both heading for the infirmary.

'Father John is in his element,' said Malcolm. 'He loves dabbling in politics. But this business of entertaining the king is, frankly, a bit of a bore and a distraction. Though I cannot say that to father. We shall be required to leave our normal duties for others, all ceremony, flimflam and formulaic courtesy; necessary, perhaps in the scheme of things, but a frightful waste of time too.'

'A pity our young man isn't here to help with the young squire,' said Peter. 'Good experience for him, but Fergus is also an excellent example of what we can achieve.'

Malcolm put a hand on Peter's shoulder. 'Only a matter of days now, and he'll be back.'

'Well, he is yearning for a visit to his home in Islay, and that would be good for him before embarking fully on his novitiate. Do you think one of us could go with him?'

Malcolm looked at Peter in some surprise. 'You would like to do that?'

'Me? Great heavens, no! I'm no traveller, and I would hate to leave my work here. I was thinking of you, brother. You love travel and you're a good horseman. And you have earned it, some time off from the daily round. A sabbatical trip, one with research at its centre, would be perfect. You could take a look at their midwifery practice, vastly better than ours.'

Malcolm was touched. 'It's very generous of you to put it like that. Such a trip to Islay would have to be in the summer months, and be completed before winter sets in. We'll have to wait for the youngster to return from Lanark.'

They had reached the infirmary, where James and Thomas had laid out materials, splints, bandages and an array of medicinal herbs, potions and unguents, and had made up a bed near the fire for the wounded squire. Peter and Malcolm nodded their approval as they supervised the preparations.

Chapter 15

At the very time that Peter and Malcolm were discussing him, Fergus was striding alone over the moorland on his return journey to Soltre. The spring day was chilly but bright, and he listened happily to the sound of larks singing above.

He and Callum had reached Callum's brother's farm on the hills near Lanark the day before, finding an expectant gathering of family and neighbours. There had been greetings, tears, exclamations, introductions, thanks and blessings. Callum's brother, James, had a wife and a child, and his tiny farm was yielding a living, and no one was in any doubt that Callum's pilgrimage had brought about this success. They had sat down in the farm kitchen to a meal of bannocks, haggis, eggs and a broth of kale and potatoes, with plentiful ale. There was merriment, singing and storytelling; Callum was called upon to relate the adventures of his pilgrimage, with his audience hanging on every word, while he gently rocked his little niece on his knee.

Fergus had found, to his relief, that he was not peppered with questions as to events in the abbey garth with Sir Colin. On their journey, he had been the object of intense curiosity, and although he had done his best to deflect the stories, as if the central figure were someone else, he knew his interlocutors were not deceived. He was uncomfortable with the idea of his fame as a miracle worker.

In spite of the huge wrench of parting with Callum, he knew he must return to Soltre the following day. The journey had not been a hardship, people had been willing to feed them and give them shelter, but he was aware that Callum's family, though no longer starving, lived a hard life with little to spare.

'James disna really need my help on a ferm this size,' said Callum. 'I had a guid talk wi' the priest yestreen. He will learn me to read and write. I could become a dominie. I could work at Soltre. The world is a big place, Fergus. You and I live richt near each other, and we shall forgaither. I want tae ken how life treats you. Maybe we'll tryst often, as friends should.'

With such vows, this was no real parting. They eventually separated and Fergus strode down the hill, his heart full.

He had much to think about as he walked. Here he was, in canon's robes, as if he was acting a part. He wanted to be a healer, but did he really want to become a priest? There was a kind of priestly character that would not sit well with him. The reverential attentions he had received in the last few days, and the willingness of people to believe that he was a seer, made him feel that so much of the Church's teaching was bogus. On their second night, the local priest had taken him aside and told him he was a reincarnation of St Cuthbert! The priest had said that the saint had also been a military man before becoming a monk. Such nonsense was being peddled about him, and no one would brook contradiction.

He mused on the three tenets of the monastic life: poverty, chastity and obedience. Poverty he did not fear, at least not as practised in monasteries and abbeys. He would never face real, life-threatening poverty, as Callum and his family had endured. Life in an abbey was as safe and assured as any life could be. Chastity? He had thought little about this. He thought of blood-lettings to prevent lustful thoughts, a practice new to him, and wondered if he could refuse it. That brought him to the tenet of obedience, and here he was already picking and choosing what he would do and what he wouldn't. Unquestioned obedience would be hard to achieve. However, he knew that in the Soltre community he was destined to rise rapidly, and senior canons exacted obedience from others in the main. He could cope with that.

He looked forward to working hard at studying and practical learning, and to the prospect of going to universities in far-flung places. He loved the atmosphere of tranquillity in the church, the sound of the bells and the choir's almost unearthly singing. But he had found the frequent calls to prayer and church services, as if that was the most important thing in life, distracting and even irritating. If you missed prayers, you had to confess to a sin. But tending the sick was more important than praying, and required no apology or penance. He had not discussed these doubts with Callum because his friend's faith was so staunch, sustaining him on his pilgrimage and restoring his family's fortune.

He would talk to Father John about his reservations; or better still, someone secular and sensible like Lady Mary. She would be able to give him news about his father too, not withholding news from him as the brothers did. When he reached Soltre he would write to her…

His thoughts were interrupted by the appearance, on the brow of the hill ahead, of a horseman. No – a horsewoman! Even at this distance, he knew the elegant silhouette. It was the Lady Mary herself. Fergus was rooted to the spot by astonishment and a surge of extremely destabilising feelings. He had been thinking about her and she appeared! Was he dreaming? But no, she had seen him and was now waving. He returned the wave as she deftly steered her cob down the scrubby moorland slope towards him. Momentarily, he thought as Callum might have thought: that he had the power to conjure up in his presence the very person he wanted. It was only a moment, however, and he shook himself free of such nonsense. Two other riders, Mary's attendants, had also appeared behind her and were wending their way down the slope.

'Fergus! I've found you at last. How different you look in your habit. And I do believe you've grown since I last saw you!' She leapt off her horse with ease and grace, as one of her attendants came up and took the reins. 'You look surprised to see me!' They met and embraced without any awkwardness, like old friends. 'And your lovely hair has been chopped short! Still, only a small tonsure, I see.'

'Mary, I am so pleased to see you, you can't imagine. I was surprised because I was thinking about you and then, suddenly, there you were! Have you actually come looking for me?'

'Indeed I have. You are needed most urgently back at Soltre. I am instructed to persuade you to ride back with me, to reach the abbey by nightfall. You deserve a lot of explanation, Fergus, but if you will trust me and mount up, I can best explain as we ride on.'

One of the horses was moved forward and the attendant dismounted, preparing to help Fergus mount up, which was somewhat more difficult than usual in his long tunic.

'What will you do, friend, when I take your horse?'

The young man grinned. 'No problem, brother. I'll ride behind Neil there, then we can borrow another horse from one of the farms.' Fergus and Mary nudged their horses to a purposeful walk, heading east.

'It's not a pretty story I have to tell you, Fergus. But it must be done.'

Mary steeled herself and began to relate the story of Sir Roger fleeing to Leith to take ship for France, only remembering his own family rather late in the day, Sir Colin's pursuit and the dreadful vengeance inflicted upon the Kerr squire and the de Vere ladies.

Fergus felt a heavy sickness in the pit of his stomach; he had seen Colin at this sort of work before. Then Mary told him of the death of the young daughter, Kate. This outcome meant that

Colin would be tried for murder; he had been taken in chains to Edinburgh, where he was held with a heavy guard in the Tollbooth prison. Fergus now understood the many references he had heard in the last few days to Colin being imprisoned. He had not really believed it to be any other than a token gesture.

'Father John worried about your reaction to your two half-sisters being subject to such shocking abuse; and, even more, to the cowardly behaviour shown by Sir Roger. Perhaps he thought you might do something rash and hot-headed, like challenging Colin to a duel. This was before we knew he'd been put in chains.'

'I don't believe it is right to protect people from the truth, however it affects them,' said Fergus. 'So Colin really is going to stand trial. Will it be rigged? Will he get the death sentence? I can hardly believe his father would not be able to prevent that.'

Mary turned and looked at him. 'Do you think he should die, Fergus?'

'Whose moral code should I consult? You might ask, should any man kill another, or consent to his death? In this world of warring and violence, it is difficult to be a pacifist. My gut feeling is that the world would be a better place without him in it. If I came upon him alone out here on the moor, I would react as any man would.'

There was a pause. Then Mary said, 'Well, the story is not finished yet. The Earl Douglas is in a difficult situation. He is actually staying at Galagate with Donald, who is one of the justiciar's men. The de Vere ladies are related to the Armstrong family, almost as powerful as the Douglases hereabouts, and the young squire is a Kerr. So the earl needs to do some propitiating. If he pulled strings to release Colin, there would be pandemonium. And there is another complication.

'Maybe you know that Scotland's King James has just been released from captivity in London? He is to travel north very soon with his new queen, Joan. When he was captured eighteen years ago, the Douglas clan rather favoured the Duke of Albany as a future monarch, and may well have been complicit in King James's capture. However, they have changed their tune now. The Earl Douglas has been negotiating the King's release for some two years or more, and wants to be known as a close supporter.

'There are mixed feelings among the nobility towards the King: they will have to cut their own power, they will have to give up lands they previously seized that belong to the Crown and, worst of all, they will have to find money for his ransom, and hostages of rank to ensure that this is paid.'

'Ahh,' said Fergus. 'Now I see. Colin could be one of the hostages.'

'If the earl can negotiate it, yes. Now, it may sound like the old story of privilege enabling escape from justice, but it's not an enviable situation, to be a hostage. Colin will no longer be the heir, he will have no freedom and he'll be at risk every time there is a change of political climate. The chances are he will never be freed. Who is going to be motivated to pay sacks of money for his ransom? Anyone who comes to power with a grudge against the Douglas clan could refuse the ransom payments and his fate would be sealed.'

'How do I come into this?' asked Fergus, still perplexed.

'If the court gives him a death sentence, that can only be revoked in exchange for hostage status if a certain person agrees to it. The certain person is the nearest adult male relative to the murdered individual. On the father's side, of course. And, in the absence of Sir Roger, that person is you.'

Fergus felt a jarring sensation in his gut and a deep sense of foreboding. This man had entered his life uninvited, like an incubus, and he would never be rid of him.

Mary continued, 'You can see now the need for urgency. The earl wants things cut and dried before the king arrives, which could be any day now. He is hopeful, thinking the other nobles will be likely to agree, seeing that it lets them off the hook to an extent, as they will be less pressurised to provide a hostage themselves.'

Fergus looked ahead and thought. What an impossible situation! He held this man's fate in his hands, and he did not like it one little bit. 'Mary, I don't even know these ladies, girls, my half-siblings. I know nothing about them, even their ages. Is there no one else who can take this on? How am I supposed to respond?'

'It is a dreadful position for you, Fergus. When we get to Soltre, the earl will be there, waiting to talk to you. We rode over from Galagate together this morning, looking for you. When you decide, you will have to make a statement, with witnesses in attendance, and a signed record made. I do not think you will even be allowed to talk to Father John or the brothers beforehand.'

Fergus was incensed. 'Why should the earl arrange things to suit himself? Yet again I am to be intimidated. I wish Callum were here. He has such a capacity for clear thinking.'

And suddenly, having thought about Callum, Fergus knew what his reaction should be. He thought of Callum's family and all the others who had suffered at the hands of the Douglas clan, and how they would best be served. Why should the common people's interest not be favoured for once? Churchmen might turn the other cheek and show pity on Colin, but on this occasion, his compassion was needed more urgently elsewhere.

'We should push on a bit, Fergus,' said Mary. 'There's a road here that's reasonably level, let's have a gallop.'

At Soltre, Father John met Fergus, greeted him hastily and led him towards his residence.

'This is a trouble I would have spared you, brother,' he said. 'Terrible business altogether. Don't be cowed by the earl. Follow your conscience.'

They entered the parlour of the residence, where a large, impressive-looking man stood with a flagon in his hand, dressed in fine clothes, bearded, dour and authoritarian. The earl greeted Fergus with a stare, inspecting him as if sizing up an adversary. Father John left.

'I began to wonder if you had broken your journey and would not return tonight,' complained Earl Douglas, who seemed to occupy a huge space in the room.

'My Lord, we have ridden without pause for several hours and did not even stop for food or drink,' replied Fergus, who was tired, hungry and very thirsty.

The earl turned and rang a bell hanging near the fire, whereupon a servant appeared in the Douglas livery and was ordered to bring ale, which was promptly done.

Fergus did not stand on ceremony, but lifted the ale and drank deeply. The earl shifted his weight and said, 'You know why I have sent for you. I regret certain… actions that my son has been responsible for, and which have affected you and members of your family. Bad, very bad. But you can now assist me in rectifying these matters. We wish to have things agreed before his grace, King James, arrives.'

Fergus, whose anger had been mounting throughout his ride, recognised this evasive form of speech and was determined not to accept any dumbing down of the enormity of Colin's sins.

'What is it you wish of me?' he asked. Douglas looked at him in angry astonishment.

'I thought the Lady Mary had explained all that to you.'

'I find her story difficult to comprehend. I require you, my lord, to explain it to me yourself.'

The earl growled angrily and began to stalk to and fro. 'My son Colin has been apprehended. He is to stand trial. He will be found guilty; he is guilty. I wish to have the probable… the inevitable… death sentence commuted to hostage status, replacing the king's person in London. This will benefit the King and all concerned. However, I have to have your consent.' He sounded contemptuous and accusatory. 'You are this unfortunate girl's brother, are you not? You must give your consent to me and to witnesses gathered in the next room. We will sign the testament and then it will be taken to the council of the court in Edinburgh. That is all you have to do.'

'And if I say no?'

'You are not in any position to say no.'

'If I have no choice, why are we both here?'

'There are formalities to be conducted, papers to be signed, to record for the future that due process has been observed.'

Fergus said, with a bitter smile, 'Forgive me, but you know as well as I do that "due process" means my agreement or my disagreement, and that I alone must make this choice. I do not wish to make it; I know nothing of these things. I do not – did not – even know the young lady who has been raped and murdered by your son. I do know of numerous similar things Sir Colin has committed, multiple sufferings he has caused to many people. I know of a great many people who welcome the prospect of a death penalty for him. Nevertheless, I do not feel it is for me to judge him. I do not wish to have anything more to do with him.'

Here the earl interrupted. 'Quite right, quite right, you have probably had enough of his wild ways. So let us just get this finished. Come, young man, let us go and sign this document and have done with it.'

'No, my lord, you misunderstand me. It is not my place to sign any such document, commuting his sentence from the death penalty to hostage status. I shall not do it.'

The earl's lowering expression grew, if possible, even more ugly, and he took some steps towards Fergus, thrusting his face forward and glaring. Fergus stood his ground without flinching and met the earl's gaze.

'So all this…' He gestured with contempt at Fergus's garb. 'All this dressing up is for show only. You would commit a man to his grave! And go and say your prayers afterwards, I suppose?'

'As you very well know, my lord, it is not I but the court judge who commits your son to death. If that is seen to be justice by legal heads better than mine, then I shall not interfere.'

'You clever young upstart,' snarled the earl. 'You know this action would help your king, your country, your community here at the abbey. You will be judged severely if you do not sign. You will be sent away from here, you will be shunned, hated, despised…' There was a pause as the earl ran out of bluster and stood fuming in impotent rage. 'Is this your notion of Christian compassion?'

Fergus laughed mirthlessly. 'You talk of compassion? What compassion was shown to all the ordinary people in the countryside whose livelihoods your son wrecked, the women he misused, the men he slew in supposed legal redress?'

'Pah! Who cares for such peasants? What are they worth?'

Fergus looked at him in disgust. 'But the one for whom he stands trial was not a peasant – if that is your level of morality. What mercy was shown to her, to her sister and mother, or the young squire who tried to save them? There is no twist or turn you can make to persuade me that I should do your bidding, my lord.'

Fergus lifted his tankard and drained the last of its contents. 'If you will excuse me, my lord, I have nothing else to say.' He stood, bowed slightly and strode to the door. But the earl stepped in front of him, looking like a bull about to charge.

'You will go when I say so, young man. I've not finished yet.' He pointed a finger threateningly at Fergus's face. 'Do you know what I was doing, not much more than a week ago? I was fighting at the head of an army in France, fighting for the dauphin in his war against the Burgundians – and the English. We won that battle. And do you know what men do when they have won? They run amok, rampage, pillage, rape – yes, violent, vicious rape, even murder. And no one stops them. It is expected, it is their reward for the hard life they lead. And after all this, I come home and find my son on trial for his life for doing the very same thing, only on a lesser scale! Do you think I am going to stand by and let that happen?'

'I am very glad we have an enlightened society where such acts are not tolerated in civilian life, whatever happens in the madness that is war. Nor are such acts acceptable in the islands I come from. There it would be considered my duty as the victim's kinsman to seek redress myself, in person, not even waiting for the due process of the law. And I tell you my lord, I am weighing in the balance of my conscience that obligation. It would most certainly not sit well with me if I connived at this attempt to save him.'

'You will find it is a very bad thing to make an enemy of the house of Douglas,' snarled the earl.

'I have friends in high places who are even more powerful than you,' said Fergus, realising as he spoke that his words might be taken to mean supernatural friends, whereas he was in fact referring to the Lord MacDonald of the Isles and his clan. He saw Earl Douglas start and blanch even as he spoke, no doubt thinking of Fergus's reputation as one endowed with special powers. 'I do not fear you, my lord. Now please let me pass.'

The earl, breathing heavily and sweating on his brow, made an effort to take command of himself.

'Look, young man, I have no doubt that you are a fine fellow, well-meaning and upright. But my son has been bred for the battlefield from a babe in arms. You cannot make soldiers who are not rough-hewn. They learn to react with violence; it is their purpose in life to kill. He has been allowed too much licence too soon. But he can reform. He is not a lost cause. What about the sinner that repenteth, the... the... prodigal son? I will do anything to save him. Why will you not help me?'

Of all his lordship's tactics, this was the one most likely to succeed.

'My lord, I cannot – will not – do this thing. But surely there are other people in the family who qualify? Either on Sir Roger's side of the family or on Lady Kathleen's? I am an illegitimate son of Sir Roger and only a half-brother to the late Lady Kate. There must be other choices.'

Douglas walked to the fire and leaned both hands on the mantelpiece, deep in thought and perhaps in despair. Fergus waited for a moment, then turned and left.

Chapter 16

Glad of solitude after the fraught encounter, Fergus directed his steps to the church, from where he could hear singing. Going into a service late was not approved, but he needed a tranquil atmosphere. The church doors were heavy and a few heads were raised at the metallic clunk of the latch as he entered and slipped into one of the pews of the central nave.

Kneeling and bowing his head in an attitude of devotion, he felt withdrawn into himself, and did not immediately see Brother Peter sitting in his accustomed place near the door.

When Fergus at last looked up, Peter was looking his way, giving him a covert smile and nod of welcome. Soon after, another entrant made his way over to Peter – Thomas, from the infirmary. This service of compline was often interrupted for the infirmarer, and Peter got up. He nodded to Thomas, then silently made his way over to Fergus.

'When compline is finished, come to me in the infirmary, brother,' he murmured in the softest voice. Fergus nodded, pleased. The prospect of time with Peter made his worries drift away. The service was brief, little more than half an hour, and he slid out of his pew at the end with haste, not wanting to be collared by Brother William, and headed for the infirmary.

Peter and Thomas were tending an inmate in the bed he had himself occupied near the fire. He noted that the patient was a young man with a face of pallor, pain and suffering, in a semi-conscious state. Peter beckoned him close.

'This is Dougal Kerr, brother. Injured in a violent attack by – well, unfortunately, you know too well. He's just arrived today after an uncomfortable journey, so we've given him some heavy pain relief. He's quite drowsy, as you see. Thomas was worried because, as he's got broken ribs, we fear his breathing is disordered. The risk of congestion in his lungs is high. I'd like you to be involved in his case; it will be excellent experience. We need a rota of folk sitting with him through the night, because of the breathing problem. Would you be prepared to join in, Fergus? It's a lot to ask, I know.'

'Brother, I'd be delighted. I'll sit with him right now if that suits. Do you mind if I just go to the kitchen first and get some food? I haven't eaten all day.'

Fergus felt quite joyous to be back in the midst of work he knew and among colleagues he respected. He sped to the nearby kitchen, where they gave him a bowl of broth, which he ate standing, then loaded up a wooden platter with bread, cheese and flagons of ale, some for Peter too, who had, as usual, missed supper.

Back at Dougal's bedside, Peter explained to Fergus the things he should look out for: any irregularity in rhythm or alteration in speed of breathing; any quickening of the pulse; serious dropping of the level of consciousness; and any change in skin temperature or colour.

'We're also concerned about the head injury,' he said. 'We hope it's just bruising, but if there is bleeding inside the skull we may need to do a trephine to release pressure.' Fergus indicated the food he had brought for Peter, courtesy of the kitchen. They sat down on stools near the fire and made short work of the provisions.

'When he is able to converse,' Peter said, munching appreciatively, 'he will benefit very much from contact with you. You are an example of our expertise in healing those with injuries. That really will help him to believe in his recovery. He was rather depressed and miserable when he arrived.'

'Do you go and get some rest, brother,' said Fergus. 'I know how you don't spare yourself. I am happy to stay for as long as is needed. I have been taking a holiday, after all.' But Peter showed no haste to be away to bed. The patient seemed to be settling into a quiet sleep, with all vital functions steady. Peter took Fergus's arm and indicated they should move away a little distance, to keep an eye on Dougal while conversing quietly.

Fergus described his journey, finding enormous relief in sharing his moral dilemma over his response to the earl's plea. Peter was outraged that they had put such a responsibility on his shoulders.

'I don't usually go along with capital punishment,' he said. 'And yet I doubt that Colin Douglas could reform. But your response was the right one. It is not for you to interfere with the court decision. There is a strong feeling among other noble families that this vicious person should meet his end.'

Fergus talked of his embarrassment at the reputation he seemed to have acquired, being treated as a saint by most of the country folk he had met, including one of the priests! This had brought home to him, as much as anything, that he did not feel cut out for the priestly role.

'Is it possible,' he asked, 'to be a canon here, and a doctor, without actually becoming a priest?'

'For sure,' said Peter, without hesitation. 'The Church is still rather uneasy about priests being doctors and at one time it was forbidden altogether. Our present almoner is not in holy orders. He feels better able to stay in touch with the outside world in a secular capacity. I can understand; you are an individualist, a thinker. I knew you would have problems with the obedience rule. Of course, it still applies to you as a novice canon.'

Peter then talked about Malcolm's proposal to accompany Fergus to Islay. It would be a double-function trip, for Fergus to see his family and as a fact-finding mission to enable them to plan better obstetric care for their female patients. Fergus was enthusiastic and offered to write to his Islay family to prepare the way.

'There's one snag,' said Peter. 'The coming of King James. We shall all be expected to be here to greet him. You are our prized pupil and Malcolm as medicus is an important presence. You'd have to delay your journey until after the ceremonials.'

They both glanced over at Dougal, who had stirred slightly, groaning in his sleep as he moved. Fergus got up and went to check him over. He gently felt his pulse. Looking towards Peter, he said in a low voice, 'He is well settled, brother. Why don't you get some rest? I'll stay here.'

Peter got up and stretched. 'I'm more than happy to leave you in charge. I've got a pallet in the pharmacy there, where I can get a bit of sleep. If you are at all worried, come and get me.' Fergus noted then just how tired Peter looked, and was cross with himself for not making him go and rest sooner. Peter showed him where there was peat to build up the fire if needed, some extra candles, and a container of boiled water and a cup if Dougal wanted something to drink.

'Have water yourself if you need it to stay awake,' said Peter. 'Thomas will be along at midnight and you should get some rest then. I give you leave to miss matins.'

After Peter had gone to his pallet, Fergus examined the young man carefully: breathing regular if a little shallow, and the right tempo; generally still and settled; colour pale but not unduly so; no sweating. The left forearm was splinted, the left side of the face showing the yellow of an evolving bruise, the eyelids still swollen. The young man looked not much older than himself, and Fergus thought wryly that they had both been injured courtesy of Sir Colin Douglas. He poured himself a cup of water, still feeling thirsty from his earlier abstinence. He thought of Mary, aware that he had left her without a farewell. And what had the earl done after their conversation?

He thought of the proposed trip to Islay with great delight. That would be far more exciting than meeting the king. He had seen a fair amount of aristocratic ceremony back in Islay, when the Lords MacDonald held feasts at Finlaggan for military feats and family events. Thinking of past and future, he was glad of the time to sit quietly and ponder.

The minutes and then the hours passed. At times, feeling he was at risk of falling asleep, he got up and paced silently to and fro, not going too far from the bedside. He saw there was a morsel of bread and cheese left from their supper and ate it with relish. He sat for a while, looking into the fire and creating fantasies out of the shapes of the smouldering peat. He thought that midnight would not be too far off.

Looking back to his patient, he saw that Dougal's eyes were open and watching him.

'Hello!' said Fergus softly. 'How are you feeling?'

'I'm fair... if I don't move. Or talk. My ribs are so sore. I'd like to take a really big breath, but I'm scared to.'

'If I support your ribs where they are sore, would you be able to breathe better?'

'Yes. Can you put your hand here?' He indicated towards the left of his ribcage. 'The others have been doing that.'

Fergus put his hand over the sore area and gently applied pressure. 'Is that enough? Take it gently now.' With his assistance, Dougal was able to take a few deep breaths without too much agony.

'Would you like some water?' asked Fergus, pouring some into a fresh cup. He supported Dougal's head as he drank.

'I haven't met you, have I?' asked Dougal. 'You look young to be a brother and in sole charge.'

Fergus laughed softly. 'I am – just fourteen. But don't worry, Brother Peter is just a few yards away. I think I can hear him snoring.' They both listened to the deep, rhythmic sounds coming from the pharmacy and grinned at each other. Fergus then introduced himself and explained who he was.

'Is there anything else I can do for your comfort?' he asked.

'Err… yes, I really could do with a piss, I think that's what wakened me.'

'Right, you'll have to tell me how we manage that. Do I need to get you up?'

'No, there's a few pots they keep for the purpose. Look, there's some stacked by the fire over there.' Fergus followed the direction of Dougal's eyes and collected one of the clay, spherical containers, remembering he had had to relieve himself in this rather awkward way when he was a patient.

'Now, I haven't done this before, so tell me how much I should help…' Fergus eased back the covers and gently pulled down Dougal's breeks.

'If you can just pull my shoulder over a bit…'

They found a position for Dougal in which he could release his bladder, which he did with a groan of relief. Fergus took the full pot and placed it on the floor while continuing to support the young man, and then eased him back on the bed, arranging his clothes and covers.

'Just great, thank you, that feels so much better.'

There was a bowl of water on a stand for hand washing, so Fergus rinsed his hands and dried them. Returning to his stool he saw that Dougal's eyes were watering. 'You all right?' he asked.

'Sorry, I'm just miserable at having to get all these things done for me. Will I ever be normal again?'

Fergus put a gentle hand on his shoulder and smiled encouragingly. 'You are in the very best place, my friend. They work miracles here. I can tell you that better than anyone. I was lying right where you are not many months ago, and in as bad a state. Worse, in fact, because I had a wound that refused to heal.

You've probably never been laid up before. It feels like the end of the world, but believe me, it isn't. From what I've heard Brother Peter saying, they expect you to make a full recovery, and quite quickly, too.'

Dougal drank in his words, desperate for something to give him hope. So Fergus related his own story, although tactfully not mentioning the dreaded Douglas name.

'Do you want to see my scar?' he asked. 'I warn you, it's not pretty.' Fergus lifted his tunic and showed the lengthy scar, puckered at one end, on his left chest wall. 'The spear went in diagonally, see, up towards the armpit, luckily for me, but took bits of my clothing with it. That's what was preventing healing. The brothers worked that out somehow and did a wee operation to get the stuff out. Once that was done I got better by leaps and bounds.'

Dougal seemed impressed, and definitely more cheerful. 'So then you changed your mind about soldiering?' he asked.

'Yes, I certainly did. I think I was young and daft to go in that direction.'

'I'm not sure what I'll do now,' said Dougal. 'Sir Roger de Vere has vanished to the continent.'

Fergus thought it was good that Dougal was thinking of his future. He decided not to mention his own connection with Sir Roger. 'Do you want to go to sleep again?' he asked. 'I mustn't keep you awake if you want to doze.'

Just then, Fergus became aware of a person moving across the dark expanse of the hall towards them. It was Thomas, come to relieve him. He was surprised to see the patient awake. 'I thought the knock-out drops we gave you would have kept you under till morning!'

Fergus reported that Dougal had done some deep breathing with support, had emptied his bladder and had a drink.

Thomas cast a practised eye over the patient. 'You look better already,' he said.

'Brother Fergus here has cheered me up a lot,' said Dougal.

'For a young 'un, you've done well, brother,' said Thomas. 'I don't need to ask where Brother Peter is, I can hear him. That's good too. We'll try not to wake him. Off you go now, brother. Get some sleep, or we'll have you back in here under our thumbs again.'

At sunrise the next morning, Earl Archibald Douglas set out to Galagate with his retinue, accompanied by Lady Mary. She had expected him to be in the blackest of humours after the failure of his mission. However, he was no more dour than usual and seemed disposed to conversation.

'Lady Mary, it was good of you to help me find Fergus MacBeath yesterday. I've put you through some strenuous journeying; all on a fool's errand.'

Mary's courtesy forced her to say, 'I'm sorry my lord. Is there no one else to help over the hostage status for your son?'

'No, none. Father John consulted some legal tomes from his library. It seems that a condemned man cannot stand as hostage for anyone, and certainly not a king. Logical, I suppose.'

They rode in silence for a while.

Mary said, tentatively, 'I hope you are not too vexed with Fergus, my lord?'

'No. I am impressed by him. He bore himself in a manly way. Stood his ground. Most Highlanders fight with swords rather than words, but he has no need for arms when he can command the elements as he did. Colin's men were scared witless. Soltre is sacrosanct and they know it now. MacBeath's powers come from his Celtic ancestry, from the Druids maybe, but he seems to be approved by the Holy Trinity too.' He sketched the sign of the cross on himself and glanced at Mary. 'I am going on south to Durham after Galagate. The King will be there very soon and I hope to be the first to greet him. I shall throw myself on his mercy and beg a pardon for Colin. I do not think he will refuse me – he owes me for negotiating his release.'

Mary was startled at the news, and disturbed, but concealed her feelings. 'He will be released?' she asked, keeping her voice neutral.

'He will need to leave the Borders,' said the earl. 'Too many enemies here. He would get a dirk in the ribs one dark night. Probably he will go as a mercenary overseas.'

Mary, fascinated, kept quiet, for Douglas seemed to be in a mood to confide.

'If we get the king's pardon, I shall be his to command. King James will be as defenceless as a kitten, returning from exile. He is in desperate need of money. And friends. He comes knowing nothing of diplomacy or government. He must unlearn the ways of the English court, come down to our level. Learn economy, eschew luxury. Scotland is a poor country and can't afford courtly grandeur. Can't afford wars either, cripplingly expensive. We must keep on good terms with the English, but not offend the French.'

'Is Scotland really so poor?'

'I fear so. The Lord Chancellor, Bishop Lauder, says eighteen years of anarchy has bled us dry.'

Mary knew well that women did not offer political opinions, and certainly not to powerful earls. But she thought of the little realm that was Soltre, and how prosperity really did get handed down to the poor. Why could the country not be run on a similar basis?

Chapter 17

Fergus soon adjusted to the nightly interruptions for prayer by sleeping even more deeply than normal. One night, he was wakened from a profound sleep and was briefly disorientated. He remembered falling into his bed in the novices' section of the dormitory after matins, but nothing after that. Right now in the pitch dark someone was hissing urgently at him, with a hand shaking his shoulder none too gently. 'Brother Fergus, wake up! You are wanted immediately!'

With a groan he sat up and registered one of the infirmary assistants leaning over him and a crusie lamp on the floor.

'You took some waking, brother. Come, Brother Malcolm is down there and will explain.'

They sped down the dormitory stairs and into the cloister where loomed the tall figure of Brother Malcolm, well wrapped against the chill night. 'Thanks, Jake,' he said. 'Fergus, sorry to wake you. We've got a real emergency on our hands and we're really stretched for staff. Come, sit down for a moment while I explain.' They sat near a pillar, out of the wind.

'We've received a message from Galagate Castle that your mother, Lady Catriona, is near term and has rather suddenly become seriously ill,' said Malcolm, looking at Fergus closely. 'One of their guides is here, who'll take us a safe route, but it's not for the faint-hearted. Now, it isn't at all fair to ask you, given your relationship, but we need someone of medical background who can manage a horse on rough terrain. Will you help, please?'

'Brother, of course I will. I'm proud to be asked.'

'Excellent. Now, they are getting the horses ready. Have you got enough warm clothing on? You'll need your cowl – good, I see you have it, it's a cold, raw night. I've to gather things we need from the pharmacy and store, hopefully without disturbing Peter. He and Thomas are needed here for the young squire, so there will be you, me and James going to Galagate.'

They hastened through the infirmary hall, where Dougal seemed to be settled with Thomas in attendance. In the well-organised pharmacy, Malcolm gathered his requirements, filling two saddlebags with bags, bottles and other mysterious implements. All the time, Peter slept on, on his straw-filled pallet on the floor. As they left, Malcolm murmured, 'He'll be furious we didn't wake him. But he needs his sleep!'

Out in the garth, Fergus's eyes were beginning to adjust and he could see James with the horses and the guide. They fixed the saddlebags and mounted up as the gates were opened.

Moving southwards along a good road, they broke into a canter: speed was of the essence. Fergus's horse surged forward after the leader, going at speed into the murky shadows. In less than two hours, with dawn breaking, they reached the castle grounds. They were led without ceremony into the castle and up the stairs, where they met Sir Donald Dampierre, Lady Mary and an elderly man, the local physician. The atmosphere was tense. Mary put her hand on Fergus's arm with a concerned expression. 'I am surprised they brought you, Fergus!'

Malcolm was already in deep professional conversation with Donald and the physician. He turned to Fergus, drawing him off from the others. 'Brother, this is a life and death situation. Can you cope? Please be honest. You mother seems to be dangerously ill. We may have to take extreme measures. She may die. It's not easy…'

Fergus looked him in the eye and said firmly, 'Brother, I can cope. Don't worry about me. Just tell me what is required and I'll do it.'

The family physician explained that Catriona had been perfectly well until the previous day. Her time was due and they expected an uncomplicated labour as in the past. However, on waking she had complained of a terrible headache, with visual distortion. He, Adam Scott, had been summoned, and found Catriona most unwell, with stomach pains and weak contractions. Then her conscious level seemed to deteriorate and she became confused. Adam Scott felt that professional reinforcements were called for, fearing a fatal outcome, and so the messenger had been sent to Soltre.

Malcolm asked for and inspected a urine sample: scanty, brown and foul-smelling. 'How do she and Donald feel about the child? They have a big family, don't they?'

'The life of the mother is paramount,' replied the doctor.

Fergus had been prepared, but was still alarmed at his mother's appearance. Her shock of red hair was tied back and her face was almost unrecognisable, puffy and streaked with sweat. She opened her eyes but showed no signs of recognition, moaning softly, anxious and restless.

Malcolm drew Fergus away a little. 'Probably the infant has died in utero. We'll check that out with this trumpet here.' He showed Fergus an instrument that James had produced. 'If so, it makes the treatment decision straightforward.'

Mary had arranged Catriona so that her belly was exposed, and remained by her side. Malcolm applied the wide end of the instrument to the dome-shaped belly and listened carefully with his ear applied to the other end. The silence in the room was extreme. Malcolm asked Fergus to do the same, muttering to him, 'I hear nothing, brother. Listen for tiny heartbeats all over. Your ears will be much better than mine.'

So Fergus listened deep, deep down, closing his eyes to concentrate. At last, he stood and shook his head. 'Not a thing.'

Malcolm said they should deliver immediately. Mary gave orders for hot water and sheets and stayed to help, while Malcolm explained the plan to Donald, who left the room.

'I'm going to try to deliver naturally,' Malcolm said. 'But if it doesn't happen, we insert instruments and remove the foetus piecemeal. It's not pretty. If you feel unwell, better to retire…'

Fergus was staunch and sturdy. 'I'm fine.'

After massaging the swollen belly, Malcolm gently lifted Catriona's legs so that they bent at the knee, then let the knees fall apart, leaving the sheets partly covering her person. He inserted an instrument between her legs then peered inside the birth canal. Mary briskly produced some lamps, positioning them at the foot of the bed. Malcolm said to Fergus, 'Very good so far, the cervix is quite open, so there is a good chance we might get a speedy delivery.' He looked round to where James had lined up a series of preparations on a table. 'We'll break the waters, then start with the buttercup root, please, James. Fergus, can you hold this speculum, please, just so, that's good. It frees my hands.'

He broke the waters with pincers but not much flowed out. He took the jar from James and inserted a dollop of the unguent. Almost immediately, Catriona became restless, reaching out and staring wildly. Malcolm wiped his hands and returned his left hand to her belly. 'We're getting contractions.'

After some minutes he called for the next preparation. 'We'll pop in some fairy flax now. A bit stronger.' Malcolm continued to knead the belly and periodically to check Catriona's pulse. After the flax paste had been inserted, contractions seemed to be coming regularly for some minutes, then they subsided.

'Right, another step up in strength. Clubmoss, please, James.' The green paste was put in. 'I doubt we'll need anything else,' said Malcolm as he bent down for another view. 'Kelp or ergot would be next.' But Catriona's need to push took over, and even when Mary and Malcolm tried to get her to ease off, she took no notice. The speculum was taken out, and in a short time, with a final strain, a slippery red-blue mass appeared. Quite unlike a healthy newborn, it could still be seen to be female. Malcolm quickly wrapped it in a sheet with a brief nod to Fergus and Mary. He tied the cord and cut it, then waited for the afterbirth, which followed speedily.

After that, all attention was focused on the mother, cleaning up the bed, removing blood-stained sheets and making her comfortable and dry. Mary accomplished all this like a practised nurse. To Fergus, Catriona looked better almost immediately.

'Is that really you, son?' she asked, taking his hand. Shortly after, she seemed to fall into a light sleep, breathing steadily and with ease.

Malcolm beckoned him over to the table, murmuring, 'The infant was dead, as you saw, but also macerated and deformed. It has been dead for some time. We'll take the tiny corpse back with us and give it a Christian burial. I've performed a brief baptism just now. James, bless him, remembered to bring some holy water.'

The crisis atmosphere subsided. Malcolm washed his hands, then went to talk to Donald, who was overwhelmed with gratitude and relief that the worst was past and his wife had survived.

'We're not quite out of the woods, Sir Donald. My team will stay for a few hours if you can bear with us. Just to check no complications arise.'

To Fergus, he said, 'We must watch for bleeding and fever. If she's well enough later today, you and I can ride back to Soltre. James is away already. This physician, Adam Scott, is a good man and will take over when we go. I am just so relieved it was straightforward. It was useful experience for you. Our medicines work pretty well, as you saw, but I'm keen to know if your Islay family have better instruments than we have.'

They were given some refreshment, then Malcolm suggested to his younger colleague that he should catch up on some sleep. 'I can keep an eye on Lady Catriona meanwhile.'

Later that day, Fergus could see the transformation in his mother's appearance. She was propped up on her pillows, alert and calm, and already her face was less swollen.

'Here he is,' she said, looking at him with a mix of wonder and respect, and holding out her hand to him. 'My saintly boy. You have helped to bring about another miracle. I thought my end was come.'

Fergus took her hand, leaning forward to kiss her brow. 'Mother, I am so sorry about the child.'

She made a resigned face. 'It's a sad outcome after all these months. But at least I am still here. I've never lost one before, you know.'

She began to fish about under her pillow and produced a tatty roll of parchment. 'This prayer roll has been with me for every confinement. But it didn't do its work this time. I think it has lost its power. No more childbearing for me.' She tossed it away. Her eyes moistened and she squeezed his hand. 'You have grown up so fast, Fergus. I wanted to forget about you, you know. You were something of an embarrassment. But I'm very proud of you. And grateful.'

'I didn't do much, Mother. It was Brother Malcolm who saved you and I am so lucky to be one of his students.'

'And he tells me you are going to travel to Islay together? I must give you letters for your grandmother and all the family. With such a close call I am thinking of them all. I wish I could go with you.' She looked at him closely. 'You are a real islander, Fergus. You have all your inheritance from me, not much from Roger. Maybe that's as well. I'll probably never see him again.' She paused. 'There's something I'm going to tell you. I've never breathed a word to anyone before, but… the man who sired you probably was not Sir Roger, the Lord rot his cowardly soul. I believe it was Euan MacDonald, who I used to run wild with on Islay. Even in the midst of my infatuation with Roger, I had congress with him. He could seduce me right now; he was the ultimate lordly man, a true son of Somerled.' She looked pensive. 'So you don't need to be ashamed of your father, my son. The combination of MacBeath and MacDonald – what power you have! Medical mystique and military might! Take care how you use it.'

Fergus hardly knew whether or not to take this seriously. He knew his mother was free-living, free-loving and completely amoral. But maybe she had told him this tale to obliterate the stain of Sir Roger's appalling disgrace.

Seeing his expression of doubt, Catriona added, 'No one knew, and everyone assumed Roger was the father as we had been consorting openly. I was bundled into a marriage with Donald; the negotiations with him were already underway. He knew of my misdemeanour but was happy to take me – without the encumbrance, of course.'

Fergus stored this away to think of later. At present his mind was occupied with his recent medical experience. He was also relishing the new interaction with his mother, so different from her imperious treatment of him at their last meeting. He felt he had had a baptism of fire in his chosen profession, and his foot was placed on the bottom rung of that ladder. He was filled with an urgent desire for more learning and the power to heal, as well as the respect and awe those skills brought him.

Malcolm and Fergus rode back to the abbey as the sun sank. The spring evening was balmy, with birds singing and a soft breeze stirring the fragrant air. They took a measured pace, relaxing after the rigours of the day. Fergus was glad of the chance to clarify his impressions.

'At home in Islay, midwifery is all in the women's sphere. We have skilled midwives but also lady doctors who cope when things go wrong. Like today. There's no question of any man being involved. Even the male doctors confess themselves excluded and ignorant. And I had thought that priests were strictly not allowed to have anything to do with childbirth. To find you so skilled and obviously familiar and experienced with the process comes as a huge surprise. Today, there was no place for embarrassment or worrying about modesty, or doing everything under covers, averting the eyes and all that. And it is right, there ought not to be. If you hold back for reasons of modesty or delicacy, you can't address properly what is happening.'

Malcolm nodding his agreement. 'You have got it exactly right,' he said. 'If a man has something wrong with his genitals or his bum, we are not mimsy about examining him. It should be the same with women. We are detached, sexless in this matter.

'You are fortunate on Islay to have skilled women practitioners. Here, where no male doctor usually has any idea about even a normal delivery, always the province of women, he cannot hope to be of any use when things go wrong. Like our good friend Adam Scott.

'And you are right about the Church's stance. Midwifery is strictly forbidden to us. But as you know, I have an interest – partly because of my poor mother, who died in childbirth. She had something we call the toxic pregnancy syndrome. So, I've quietly broken the rules and made sure I do know about uncomplicated childbirth. I've taken a risk. The Church sees women as tempters and the source of original sin; and so some queasy men are afraid of being soiled by them. Some church leaders even consider that women have no souls; did you know that? I think these attitudes are a form of phobia. But I could get excommunicated for saying so. I've made Father John a little uneasy, but he tends to trust me and turn a blind eye.

'I have befriended some of the midwives in the community, and learned from them whenever I could. They are often hounded by their priests and can go underground. If you can find one, make use of her, but be sure you are very careful. We have protected them when someone in the village gets a grudge against them, as they sometimes do. Superstitions abound in these wells of ignorance, and chance happenings to a family's animals or produce can cause accusations of witchcraft. Then the local priest gets called in, who is often no wiser than the rest. But if we at Soltre have had dealings with the wise women, it can raise them above suspicion. We tell the priest that they have our sanction, and that is enough to get him to back off.'

'I was also very surprised at how quickly your medicines had their effect,' said Fergus. 'It was almost instantaneous.'

'That's right, and we have to be very careful not to overdose. Those tissues in a pregnant woman are very rich in blood. It can be a problem if things go wrong – severe haemorrhage may result. But there is rapid absorption of medicines, which is useful in an emergency. It tells us something about the anatomy of blood vessels, and Muslim medicine teaches theories about how blood circulates which are very different from what was described by Galen. I believe they are more advanced than ourselves. But, again, I find myself at cross purposes with the Church's teaching here.'

'You mentioned the toxic pregnancy syndrome. Was this what my mother had?'

'No, but the signs were similar. When a child dies in the womb and is not immediately expelled, there is a kind of accelerated toxic process that seems to attack all the body systems and is very dangerous. I am hoping that this particular success of saving the life of Lady Catriona will be a kind of certificate of approval that will get us an opening into the closed female ranks of childbearing experts on Islay. Do you think it will?'

'Yes, I do. My mother is prepared to send letters with us when we go. But the Islay medical scene is an open-minded one. I am sure we will be welcomed.'

'You conducted yourself well today, Fergus. You remained very detached. How did you feel?'

'I braced myself before we went in. I think it was not difficult because I know my mother so little. I've only met her once since my birth. But now I seem to have risen in her estimation!'

Then they moved off at a trot in order to be back before dark.

Fergus and Malcolm carried out a burial ceremony of the still-born waif. The tiny corpse, being repellent to view, had been tenderly wrapped in linen and canvas and carried carefully back in one of the saddlebags. They buried her in a corner of the cemetery where a site was dedicated to young persons, at present with only two small graves in it. They dug a pit, lined it with stone slabs and reverently placed the bundle inside. Malcolm said a few short prayers for the soul, rescued by its hasty baptism after birth. They filled the pit with soil and carefully fitted two layers of stones on top. 'We must be sure,' said Malcolm, 'that no marauding animal can ransack the grave.'

'Tomorrow, I shall return and put some plants and flowers on the site,' said Fergus. 'And a date and dedication stone. Poor wee mite shouldn't be left alone and uncared for.'

Chapter 18

The arrival of King James at Soltre, eagerly anticipated for some time now, had been delayed because of the protracted stay he and his retinue had made at Durham Priory. Many of the Scottish nobles had travelled there to meet with the King and swear allegiance, and perhaps iron out some of the 'misunderstandings' that had arisen during his enforced absence in England. They also needed to agree a substantial ransom treaty for his release, and the selection of the hostages needed to guarantee the ransom was left undecided for the present.

The most prominent of the Scottish nobles at this time was King James's kinsman, Murdoch Stewart, Duke of Albany, acting governor of Scotland. Neither Murdoch nor his father, Robert, before him had exerted themselves to the full to secure their king's release. This was logical enough, since the Albanys, being men of the world, preferred to keep the power and revenues themselves. However, they had been less canny than the Earl Archibald Douglas in foreseeing the King's imminent return. The new regime in England, a regency council of an infant king, was motivated to release the King of Scots at a time when it was relatively weak; England lacked a strong monarch, needed cash and was engaged in intermittent warfare in France. A trouble-free relationship with their northern neighbour was much desired.

Douglas had been in regular contact with James at the English court for two or three years, offering his allegiance during the tricky time of his return. With his own agenda concerning his son Colin, he had hastened to Durham to meet his monarch. Albany, on the other hand, was holding out, hoping for hitches and delays, but belatedly realised he had no choice, the king's return having been set in motion, and decided to meet his king on the next major halt on the route: Soltre. He seemed to have accepted that here he would relinquish his governor's seals and insignia of office, as well as the revenue that went with them.

The third most powerful man in Scotland, whose presence was neither expected not invited, was Fergus's liege lord, the elusive and semi-autonomous Lord MacDonald of the Isles.

It seemed that Father John was to have his wish, and that great political events would happen at his abbey and on his watch.

Elaborate preparations had been underway for weeks. The king and Queen Joan were to be accommodated in the master's residence, and a suite of rooms was prepared with suitable furnishings, wall hangings, carpets, closets and bed linen of the very finest. The residence would also need to house the king's closest servants and his bodyguards. Most other guests would be housed in the guest house with a slightly lesser degree of luxury. Besides the royals and nobles, the abbots or priors of the most prominent Augustinian houses in the south-east of Scotland had been invited. There would be armies of servants and attendants for whom the non-clerical abbey staff would make ad hoc sleeping arrangements. The huge number of horses would also require due consideration; barns and outhouses could be made to serve as stables. One of the busiest departments was the kitchen, where not only meals for royalty and aristocracy were to be prepared, but also gargantuan quantities of humbler fare for the workers, not forgetting the usual inmates – the canons themselves and the patients in the infirmary.

The army of novices were let off hours of study to help with preparations, such as carting in the enormous quantities of supplies that arrived each day by oxcart: sides of beef, pork, venison, carcasses of poultry, game birds and swan, sacks of grain, barrels of ale and flagons of wine. The church was given a thorough clean and all the ceremonial vestments and hangings were taken out for a shake and an airing. The precentor and choirmaster summoned the choirboys from the local choral school every day to practise their harmonious chanting to a high level of heavenly sound.

The local population was well aware that great events were about to happen at Soltre, because most of them were involved in the preparations. All the ancillary suppliers on abbey land and in nearby towns such as Lauder and Haddington, all the farms, mills, breweries, tanneries, bakeries, blacksmiths, butchers, fishmongers and wine suppliers, were working overtime according to instructions from the cellarer and the hostillar to ensure the king's visit was a memorable success. The bursar had a list of people, men and women, whom he could call upon for extra staff if they were needed in the kitchens, stables, laundry or workshops.

In spite of all the excitement and frenetic activity, the raison d'être of the abbey, its medical work, continued as it always did. People came to the morning clinics in the garth; indeed, there was a noticeable increase in numbers, no doubt as a result of the curiosity factor. Brother Peter and his team soldiered on as always. Fergus was often there, as the squire Dougal was well on his way to recovery and no longer causing anxiety.

Father John welcomed an advance delegation of the King's close advisers, who came to inspect the arrangements and to discuss the programme of events. The main ceremony would be the handing over of the governor's seal of office and the swearing of allegiance to King James. Besides the approved guest list, the king had expressed a wish to meet some of the ordinary folk of his kingdom. Father John mentioned their recent celebrity Callum, who had successfully completed the Santiago de

Compostela pilgrimage. King James would be delighted to meet him, came the response. So Father John's scribe set in motion the arrangements to bring Callum back for the royal visit.

King James, it was reported, besides being an adept sportsman and a cultured lover of the arts and music, was very devout. Father John decided that Callum should attend the splendid banquet that was to follow the ceremony of the transfer of power from the guardian, and that Fergus should come too. The king's one-time MacBeath physician, alas, had died while in his service. Now he had returned to his own kingdom, he was expected to renew this old custom of appointing his doctor from the illustrious Highland medical family. Both of these young men, it seemed, would enjoy the full light of the king's interest, and perhaps his influence in their lives.

Father John gathered his most senior colleagues together to discuss the responsibilities raised by the king's agents. The return of the monarch from exile roused tensions between the noble families, all trying to test which way the winds were blowing. There were those who would inevitably lose power and wealth, those whose loyalty had been in doubt, those who feared losing everything, including their lives. Such men might plan desperate measures, and it was imperative that these were not given a chance to unfold at Soltre. The fidelity of the Duke of Albany, the governor of Scotland, was in considerable doubt, not least because he had delayed his meeting with the king until it could take place on Scottish soil. In no doubt at all was the attitude of Albany's son, Walter, who had actively opposed King James's return. If he were planning some act of rebellion with violence, would he not be more likely to attempt this on home territory?

Albany would of course be welcomed, but he would not be allowed to bring any of his henchmen – certainly not his son, Walter. There would be a strict veto on him, or indeed anyone, carrying arms into the abbey precincts. This strict abbey rule could be flaunted by determined military men, as Sir Colin Douglas had done, but when the high profile of royalty was involved, it would be enforced. The only men who would keep their arms with them throughout the ceremonies would be the King's personal bodyguards, men whom he could trust absolutely. The great gate to the abbey would be manned by another contingent of his men, who would monitor all entries. This went against the grain of the Augustinian philosophy, but there was nothing to be done but submit. The King's person was sacrosanct.

Chapter 19

Finally the great day arrived, when King James came to Soltre. All were deeply conscious of the honour of welcoming back their monarch from exile, and most felt the anxieties related to the onus of entertaining the king in royal style. The road leading to the abbey was crowded with well-wishers, cheering and eager for a sight of the royal couple. The watch in the tower over the gate performed his duty of announcing the arrival with even more panache than usual.

The royal party swept into the abbey garth, the king and his wife as richly dressed in furs, velvet wrappings and sparkling jewels as anyone could desire. And the man himself! He was a king to be proud of, young and tall and comely, with a look of delight and dignified pleasure in the hearty welcome he was receiving. He emanated goodwill, and everyone relaxed a little, so that the formalities of welcome flowed sweetly. All the members, lay and clerical, were present in the garth, but as the royal couple were conveyed by Father John into the residence, they melted away and back to their duties. For some, it was the only sighting they would have of their king and queen.

The ceremony of the handover between King James and the Duke of Albany was to take place in the chapter house at the hour of the chapter meeting, and was attended by all the canons, including the novices. The meeting between the two men was simple and dignified, with no outward show of hostility. Albany sank to his knee and declared his allegiance in a most honourable manner, the seals of office were handed over and everyone present recorded mentally the sense of relief and of occasion. Father John then spoke briefly of the honour of being the first to welcome the king from exile back to his rightful place, and the king replied, at greater length and with considerable fluency and wit. He was a modern monarch with all the polish and education that should accompany such a role. He expressed not only gratitude but interest in the activities of the famed Soltre, and expressed his wish to visit various parts of it during his stay.

Then the company went into High Mass in the church, celebrated by Father John himself. The choirboys came into their own and sang their exquisite harmonies in a manner befitting the grandeur of the occasion.

Father John was not one to leave anything to chance. He had established long ago a network of spies and informants, who provided advance information of any turbulence in the surrounding countryside that might affect the abbey. In addition, he could swiftly call up a number of staunch countrymen who could give a good account of themselves in any roughhouse. Many of these men had had in the past some need of the abbey's services and reason to feel beholden to it; their loyalty was absolute. Father John had, without consulting anyone, installed a goodly number of this unofficial pool of guardians around the various parts of the building to observe any unusual activity, or signs of plotting or trouble, during the king's stay. And although these men were not armed with conventional weapons, they had hidden dirks and sticks for use, should they be needed.

The good father considered that any planned trouble would most likely erupt at the grand banquet after the handover ceremony. With good food and wine, company and conversation, people relaxed into enjoyment whilst barriers and states of alertness dropped. The banquet would take place in the hall of the guest house, and here John had deployed the core of his strongmen. Some would attend the doorways and windows, some would double up as waiters and servers, others would patrol the outside precincts and the various corridors, nooks and crannies of the guest house.

Meanwhile, his spy network had been put on full alert also, to report any unusual gathering of mounted riders within a ten-mile radius. The band of guards at the great gate was tripled, and reinforced by the King's own guardsmen, while other possible entry points were blocked and guarded. Many of these arrangements had been established centuries previously, at the turbulent times of the wars of independence. Nowadays they were relaxed for the most part, but with the reserve force available, they could be put into action very speedily.

The company assembled in the guest parlour, adorned with tapestries and brightened by numerous candle flames and a crackling fire. The last to arrive would be the king and queen. Fergus and Callum had entered together and now stood waiting among the other guests. Fergus glanced around and, to his surprise, saw his mother standing near the fire, looking well and almost radiant in her grand attire and elaborate headdress with flimsy veil, through which her bright hair shone. With her were Sir Donald and Lady Mary. Across the room was Sir Archibald Douglas, standing alone, with his habitual stern expression. Fergus also recognised, because of his grand robes and mitre, Henry Wardlaw, Bishop of St Andrews, the most senior churchman in Scotland. He was conversing with three elderly clerics dressed in Augustinian attire, whom Fergus assumed would be abbots and priors. He recognised the Abbot of Jedburgh, Father Patrick, a close friend and associate of Father John's.

The air of expectancy was turning to tension and anxiety; looking around, Fergus could see why. He murmured to Callum, 'Albany's not here.' Father John was speaking in a hurried manner to two of the attendants, who, Fergus could see, were part of the protection group. They left the room and, shortly after, Albany entered, looking irritated. He was greeted with immaculate politeness by the father, to whom his response was distinctly surly. 'Don't suppose he's used to being ordered to get a move on,' muttered Fergus.

Father John stood forward, unruffled as ever, and said, 'Welcome to you all, My Lord Bishop, abbots, priors, lords, ladies and gentlemen. I am now going to escort their graces, King James and Queen Joan, to this place to meet you. When they come in, everyone will of course show their due reverence with a bow or curtsey. The servants are just about to go round and supply everyone with a wine. We shall raise a glass to their graces and drink a toast of welcome, which I shall propose. His grace the King will be pleased to have a short conversation with a small number of you before we adjourn for dinner. I shall beckon those of you who are to be so honoured to come to the gracious presence. But if you are not called, please don't be disappointed. The king loves meeting people and conversation, and there will be other chances during and after dinner.'

Father John left the room and there was a buzz of conversation while the flagons of wine were being handed round. Fergus watched Albany, who did not look happy, and wondered what was going on. Soon, the door was flung open by two of the king's guard, armed to the teeth, it seemed, and while they stood to attention by the door they were followed in by their graces in their gorgeous robes, accompanied by a fine-looking elderly gentleman, clearly a close friend. As they all walked in, followed by Father John, Malcolm hastened forward to lead the royal couple to the centre of the room in front of the fire. Then there was a swish and rustle of everyone's best clothes as, with one accord, the men swept their hats off and bowed deeply while the ladies sank to the floor amid their voluminous skirts. Fergus saw that his mother relied on her husband's steadying hand under her arm to raise her from the floor.

John raised his flagon and said in his most resounding voice, 'All hail and welcome to their graces, King James and Queen Joan. May they enjoy good health, long life and a happy, long and peaceful reign. God bless them, now and always.'

The company raised their flagons and said in chorus, 'To King James and Queen Joan,' and drank deeply. Callum murmured in Fergus's ear, 'First time I've taken wine.' The king was genially raising his flagon to the company in all directions, and saying, 'Thank you, thank you, my good friends. This is a memorable homecoming.'

Fergus's sharp eyes noted that, although Albany raised his flagon, his lips did not move. The first to greet and speak to the king was Bishop Henry Wardlaw. He had tutored James as a child and had engaged with the Earl of Douglas and others in negotiating to bring the king back to Scotland. It was clear, watching the two men together, that there was genuine friendship between them.

Meanwhile, the company broke up into little groups to chat, all still keeping an eye on the central figures, each hoping they would be called by Father John to meet the king. Fergus, looking up from his conversation with Callum, saw his mother in deep conversation with the king while Sir Donald engaged with the queen. He could see that his mother was working her legendary charm and that the king was entranced, seeming to be in no hurry to move on to someone else. However, soon the Earl of Douglas was called forward, and Lady Catriona, with a last flirtatious smile to the king, moved towards Fergus and Callum. She greeted Fergus with an affectionate kiss on both cheeks, then smiled at Callum and took his hand as they were introduced.

'Did you notice,' she said to them, 'that there is some... antagonism with the Duke of Albany? Why can these men not enjoy a grand party without getting hostile and political? Hardly surprising, though, if he's sulking a bit, having lost his position as Big Chief.'

Donald had followed her and greeted the two young men, telling them that the fine elderly man, the friend of the king, was none other than the Lord Justice of Scotland, Sir Robert Lauder. As he spoke, they turned to watch the Earl of Douglas greet his king with elaborate deference, down on one knee and bending his head to kiss the royal hand. Donald murmured to the group around him, 'Archie's emphasising his devotion in contrast to the other one! I think Albany had hoped he might find the king weak and undefended, and so could seize the chance to challenge him. Father John's outer network has warned of activity nearby – a band of armed men on horseback. The fear is that this is Albany's son Walter, who has been strongly antagonistic to the king's return.'

'Do you think there will be trouble?' asked Catriona, sipping her wine. 'Even in the abbey precincts?'

'In past times there have been murders even in churches when it is a question of rivalry for the crown!' Donald replied.

As the little party gossiped, Callum was beckoned over to speak to the king. Fergus watched his friend with pride as he bore himself well and responded to the king's questions while Father John hovered in case Callum should be floundering under the awesome royal interest. But he seemed to be speaking confidently, and the king was clearly genuinely fascinated at his account of the pilgrimage, and kept him talking longer than any other person so far. Meanwhile, Malcolm was beckoning Fergus over to meet Bishop Wardlaw. He had not anticipated this and had a moment's anxiety. How did one behave towards the most senior man in the Church when one was probably the most junior? He need not have worried, for the bishop beamed upon him and took both hands, holding him up as he prepared to kneel.

'My son, Fergus! I have been hearing about you from your friends and am delighted to meet you. Malcolm here tells me we shall expect you at St Andrews in a year or two as a student at my university there. You are indeed fortunate to have been guided to Soltre; there is no better place for learning and care of souls. I have been discussing with Malcolm a prescribed course of reading for you to prepare for your time with us at St Andrews. You'll be with us for perhaps three or four years, then back here fully trained.'

Fergus found that he was not required to contribute much to the conversation, as the bishop preferred to discourse himself. He glanced at Malcolm, who gave him the flicker of a wink. Then, quite suddenly, Callum was leaving the royal presence and Father John was beckoning to Fergus. He was even more surprised, not having expected to be one of the honoured ones. He bowed respectfully to the bishop and moved forward, kneeling to kiss the king's hand. He looked up and smiled; King James met his gaze with friendly eyes and Fergus felt immediately at his ease. Secular majesty was easier than the sacred variety, he found.

'We can tell who is your near relation!' said the king. 'The charming lady we were speaking to earlier! Are we right?'

'Yes indeed, sire, she is my mother.' They both glanced over to where Catriona stood. The king continued, 'But before we come on to your family, we must mention your friend, the pilgrim – Callum, is it? We are completely astounded that a young man would have such faith and determination, not to mention powers of endurance. It shows what an iron will can do. We should like to have such a uniquely endowed young person in our entourage. To be accompanied by a man so in touch with holiness would be a blessing indeed. Do you think he would agree?'

'Sire, he would be most honoured, I am sure.' Fergus actually wondered as he spoke whether that was true. Would Callum, of straight and simple principles, want to be part of a king's court, with all the attendant deceit, intrigue and backstabbing? He perceived that Callum, like himself, was seen as something of a spiritual being, clothed in myth and destined to be treated as a token holy man. But the king had moved on and was asking him about his MacBeath family. Did he remember the king's erstwhile physician, the late Brian MacBeath?

Fergus had indeed heard the name, and thought he was a distant relation, a second or third cousin. The king said that he wished most earnestly for another MacBeath doctor. 'What a shame you are not a few years older, Brother Fergus, and fully trained. We have heard remarkable things of you. However, there must be others?'

'Indeed, we are a prolific family,' Fergus admitted. He mentioned his forthcoming trip to Islay, whereupon the King eagerly instructed him to liaise with his own personal secretary to find a suitable physician for the royal person.

'And now, an even more weighty matter, brother. Your liege lord, Alexander MacDonald, who calls himself Lord of the Isles, we should have liked to see here or even at our earlier gathering at Durham. He is not easy to make contact with. But we want to meet him soon, as one of the most influential men in the kingdom. We should like to offer the hand of friendship to him. You would be a most suitable ambassador, carrying a message to him from ourselves, by word of mouth. Request him to come to us at Perth. We are advised by those close to us to hasten there and have the coronation at Scone arranged with all possible speed. Probably within the month. If he comes to us at our coronation, he will be welcomed – and rewarded. We hope he will join our parliament. The MacDonalds have their headquarters at Finlaggan on Islay, is that right?'

'Indeed it is, sire.'

'Your family, as we understood from your kinsman Brian, is close to the MacDonald clan? And now we see you, brother, in the full glow of candlelight, we perceive you have the lineaments of the MacDonalds. We met Donald MacDonald, the previous head of the clan, as a boy when our father was king. A striking man he was too. Have you MacDonald blood mingling with the MacBeath?'

Fergus was nonplussed at the question, especially in view of his mother's recent admission. He flushed and smiled. 'Sire, I cannot say. It is most probable.' The king laughed. 'A prudent answer, young man. All those long, cold nights in the north-west... You have a noble heritage. Good luck to you, and remember our commission!'

Fergus knew he was being dismissed and, with due reverence, replied, 'Sire, I shall carry out your instructions as well and as promptly as I can.'

Father John then invited the royal couple to lead the way to the next room, the dining hall of the guest house, and the other guests followed in twos and threes. Guardsmen had appeared at this doorway while others were disposed around the room. Fergus found himself moving slowly forwards in the company of Sir Archibald Douglas, who greeted him with surprising courtesy.

'I have to apologise for my rudeness at our last meeting,' said the earl. 'I made an impossible demand, which you were justified in refusing.'

'My lord, that is very gracious, I thank you,' replied Fergus, very surprised. Douglas didn't seem to be a man much given to apologising.

The earl continued, 'You probably want to know how events have turned out. His grace cannot be replaced as hostage by a man under sentence of death, no matter who concurs; it seems that such a sentence reduces the man's value. However, the king in his graciousness has given Colin the king's pardon.'

'He's been reprieved?' Fergus exclaimed in horror, clear in his voice as well as on his face.

Douglas glanced at him, unperturbed. 'Not altogether. The sentence has been commuted to banishment from this country – these islands – for life. He will be transferred from the Tollbooth in Edinburgh in the next day or two to a prison ship in Leith and taken to France. I have more business in that country shortly; I mentioned to you that I have been fighting for the dauphin's cause. Colin will join my army. Thereafter he will continue to do what he is good at – fighting. There is no shortage of opportunities for trained soldiers such as he. He may redeem himself yet.'

Fergus hardly knew how to respond. Natural courtesy surfaced, and he said, 'My lord, I am sure you are relieved at this improvement in his prospects.'

'Well, he will need to look to himself,' said Douglas. 'He has made plenty of enemies among influential people in this recent escapade.'

'Perhaps I should mention, my lord… It seems that I do not – did not – in fact qualify to speak on behalf of the late, young de Vere lady.' Fergus hesitated, wondering whether to divulge the delicate issue of his parentage. 'It seems that….. that although it was popularly supposed Roger de Vere was my father, in fact that was not so. My true father is Euan MacDonald, younger brother of the current clan chief, Alexander.'

'Is that so?' said the earl, looking at Fergus, it seemed, with renewed respect. 'Well, in spite of the irregularity, you come of two lines of heritage that command high respect. You will be glad not to be living under the shame of Roger's behaviour. I saw that his grace the king showed you marked signs of favour.'

They found themselves being shepherded to their places at the banqueting table. Earl Archibald Douglas was among the guests to be seated with the royal couple at the high table. Catriona and Donald were also placed in the royal company, and Donald was soon in close conversation with Sir Robert Lauder, no doubt on legal matters. Fergus made his way to where guests were milling about, finding seats as near to the top table as they could without overtly pushing their way in front. He saw Lady Mary and Callum together and joined them at seats somewhere in the middle. He was eager to talk to Callum about his prospects in the royal household, and to ask him if he would accept the job.

'I dinna think I have much choice, do I?' said Callum. 'Not if the king expects it. I've nae too many other prospects in life, either. I should see whaur this yin gaes. D'ye think I'll be able tae continue my education? I've started tae read and write. But ye ken, the king's got a lot on his mind. Mebbe he'll forget.'

'No, I don't think so,' said Mary. 'I heard him giving instructions to his secretary. He's been hovering close at the royal elbow while his grace works out his personal entourage. I hear you've been given some instructions too, Fergus.'

'I have indeed. Malcolm will be pleased, for it gives us every reason – two new reasons, actually – to hasten the trip to Islay. The king seemed very determined to engage Lord MacDonald as his henchman.'

'He needs another strong band to oppose the Albany Stewarts,' said Mary quietly, quickly looking around to make sure the duke was not within earshot. 'Douglas has come to heel, but the king has alienated the Duke of Albany by proposing that his son Walter should become one of the hostages needed to secure the ransom. You can imagine how that was received! I think that was why the duke was late at the reception and has been looking daggers ever since.'

'I heard that a band of marauding soldiers was intercepted on its way here, and that it was possibly Walter preparing to join or lead a coup,' said Fergus. 'All these heavy military types suggest that there is risk of a challenge. Indeed, the king said to me that he was going to expedite his coronation. I suppose that once that is achieved he'll feel more secure.'

'I also heard that his stay here at Soltre is probably going to be cut short,' said Mary. 'Depending on what's going on in the countryside and the strength of his forces, he feels he should waste no time in heading north and securing his crown. There had been a plan to go hawking on the moors tomorrow, but they will probably depart instead.'

'That's a terrible shame, in view of all the work gone into preparations,' said Fergus. 'Still, prudence and safety come first.'

'Until the king has secured his reputation and made solid friendships,' said Mary, 'he's extremely vulnerable. Even though he has his own guards to take him north, they are just borrowed English soldiers who are probably hankering to return home. Father John's little army of volunteers is probably the most secure force, and I'm sure father will allow them to accompany the king. Then there's a number of Douglas's men too.' She lowered her voice. 'But the king is not completely sure of Douglas's fidelity. Ultimately, everyone is out for himself.'

As they talked, food was appearing in great dishes on the tables: stews of venison and mutton, enormous pies of game birds, roasted swan, goose and capon, piles of mixed vegetables, dishes of oysters and salmon. Each guest had a platter and could help himself or be waited on by the servants. Wine and ale were available in large jugs. Callum's eyes were popping out of his head with amazement.

'The good father has put on a fine show!' said Mary.

'If the guests do indeed leave tomorrow,' said Fergus, 'we'll have to forgo our vows of poverty for several weeks. Look, here are more dishes. Tarts and jellies, fritters, eggs, sugared fruits with honey. Have you got a sweet tooth, Callum?'

The eating and drinking went on for some hours, and after the first hour or so, musicians arrived and settled themselves near the royal group at the top table; a select gathering of local talent including singers, pipers and fiddlers. The king looked happy, not least because he was seated next to the Lady Catriona, and was enjoying and warmly applauding the musicians. The Duke of Albany, who sat in silent solitude, left the party early, but not unnoticed. Father John intercepted him at the door to bid him a courteous goodnight; this was the signal for two men in dark garments to follow him to his room and remain on vigil outside the door, while two others left the guest house to remain on watch by his window.

With such a thorough guardian force, no further alarms occurred internally at Soltre that night, although a number of lurking bands were challenged, melting away into the night when they realised that they were seriously outnumbered.

Chapter 20

The good father did not go to bed at all that night, for the practical reason that all the accommodation in his residence was occupied with honoured guests, the royal couple and his lordship, the bishop.

There were a few midnight roamers in the countryside around Soltre. Father John's network of spies reported back to the gate at intervals, and from there the information was carried immediately to the father as he sat in his study. The band of soldiers who had advanced and retreated in the middle of the night were stealthily followed by the most experienced of his sleuths: a tough, grizzled man called Gil, riding a sturdy, sure-footed Border cob. The pair were famed for their ability to stalk anything on legs, to move in total silence and melt invisibly into the shadows. The soldiers made enough noise to be easily followed, relying more on speed than cunning.

Gil was armed with a vicious dirk, which he had no intention of using unless absolutely necessary. He followed them for about twenty miles, to woodlands at the base of the Pentland Hills, where they came to a halt, clearly thinking they were not pursued, and prepared to rest for the remainder of the night. They spoke to each other in voices that carried well enough to where Gil had found concealment in a thicket, having left his horse tethered a little way off. He listened long enough to establish the identity of the band; that this was indeed Walter Stewart and his men. From snatches of conversation, it became clear to Gil that the riders had been surprised that Soltre was so well defended. They had intended some action, it seemed, if it had proved possible. He heard them mention the duke, but it was not clear if he was privy to their plans of attack. Their intention now was to travel north early in the morning.

Gil waited for an hour or more, memorising all the talk that he heard and the identities of some of the men present, which included Walter himself. Then, as the group settled to sleep, and carefully avoiding the man they had left on watch, Gil glided away to his horse, led him to the edge of the trees, mounted up and rode off at speed. He was back at Soltre as dawn was breaking.

The king came to Father John's study at around six in the morning, as had been agreed the night before. John had reported the outside happenings to the king the previous evening before they all retired, and they had debated the wisdom of their graces travelling north when possible danger threatened. It would certainly be folly to be enjoying sport out on the moors under such conditions. The loyalty of the English guard was waning as time and distance passed, and it seemed prudent to hasten to Perth and, with the bishop's assistance, to expedite the coronation at Scone.

With the king settled in front of the fire, necessary even on that summer morning, John shared the news brought in by Gil an hour before. King James nodded sombrely as he digested this.

'Gil was sure their intention was to travel back north at first light,' John added. 'He heard no plans for an ambush or any further challenge.'

'I believe we must travel ourselves with all possible haste, whatever the conditions,' said the king. 'Good, Father John, we are very grateful for your hospitality, and astounded at the establishment here at Soltre. We have never encountered another monastery or priory like it. We would dearly have liked to see the infirmary and other areas of activity, but most impressive is your capacity for defence. We understand how this has been born of troubles in past centuries. Such loyalty by your men is something we should wish to emulate – not just your community here in the abbey, but in the countryside surrounding. We feel strongly the need to surround ourselves with people of similar commitment and fidelity. Do you have any advice for us, father?'

Father John could well perceive how vulnerable the king felt at this moment; nominally a king but, having been a helpless captive for most of his life, needing to build a regal reputation and authority almost overnight. Meanwhile, he was faced with a number of powerful nobles with their own armies who wanted the crown for themselves, and who would only be stopped by superior forces, or by the conviction that James had the divine right to call himself king – a belief that would be enhanced by his coronation, seated on the famed Stone of Destiny at Scone.

'I do believe, sire, that your plan to hold your coronation with speed is correct. You need friends you can trust, and Bishop Wardlaw is your right-hand man, Sir Robert Lauder also. You have won friends here, sire, there is no doubt about it. My warriors, tough unpolished Borderers as they are, would die for you already. And they are at your disposal, to augment your forces as you travel north and arrange the coronation. I believe, sire, although you mentioned doubts about my lord Archibald Douglas, that he is confirmed in his loyalty too. It was a stroke of genius to pardon his son, sire. I am sure you can accept with every confidence his offer of extra men to accompany you north.'

'We certainly did not gain the loyalty of Albany by suggesting his son be a hostage on our behalf! However, the Albany son is a lost cause and will have to be dealt with. Do you think we should offer a place in our company to the Duke of Albany? It would be expected normally, and perhaps be seen as hostile not to do so?'

'I think it would be prudent. It is always good to be charitable where you can, and he has no forces with him. You asked my advice, sire, about gaining loyalty. It sounds very worldly to say so, but it is all about give and take. Here at Soltre we have power to benefit men, whole families, indeed dynasties, with jobs and security. We run a feudal estate, in effect. The reason for the gratitude of most people, though, is the medical attention they get from us. Most families have benefited from our service in this respect. Our rolling experience dates, as Your Grace mentioned, from the treating of injured warriors in past warfare. While the Church teaches that all sickness is punishment for sin, you cannot say the same for injuries incurred in fighting for king and country. I hope and believe that the orthodoxy connecting illness with sin is gradually changing. We do not treat the sick on that basis; we prefer the philosophy of the ancient Greeks, that there is a cause for individual ills and a way to cure them. And the Good Lord has given us the wherewithal to find causes and cures – using our intellects, natural compassion and the bounty surrounding us.

'So you might say, sire, that our medical philosophy arises out of past loyalty to the Crown. And our present loyalty is entirely yours, Your Grace.'

So saying, the father stood up and bowed deeply, and the king was visibly moved. Father John had his own agenda for emphasising his loyalty and that of his establishment in its widest extent. The medical practice of Soltre was sustained by its fame, but it was, as he had hinted, out of step with the Church's current attitude. But the Church was feudal also, and all it required was a change of papal opinion to an old-fashioned orthodoxy and Soltre might come under fire. If he had the king's sponsorship, born out of loyalty at this difficult time, it could be protective.

Meanwhile, the combined forces that could be assembled would ensure his grace's safe passage to Perth, and instructions were sent out with the father's scribe to put these arrangements in place. Then the king had further points to discuss.

'Do you think it a good thing for us to take this young pilgrim, Callum, under our wing?'

'Sire, I do indeed. He is an illiterate country boy, but is an excellent young man of courage and principle. However, he is not the stuff of which courtiers are made. Your Grace would need to find him some honest toil to undertake. Might I suggest that for the time being you keep him near your person as an unofficial bodyguard? Apparently unarmed, but charged with keeping his eyes open for potential dangers? Once Your Grace knows him better, then it will be clear in what way he can serve you best.'

'We hope the holiness he has earned from his pilgrimage would extend to ourselves, so the role of unofficial bodyguard would seem apt.'

After all the elaborate preparations, the king and queen only stayed at Soltre for twenty-four hours. However, Father John was content with what had been achieved. He had the fulsome gratitude of the king for his arrangements, which had witnessed the handover of the seals of office from the present governor, averted an attack from the governor's son and exposed beyond doubt the continuing disloyalty of the same. He had seen Sir Colin Douglas receive the king's pardon, with the beneficial outcome of consolidating the loyalty of the Earl Douglas. Meanwhile, that young firebrand had been consigned to banishment, so would be stirring no more trouble locally. He had instigated measures that would provide the king with a MacBeath doctor and at the same time would bring the Lord of the Isles to a position of allegiance. And he had found an excellent position for Callum. All in all, he felt good work had been accomplished, and once his servants had put the residence back in some semblance of normal order, Father John took his siesta with sweet dreams of self-congratulation.

With commissions from the king himself, there was every reason for Malcolm and Fergus to hasten their arrangements to depart for Islay. The round journey would take them several months, and it was desirable that they should return before the worst of the autumn storms threatened. Fergus was filled with delight and anticipation, both for the journey and the prospect of going home, made all the more sweet by the new roles he had – particularly as envoy of the King, charged with two messages of great importance.

Having not seen much of his best-loved adviser, Brother Peter, during the upheaval of the royal visit, Fergus made a point of joining him in the infirmary late one evening after compline. They talked of Fergus's journey.

'I must not neglect my studies, even as we travel,' said Fergus. 'I am to become proficient in Italian and French, perhaps Spanish too. My Latin is already quite good. Brother Malcolm says we shall speak a different language each day.'

'This is in preparation for university?' asked Peter.

'Yes. Brother Malcolm wants me to go to Paris first, then to Bologna; perhaps a visit to Salamanca after that. I believe this is what he did himself. What I don't understand is that he seems to be disobeying Bishop Wardlaw's instructions. The bishop seemed to think I would do all my studies at St Andrews.'

Peter pulled a wry face. 'Malcolm mentioned that the bishop took a rather high-handed line with you. We are not bound to obey him in this. You would learn nothing at St Andrews except doctrinal detail and theology. You need to meet men who keep their minds open – to both ancient wisdom from Greece and modern oriental discoveries, from Muslims and others. Your own kin, the MacBeaths, have regularly found their way to these far-flung places.'

'I suppose all monastic communities that provide care of the sick are out of step with official doctrine?'

'Yes, but at Soltre we are more active than most in trying to cure as well as to comfort. We will be in the firing line if anyone starts to stir up hunts for heretics. Showing our loyalty to the king at this moment has hopefully earned his protection. And with the bishop there to see this! Father does not anticipate any immediate crackdown on our practices by the Church's policy-makers, but that can be unpredictable. There was a massive heresy hunt in France once, when a group of people, devout and pious, started thinking things out for themselves. The pope even took arms against them. It could happen again.'

Chapter 21

Fergus's special joy in returning home to Islay was that he came not as a sorry failure but as a man who had overcome adversity and found his own calling. He came with a purpose, in noble company, as a messenger of the king.

He enthused about his homeland to Malcolm; the green island that bore the wild ocean battering its west coast, while the mountains in the east, facing the mainland, seemed to have pitched up in the wrong place. Luckily, Malcolm proved as strong a sailor as he was a horseman, for the passage across the sea in an open longboat, a birlinn, was rough and wet. But the welcome was rich, warm and as comforting as the usquebaugh, the spirit distilled on the island, could make it.

Fergus was pleasurably aware that he had onerous duties to perform. The most delicate was to approach the Lord Alexander MacDonald in such a way that the lord would not feel himself commanded to attend the king. A good opportunity occurred when, amid the rejoicing on his return – and the rejoicing was ebullient and island-wide – he met Euan MacDonald, brother of the Lord Alexander, whom he had hitherto only known as a distant and rather august presence at formal gatherings. Now, at an informal party at the house of his own grandparents, he approached Euan, seeing him in a new light and closely inspecting him. He appeared remarkably young – not much older than I am, thought the lad – strong and muscular, with dark, red-tinged hair and beard, freckles and grey eyes.

Right hands firmly clasped, they engaged those eyes of identical colour in frank contact.

'Hello, son!' said Euan cheerfully.

'Hello, father. You knew, then.'

'I was fairly sure. I take it your mother told you.' Then the two hugged long and strong, and the other merrymakers – those who were in any condition to observe – made their own inferences. So the erstwhile father figure of Sir Roger de Vere was firmly replaced by one of the lordly MacDonalds, and Fergus was thrilled and swelled with pride. He remembered that, even though Roger had until recently been loving and attentive, he had always seemed distinctly foreign and 'other'. His MacBeath family had never approved of Roger at all, not least because he was unremarkable and mediocre in all things other than Catriona's affection. They despaired when he had claimed Fergus for the Douglas clan, and were now overjoyed that de Vere had been banished from the family.

'If we had only known,' said Grandmother MacBeath, shaking her head in regret. 'Euan was unmarried at the time. A match might have been made.' In no time, it was accepted around the island that Euan was Fergus's father. Even Euan's wife, herself the mother of two young boys, smiled upon him. But Euan had indeed been very young when Fergus was conceived, scarcely more than a boy, sowing his wild oats.

So it was quite natural that Fergus should be invited to Finlaggan to meet with Lord Alexander MacDonald. Before the visit took place, he asked Euan about the best way to deliver his message from King James, in such a manner that it would be taken and responded to in the spirit of goodwill in which it was made.

'If you deliver the message quite frankly, in the way you've told me,' said Euan, 'including the trouble with the Albany Stewarts, and the need the king has for powerful allies, I do not think there will be any difficulty. And the message is conveyed by a friend, ally and kinsman – one of complete trustworthiness!'

Father and son rode over to Finlaggan on rough-coated, sturdy Highland ponies. The grey, compact stone castle was situated on an islet in the middle of a lochan, barely visible in the dripping grey mist as they crossed over the causeway on their sure-footed mounts. They were greeted heartily by the Lord Alexander and a dozen MacDonald men. Fergus was treated as an equal among them, respect being given him as kin and as an Augustinian canon as well as a personal messenger of royalty. The discussion was carried out at table with all due hospitality, and it was agreed that Lord Alexander would immediately leave the island with a retinue in order to wait upon the king at his coronation, or soon after, for time was short.

'I do not want to meet the king empty-handed,' said Alexander, looking round. 'I am not begging for favours from him. I should take a gift of some value.' Fergus caught Euan's eye and his father gave a brief, encouraging nod.

'My lord,' he said, not quite ready yet to address Lord Alexander as uncle. The great man looked his way and gestured that he should continue.

'Another task I am requested to perform for his grace King James is to find a personal physician for him from the MacBeath family. The king used to be attended by Brian of our ilk, until his recent demise. I have discussed this with senior members of the MacBeath family and there is a very obvious and willing candidate for the role. Hamish, who is young, recently returned from France, where he has been acting as field doctor to the troops there to gain experience after his medical training.'

'And I can take this medical treasure with me to offer to King James! This costs me nothing, and yet I can see that his grace would welcome such a gift as being beyond value. It would certainly assure him of my best intentions and be a splendid diplomatic move. What do you think, men?'

There was general assent and acquiescence, and Lord Alexander nodded his approval at Fergus.

'Nothing short of brilliant, nephew. My hearty thanks. I shall be glad of Hamish's company on our travels, and no doubt he will be glad to travel in our band. Can he be ready to go immediately, do you think?'

Fergus was sorry there was so little time to spend in Hamish's company. He wanted to know all about his kinsman's experiences in his training years.

Hamish had one particular nugget of advice: 'Don't waste your time going to St Andrews University,' he said. 'It was established by Bishop Wardlaw and all the education is fenced around by Church law. I know you are a man of the cloth now, and I know about the reputation of Soltre, otherwise I would say you are wasted in that garb! The bishop doesn't like medical men who are not also churchmen; he thinks we are too free-thinking and prone to devilish theories. I left St Andrews in disgust after a few months. All the treatments they taught were about shriving sins and penance and looking deep into souls. It's as if they are obstructing the way of real progress. You and Brother Malcolm are sailing near the wind in your researches into the problems of pregnancy. Mind you, I do think it is an excellent work; the whole subject is steeped in ignorance and superstition. Churchmen would like all men to be spontaneously generated, I think, without any female intervention. But I wonder how much you will get away with in a church-based establishment. Don't be advertising your successes too much!'

'Malcolm has explained some of this to me,' said Fergus. 'But, as you say, Soltre is somewhat immune from clerical repression by its reputation.'

'All the same, take care. Watch your back,' said Hamish. 'I am enormously grateful for this opportunity you've brought to me, cousin Fergus. I shall keep in touch from the royal court and watch your career with interest. It is my view that you should not commit altogether to Soltre. Don't join the priesthood, whatever you do. If you are a canon, it is possible to leave. If you are a priest, well, it's more difficult.'

'You will find a good friend of mine in attendance on the king,' said Fergus. 'Callum, the pilgrim.' And he explained about how Callum had become locally renowned and how the king had adopted him as his holy man in residence.

'I am not sure how Callum will adapt to court life,' he said. 'Can you look out for him, help him to find a niche that suits him? And keep me in touch with him?' Hamish readily agreed to do this.

Once the MacDonald party, with Hamish, had departed, Fergus and Malcolm could concentrate on their medical explorations. Fergus's family was able to summon the best and most experienced practitioners in childbirth on the island, all women, to a conference. One of the most important proposals was that Fergus should attend some normal deliveries. Not all mothers would be willing to be attended by men, but word had got round that these two canons had saved the life of Lady Catriona, one of their own Islay women, in childbirth, and under extreme circumstances. That would be their passport into cottages where births were imminent; and so it proved to be.

After some weeks, their various aims having been accomplished, Fergus and Malcolm set off on the journey back to Soltre. News had already filtered through to them that Lord Alexander had reached the king's side in time for the coronation in May, and had been rewarded for this expression of loyalty with the earldom of Ross and an invitation to join the new parliament when it met at Stirling. The earldom was a most generous gift, giving MacDonald a huge swathe of the north-west mainland and significantly increasing his power. The reward was also a snub to the Albany Stewarts, who had not shown conspicuous loyalty to the Crown. In fact, King James had had Walter, the duke's son, imprisoned on account of his disloyal plotting.

Fergus was aware that the sudden and unexpected increase in Lord Alexander's fortunes had been brought about, in part at least, by his own intervention and felt very proud indeed. With the loyalty of the Albany Stewarts and the Douglases somewhat uncertain, perhaps the king was relieved to feel that one of the big three nobles of Scotland would show undivided allegiance to the Crown.

Back at Soltre, Fergus received messages from Hamish and Callum at the royal court. But these tidings were soon superseded by momentous news from France. Earl Archibald Douglas had taken his army to France to support the dauphin in his civil struggle against the Burgundians and their allies, the English. Douglas was joined by his exiled son, Colin, and John Stewart, half-brother to Murdoch, the erstwhile guardian of Scotland. At a bloody battle in Verneuil, near Normandy, Earl Douglas and John Stewart had been killed – as well, said the news, as one of Douglas's sons. Their Scots armies were completely wiped out.

Although this Douglas son was not named, it was assumed that he was none other than Colin, who had certainly been in action there. The people of the Borders rejoiced unashamedly that this much-to-be-desired death had at last taken place. However, many of Douglas's army men were Borders people, so there were many bereaved and mourning families also.

At Soltre, just before chapter meeting, Father John gathered the senior canons together to discuss the political as well as local connotations of the battle and its outcome. Fergus was included among their number.

'There are many of our local families who have lost someone. We must remember them in our prayers. However, the news will come as a great boon to the king,' said Father John. 'So many of the Albany Stewart henchmen have been lost, as well as

Murdoch's brother, the Earl of Douglas and his men. Two of the king's challenging power bases completely wiped out.'

'But Douglas was one of the king's allies,' said Peter.

'I think the king knew he could not completely trust Douglas,' said John. 'His loyalty was always conditional.' Fergus nodded to himself. His kinsman, Lord Alexander, was now still more important to King James.

Events soon proved John to be correct in his insights. King James felt he could act with royal ruthlessness, and imprisoned Murdoch and another of his sons, who joined Walter behind bars – not for long, however, as all three were put to death, while James seized their estates and castles for himself. He had begun to build a modern palace at Linlithgow.

'He's setting himself up as quite an autocratic king,' observed Father John. 'It's not something we've been accustomed to in Scotland. But with so many ambitious men around, who would stop at very little to gain their ends, maybe it's just what we need for stability.'

PART 2

Chapter 22

1432

Fergus, on horseback, manoeuvred through the thick green forest to the east of Soltre. In the height of summer, the scents of woodland and wet earth, with an occasional sharp whiff of fox or badger, filled his nostrils. He had thought he knew the paths through the forest fairly well, but had forgotten how the structure changed even from year to year, with storm damage, growth of trees and shrubs and the constant battle between various ground-level plants to gain an advantage of light and warmth. Percy, his horse, would easily find the way back to Soltre if he was allowed his head, but Fergus had an urgent visit to make to a cottage somewhat off the beaten track. Trying to make a short cut, he had definitely got them lost. If it had been winter, he might have been guided by the smell of woodsmoke. He pulled Percy to a halt and listened for any workaday sounds, such as chopping or hammering or farmyard noises.

Even the remnants of a path were difficult to make out in the dense undergrowth. All he could hear was the rustling of leaves in the slight breeze and Percy's occasional headshake to scatter the flies. Then… did he imagine it? No, there it was; it sounded like a baby's cry. He nudged Percy forward, towards the sound. Quite suddenly, the greenery parted and he found himself in a woodland clearing. Crossing it from the opposite side, and startled to see him and Percy suddenly emerge from the trees, was a young woman. She stopped in her tracks and stared at him.

Probably reassured by his clerical garb, she nodded and said, 'Good day, brother. Are you lost?'

Fergus took in her appearance. She was around thirty, certainly comely from a distance. She had long brown hair appearing from beneath her white cotton cap; her dress was plain and grey; she had a coarse shawl thrown around her shoulders; and she carried a covered basket.

'Yes, sister, you are quite right. I should have come by clearer paths. I'm looking for the cottage of a Maggie Burn, quite near the village of Dunfrae.'

'I've just come frae there myself.' Just then, the infant cry could be heard nearer at hand, and she briefly turned her head.

Fergus said, 'I'm the doctor from Soltre. I had a message that Maggie was having trouble giving birth. From the sound of it, maybe my work has been done for me.' He paused. 'My name's Brother Fergus.'

She brightened at the name and gave a respectful little bob. 'Brother Fergus, I have heard tell of ye. I am honoured. My name is Jan – Jan Eliot. Come away, I'll take you to Maggie.'

She led the way out of the clearing and Fergus found himself on a well-defined path that led to a small hamlet of three cottages. He dismounted and loosely tied up Percy to a post. Jan led the way through the front door of the first cottage, respectfully calling first, 'Hey there, Maggie, it's me again, with a visitor for you.' She peered in to make sure all was in order before beckoning for Fergus to enter.

After introductions had been made, and Maggie, lying in bed, had been suitably abashed by her eminent visitor, Fergus was shown the infant, now soundly sleeping in a rough basketwork cradle. He told Maggie that he had received an urgent message that morning.

'Aye, that was the neighbour Jem,' interjected Jan. 'He went up to Soltre early because Maggie's husband was worried; she'd been in labour for twenty-four hours and was getting exhausted. Jem's wife came and called me. I live close by and am often called for childbirths.' Fergus's eyes widened with interest. Here was the answer to his prayers.

'How did you manage to help her?' he asked. Smiling at the mother, who did indeed look very tired and drawn, he gently pulled down the coverings in the cradle and looked at the sleeping infant, wrinkled and red, but seemingly none the worse for wear. There was a pause; Fergus looked up at Jan and saw her doubt and hesitation.

'Believe me, I ask with respectful and true interest. You wise women have knowledge that I wish was known to us, known more generally. Please do tell me. You've done a good job as far as I can see.'

'I felt her belly. This is her first, ye ken. It was clear to me that the baby wisna well positioned for a good birth. You should be able to feel the back of its head just here.' She indicated Maggie's lower belly area. 'I ken how tae massage the infant, so it kind o' rolls round. It's easier with a woman who's already had a wean. But Jem next door had a wee drop o' the barley bree and I had some relaxing herbs. So I made her a brew wi' those and we got her a bit softer and looser and after about an hour o' encouraging, the wean just turned, like ye would in a bed!' She and Maggie grinned at each other and squeezed hands. 'And after that, the birth was normal.'

'Let me see your hands,' said Fergus. She showed him a pair of hands that, though roughened and calloused in places, were surprisingly slim and elegant. 'You have had plenty experience, Jan, I can see. I am amazed. I have never seen this done before.'

He asked Maggie a few questions and established that all was well, after which there was nothing to do but let mother and child sleep. He asked if he could walk with Jan towards her home and talk further. Unhitching Percy, he led him as they walked together. Fergus was so dumbfounded at what he had heard and seen, he hardly knew where to begin.

'Do you have children of your own, Jan?'

'Yes, I've a daughter, eight years old. She's called Annie. My neighbour is watching her. I came here in the middle of the night.'

'Is your husband not at home?'

'I've nae husband,' Jan replied bluntly. After a pause, she added, 'Until two years ago, I lived near Gifford. I worked up at the big Yester estate house like my mother afore me. Ye will understand when I tell ye that all women who work there have to do what they're tellt. If the maister or his sons tak a fancy tae ye, ye canna say them nay. A' the same, when ye get a bairn, as I did – and as my mother did in her time, several in fact – they dinna turn ye awa'; which happens in other places.'

'But you decided to leave?'

'Yes. My Annie was getting to the age when the men of the house would start gowping at her. And she's a bonnie lass. I thought we would be better awa' frae there.'

'But she would have been only six when you left!'

'Ah, weel. I felt she was in some danger. I bide in a cottage that belongs to the bakery where I work now. It's a wee step frae here, brother, the next village.'

Fergus paid no heed to the hint, there was too much he wanted to know. 'Tell me how you came by your knowledge of childbirth.'

'Frae my mother. She was widely kent over Gifford way. Even the quality would bring her in. I went with her every time when I was wee. I had to, otherwise I was left alane. She got her skills frae her mother afore her, and so on back, back in time, I dinna ken how far. I ken some other plants that are used for healing wounds and suchlike, so I'm called for those things too.' They walked on in silence, Fergus deep in thought.

'Do you get called much around here for births?'

'Not much, so far. You have to get known. I think some women are feart to call in a wise woman like me, unless they're desperate – like Maggie and her man were. There are some priests around who look upon the likes of me as a witch. I've had the local priest at our village, poking around my place and asking if I do spells and warning me not to consort with evil spirits and suchlike. I had some kelp that I'd gathered from the beach for medicine making and he took it away.'

'Well, now, that is where I could help you. We can persuade the local priests to back off if they know that all you do is done with the approval of Soltre. Some priests are both ignorant and afraid of women. Where do they think they came from themselves? Discovered under a font, perhaps!'

Jan burst out laughing, and Fergus thought then how pretty and young she looked. He had a thousand questions buzzing in his brain.

'Mistress Jan,' he said, 'Do you mind me asking a personal question? Were you fathered in the same way as your daughter was?' She nodded, not at all perturbed.

'Aye, and so was my mother. You just kind of accept that all the women there belong frae their birth to the big house. My mother was there from birth till her death, only a few years ago. She was very young to die, probably tired from her own child-bearing. She had ten weans; several sons who ran away. The lads were nae sae welcome in the house.'

'And have you just had the one child?'

'Aye, Annie is my only one.' She paused. 'Ye may wonder why. There are ways of stopping yerself falling pregnant. They dinna always work, but they did wi' me.' Fergus gazed at her in amazement. How many valuable nuggets of know-how were lodged in this head?

'Where did you find that out?'

'My mother again. There are things that are handed down. Some work and some dinna. I was determined not tae end up wi' a brood like my mother, one a year like the farm animals, and all the work and then the heartache when the lads scarpered. Basically, you use the plants that are good for bringing on labour, but only in small amounts, and best taken afore the man gets at ye. Some can make ye very sick, but it's worth it.'

'How did you manage to get away from the Yester estate?'

'It's not hard to walk away. The difficult thing is to find a place to stay and a way to make a living. One of the men from the bakery who came to the big house wi' bread and goods got me a job at the bakery near here, at Fala. They've let me have a cottage too, though not for long. It's hard to find the rent, so they take something off my pay.'

Fergus questioned her about the plants she gathered, and where she found them; some were not familiar to him. Soon they arrived at the little row of thatched wattle-and-daub cottages where she lived. A small girl appeared at the door of the next cottage; a sweet-faced child with long, wispy light-brown hair, whose delight when she saw Jan left Fergus in no doubt that this was Annie. Jan mussed her hair then went inside to thank the neighbour, leaving the child gazing inquisitively at Fergus and his horse. Like her mother, she was more curious than shy.

She smiled up at him, brushing her hair from her face. 'I like your horse,' she said. 'What's his name?' She patted his neck and put her hand under his muzzle, like one accustomed to animals. By the time Jan reappeared she had been hoisted up and was sitting astride the horse, asking to be taken a walk, much more interested in Percy than in Fergus.

'Remember your manners, bairnie. This is Brother Fergus. Say "How d'you do, brother? Thank ye for letting me sit on your horse."'

Jan allowed Annie some minutes on horseback, but then made it clear she needed to get organised for her day's work.

'I must go too now, Mistress Jan,' said Fergus. But I shall come and talk to you some more, if I may. I think we can help each other. Tell me, who is this troublesome priest and where can I find him?'

Chapter 23

Fergus digested all he had seen and heard as he rode back to Soltre. He remembered Malcolm's advice to him, years ago, to make friends with one of the local midwives. Here was the ideal person. Jan seemed, from her conversation, an intelligent and capable young woman, observant and skilled as well as compassionate. He had noticed how her speech at times almost sounded educated, presumably because of her upbringing in the big house; although most of the time she used the vernacular. He dwelled too on the situation where serving girls doubled as comfort women for the men of a well-to-do household. He had heard of the practice, but had never come across it so frankly spoken of before now. Although it seemed good that at least the women were not turned away when pregnant, he wondered if this indicated a certain tendency among the men at Yester to favour the very young with their sexual attentions.

Striding over to Father John's office, Fergus continued thinking about Jan. He'd seen enough of the world in his student years to know that poverty drove people, women especially, to do desperate things. He thought it very probable that Jan had used her womanly ways to get her job and her cottage, and perhaps also to pay her rent. It seemed intolerable that she should have to resort to such means when she was endowed with much rarer skills and knowledge. Well, if he had any power at all, he would remedy the situation.

Fergus had completed his studies in Salamanca a few years previously. He had studied first in Bologna, then Paris, before spending a final few months in Spain. His student years were filled with study and discovery interspersed with the excesses, high spirits and transgressions of youth. He would remove his canonical robes and join his friends in visiting the fleshpots of the city. He even had to physic himself after encounters in the brothels. The folk wisdom that circulated among the medical students for such events proved to be efficacious. He told himself it was practical learning that he wouldn't have got at St Andrews.

After Salamanca, he felt more exploring was needed. He still compared himself to Callum, remembering how his friend, an ignorant, penniless farm boy, had managed to get to Spain and back on his own resources. Fergus could never match that for courage and achievement. Indeed, with his degree in medicine as well as skill, experience and contacts in the Augustinian world, travelling and living on his wits should be easy. The art of medicine in distant exotic lands beckoned, and he set sail for Egypt, travelling across the Mediterranean Sea with a group of clerics – experienced travellers who smoothed his way.

Fortunate to reach Egypt a year after a severe plague epidemic had subsided, as well as during a comparatively stable period of government under the Sultan, Al Ashraf, he was hospitably welcomed as a doctor in one of the hospitals that treated diseases in people of all faiths and classes, free of charge. This hospital was, as was typical, well endowed, and he earned a high salary. True to his calling, he put this aside for Soltre's use at a future date, though did purchase a copy of the famous Canon of Medicine by the ancient Persian physician and philosopher Ibn Sina, and manuals of medical plants that were in use. He warmed to the Islamic philosophy that 'There is no disease that Allah has created except that he has also created its remedy.' If only, he thought, we could disseminate such a liberal philosophy back home in Scotland.

At last, he returned to Soltre, feeling that he had mastered his subject as far as lay in his power. His coming caused a stir, for he was not forgotten. His memory had been perpetuated by stories – some true, some fanciful – among the abbey residents, as well as the Border folk. Mostly they remembered him as the one who had vanquished their own particular devil in the shape of Colin Douglas. Fergus was now in his early twenties, no longer the slender boy of the past but a tall, broad-shouldered, well-favoured man. His complexion was darker and more rugged, his hair a shade fairer following his travels in distant lands. The women liked his manly appearance, and thought his hair resembled a bright halo, already well earned.

His saintly reputation, he was aware, was very far from the truth. As a man who had seen and studied the world across several countries, his faith in God was intact; but his opinion of the Church's organisation and teaching was lower than ever. It was a self-serving, power-based institution, steeped in worldly concerns and venality. But there were good men and women and there were oases of holiness, of which Soltre was one. He was glad to return and to commit to its clean, clear-cut principles.

His old friends welcomed him back with warmth and delight. Or most of them did. To his dismay, he found that Malcolm was no longer at the abbey. They broke the news to him gently. Malcolm had developed a terminal illness which he had quietly diagnosed himself, and, too ill to continue until Fergus's return, had taken himself into retirement at a priory over to the west. He had died shortly after, only a few months since.

Fergus found himself immediately elevated to the position of medicus, but unable to rejoice, so torn apart was he by the death of his excellent friend. He had been such a tower of strength and wisdom, full of down-to-earth common sense, humour and understanding of human nature. How could such a powerful presence and force for good be dead? Blown away as if he never had existed. Fergus mourned as he had never done before. He had subconsciously felt that the triumvirate of John,

Malcolm and Peter, such powerful influences in his life, would be immortal. Fergus thought of Malcolm's endeavours to help women, going against the trend and the creed of the church, and hardened his own determination to follow on with this work, however much courage it took.

As Fergus returned from visiting Maggie, Father John greeted him and invited him into the office, while giving his clerk instructions for dealing with other pressing business. 'Brother Medicus, you were out at first light, I believe, attending a woman in childbirth.'

Fergus was never surprised at how much father knew about what was going on around him; his information network was second to none. However, he had already decided to give John an edited version of his encounter in the forest that morning and hoped that certain sensitive details would remain hidden. Not only did he wish to respect Jan's confidences, but he knew father to be less worldly wise than himself.

He paused before responding, and John asked, 'Is all well with mother and child?'

'Indeed it is, father, and not in any way owing to me.' He described his meeting with the local midwife, and her extraordinary knowledge and skills. Father John, who had listened with an inscrutable expression, said with emphasis, 'It must be a source of relief to know that such a person is available to fill a role forbidden to us.'

Fergus looked at him in horrified surprise. 'Malcolm advised me to find such a wise woman and collaborate with her!' he said. 'She is vulnerable, working without status or protection. Indeed, she has already found the local priest to be antagonistic and interfering.'

'What would you hope to do by way of collaborating?' asked John.

'I had hoped to take her under the Soltre wing, let it be known that she was acceptable to our medical team. This way, people would trust her, the local priests could be held at bay with their suspicions of witchcraft. And to be frank, she probably has a lot she can teach me.'

John leaned back in his chair and looked up, as if seeking inspiration or help. He gave a big sigh and leaned forwards, his elbows on the desk. 'My dear Fergus, I know you to be the epitome of compassion and rectitude. I know you wish to follow in the ways of Malcolm, God rest his excellent soul. But we live in difficult times and I cannot be wholehearted in endorsing your plans. I am aware from our discussions that in your travels you have come across free-thinkers and have yourself learned to question orthodoxy and to follow your own thought-out ways to the truth, but our Church is not yet ready to let its hallowed creeds be challenged. And it is fighting a rising tide of such challenges, and perhaps behaving in ways not altogether logical or… benign. Here at Soltre, in all my time hitherto, we have been able to act more or less autonomously. We have our own rule, but we are aligned with the Church. I recognised years ago that the time might come when the Church's ruling hand could become more despotic. It was the reason why I was so keen to engage the king on his return from England, to gain the power of his protection. But he and Bishop Wardlaw are intimate friends, and the king has joined him in his war on heresy. A war which is rapidly becoming the bishop's raison d'être.'

'I heard about the terrible case of the French peasant girl who had visions, and was burned as a heretic,' said Fergus. 'But I wasn't aware such phobias were gaining ground over here.'

'I am afraid they are alive and burgeoning here, my dear Fergus. "Phobia" is right; senior churchmen fear the empowering of the ordinary person by too much knowledge. Twenty years ago, Bishop Wardlaw permitted the burning at the stake of an English priest, John Resby, for teaching the words of the dissenter Wycliffe. Wardlaw now has persuaded the king in an act of parliament to commit all bishops to root out heresy as a prime duty. And he has appointed a "papal inquisitor of heretical depravity" here in Scotland. We offended him by not sending you to his own orthodox university, so we are already marked down as potential candidates for inquisition. And I should emphasise that the fear among the Church's hierarchy is magnified tenfold when extended to women; a fear that defies logic.'

Fergus leaned forward, eager and animated. 'But are they not now thinking that they were wrong in condemning the French girl, Jeanne d'Arc? If in papal circles they can retract and accept they were wrong...'

'They do so by creating a scapegoat, which in this case was the Bishop Cauchon, who had condemned her. In times of war, even bishops can be misled by heavily vested secular interests.'

'Father, it is clear then that orthodoxy can go wrong. The decisions are those of men, however exalted, and they make mistakes. Especially when they have conflicting agendas. Should we fail to do something good because it is not currently approved doctrine? Shall we not lose moral authority here if we fail to strive for that good progress?'

'Brother Medicus, you argue exactly like Malcolm did. But consider this: if we all decide for ourselves what is right and what is wrong, where is the authority? We shall descend into anarchy. Still, I confess the world is lacking moral leadership at the moment on account of this terrible papal schism. Our leaders are showing just what frail creatures men are, even those who should be faultless.

'I have to compromise, my dear brother; I have to keep an eye on the political world and try to shield my charges from the worst consequences. I gave Malcolm more freedom than I can give you, because of the changing times. However, under his persuasion, I did try to improve the education of women in the areas where we have influence. Which are, as you know, extensive. We have managed to get schooling for girls locally, which is key to improving their status. It is my view that midwifery should remain a female sphere, but that women should be equipped to deal with it.

'So, you may let it be known that Mistress Jan does her work with our approval, and tell the priests they should not interfere. By all means, communicate with her. But she must not come to Soltre and none of her activities can take place here. We cannot step too deeply into an area the Church has instructed us to distance ourselves from. You admit this young woman has skills you could not now acquire in a lifetime; then make the most of her! Let her do the work while you are the enabler.'

Fergus had no choice but to bow obediently and say, 'Yes, father.' Then, after a moment's hesitation, he said, 'There will be occasions, like today, when childbirth goes wrong, and becomes a medical problem. I am likely to be called out, and cannot refuse to go.'

'You must follow your own professional conscience,' acknowledged Father John.

That same day, Peter and Fergus sat in the late evening warmth in the cloister, enjoying a few moments of respite and time to chat. Fergus had described his encounter with Jan, and Father John's muted response.

'It worries me that he is prepared to bend to accommodate these doctrinal edicts, when what matters is how best we can help vulnerable people. Do you think it's because he's getting old?'

'That tension has always been there, you know, and father has been skilled in bending rules rather than breaking them,' said Peter. 'You know he wants us to abandon the bloodletting sessions to suppress lust? There have been instructions from on high about that too. I know you think it is an illogical practice, to take blood away and then pamper the subject with rest and food to restore his strength, and I agree with you. Frankly, if unnatural affection arises between men here, I don't believe anything will stop it. I have found it better to look the other way.'

'Father reproved me for choosing my own morals, Peter! But the more you read and listen and learn, the more you doubt the teaching of the Church. It is given to us in a way which is so patronising, so oversimplified; it's fed to us like milky pap and infant food.'

'Everyone has doubts at times, brother. Your discomfort and doubts are the cross you have to bear for greater knowledge and insight. For me, I choose an easier path. I just focus on the work before me and do the best I can. Understanding holy mysteries is not something I worry about any more. I fret about understanding the nature of humankind. Which is a murky mystery enough.'

When Fergus next found time to ride down the hill to Jan's cottage, a week had elapsed. He knocked at the lintel of the cottage but no response came. He called in next door, and the neighbour told him that Jan and Annie had flitted just a few days ago, but could not say why. He got the impression that she knew but would not give away confidences.

'I need to find her, mistress. Can you tell me where she has gone?'

A shake of the head and a bland expression told him that here was an impenetrable wall. He was vexed. Did Jan wish to evade him? Had he done her a disservice? He was aware of how vulnerable she and her daughter were.

Knowing the priest's name and home, he headed there. Father Leonard, who lived in a cottage only slightly more comfortable than the ones he had just left, received him courteously enough. He knew Jan Eliot. 'Oh yes, who does not?' he asked with a sneer. Fergus gave him a cold stare. He asked if the priest knew of her current whereabouts, but he was not able to help. Fergus got the impression that Jan's recent house move was news to him.

Fergus rode into the village of Fala, enquiring for bakeries. He discovered the sites of two, but no one seemed to have heard of Jan. Again, he thought it was possible he was being stonewalled. He thought of Maggie Burn, whose delivery Jan had managed so professionally, and retraced his steps there. Maggie was rocking her baby and feeding him when he arrived, asking for news of Jan. 'Brother, I canna tell ye. If Jan hauds awa', it's wi' good reason, and even if I kent, which I dinna, I couldna gie her awa'.'

'But Mistress Burn, I want to help her! I wish her nothing but good. I thought she trusted me.' Fergus was so frustrated; there must be some way to find her. 'Mistress, can you do one thing for me, please? If you see her, will you tell her I was looking for her? Please beg her to trust me! I just need to talk to her, persuade her of how much use she could be with her natural gifts. They are too valuable to waste. You saw yourself how skilled she was!'

Maggie smiled docilely and nodded. 'Aye, I'll do that for ye, brother.'

'And are you likely to see her? And soon?'

'Aye, like enough she'll drop by in a day or two.'

Fergus returned to Soltre pondering the mystery and the strange and unpredictable ways of women. And yet, he thought, with such a history as hers, why should she trust anyone? Especially a member of the Church – someone who, to her, was part of the establishment. She could not have gone far, he thought, and surely he would hear news of her soon enough.

But it would be nearly three years before he heard or saw anything more of Jan.

Chapter 24

1435

Some three years had passed when, one spring night, chilly with a late frost, the canons had all returned to their dormitories from midnight Mass and wrapped themselves as well as they could in their cowls and blankets against the cold. Only Peter had fallen immediately asleep; all the others were alerted by hasty steps on the night stairs, and all thought, 'Poor old Fergus. Who'd be medicus on a night like this?'

Fergus, as usual, took some time to regain full consciousness. The messenger shook him, whispering, 'A message from Lady Mary!' Fergus groaned, thinking at first of his mother, then realising that Mary, now married and living in Lauder, was no longer his mother's companion. He had not seen her since his return to Soltre some years before, though they had exchanged messages. He wrapped himself in his cowl and followed the man downstairs.

Soon he was riding through the clear, moonlit night, heading towards Lauder with his guide. There was little wind and the temperature was near freezing. At Mary's written request, he was hurrying to the house of her new husband's cousin, who was suffering a protracted and perhaps obstructed labour. Fergus had not attended any sort of birth since his meeting with Jan three years ago. He thought hard of what she had told him, hoping he would be as effective as she had been.

Mary was waiting for him, and Fergus was thankful for a woman with at least some midwifery experience! She was now

Mary Gordon, married to David, a landowner and friend of Donald Dampierre. Her cousin, Sarah, had been labouring for more than twenty-four hours with her first baby. She was tired and a little weepy, but far from exhausted. Fergus talked in his gentle, easy way as he palpated her slender belly, closing his eyes and seeing through his sensitive fingers. Relief flooded through him, for he could picture the baby, and it was lying the wrong way, trying to emerge tail end first. He had brought some poppy extract, some tincture of lady's smock and some usquebaugh – what Jan had called barley bree. With Mary's help, he warmed a suitable mixture over the hearth, designed to relax muscles. He wanted to slow down labour only enough allow manipulation of the infant, but not to delay it unduly. Sarah drank the concoction and soon became quite drowsy and tipsy.

Fergus gently, gently massaged while murmuring small talk to his patient, who smiled and gave herself into his care. 'Ideal, trusting patient,' he thought. Contractions from the womb were coming regularly but not forcefully, and quite suddenly there was some boisterous activity under his hands as he felt the infant roll over. He still had his concerns, and continued to knead gently until he was certain the position was correct. Then his concern was that labour should now progress with expedition, and he had his supply of stimulants with him should they be needed. But to his relief, nature took over, and in the small hours of the morning, a healthy baby girl was brought into the world.

In the general euphoria that always follows such an event, Fergus's pleasure was as great as any. Mary said to him, with genuine admiration, 'You are obviously as experienced now as Malcolm ever was!' He told her what he would have told few others: that this was his first attempt to turn a child in the womb. He told her about Jan, how she had seemed to disappear from the face of the earth, and how much he had hoped would be gained from her extraordinary know-how.

In his attempts to find Jan, Fergus had sometimes visited the cottage she had occupied and places she had mentioned as sources of the herbs she gathered. He had gone back to Maggie's cottage, but she still could not, or would not, give away any information. Sometimes in the woods he had felt he was being watched. He might have dismissed this as fancy, but Percy, the horse, also seemed to sense something; his head would lift, he would prick his ears and flare his nostrils.

After the birth of Sarah's child, Fergus thought he would very much like to tell Jan of his success; surely it would please her to know her teaching had had such good effects. He resolved to renew his searches for her.

Chapter 25

Some months later in the woodlands, when falling leaves had covered the ground with a crunchy carpet, Fergus and Percy became aware of a presence, close by. There was a scuffling sound. It could have been a deer or other woodland creature, but there had been no panicked noise of swift escape. Fergus felt sure it was a human presence, and they stopped and listened. Fergus pressed his leg to turn Percy and his eye caught the movement of a small figure hiding behind a trunk. He kept very still and waited. A head and face appeared furtively, then vanished again. He began to move forward, calling, 'Annie! I can see you, hiding there. Come out and say hello!'

After a few seconds, Annie emerged from her hiding place, laughing, and only half reluctant. She ran over and greeted him, perhaps a little more shyly than before, giving Percy her friendliest attention. Fergus knew what would best promote her confidence and dismounted, offering her a ride. She beamed at him as she clambered up with nimble ease. 'I can ride quite well now, Brother Fergus.'

'I've been looking for you and your mother, Annie. It's a long time ago we first met.'

'Mum couldn't pay her rent, so her friend at the bakery said we could live with him.'

'And do you live with him now?'

'Yes. He's *quite* good to us.'

Fergus noticed her emphasis. 'Would you like to take me there now? You can ride all the way, if you like.'

'I don't think Mum would want you to go there.'

'Right, I won't go if you think I shouldn't, Annie. But I would very much like to talk to your mother. Do you think she would be happy to talk to me?'

'Oh yes, she would. She's working just now. I'm not supposed to wander far off. I'll show you the way, then you can hide and I'll go get her.'

So they stopped a short distance from one of the bakeries that Fergus had visited before, and Annie pointed out the cottage next to it, where they lived. Then she slithered off Percy, asked Fergus to wait, and ran off to the ramshackle bakery building, where she vanished from view. Although Annie had grown in height, she was still thin and waiflike, still very much a child, although she must be now about eleven. She was also, he noted, rather poorly clad for the autumn chill that prevailed.

He had half expected he would not see Annie again, but soon she reappeared with Jan hot on her heels. They ran into the woodlands, hair flying in the wind, clearly trying not to be seen.

'Mistress Jan, I am overjoyed to see you again!'

'Brother Fergus, it is good to see you too.' She gave him both her hands. 'I'm not supposed to be out o' my work, ye ken, brother. But I did hear a while back ye were trying to find me.'

'How long have we got to talk?'

Jan turned to Annie. 'Tell you what, bairnie, will ye go and stand in fer me fer a while? If anyone asks, just say I wisna feeling well and needed some air.' Annie nodded, smiled winningly at Fergus, patted Percy and scampered back to the bakery.

'Brother, I am sorry I vanished all that while back. It wisna that I didna trust ye. I couldna pay my rent, I wis behindhand in fact. My friend at the bakery, Hughie, him that got me the job, said Annie and I could bide wi' him. He didna want me as a wife or a bidie-in, ye ken, he's no that way wi' women. It wis the only solution at the time. I didna want to sink back into the auld ways o' payin'.'

'And does he treat you well? And Annie, too? You both look thin and pale.

"Aye, weel enough. I've nae worries aboot money and finding food. We've a roof ower oor heads. But Hughie works me hard, ye ken. And disna let me go to ony birthings. I havena done ony since Maggie Burns, ye ken?'

'Would you like to be doing birthings and the like again, Mistress Jan?'

'Oh, Brother, would I? Would I? It's what I wis made fer, I believe. If I could do that and make a living, that would be the best thing ever. But I hev wee Annie to think o', and canna tak risks. By the by, brother, please cry me Jan. If you say mistress, it gies me ideas above my station!'

'I could make it possible for you to work with the support of us at Soltre. You could make a living out of birthings and caring for pregnant women. You'd be working under our protection, and we'd see there was no trouble with priests or bosses either. We really need you!'

Jan bit her lip. 'It would be so wonderful, brother. When I didna try to find you again before, partly it wis because I thought ye'd have made enquiries and heard mair aboot me than ye liked. I couldna believe ye'd want to hae much to dae wi' the likes o' me. Ye ken, in the past I hae used ma body to pay the rent.'

'Jan,' he said gently. 'I have seen enough of the world to know how things are stacked against single women. I know, when there's a child to feed and clothe, a mother will do anything. How would you get away from Yester, how would you pay rent even for a month without resorting to the obvious way of paying?'

'I did another thing I'm ashamed o'. This is turning into ma confession, brother! Ma mither telt me never to use witchcraft. She said it aeways comes back at ye. People fear ye, but they blame ye too for a' that gaes wrang. And I didna use it, but I did threaten to when they wouldna pay me properly at the bakery. See, Hughie didna want ma body, but his brother, the owner, did. Onyway, even with mair pay, I fell behind wi' the rent, so that's when I said I'd live wi' Hughie. Hope you can follow a' this blether, brother.'

'Jan, I get the picture full well. I didn't know about the witch-craft story. But nothing you've told me comes as any surprise. I think it only fair that I should tell you about myself, since I know so much of you. I was born out of wedlock too, you know. In fact, until a few years ago, I didn't know who my real father was.'

'But you come from folk who are high heid yins. They can get awa' wi' it.'

'Maybe so. But in moral terms, I have no right to hold you in contempt for your origins, or how you have had to live. I have myself visited women of the night as a student. I befriended one of them, who was as articulate as you, if not as skilled and clever. I learned so much from her about how the world works. She helped me out when I was low on cash, and I did the same for her when I could. This was in Paris. And I was under a vow of chastity at the time.'

'Most men dinna see it like that. They want ye, they tak ye, then they look on ye like scum. This is why I found it sae unco that ye wanted me to work for ye. I still canna believe it. And I tell ye, brother, that I would be so happy if I never, ever had to service ony man ever again.'

'Alas, I cannot change the nature of men, but I shall show you that we are on equal terms, Jan. That is why I've made my own confession to you. But let's talk practicalities.'

As they talked, Fergus became aware that Jan was actually frightened of Hughie, who seemed to be sternly controlling and regarded her as his property. If he should discover Jan's new prospects, he might turn unpleasant and even violent. The full extent of the suffering of vulnerable women was becoming clearer by the minute to Fergus. It was also clear that he would have to go and face Hughie and his brother, and spirit away Jan and her daughter from under their noses, so that they were not left at the mercy of these men.

Thinking fast, he knew that a cottage on Soltre's land might not be immediately available. What would he do with two women meanwhile? Never lost for a solution, he realised he could put them in the guest house, which might raise a few eyebrows, or, in extremis, he knew that Mary would lodge them.

So they returned to the bakery, causing consternation as he tied up Percy outside and walked in with Jan. Hughie and his brother, Greig, the master baker, both covered in flour, looked at him open-mouthed. Fergus asked if they could talk in a side room, away from the attention being showed by the rest of the workforce. He ushered Jan in with him. Annie was nowhere in sight.

After polite introductions had been made, and the two men had changed their half-hostile, half-perplexed expressions for respect and even anxious reverence, Fergus explained that he had been looking for Jan for some time because he knew of her medical skills and wanted to make use of them. From now on, she would work for Soltre and he would find her lodging. She would not finish her shift, but they could give her any pay that was due. Hughie began to speak, but Greig nudged him and hastily found some coins in a drawer, which he handed to her.

'I'd like to thank you for looking after Mistress Eliot and her daughter,' said Fergus. 'Now she will be a valued member of our team.' And then they left, gathering up Annie, who had reappeared, rubbing dough from her hands. Fergus told Hughie that the ladies would come with him, and he would send a cart later that day for their belongings.

Fergus left the two women in the guest house in the bemused hands of Brother Kenneth, explaining to him that they were in some danger from male abuse and had needed urgent removal.

Later, Kenneth came to find Fergus to tell him that the two women were so poorly dressed he wondered how they would survive the autumn winds, let alone the coming winter. He had some stores of clothing for travellers and proposed getting them dressed more suitably. 'It might have to be men's gear until the tailor comes, as I don't have much women's stuff,' he said.

Fergus advised him not to give them very rich food, for it could make them ill, as they were so unused to it. 'Give them vegetable broth, bread, ale, much as we have in the refectory,' he said. 'At least at first.'

Kenneth asked, 'How long do you propose keeping them here, Brother Medicus?' Fergus said he hoped there would be a suitable cottage on Soltre's land, if Brother Robert, the bursar, could find one. Meanwhile, he saw no reason why the ladies should not stay at the guest house. Kenneth looked doubtful and worried. 'What if there is no cottage, brother? They can hardly stay here indefinitely.'

Fergus visited the ladies in their quarters and found them dazed at such luxury. 'Living under a solid roof reminds us o' Yester,' said Jan. 'But we never got to sit by the fire. I dinna think I've ever been sae warm afore, or sae well fed.' Jan was sitting with some dun wool stuff, making a dress, while Annie was cutting up blankets for shawls. She was dressed in men's trousers and tunic.

'D'ye ken, she went to the stable dressed like that!' said Jan, half severe, half laughing. 'She looks like a tinker laddie.'

'I wanted to see Percy and the other horses,' said Annie. 'I was properly dressed for a stable.'

Peter was waiting for him outside the guest house, and, taking his arm, led him gently across the garth. 'Fergus, I am afraid there are problems arising from the two ladies. Several of the senior brothers are uneasy. Frankly, so am I. Father John is away visiting and would most certainly not approve, I am sure you understand that. There was consternation when young Annie appeared at the stable, dressed like a boy! Is there no other place they could dwell for the time being?'

Fergus suppressed his feeling of rage. He could never be angry with Peter, but the collective attitude of the others was so typically antipathetic. 'I suppose it was tactless of me. They did need urgent rescue. But I am sure Mary would find them somewhere to stay.' Peter led the way to the bursar's office.

Brother Robert assured Fergus that their concern was for Father John's attitude and not lack of compassion. 'We can find a cottage on the slope below Lindean for them in time, brother, but not immediately,' he said. 'It's very small. They will need some bed bases and pallets, blankets, chairs, pots, kettles, the basics. We'll supply those, no bother.'

Peter said, 'They both look thin and under-nourished, brothers. We should include them on the food round that we supply to our workers once they move to the cottage.'

Fergus shot him a look of gratitude. 'It makes you realise what real poverty is,' he said. 'Our poverty rule is a mere pretence by comparison. However, I shall take them over to Mary's place in Lauder for the time being. She is one of those souls who can solve problems instantly.'

A pony and cart were loaded up with the ladies and their meagre belongings, as well as the stuff for their clothing needs, and Fergus drove them to Mary's new residence, a modest mansion with surrounding farm and woodland that she occupied with her husband. If Mary and David were surprised at this eccentric request to accommodate Jan and Annie, they did not show it. Mary greeted them as warmly as any well-to-do guests, and while they were being refreshed began turning out cupboards for suitable clothing. She was shocked at the worn pilgrim's male garb that had been offered them at the abbey.

'Scarcely decent!' she snorted. 'No wonder the poor brothers couldn't deal with it. Mind you, Annie looks rather well in her boy's gear. But she'll look better still in a becoming dress.'

'Mary, you are an angel,' said Fergus with feeling.

'I am delighted, Brother Fergus,' said Mary. 'After leaving your mother, with all her demands, I still sometimes feel rather underemployed. Did you know that I have joined the local dominie's wife in opening a school for girls? Do you think Annie would like to join it?'

'Let's ask her,' said Fergus. 'I imagine she will be delighted.'

The prospect of some education was greeted by Annie as a prize beyond imagining. Although the local school at Fala had taken some girls, Jan would not trust Annie to Father Leonard, who ran it.

Fergus looked questioningly at her.

'Aye,' she nodded. 'He came tae visit before I bided at Hughie's, with his smarmy ways and hands going everywhere, and whispering about ways of *managing*. He made his intentions clear. He was efter wee Annie as weel as me. Once I'd refused him he took against me, came and searched the cottage for plants and things.'

Jan turned away, feeling her eyes welling with tears. 'We feel so safe and happy, Brother. I hope it'll last a while. I am truly grateful, ye ken. But I am not one whose life was meant to be easy.'

Chapter 26

Mary was as blithe and happy as a lark with her new charges, and David found them a cottage close by the house. Not only Annie but Jan herself attended the girls' school, and in return they gave help both on the farm and in the house. Mary and Jan had a common interest in midwifery, and Jan was introduced to some women in preparation for assisting at delivery.

After a month, Fergus congratulated Mary on doing his work for him, reflecting it was a very happy outcome for all concerned. 'You have made such an improvement in their health and appearance,' he said. 'Annie especially has lost that fragile, waiflike look.'

'Jan is an attractive woman,' said Mary. 'And you both seem to be close friends already. Are you not afraid of gossip, Fergus?'

'There will no doubt be gossip, it's a human habit as ingrained as eating and sleeping. As long as there is no true substance underneath...'

'And you are impervious, Fergus? It's a bizarre life, the celibate one. Might you not be ensnared? Please don't be offended with me.'

'No, I'm honoured you are concerned about my soul, Mary. I have confessed to you that I dropped any pretensions to celibacy in my student years. I think I sowed all my wild oats then. Nowadays hard work keeps such needs at bay.'

'You are a man in control of himself, I know. A man on a mission. But it's not just physical needs I mean. Have you never fallen in love, Fergus?'

'It has always seemed to me that falling in love is something women do, not usually men. Women love absolutely and commit completely; it is admirable, but makes them vulnerable. With men it's either a pretence or a deception, a means to an end. I certainly have never experienced it and can't envisage what it's like. I like women, of course; I enjoy their company and ways. That is something not many of my celibate colleagues do.'

Mary's expression as she listened was sceptical, but she did not pursue the topic. However, she did report back to Catriona, Fergus's mother. Their husbands were close friends and colleagues now, and meetings were frequent.

'He is a fine man, Kitty, a son to be proud of. Tall, well built, with such an air about him. You should see how the women look at him; it's a shame he's unavailable! With so much female adoration, I wonder how staunch he will be. His relationship with this new discovery, Jan, is a working one, but there's quite a buzz between them. It's clear she worships him.'

'Isn't she a bit older than him?' asked Catriona. 'I always thought you were close to him too. Perhaps, like all these holy men, he enjoys being worshipped one-sidedly, and saves his passion for his work.'

Mary shook her head slightly. She felt she knew Fergus better than his mother did. A man of such strong feeling and purpose, she felt, could be a victim of the unforeseen, the wayward lightning strike of fate.

When the cottage below Lindean finally became available, after some months, David made the Eliot ladies a present of a couple of mules so that they could continue to attend the school, and Mary and Jan could pursue their own tasks.

The winter evenings were short, but Fergus and Peter would still amble round the cloister after compline and before bed, well wrapped in their cowls, deep in conversation.

One evening as they were thus occupied, the peace of the evening was disturbed by the sound of busy footsteps coming towards them. Brother Robert, the bursar, slowed his pace as he saw his two colleagues, a worried expression on his face.

'Brothers,' he said as he approached. 'I am very sorry to disturb you. One of the factors is here, one of the men who collect the cottage rents. He had business with me this evening, and I told him your instructions, Brother Fergus, about Mistress Jan Eliot – no rent to pay and to receive regular food supplies from us. He has something to say. I tried to put him off, but… he's still here. Shall I call him?'

Fergus frowned, knowing trouble was coming. 'Of course,' he said shortly. The factor, who had been lurking in a far corner was summoned by a wave, and came strutting forward. He was a short, stout man with a truculent look about him. He was introduced as Jock Stephen.

'Brother Fergus, pardon my presumption. However, when Brother Robert told me this evening that Jan Eliot was installed in yon shepherd's cottage, I thought you should know what kind of a woman this is. She is widely known to be a… a limmer. A woman of ill repute. A strumpet, in plain words.'

Fergus stared down at the factor, who began to shift uneasily in the silence.

'You ken what that is, brother, I'm sure. Even you, a man of the cloth. She sells her body for material gains. And I happen to know she has done that to pay her rent.'

'And how do you know that?' asked Fergus coldly, as the factor's face took on a red tone about the cheeks and neck.

'It's just common knowledge. The priest told me lang syne, Father Leonard…'

'How does the priest know?'

'I dinna ken, perhaps through the confessional…'

'I should hope not. That would be breaking the vow of confidentiality.'

'Brother, how can I tell how these things get around? All I can say is that her reputation is bad. She's a fallen woman.'

'You still have not explained to me how you believe she has paid rent by prostituting herself. Have you yourself had carnal knowledge of her?'

'Brother, of course I havenae. I'm a married man! I ken the man she used tae work for. He tellt me he's helped her out when the rent was due – in exchange for her favours.'

'And he didn't tell you he paid her so little in the bakery that she was at his mercy! So you men discuss her in the tavern over your ale, and soil her reputation, and then come here and try to ruin her prospects of lifting herself out of a life she is trying to leave behind. And all the time, any man who has taken advantage of her poverty is every bit as guilty of immoral behaviour as she. Worse, in fact, because she is trying to keep her child and herself alive and aim for a better life. And who are you to come here and tell me who should occupy Soltre's cottages and who should not? Who are you to cast the first stone?'

'Brother Robert here says that cottages are only for people of good character. It's in the rules I'm supposed to follow! She should be told to quit.'

Fergus was outraged. 'What? On hearsay evidence only? Is that what our care and compassion has come to? I tell you both, I shall guarantee that this young woman's conduct from now on will be untainted, whatever it has been in the past. And furthermore, any man connected with Soltre who makes any attempt at mischief making and forces himself on her will be dismissed from his post. Now leave us.'

Fergus was so boiled up with indignation that he had to stalk around the cloister to cool off after the two men had left. He finally came and sat down beside Peter.

'I am right, aren't I, Peter?'

'Yes, you are right, if a little high-handed.'

'I cannot bear the hypocrisy of men who take their pleasure and then condemn the women who service them. I would bet a large sum that that factor fellow himself has used her, or tried to. Did you see his flushed, shifty look?'

Peter remained silent, waiting for Fergus to carry on.

'I haven't told you all about this young woman, Peter. I was fully aware that she must have sold herself at times to get out of her slavery at Yester estate and to pay her rent when she earned so little. You know, I have seen plenty of low life in my travels abroad, and I confess that I have used the services of ladies of ill repute, as they are so called. But mostly I valued those encounters for what I learned. They are not sunk into depravity, as the general opinion would have it. They are nearly all mothers, usually as a result of rape – often rape by the men of the house they serve, just as happened with Jan. And it is usual for them to be put out once they have a child. Just put out onto the streets to survive. Or be taken into slavery by someone else. Most of them said, as Jan did, that they would give up on sex altogether if they could. It is loathsome and rough in most cases. Men are such brutes.' He paused. 'I shall have to go and see her tomorrow, Peter. Make sure this factor oaf has not been bullying her.'

'You'd better see Father John in the morning too – before Brother Robert gets there.'

'We'd better turn in soon, Peter, we're both tired.'

Chapter 27

Peter had never seen Father John so inflamed with anger; he seemed on the point of losing control.

'This woman Fergus has found for us to employ is a streetwalker! In the name of Heaven, Peter, what was he thinking about? We cannot under any circumstances accept her. Where is he, where is he? He must see me at once!'

'He has gone out to see her. He went before daylight. It is hardly fair – or accurate – to call her a streetwalker, father.'

'I don't need to tell you, it's what she will be called and condemned for; and worse! Oh, merciful God, how I am tried and tested! Peter, can we reverse this? Can we bring him to see reason? What in the name of all that is holy will Bishop Wardlaw say when he hears we have linked ourselves with a woman of loose morals?'

'Does the bishop need to know?'

'He probably knows it already; his spy network is second to none. No, no, no, Peter, this I cannot condone. Do you not see what it will do to Soltre? It is all very well to be compassionate over a fallen sister, but we have our entire establishment and its credibility to consider, first and foremost.'

'Father, remember our Lord Jesus and his treatment of Mary Magdalene. And how he said to the multitude, "Let him that is without sin cast the first stone." These are the things we shall have to remind the bishop of if he condemns us. We are to welcome the sinner that repenteth, the prodigal son – or daughter. Fergus was in no doubt at all that Jan would completely eschew her former woeful ways once she was established as a Soltre servant. Of course, without question, she must do that.'

Peter was amazed to find himself preaching to the father. 'You will recall that even before Fergus left for his studies, he, Malcolm and I searched for our ideal midwife and could not find anyone suitable. One hears tell of wise women, but where are they? It's clear now that clever and capable women are all employed at big estates and establishments, where they live and survive just like Jan did. Most of them probably never emerge. Some get married and some are intimidated by their parish priests.'

But Father John continued to look distraught and agitated. 'Peter, there was a time when I thought like you. Alas, no longer. I dearly wish the world was still as simple, as clearly demarcated into black and white. It has been my life's work to build and maintain Soltre as a centre of medical excellence, based on the ethos of compassion for the sick and needy. We have done so, and we have gone from strength to strength. But we have done so from within the Church and the Augustinian way; we have steered our course in spite of hazards.

'And now the Church is under attack, and the assailants are from within its ranks. And so the pope and the cardinals and the bishops are armed to the teeth against that enemy within, the enemy that they call heresy. So fearful are they that they look for this intruder everywhere. And their zeal undoubtedly misleads them.

'But know this, Peter. There is a ruthlessness amongst the Church's princes that condemns and destroys before it examines. It is steeped in fear. And it is all about challenges to a doctrine that has been devised by themselves – by men, not by God. How do we know He condones it? He cannot, when it involves such cruel and violent acts.

'And the worst is that our bishop, Wardlaw himself, in whose see our own abbey church lies, has been infected with this same paranoia. We offended him with Fergus's rejection of his tuition at St Andrews and he is deeply suspicious of other medical schools that are run on different principles. One of the reasons I courted the king so carefully was to win his sponsorship and protection. But alas, he and the bishop are hand in glove. The king has taken no notice of us since he came here on his return from England, though he was full of gratitude and plans to visit and support us.'

'Father, what evidence is there that Bishop Wardlaw is so militant in the matter of heresy?' asked Peter, wondering if the father himself was not getting paranoid. 'I know that in France long gone, certain sects rejected the Church and were slaughtered in vast numbers. But not now, not here?'

'There you are wrong, Peter. Pursuit of heresy in all its nastiness is very much alive here in Scotland and our bishop is its leading light. I wonder sometimes if he's ambitious for a cardinal's hat and is making his mark for that purpose. You know he condoned the burning of a heretic twenty years ago? His university declares its purpose as "an impregnable rampart of doctors and masters to resist heresy". Nothing about learning and studying for its own good. He's appointed Lawrence of Lindores as his papal inquisitor in Scotland. He has persuaded the king and the Scottish parliament to charge all bishops with rooting out heretics as their top priority.

'And most sinister of all – only two or three years since, he committed to burning at the stake, at St Andrews, a Bohemian doctor called Paul Crawar, accused of heresy by supporting the teaching of Wycliffe, Huss and other radicals. Such a man has lost touch with any tenderness or pity.'

'These free-thinkers preach so openly, they almost have a death wish,' said Peter. 'Or a martyr wish. But Fergus isn't like that. He is just in favour of people thinking for themselves and not being spoon-fed. And he has compassion written all over his soul; that and a bottomless curiosity about how things work.'

'Someone as clever as Fergus is not going to be reined in and restricted by the tenets of the Church, especially after being exposed to free-thinking modernists on his travels across the world,' Father John said with an agonised expression. 'And I wish he would be guided by my diplomacy. He is too hot-headed and stubborn and idealistic and naive. Believe me, Peter, I am moved as much by anxiety for him as for our establishment.'

'You must know, father, that Fergus has very severe doubts over his faith at the moment. To him, the Church is not a compassionate body.' Peter was amazed at himself for his unaccustomed contrariness. 'If you intervene over Jan, I don't think he will stay here at Soltre. He will not renege on good work because of the twisted thinking of the Church elite – an elite that sits in palaces, consorts with aristocrats, dresses in silks, gorges on fine fare and spends its time debating theoretical trivia. Fergus would be welcomed in almost any prestigious medical post. His kinsman, as you know, is physician to the king. His uncle is Lord of the Isles. He has prospects out there. Don't drive him away.'

Father John sat with his hands over his eyes for several minutes. Then he said, 'Peter, I wonder if that might be the best thing for all of us. That he goes away.' Peter let out a cry, almost a howl, of dissent. He stood up and regarded Father John in astounded disbelief and horror.

'If you believe that, father, you must seriously believe that Armageddon is nigh. How much have we given thanks that Fergus was delivered into our hands? A great gift from the Lord. We have pinned all our hopes and aspirations on him for years past. We have seen nothing but good in him. And now you want to be rid of him?'

Agitated beyond belief, Peter was so disorientated that he failed to observe his friend and colleague clutch at his chest and inhale sharply.

'I could not answer for the response of our local population! They would invade us, they would be consumed with rage, they would pull the place apart. Fergus is their saint, their saviour. Have you not seen how they flock to the garth – the numbers are sky-high ever since he came back. All want to see him, to touch him, talk to him. Father...' Peter turned and stopped in his flow of rhetoric. Father John was slumped, grey and sweating, groaning, hands pressed to his chest.

'Oh God, oh God, forgive, forgive, Lord, take this cup...' John's words became an incoherent mumble of agony so terrible it seemed he could not bear it.

Peter dived forward and reached him just as he sank in a lifeless heap on the floor. 'Father, father...' His instincts kicked in and overrode all that had gone before. Grabbing a little bell that sat on the desk, he rang it frantically, shouting, 'Come quickly! The father is taken ill!'

As Fergus entered the abbey by the open gate he was immediately aware of a frenetic atmosphere, with shouts and people running to and fro across the garth, and there in the middle was a stable boy on a horse coming in haste towards him. 'Brother Fergus! I was just coming to find you. Father John is ill, you are urgently needed.' Fergus leapt off his horse and sped to the residence as the boy grabbed Percy's reins.

He found Father John lying on the floor in a state of agitated semi-consciousness, clearly distressed, groaning and muttering, his face grey and clammy. Peter and his helpers had tried to make him more comfortable with pillows and blankets and Peter had sent Thomas to bring some calming medicine. However, such was the father's agitation that it was impossible to get him to take it.

Fergus knelt down beside him and spoke gently. 'Father, it's me, Fergus. Let us help you.' He took the father's hand, feeling his pulse, and the combination of his touch as well as his voice seemed to bring the patient back to a better state of awareness. 'Oh, my son, it's you,' moaned John, opening and closing his eyes.

Between them, Fergus and Peter managed to lift him onto a couch. Peter gave a swift account of events while Fergus made a rapid examination.

'Heart shock,' Fergus said briefly to Peter, who nodded. He held Father John's hand and put his other on the chest, which seemed to control some of the distress. 'It would be better to get him to the infirmary where we have all our supplies. Thomas, James, can you get a stretcher, we'll move him as quickly as we can. What is in this medicine, Peter? Just opium? We may need more than this.' With great tact and tenderness, Fergus persuaded the father to take a dribble of the medicine.

Some time later, with the father in the infirmary, they managed to get him to swallow enough of the prescribed preparation of opium, mandrake and hemlock to ease the pain, though he continued to be agitated and restless. Peter and Fergus, between their duties, found time to talk about the crisis and how it had unfolded – hovering alert nearby, but talking in low voices. Peter, himself looking severely shaken, had described John's horrified reaction to his story about Jan and her reputation.

'He wasn't himself, even at the start of our discussion, he seemed in a state of fear, of delusion,' said Peter. 'Almost in a post-nightmare state.'

'As if the beginnings of the attack were already under way, you think?' responded Fergus. Peter paused, looking haunted and undecided. 'Tell me,' said Fergus, who could read his friend's body language like a book.

'He was worried about the effect on Soltre of employing Jan, and what the bishop would say,' said Peter slowly. 'But even more, he was fearful for you. He even thought it might be better if you decided to leave! I could not believe my ears. I reacted rather strongly, I fear. It was then the collapse occurred.'

'Did he think I would be led into libertine ways?'

'No. Not that. He told me a tale of how Bishop Henry Wardlaw and others are working themselves into a lather about heresy. And finding it everywhere – everything that goes outside the strict teaching of the church qualifies as heresy. So perhaps he was not altogether irrational in worrying about you.'

Father John had become suddenly still, and Fergus moved swiftly to check his heartbeat and pulse. He looked back to Peter, anxious and worried. 'I can't feel his pulse and the heart is fast and weak. I'm not sure the mandrake was a good idea, after all. What was the rationale for including it?'

Peter, at the other side of the bed, said, 'It's supposed to scare demons away. Thomas and others queried whether the father was possessed – the attack happened so suddenly.'

'I am afraid that superstition will take hold...' murmured Fergus. 'But no more of the mandrake, I think. We'll use ointment with opium, black henbane and hemlock; rub it on his chest. We're not going to get it in by mouth, I suspect. We can try it by enema if we have to.' He sat down and, holding John's hands, began to talk softly, close to his ear. 'Father, can you hear me? Don't give in! Can you wake up and talk to us? You cannot be ready to go yet!'

Turning to Peter, he said, 'He's so cold! Can you ask Thomas to bring another blanket and make up the fire? I fear we are losing him, Peter. I think we need to support his heart with foxglove – it's so weak. Can you make up a preparation, please? We'll give it by enema.'

Over the next few hours, Father John's condition alternated between a near coma and distressed agitation. In the latter phases he gabbled in confusion and fear, and few words could be made out: 'Go, go, go... It's over... Save me, oh Lord, miserable sinner.' It seemed that no treatments could stabilise him between these extremes, until, at last, he sank into oblivion and it looked as if the end was nigh. Fergus hurriedly sent for Prior Richard, who had spent his time between praying in the church and hovering near the infirmary.

The community of canons was sent for and as they assembled around the bed, the ceremony of the last rites began. But as the prayers and touching of the lips with wine progressed, signs of agitation, of twitching limbs and staring eyes and mutterings, recurred. The community expected to stay in prayer as the beloved father slipped away, but it was clear to Fergus that this was not going to happen yet. He murmured to Richard that it would be better if they moved the father back to his own residence to die in peace, so John was moved to a stretcher and carried back across the garth to his residence, followed by a procession of sorrowing canons.

Once Fergus, Peter and Thomas had settled the patient on his couch and everyone else had moved to the church, Father John moved to a new phase: harsh, almost violent breathing, gradually subsiding to almost total inertia. The cycle would then be repeated after some minutes.

Fergus shook his head sadly. 'He is not having a good death, Peter, is he? He of all people deserved that. I thought it better to get him away from public observance; things can be so mistranslated. I hate this idea of possession by evil spirits. Born of ignorance! I've seen this distressing pattern of dying in others having a heart shock. I do hope it ends soon for him.'

*

The good father defied predictions and clung on to life. Peter and Fergus took it in turns to sit with him, while the other attended to medical duties in the infirmary and in the garth at the morning clinic. Neither took much rest, and devotional duties were completely forgotten. At times, Father John seemed to sink peacefully into deep coma, while at other times the cyclical breathing disturbance returned.

Then, early one morning, as dawn was breaking and with Peter sitting drowsily beside him, John opened his eyes, seemingly conscious and tranquil.

'Peter,' he said, in a normal if weak voice. 'Good brother. Can you ask Fergus and Richard to come?'

Quite overcome, Peter went down on his knees, his eyes moist, as he gathered John's left hand in his own. He kissed it fervently, then arose and alerted the sleeping clerk outside the room to fetch the others. Prior Richard was the first to arrive, sinking on his knees at the bedside. 'Richard,' said John. 'I need you... hear my confession. But first... I must talk... Fergus. Ah.' Seeing Fergus coming towards him he tried to raise himself, but was too weak.

'Fergus, I have been to the gates of Hell. And I saw... the future. Black and dreadful. I gazed into the abyss. Worse than anything we imagine. Then they mocked me and... drove me away.' After this speech, he was breathless and had to pause. Fergus offered some water, which he took, spluttering.

'I hope... they take me at Heaven's gates since they refused me at Hell,' he said with a ghost of a smile. 'Fergus. Beware the bishop. Your new magister... vote for him... from among you. Don't let Wardlaw impose. Vote among... here and at... Jed...'

Fergus, holding the father's hand in his, helped him out. 'Jedburgh?'

'Yes... and other Augustinian places. You have that right. Don't let... bishop bully you.' John sank back, exhausted. He beckoned to Peter, and he and Fergus knelt as John put a hand on each head in blessing. Then John beckoned to Richard, saying, 'C... confess...'

After his confession and a brief repeat of the last rites, John sank into a peaceful sleep from which he never awoke.

Chapter 28

1436

Throughout the solemnities of grieving and ritual, the singing of the Litany for the Dying as the father's body was sprinkled with holy water and reverently wrapped in a winding sheet, the processional removal of him to the church and the singing there of the Mass for the Dead, the muffled tones of the church bell tolled out over the abbey and beyond. People going about their daily business in the farms, woodlands and fields stopped in their tracks at the sound and made the sign of the cross. The bell continued its mournful beat up until the moment of interment in a place of honour in the abbey cemetery. When it stopped, the silence seemed momentous.

But after the ceremonies were over, the atmosphere at Soltre was one of bewilderment, like a beehive that has lost its queen. How could it continue to function with no Father John? Poor Prior Richard was the nominal magister until a new one could be appointed, but he had no natural authority or presence, and his organisational skills were minimal. The father's chief clerk fortunately knew the intricate workings of the abbey, and with the help of his two assistants and the senior brothers, somehow things muddled along.

Most urgent to be set in motion was the process of electing a new magister. Richard quickly let it be known that he did not wish to be a candidate. Among the others there was no outstanding leader. Peter, Richard and Fergus recalled the father's last instructions: to choose a leader from among themselves, or at least the wider Augustinian community, and not have someone imposed by the bishop. They were all aware of the increasing tendency for such roles to be seized for a relative of royalty, whether of Church or state.

'Can we proceed without letting Bishop Wardlaw know?' asked Fergus. 'He'll want to take over and organise us. We need a second Father John – a working intellectual, not an aristocratic despot.'

'I'm afraid we have to inform him,' said Prior Richard. 'It's prescribed procedure. We have to go through the bishop to request from the king a licence to proceed to election. Then, once the election has been held, we have to ask permission to install our magister-elect.'

'It sounds as if it's designed to invite meddling from on high,' grumbled Fergus.

The clerks hastened to write and send off the formal notifications and request for a licence. Meanwhile, all other Augustinian establishments in the south of Scotland were informed of the father's death by the sending round of an obituary roll, requesting their prayers for the father's soul. Private notes went post-haste to the abbots of Jedburgh, Holyrood and Inchcolm in the first instance, these being the closest sister abbeys, seeking names of possible candidates for the post. Richard, who had gone on diplomatic visits on behalf of Father John to these abbeys, knew of at least one suitable man at Jedburgh and possibly another at Inchcolm.

In all the events of the last few days, Fergus had not forgotten Jan. He had, early on, sent a message by word of mouth with one of the messengers saying that the father's serious illness was keeping him fully occupied. He had given instructions to the land agent that Jan was to be included in the round of recipients of foodstuffs from the abbey stocks, and reiterated to Brother Robert that she was not to be charged rent.

At last, one morning, a week or two after the funeral, he found time to mount up and visit, going early in the morning to be sure of finding her. As he appeared at her door, she looked pleased.

'Brother Fergus, welcome. Good of you to come, you must be so vexed now with the father gone, God rest his soul.'

Jan could hardly wait to thank him for the new arrangements, and to report that the women in the villages and cottages round about were treating her with greater respect, and that she had already been introduced to two local women in mid pregnancy; both well, but interested in being supervised and checked.

'My boss as was at the bakery came by,' said Jan. 'He's offered to raise my wages if I go back! I shuddered even at the sicht o' him.'

'Let me know if he makes trouble for you,' said Fergus.

'Oh, I doubt he'll dae that. It's your name, Brother Fergus. It opens all doors and sweeps aside all trouble. Can I ask you about an odd crack that's going the rounds? And causing a stir. They say that the good father was haeing an airgument wi' anither brother, and he was heard to say you would dae well to leave Soltre. And it was at that moment he was struck down wi' mortal illness. They are saying that it was a divine judgement for even thinking you should go away.'

Fergus groaned as he heard this. What a tragedy that the father's dying name should be so besmirched.

'That is nonsense, Jan. The good father doesn't deserve that. He was the best of men, goodness through and through. He was only thinking of me – he feared I might get into trouble for some of the things we are trying to do, that go against the Church's teaching.'

'Aye, weel – a' I can say is that folk willna hear onything against ye. You are their champion. I am richt glad to be assistin' ye.'

Fergus said, eager to change the subject, 'How are you getting on with the schooling?'

'Brother, I canna thank ye enough. Annie is a bright lassie and looks set to hae a better start than I did. She picks it a' up faster than I dae. See here – Father Leonard, who cam' to visit and is gey mindfu' o' his manners noo, has gi'en me a book for learning my letters.'

This made Fergus think of Callum. Explaining to Jan who he was and how an illiterate farm boy had come to attend on the king, he described Callum's learning of reading and writing, to the extent that he now wrote poetry in the vernacular Scots language.

'And the king was so charmed that he asked Callum to write a love poem to his queen, Joan. He told him what the content should be, so everyone thinks the king wrote it! And everyone talks about how cultured King James is. But it was Callum. He's now a sort of unofficial poet laureate. And since he learned to speak Spanish when he was on pilgrimage, he can now read and write in that language too. He's a man of letters! And I think he's even done some diplomatic letter writing for the king. So if he can do it, a clever lady like you certainly can!'

She beamed and said, 'Whit a story!' Then she sighed. 'But he earned his good fortune on the pilgrimage. Whit have I done to earn your favour, brother? I feel I dinna deserve all this ye are giving me. Dinna get me wrang but… are ye sure there's no' gonna be payback time?'

Fergus was struck at how ingrained was her lack of self-worth. It would take time to gain her trust. 'Believe me, you will indeed earn all these good things by working with us. That will be the payback! And do remember that as a canon I'm supposed to be celibate.'

'Disna stop most of they priests wanting their way wi' ye.'

Fergus laughed and said, 'You don't think I'm a saint then?'

'Brother, I'm fu' sure ye are a good man. But I've learned that a' men – those that are men – have urges that canna be stopped. And they will want ye sooner or later if they hae you in their power.'

This was said teasingly, and Fergus was strongly aware of chemistry between them – indeed, that had been there from the start, but which was activated by her frank directness.

'I have put myself in your power by telling you things about myself that I haven't even told in the confessional. Jan, believe me, you will certainly earn every scrap of privilege I've put your way. Is there anything you need at the moment?'

'Aye, weel, I need to go a-gathering. With my work and the move I've nae stocks of plants and stuff. I could do wi' some kelp and there's nae way I can get to the beach.'

'Well, I can get a cart and horse to pull it. We can go together and Annie could come too. The problem is when? At the moment, things are upside down at Soltre. Still, I badly need to stock up on some things too, things only Peter or I can identify. I'll organise something. And I suggest that while you are sitting learning your letters, you can practise trusting me, all right?'

Chapter 29

A few weeks after the interment, Fergus returned from outside duties to find Soltre abuzz with activity. The messenger network had reported the approach of a party of clerics coming from the north, and it had every appearance of being Bishop Wardlaw himself, with attendants.

Richard was restless and pacing the room with anxiety as Fergus went in to see him in his office. 'Why is he coming in person?' asked Richard. 'It bodes no good whatsoever. We must greet him in here with the senior canons in force. I can't manage him on my own. He'll no doubt want to stay, and we are all at sixes and sevens.'

'Brother, stay calm. Let's take it one step at a time. The organisation for welcoming is well practised; you've seen how father did it, times without number. I'll stand by you, as will Brother Kenneth and the others. Once we've taken him to the guest house we can find out what his wishes are.'

The bishop swept into the garth on a fine palfrey, with an armed guard of four and three accompanying clerics. He was dressed for travelling comfort with a long, woollen, fur-lined cloak, capacious biretta and leather boots; looking more like a well-to-do gentleman than a church grandee. Fergus added a more hearty welcome to the nervous one of Richard, meanwhile observing that the bishop was overweight and fleshy about the face, seemed grey and tired after the journey and needed to be helped from the saddle.

When he was ensconced in the guest house by a fire and with a goblet of wine, Bishop Wardlaw said to the three gathered brothers, 'I am profoundly sorry to hear of the parting of our dearly beloved John. My commiserations to you all. We have been remembering him in our prayers.

'But my purpose here is more than that. I have not visited Soltre for many years, and I am making it my business to go around all the clerical houses in the see of St Andrews, as and when I can. I thought this juncture a suitable opportunity to pay you a visit. I should like a rest now, to recover from the journey. Please do not let me interrupt your usual routine. Then, after suitable refreshment, which I shall take here, I shall wish to meet the senior canons, perhaps in the chapter house. You can let me know when you are all gathered. We shall discuss plans for electing a new magister. I'll stay for a couple of nights so that I can take time to inspect the work of the abbey and how it is run; and also, of course, how the Church liturgy is followed. Now, will you ask my chaplain to come in to me?'

With this he made a dismissive gesture and raised his flagon to his lips. Fergus was so affronted he did not immediately rise as the others did, but stared in amazement at Wardlaw. He put out a hand to detain Brother Kenneth and said, 'We dine at midday, my lord. Brother Kenneth here will make provision for you and your company. We shall take vegetable broth and bread. Will that suit your lordship?'

Wardlaw flashed him a look of annoyance. 'No. Something more substantial, please, since I have been travelling.'

'Did your lordship come all the way from St Andrews today?' asked Fergus, affecting surprise.

'Of course not,' snapped the bishop. 'We stayed overnight at Holyrood. We have been two days on the road.'

Fergus withdrew with the others and walked in silence to the residence. Once inside, they all began talking at once, furious and incensed about his arrogance and dictatorial speech.

'You nettled him, Fergus. Good for you, though I don't know how you dared,' said Kenneth.

'Listen, brothers,' said Fergus. 'We must do our best to follow father's dying wish. Let us, the office bearers, stay on after chapter meeting and discuss how we are going to face the bishop. Richard, can you tell us just what rights we have to choose our own magister?'

'The procedure has historically been by vote or consensus, an internal affair,' said Richard. 'This business of licensing and approving has all sorts of political overtones. I've heard some horror stories about newly elected abbots having to chase round the countryside to meet the king and even having to go to the pope – and meanwhile the temporalities go to the king's own pocket.'

'Temporalities?' asked Fergus, alarmed.

'Yes, the income derived from the abbey property. It can be stopped until the elected abbot is in place and approved. And the process has undoubtedly been slowed up at times, certainly in England, to benefit the king.'

'But the income for Soltre is often in kind, and is immediately ploughed into upkeep costs. It didn't go to benefit Father John,' said Kenneth. 'I don't see any way the products of our lands could be directed to the king's pocket. And they could hardly stop us functioning as a hospital while bits of paper fly around the country and wait for scrutiny.'

'Let us meet the bishop in the residence, where we can all sit around the table, on an equal footing,' said Fergus. 'If we go to the chapter house, he will expect to take father's seat and be the dominant voice. I couldn't bear that.'

And so all the office bearers of Soltre gathered, in a sombre mood, in the residence after the midday meal, a message having been sent to Bishop Wardlaw in the guest house that they were ready to meet him. They rose to their feet as he swept regally in. It had been agreed that Fergus should be the spokesperson, since he held the senior post of medicus, even though he was the youngest. During the preliminary polite exchanges it became clear that Wardlaw was in a rather more conciliatory mood, and Fergus wondered if his previous brusque manner could be due to poor health, of which he saw clear signs.

'Dear brothers, my thanks for your hospitality, which is legendary. As I mentioned earlier to those who kindly welcomed me, I am here for several purposes: to commiserate with you; to help you find a new magister with all possible expedition; and to carry out an episcopal duty of periodic inspection.

'Now, may I ask, is there one among you who has the confidence of the majority as future magister?'

Fergus quickly glanced around his colleagues and said, 'No, my lord, not at present. Prior Richard, Father John's deputy, has indicated that he would not wish to take on this role. However, we are all in agreement that the future magister should come from the Augustinian community, the wider one if necessary. We are in communication with our brothers at Jedburgh and at Inchcolm, and believe we may resolve the issue in this manner. We agree that Father John was an ideal role model and that we should be guided by his example of duty, hard work, self-denial and simplicity, yet kindliness and compassion.'

'I agree with you,' said Wardlaw, 'that your late father was the very best. He was self-made, a profoundly well-read and educated man and one of superb organisational skills. And diplomacy! He could have graced a king's court with those abilities. We shall not find his like very easily. And I do not share your confidence that we shall find such a man within these walls or those in institutions you mention. People like Father John, natural leaders, declare themselves by their acts at an early stage. They cannot be created on the job, as it were.

'And I am sure you all realise that this post of magister of Soltre is a post of high importance now in Scotland, and although Soltre has been renowned for centuries, it has reached new heights in recent decades. To an extent, you are the victims of your own success. You are medical experts but you are also important landowners with extensive holdings. Your new magister will have to be a man of the very highest calibre; a man of the world as well as the Church.'

'My lord, we accept that our new magister will be a special man. We do not, however, agree that institutions of retreat such as ours cannot supply such a person. The qualities needed do not necessarily lead to a visible presence on a national stage. Sometimes they are sublimated in a hidden site, a sanctuary. We would wish to go through the process of election amongst ourselves. It was the dying father's wish that we would do so. We will pray for guidance, of course.'

Bishop Wardlaw made a gesture of acknowledgement as Fergus mentioned the father's dying wish. 'Well, I cannot go against the father's dying wish. By all means, go through your due process. I can give you your licence to do so. It would be well to make haste. And you will be aware that the nominated magister will have to be approved by King James? Generally speaking, your temporalities would now be suspended until the nominee is in post.' There was an uneasy stir among the company as he said this. 'However,' he continued, 'this will depend on my examination here. It may be that the organisation runs on a tight budget and there is little surplus going to waste.'

'My lord,' said Fergus, 'if his grace King James does not approve our choice of magister, what follows?'

'His grace, in consultation with me and other clerics, will recommend a suitable person.'

'No, you mistake me, my lord. I meant, what redress have we, what form of appeal, to assert our right to have our choice of magister?'

'If your feelings run strongly in favour of your own choice, your only option is to appeal to His Holiness, the pope. Your chosen man will need to go in person, at the expense of Soltre, and your temporalities would certainly be suspended for as long as it takes.'

Peter quietly observed how naturally Fergus slipped into the leadership role, and how willingly the canons accepted him – or, at least, appeared to do so. Close friend and mentor of Fergus as he was, he seldom heard any negative things said about the young man. Yet he had become aware of undercurrents of ambivalence, almost of resentment, directed at the medicus, seemingly because the father's terminal collapse had been in some way connected with a sharp difference of opinion between Fergus and himself. The canons had deeply loved the father and felt he had as much claim to sainthood as the commoners seemed to feel about Fergus. Most of the brothers were deeply conservative and conformists by nature. Not a few questioned the developments in welfare for women, uneasily feeling they were alien to the Augustinian way. They yearned for a steady hand on the reins to counterbalance the youthful impetuousness of the young Highlander.

Chapter 30

Bishop Wardlaw and his three acolytes made a thorough inspection of Soltre and its activities, as if convinced that nefarious activities were taking place there. There was a hint of accusation as they attended every department and poked and prodded into its practices, upsetting all the well-ordered routines. The morning's clinic in the garth took twice as long as normal because of their clumsy and ill-directed questions. The patients took it all in their stride, but the Soltre staff could hardly hide their irritation. Fergus's patience was quickly exhausted, and he suggested that the inspectors should stand back a little and observe, rather than crudely interfere.

Only one of the bishop's assistants entered the portals of the infirmary, saying that he had himself in a previous posting done some medical work and had the stomach for it. When he insisted that Peter should conduct him round the hall and its ancillary departments, Peter, normally the soul of mildness, bluntly refused.

'I have work to do, the sick and the dying to attend,' he said. 'In short, the suffering. You are most welcome to stay and watch, or investigate where you please – though do take care in the pharmacy as there are poisonous substances there. But I shall brook no interference with our working priorities.'

Bishop Wardlaw asked Fergus to accompany him to the cemetery, and walked him over to the corner where the three infant graves were sited.

'How do these come to be here?' he asked.

'I can only tell you about the most recent one,' replied Fergus, thinking that it would be politic to stick to the truth as far as possible. 'This was an infant who died immediately after birth. I know, because she's my half-sister. My mother gave birth to her at Galagate Castle some years ago. Fortunately a priest was available to baptise the child and they asked if she could be buried here. And since the Dampierres had been generous donors to the abbey, that was allowed. I know nothing about the others, and as you see they are very old – a hundred years at least. Quite possibly there were similar stories there.' Bishop Wardlaw digested this information in silence and they moved on to the gardens.

The kitchens and storerooms were given a careful look, for the bishop had on several occasions inveighed against priests and clerics indulging in rich food and wine.

'He remembers, I'm sure, the royal entertainment here when the king first returned,' Fergus later said to Richard. 'He wants to be sure we don't always live like that.'

'He has a reputation himself for giving lavish dinners, and one doesn't suppose he restricts himself to bread and water,' muttered Richard. The bishop's acolytes, though not the bishop himself, took their meals with the brothers in the refectory throughout their stay, duly checking that the regular fare was of the prescribed simple nature. They examined the sleeping quarters and even investigated the magister's residence, making sure that the wardrobes did not contain garments that were too ostentatious. The riding stables came next, and Walt was happy to report that the inspectors seemed surprised to find sturdy, unglamorous, working horses standing next to their own well-bred, refined animals. 'They asked,' he said with a grin, 'where we housed the falcons and kept the hunters!'

The bishop was closeted with Prior Richard in the residency office for an entire morning, looking at papers to do with landholdings, charters with details of donated land inheritance and gifts of immense value given for the privilege of Masses said in perpetuity for the donors' souls. They inspected a papal bull dated 1236, pressed with care between sheets of parchment, stating that the rule of St Augustine should be observed at Soltre in perpetuity. As expected, Father John had left all the paper-work in perfect order.

On the third day, the bishop departed along with three of his bodyguards. The three clerics, his 'sniffer dogs', as they were irreverently labelled, were left to continue the work, even riding out into the country to inspect some of the abbey farms and workshops and interviewing a number of the country people about Soltre and its inhabitants.

While the inspection continued, the abbot of Jedburgh arrived on horseback with his chaplain and a servant. The abbot, Father Patrick, was well known to the senior brothers and was greeted as an old friend. Dressed in a manner identical to all Augustinians, wearing a black tunic and cowl, he melded into the company and was soon in deep discussion with Richard, Fergus and some of the others in the residence library. He agreed the bishop's visit sounded sinister, but that Father John's last wishes should certainly be carried out. He knew the person on whom the Soltre community had fixed for nomination: his own deputy, Prior Graham, a man made very much in the same mould as John – educated, committed and deeply pious.

Father Patrick smiled ruefully at the assembly. 'You know, brothers, it is an act of extreme charity on my part that I agree he would be an excellent magister for you and am prepared to support him and you, and pave the way for his election. He is my right-hand man and I shall be hard pressed to manage without him. But he knows what is in the wind and is willing to stand for election. Let us proceed apace before Wardlaw and his cronies find someone to foist upon you.'

With Prior Richard nominally in charge, it was easy for Fergus to get a leave of absence to ride the short distance to Mary's home on the outskirts of Lauder. Mary had, according to Catriona, married beneath her rank in taking David; but she was content to be Mrs Gordon, for she had been Catriona's slave for long enough. David had a degree in law and had performed some administrative services for the Crown at Donald's behest, so had the right to attend the Convention of Estates. Fergus was well able to appreciate Father John's wisdom in staying informed with events in the world of state and politics, and the couple were a good source of the latest news in the outside world. Fergus also told Mary of the recent visit by the bishop.

'What was it all about?' asked Mary. 'Commiseration plus a hidden agenda?'

'For sure. Not heresy hunting, which is his prevailing obsession. He seemed to be much more interested in the value of our holdings, our lands and income. He seemed to imply that we were too rich. Though he saw that we don't lavish it on ourselves!'

'Indeed. You work very hard and he should be impressed rather than critical. But you know, David was saying that King James is desperate for money, and he searches for every excuse or legal loophole to deprive earls of their estates and seize their income. The latest was the Earl of March. All this is making him dangerously unpopular. Now Bishop Wardlaw is his closest friend. Do you think they are plotting an opportunistic takeover of Soltre's worldly goods?'

'We wondered. But the king has been spending plenty money, we hear. Can he really be so short of funds? I thought Wardlaw's visit was more about his own self-aggrandising and power-wielding.'

Mary shook her head. 'The king gets parliament to raise taxes to pay the ransom for his hostages in England and then spends it on other things – diplomacy, entertaining, his military adventures. His new palace at Linlithgow. He's good at spending, all right.'

'Well, I suppose,' said Fergus, 'that he may now be looking for new sources to pilfer. The inspectors at Soltre seemed to be looking for excuses to fine us, as well as making a detailed inventory of our assets. I believe that in England, the late king found it useful to confiscate the temporalities of abbeys while they dragged out the procedure of electing a new abbot. It's likely they are planning the same for us.'

'What will you do?'

'We're going ahead with an election for our magister – there is only one candidate. But then we must go crawling to King James and his friend Bishop Wardlaw and try to persuade them to agree. If they do not, it's all-out war. We could take our case to the pope. But if we do, we'll be cutting our own throats. They'd probably rub their hands in glee and seize the assets of Soltre for years to come.'

'But if they do impose their own candidate, how does that help the king financially?'

'That, I don't know. But the bishop's as wily as they come. If they have their own man as magister, they can pull strings from afar. We shall be under their thumbs, and I expect they would find ways to extort goods and valuables. Maybe even land.'

After a pause, Mary said, 'I miss my two ladies. But we'll see them regularly. I'm a rather experienced midwife myself, as you know – one very useful thing I learned from being your mother's companion! I am able to help Jan a lot in her sphere as well as teaching her literary skills. Every second woman in Lauder seems to be pregnant!'

'Your involvement is excellent,' said Fergus. 'You'll give Jan respectability and open doors for her. Father John's advice to me was to let the women get on with the work. Although I'd like to be more involved, it is a difficult time because of all this paranoia about heresy. Even some of the brothers don't like me being involved.'

'Jan and Annie are both intelligent and eager for education,' said Mary. 'I was glad to get some nourishment into them and warm clothes on their backs. Already wee Annie is looking more like a maid than a child.'

Chapter 31

Bishop Wardlaw travelled back to Holyrood Abbey, where he was expected by King James, who was eagerly awaiting his report of the Soltre visit. He met the king with Queen Joan, who took an active interest in affairs of state. After preliminary greetings were completed, with the bishop taking care to give his grace due respect but expecting a measure of reverence in return, they dismissed the servants and settled into a more informal exchange.

'My good friend, you seem weary,' said the king.

'Indeed, sire, I am getting too old for travel; I find it most irksome. But this was an important duty. I have much to tell Your Grace, and much to plan, with your concurrence.'

'Pray proceed, my good Henry.'

'Your Grace, may I have permission to speak at length?'

'Of course you may.'

'Perhaps the best news for our purpose is that there is definitely no obvious candidate to replace Father John as magister at Soltre. They have been forced to look to the neighbouring establishment at Jedburgh for a candidate, a Prior Graham, I believe. The father on his deathbed urged the company to choose an Augustinian, one from the wider community if needed, and they feel obliged to do so. I have given them the licence, but I need hardly say that we shall not endorse their elected man. Whether they will make a stand and take the matter to the papal court, I do not know. Most of the company seemed meek and accepting, though unhappy. The only one who seemed likely to cause trouble was that young Highlander, the medicus – Brother Fergus.'

'I remember meeting him, some years ago. He was little more than a boy then.'

'Indeed, sire. It would suit our purposes best if he should turn out to be a firebrand, and to oppose us in our selection of magister. We could then use delays and other tactics to take control of the income for years to come. But I suspect they will not take that route; they have too much accumulated wisdom.'

'The property owned by the community is vast, I believe?'

'Indeed, sire. I have examined all the paperwork, which goes back for three hundred years. Complete for the last two hundred, and most of it even before that. It has been stored and kept in excellent condition. Their holdings extend from just beyond the boundaries of Edinburgh right down to Jedburgh. Over to the west they go to Peebles, and to the north-east almost to Dunbar. It's the size of an earldom. I do not think there are any legal loopholes we can use to claim their land, though I've asked the chancellor to check, of course. It has all been given to them on the deaths of various grateful notables. They even hold land that was given by Thomas the Rhymer of Erceldoune, who was a famous prophet in his day.'

'When you think of the predators that operate in these regions, grasping militants like the Douglases? It is a matter of some surprise that the Soltre estate has been kept intact,' observed King James.

'They appear to have been singularly blessed, sire. There has never been a raid or an attack on them, even in the wars of independence. One may assume that this is on account of the philanthropy of their hospital practice and good works for travellers and pilgrims. You mention the Douglases; the late Earl Archibald was a donor, a most generous one – in exchange for Masses said for his family, of course. Soltre is held in great respect and affection by the entire surrounding community, of all social levels. Many of them have benefitted from the medical care it offers. Many more are employees or trading partners, and all testify to the generous treatment they receive. We could find no one to make any adverse comment whatever.'

King James wrinkled his brow. 'What can they want with such vast possessions?' he asked. 'Do they truly adhere to the poverty rule of their order?'

'It seems they do,' answered the bishop. 'We inspected the kitchens, gardens and storehouses as well as the meal tables of the canons. The brothers eat very humbly. Yet Your Grace will remember the banquet they produced at the time of your arrival back in Scotland. Guests are treated very much according to rank and expectations. They are surrounded by farms and orchards, run by local people but managed by the abbey. It is a system of benevolent feudalism. Indeed, more than that, they actively redistribute goods to benefit the poorest.

'There was no sign of grand clothing for great occasions, no evidence of expensive horses or sporting pursuits. Though their library is worth a fortune, of course, and well stocked, including the most modern medical literature.'

'You thought you might find evidence of some heretical practices,' said Queen Joan. 'This medicus, the rebellious one, could he be ensnared, do you think?'

'Ma'am, I am always alert to the possibility of heresy, but such errors are not always obvious. There is an aura surrounding this young man and we shall need to step with great care in dealing with him. He seems to have acquired a local reputation as a saint. He has been likened to St Cuthbert. You would not recognise any aspiring saintliness when you speak to him, he is not mystical in his speech or behaviour, but years ago, when he was but a stripling, he stood up to that murderous young renegade Colin Douglas and a thunderstorm broke fortuitously overhead – which has been taken by the local population to mean he is blessed with supernatural powers.'

'Sounds to me as if there is plenty of material there for a charge of heresy,' said the queen rather brusquely.

'We are not looking for heresy in the common people, ma'am, but within the abbey. This Douglas heir had been causing much grief in the countryside in those days, and the people attribute his fate of banishment and then death in battle to Brother Fergus. They are as grateful and loyal to him personally as they are to the Soltre establishment.'

Another thought struck the bishop and he turned to the king. 'You will remember, sire, that a part of the volunteer army of the good Father John accompanied Your Graces on your first hazardous trip north to Scone. Their guarding duties when needed are given voluntarily in view of benefits received. You will find no more loyal troops anywhere, and a substantial number can be raised at very short notice. I doubt very much that the Soltre community would initiate hostilities, but the common people might well do it on their behalf. The Borderers have a reputation for militancy that is second to none and you do not wish to alienate them. This is another reason for caution and tact.'

King James digested this information. 'Unfortunately,' he said testily, 'we do not have time for caution and tact. We need money now.' He began to fidget restlessly. 'I am being called upon by France to support their action against England. They wish me to attack the English enclave at Roxburgh Castle. I shall have to raise another tax to pay the army; they will not volunteer for free. At least they can live off the lands of Soltre and of the Douglases, so that is an expense spared.'

Perhaps observing the king's increasing irritation at the lack of immediate funds, Wardlaw wound up the discussion.

'In summary, sire, I would say that we have not so far found any cause for fault-finding at Soltre, and we have found many reasons to treat them with caution. For that reason, I would propose the following steps. We let them have their election, and come to us for confirmation. Then we refuse to accept their nominee. If they appeal to His Holiness, we seize their temporalities. If they do not, we propose our own candidate and have him installed. We carefully choose our own man, who will do our bidding. Once he is in the post, we can explore further whether there is any way in which we can... adjust the ownership status of the landholdings in such a way as to bring it under our own control. We can do this by charter under the Great Seal of Scotland; or we can ourselves appeal to the pope to adjudge whether or not the possession of such vast estates is in keeping with the original foundation of the hospital. Arguably, the land gifts were for sacred purposes and should be regarded as Church property. I am confident we can make our case, sire. And we can make it speedily.'

'Do you have someone in mind, Henry?'

'Sire, I do. He is a young priest called Thomas Lauder; the nephew of my colleague William Lauder, Bishop of Glasgow and the grandson of Your Grace's late great friend and protector, Sir Robert Lauder of Bass.'

The king nodded approvingly at the mention of his old friend.

Bishop Wardlaw continued, 'He is the natural son of Sir Robert's heir, also Robert, who was involved in liberating Your Grace from England. So as we see, Thomas is of sound family and connections. His origin as a natural son has impeded his progress somewhat in the Church, and he is more than usually willing to do our bidding. I believe he will grace a bishop's see at a future date if he performs this service well for Your Grace.'

The King rose, looking distracted. 'Very good, Bishop Wardlaw. Please proceed as you have described with all possible haste. Come, my dear.' He held out his arm to the queen, and left rather less cordially than at the start of the discussion.

Chapter 32

Prior Graham of Jedburgh was invited to come and stay for some days at Soltre, so that he could make himself known before his submission to election. He joined the senior canons, the office bearers, in the residency for a discussion. As with Father Patrick, there was instant rapport, with shared similar ways of thinking, values and principles.

'Brothers, I am more honoured than I can say that you are prepared to consider me as your new magister,' said Graham, speaking fluently and confidently. 'But I feel it my duty to warn you that – in my opinion, and that of Father Patrick – there is very little likelihood of my election, if it happens, being honoured by our king and bishop. The news we receive constantly is that his grace the king is desperate for sources of funds, and has made enemies amongst the nobles by extortionate practices as well as by not honouring his ransom obligations, while spending lavishly and frivolously. Here at Soltre, you are dangerously well endowed. It is a measure of your good works over centuries and the gratitude you have earned. I know of no other monastic institute with such extensive property. It is not surprising that his grace looks towards you with cupidity.'

Richard responded, 'We hear what you are saying, prior. We are all, however, agreed that Father John's dying wish should be fulfilled as far as it lies in our power to do so. We are profoundly grateful that you are prepared to stand for election in this difficult situation. We can only ask for guidance from above and trust in the power of prayer. We shall take matters step by step.'

Leaving the meeting a little later, as they made their way to the church for Mass, to be followed by a welcome meal in the refectory attended by all the canons and novices, Fergus murmured to Peter, 'Far be it from me to wish for violence, but from what I have heard, the king is in danger both from his own people as well as in these recent forays against the English. These are turbulent times. And I don't think the bishop is long for this world, by the looks of him. It is possible we shall be overtaken by events.'

'Did you hear Graham saying that the king is planning to lay siege to Roxburgh?' said Richard, joining them. 'Why should he seek to nettle the English? Brothers, it seems to me that here at Soltre we have enjoyed an oasis of peace and plenty for a long time, and we are about to see it all go up in smoke.'

In spite of the rumours and insecurity, as the company gathered in the refectory after Mass the atmosphere was one of happy expectation of a return to normality. Peter said to Graham, 'You know, we have been through our own troubles, with the father's very sudden and difficult death, and then the arrival of Bishop Wardlaw and his very harsh handling of the inspection. Even if our delight in your coming is deluded and short-lived, we should enjoy the hope of what might yet come to pass.'

This feeling was shared by everyone. There was a holiday mood, even though work continued as usual. Graham took time to speak to everyone, including the servants, and quietly visited the various workplaces, where his easy manner ensured a warm response – such a contrast from the arrogance of Wardlaw and his sniffer dogs.

Fergus quickly discovered that Graham was, like himself, a keen musician. He loved to sing and he played the flute and the recorder. Graham was invited to lead the singing in the midnight service of matins; the sound of his assured and fluid tenor rising through the stone pillars to the very roof beams caused an audible intake of breath in the choir. Eyes filled with tears and Fergus found a lump in his throat that prevented him from singing for some minutes.

Later, during the quiet time, Fergus and Graham brought out their instruments in the residency parlour and played together, trying out tunes and harmonies and finding that the clarsach and the recorder sounded very good as an ensemble. 'I'm out of practice,' said Fergus, flexing his fingers and strumming. 'But it comes back. It's great to play with another instrumentalist. Why don't we have a little concert, one evening after supper? We could have some singing too.'

The election was duly held, and the selection of Graham as the new father was enthusiastic and unanimous. The company gathered with ceremony at the great gate to send off Graham and Richard, with attendants, to carry the request to King James to honour the canons' choice. There was some doubt as to the king's whereabouts, since the siege of Roxburgh had begun, though it had quickly disintegrated in ignominious disarray among the army's leaders and the army was apparently in retreat. However, the Soltre delegation headed for Holyrood, hoping to find the king there, or at least to discover his whereabouts.

It was more than a week before the Soltre party returned, and the weary, joyless faces of Graham and Richard told their own story. Gathered in the residence with Brothers Kenneth, Peter, Fergus and Robert, they confirmed that Graham's nomination had been rejected. Graham told the story, as Richard seemed in the last extremes of travel-worn frustration.

'We thought we were in luck, as the king was indeed in residence at Holyrood. But we had great difficulty in making ourselves heard by his people; there was no one who would stop long enough to listen to us. In the aftermath of the failed siege, there was a feeling of chaos and uncertainty, and no one was allowed near the king. Eventually we met a canon of sufficient seniority to receive and understand our needs. He was good to us, and with persistence got our message through. But the king's response was that this is a matter for Bishop Wardlaw and that we should follow his instructions on this matter. Our friendly canon told us that the king was unable to focus on anything but his present military and political crisis and we'd be best advised to go on to St Andrews to the bishop's palace.

'So we continued our journey, and a weary one it was, with a huge tangle of traffic on the roads, much of it military. We knew fairly well by now that our mission had failed. At St Andrews we were at least welcomed and well lodged at the abbey there, and our request to see the bishop was received courteously. However, it seemed his lordship had taken ill through the night and was unable to see us.

'We asked to see his secretary, and explained the important nature of our need. The secretary asked if there was anyone who could deputise for the bishop. It was frustrating to be treated so dismissively. I'm afraid I got angry and suggested that all we needed was a yes, but that if it were subsequently rescinded when the bishop recovered, we would all be in trouble. I reiterated that we were there on urgent business directly from the king at Holyrood. We were invited to wait, and so we did, making our request every day and making sure we were being taken seriously. At last, we were invited to meet Wardlaw, who was sitting in his bedchamber looking very seedy; dressed in draperies covering his night gear. He said very little. To be honest, he seemed a bit muddled. There was nothing in the way of greeting or enquiries, he merely said, "I cannot grant your request. My secretary here will explain my wishes." His speech was slurred, we both noted. Then he waved us away without further ado.

'His secretary ushered us into his office and explained that the bishop had given him the task of clarifying his wishes, and apologised for keeping us waiting around for so long. His lordship and his grace the king had asked one Thomas Lauder to undertake the mastership of Soltre, and he had agreed. Thomas Lauder is, we gather, a member of a family that has served the king and the Church in various senior capacities, and has relations highly placed in the Church. His uncle William is Bishop of Glasgow. Thomas is a priest, a graduate of Paris University and has served his king as chaplain and as tutor to the young Prince James. He will be ready to come and take up his post as magister within the next month.'

The canons had expected the news of Graham's rejection, but it still came like a hammer blow. He was profoundly apologetic about bringing the awful news, while the company felt they had involved him in an unpleasant and demeaning fool's errand, and he was now going away in an aura of rejection and humiliation. With most of the group in tears, Graham took his leave, feeling they could best come to terms with their future if he left. Once his humble belongings were packed, Fergus walked him out to the garth where fresh horses and his attendants waited.

'It is not good for you to continue travelling without a break,' said Fergus. 'I think you should stay at least one night, good brother.' But Graham felt his position was anomalous and he should leave. Fergus grasped his hands. 'You are a good friend to Soltre and to me especially, Graham. You have our undying gratitude for trying to help us carry out Father John's dying instructions, to at least try to maintain our own ways against this incursion. I am deeply disappointed you are not going to be one of us. We shall keep you informed of all that happens, and welcome any advice you or Father Walter have for us.'

They hugged, then Graham mounted and was carried away.

Fergus felt sorely in need of human comfort as he watched his new friend leave the abbey. He would usually have sought out Peter's company, but as he walked slowly and aimlessly across the garth he realised that female solace was what he needed. He would saddle up and visit Jan. He would miss High Mass and dinner, but he felt numb and in a mood to reject the calls of duty.

His route, downhill to the east, took him away from the main road, but he could see that it was still busy with knots of mounted soldiers and infantry carrying their pikes, returning from the collapsed Roxburgh siege. His pathway down the wooded slope to Jan's little cottage was becoming familiar. He thought with regret about Graham's excellent attributes and how he would have graced the leadership of their community, and how Father John would have blessed their choice of his successor. What did the future hold now? Since his return to Soltre the winds of change had not stopped blowing, and a series of icy blasts they had been. After his student life, Fergus had doubted whether he truly belonged to the Church, and he still felt alienated from its present incarnation. But he followed essential Christian teaching, loved Soltre and the people who belonged there and the people who came there for help, and he would fight for its survival with all his power and cunning. Perhaps the turbulence in the country at the present time would interfere with the royal-episcopal scheming alliance. Graham was right, there were venal motives afoot. This man Thomas Lauder was a placement, a spy, an incubus, and Fergus was determined to oppose him in every way. But perhaps fate might lend a hand, as he had mentioned to Peter a while since; from the account they had heard of Bishop Wardlaw's illness, it sounded as if he would not be fully functioning in the near future, if at all.

He found Jan at home, and she was pleased to see him. Annie was even now with Mary, having lessons at her little school at Lauder. Fergus found himself disappointed at her absence. He liked it when she worked her sprightly charm on him.

'Mary knows a lot about childbearing, especially for a lady of quality,' Jan assured Fergus. 'Sad that she's none o' her ain. She has come visiting wi' me and shown concern on account o' some o' my ladies not getting proper food fer their condition. They need some meat and milk, she says.'

'That is something else we have in plenty and can supply,' said Fergus. 'You see how ignorant and dumb we men are when we are kept at a distance. I can get some milk goats from our farms for those in need. Can you and Mary make a list with addresses, and I'll arrange it? I think you and Annie should have a milk goat too. She was looking better nourished when I saw her last, but still too thin.'

Jan was able to remember the list of her patients' names, and the directions for their homes. Fergus marvelled at her memory and realised he would have to match it, for he had come out in a rush, without bringing any vellum or reed pens and ink.

'I'll remember these till I get back,' he said. 'I'll write them down then. Trouble with learning to write things down, Jan, as you'll discover, is that you don't exercise the memory so much and you lose the capacity to remember.'

'You look tired, Brother Fergus. How are things at Soltre? Do you have your new master?'

'Alas, no. King and bishop won't accept our choice. We feel they have no right to impose their own man on an Augustinian abbey that has its own ways of doing things, but in their eyes we are wealthy landowners and they are staking their claim.'

'Can't ye fecht them? That seems to be how kings settle their differences.'

Fergus laughed. 'Our king likes fighting, but you need money for that, and he has none. Our bishop likes being clever and manipulative, but he has fallen seriously sick and his brain seems addled. It's a great pity they have appointed their man already, for they both have other troubles to confront and might otherwise have forgotten about us. Still, this new master, Father Thomas, as I suppose we must call him, will be unsupported and we shall fight him in our own way.'

'Brother, whatever you do will be right, and I'm sure the Lord will smile upon ye. He seems to favour ye.'

Jan produced some ale and they sat drinking and chatting companionably at her table. 'You women are so good at seeing what's needed,' said Fergus. 'I'll see to the goats, and we'll need to send feed as well, though they can forage of course. Now, I'd better be gone. Remind me of those names and directions again.'

Chapter 33

The company at Soltre waited for some weeks for word of their new magister. They even began to hope that he might not arrive. But one morning a message came saying he was on his way, and the next day he arrived with his company of chaplain, scribe and guards. The morning clinic was in full swing, and the new father, Thomas, looked around him in bewilderment. The welcoming party of brothers, led by Richard, gathered along with hostel and stable staff to sort out accommodation and horses.

Thomas dismounted, and Fergus, still attending to a patient, an elderly farmer, paused to watch him across the garth. Indeed, all the clinic patients were agog and gaping at the arrivals. Thomas was a youngish man of medium height and build, with sparse mousy hair and no tonsure, dressed in a gentleman's riding clothes. Like Bishop Wardlaw, he did not travel in a cleric's garb.

'What is going on here?' Thomas asked peevishly, eyebrows raised, staring at the queue of country folk and the two treatment points where tables were set with medicaments and consultations taking place. 'It looks like a market! Hardly fitting for an abbey.'

Richard came forward, introducing himself and the three other brothers with him. Thomas stared vacantly, still distracted by the crowds in the garth, and did not introduce himself or his companions. Richard said, hastily, 'You forget perhaps, father, that this place is primarily a hospital. This is our daily clinic where people come to get advice on ailments. Look, here comes our medicus now, Brother Fergus, who has been working since early morning, so many folk need his advice.'

Father Thomas looked around at the stone garth and showed visible distaste at the milling people covertly glancing his way. Fergus thought, 'Poor man is nervous. Not many of our visitors are so hard to greet, and he's not doing himself any favours.'

Eventually it was clear that the chaplain and the scribe were to be permanent residents, that three horses were to remain for the father's exclusive use, but the three guards, borrowed from the bishop's establishment, would take their leave the next day. Richard, Fergus and the other brothers prepared to enter the residence with Father Thomas, to offer refreshments, to talk preliminaries and to show him the layout of the abbey. It was quickly apparent that he wished the company only of his chaplain and scribe for the present.

Fergus said, 'You know, father, there is a scribe already here in post who is fully competent and in charge of the late Father John's arrangements. Indeed, he is indispensable.'

'Maybe so, maybe so, but I must have my own man also,' Thomas said, looking uneasy.

Fergus guessed that the new scribe would be part of the spying network. 'May we know your wishes for today, father? When will you want to meet the whole company? The hour for chapter is past. Will you be taking your meals here or in the refectory?'

'Oh, questions, questions. Time enough for those. I wish to be left to settle in. I'll perhaps walk around on my own later.

Fergus saw that the father was easily nettled and decided to continue. 'Do you come from Bishop Wardlaw today, father? May we ask how he fares? I believe his health has not been good?'

'Oh, he is fair. Not yet back to his episcopal duties but there is nothing to worry about.'

Fergus observed the dissembling tone. The man was not a good liar. 'But that is now some weeks that he has been unwell. This cannot be a simple condition. Is he getting adequate care?'

'For sure he is, the best care. And I am assured that there not a cause for concern,' snapped Thomas with a hostile glare. Fergus glanced at Richard, who was enjoying the father's discomfiture.

'Father, you are new to our Border country. If I may mention that the horses you have brought – for your own use – are not at all suitable for riding in these parts, where, away from the main road, the ground is very rough. You need Border-bred cobs to cope with it; fine nags like yours will quickly go lame.'

'If I ride out, you may be sure it will be on main roads. We have more important matters to discuss than horses, I would have thought.'

'Indeed, father, we do, thank you for reminding us. This is really why we have gathered here. But if you are tired, please name your time. You will appreciate that we have not in the past ever welcomed a complete outsider into our midst, someone who is not even an Augustinian canon and who has not committed to our rule. We wish to know your intentions as well as making you aware of our ways. I raised the question of horses because it is not our custom here to have personal property. Our rule prescribes duties of poverty, chastity and obedience.'

As Fergus said this, staring steadily into Thomas's eyes, he realised it was a declaration of war, and would be recognised as such.

'Brother Fergus, I have not joined the Augustinian order and have not agreed to abide by its rule. I have come at the Bishop's behest, because you lacked a master.'

'Pardon me, father, but I do not see how you can be our magister, and be accepted as such, when you are not an Augustinian. Maybe you did not know, but we held an election, which is standard procedure, and elected a magister from our order, but Bishop Wardlaw, speaking on the king's behalf, would not accept him.'

'That I did not know,' said Father Thomas, looking honest and dignified for the first time. 'Well, this cannot be resolved immediately since the bishop is *hors de combat*. I shall no doubt receive instructions... Now I must ask you to leave me.'

Feeling that some points had at least been made, they did so.

'What an insignificant, paltry nonentity of a man,' Fergus spluttered as they left the residence, hardly bothering to keep his voice down. 'You heard what he said at the end? He admitted he is under instruction from the bishop.'

'We hardly made him feel welcome, did we?' said Richard.

'He comported himself in a way that did not invite welcome,' said Robert tersely. 'I think we should not buckle and accept this man. What are his credentials? What is his curriculum vitae? We only know of him what we heard, second hand, from Brother Graham. How can he be our magister?'

As with one mind, they moved to the chapter house to discuss their dilemma. Richard beckoned to Andrew Sinclair, the magister's senior clerk, and asked him to summon the other senior brothers – including Peter, if he could be drawn away from the infirmary. As they filed in, Richard was persuaded to sit in the father's chair next to the church door to conduct the meeting. They were soon joined by the other brothers, Peter among them, who had hastened from their various duties.

After a prayer, Richard said, 'Dear brothers, we have just received our new father, called Thomas Lauder. He has been appointed by Bishop Wardlaw without any discussion with ourselves, while our own choice, Prior Graham of Jedburgh, has been rejected for reasons unknown. We had very little time to talk to the new father; he sent us away peremptorily and, frankly, discourteously. We did learn, however, that he is not an

Augustinian and has not adopted our rule. Now, this is counter to the requirements of such an appointment, which state that a man in holy orders must have been an Augustinian canon for ten years as well as having a reputation for integrity among the members of the community he intends to govern.

'We have none of these things, brothers. We know nothing of Thomas Lauder, and he seems unwilling, so far at least, to tell us anything. We need to discuss what courts of appeal are open to us and whether we should use them. I should like to ask each of you to speak in turn, then we can have an open discussion. Brother Fergus?'

'Thank you, brother. I believe we have a balancing act to perform of some delicacy. We are outraged at the bishop's arrogance and we do not accept that he has the authority to interfere. However, we are up against powerful men, who can enforce their pronouncements if they so wish, and we must not act in such a way as to cut the ground from beneath us.

'We are in no doubt that the underlying motive in this intervention is to take control of Soltre's considerable assets on the king's behalf. If we make an absolute rejection of Thomas Lauder, we risk having those assets seized. Speaking for myself, I was so angry after this morning's encounter with the man that I should have liked to set our guards upon him and send him back to Wardlaw in disgrace.

'But we can't do that. At the same time, we must make use of what appeals we have. Brother Richard, I know you have done some research on these matters. In England there are governing chapters of our order to oversee legal disputes that have arisen in the past. We do not have any such in Scotland. Our only appeal is to our bishop and to the pope. Neither seems likely to give us much support, for a variety of reasons. But I do believe we should make our objections heard in these ways. In order to protect ourselves, we must inform Thomas, keep him aware of what we are doing and why and not reject him outright.

'We should even, perhaps, however distasteful it is, make a provisional acceptance of him, the details of which we should debate now. What do we call him? What are his duties? What should he wear? Should he be allowed to use the magister's residence? I think we should be guided by cunning and self-serving – by which I mean, Soltre-serving – and not revenge, retribution and other negative emotions.

'That does not mean we toady to him. I think we cannot undertake to obey him until his mastership is confirmed. For day-to-day management, we should continue to refer to Brother Richard. But we must treat Thomas with courtesy – cold, distant courtesy, essentially non-acceptance. He should feel like an outsider. But his official status will be, at the very best, provisional magister.'

After Fergus, the other brothers were asked to air their views. No one was prepared to simply bow down to the new man and everyone agreed that he was not to be obeyed. Many took the view that an attitude of obstructive hostility should prevail. One or two thought he should not be allowed to live in the residence. Finally, Peter was asked for his opinion.

'Brother Peter, you are the longest-standing canon of Soltre among us,' said Richard. 'What do you think?'

Peter joined his hands together, interlacing his fingers. It was a gesture that Fergus, who sat next to him, recognised as an indication of disagreement. 'It seems to me that we are all still motivated by anger, justifiably perhaps, and that we need to let a little calm prevail. I have not met Thomas Lauder yet, but, Brother Fergus, you mentioned to me as we sat down that he looked nervous. Young, inexperienced and nervous. Now, it is probable that he is quite as reluctant to be here as we are to have him. His family is eminent and every one is a bishop or holds office in the royal court, often both. One uncle is a cardinal. Why has he been sent here? The master of Soltre is a prestigious post, but not to a man of the world, used to luxuries, palaces and good company. I think he has probably been given a task to carry out, to soften us up for a takeover perhaps, and he has almost certainly been offered a boon if he performs that task. My guess is a bishopric at some future date. If that is the case, he will resist becoming a member of our order and he will certainly not commit to us for life.

'Our first task is to befriend him and find out exactly what his instructions are. He may be persuaded to confide in us. Then we can – who knows? – even join forces with him. Work out a plan whereby he does not leave here in disgrace, but one that enables us to scupper the episcopal plot once we know what it entails.'

There was a silence while Peter's words were digested. Finally, Fergus murmured, 'You wily old fox!'

'Graham mentioned that Thomas is a natural child,' said Richard, 'and that is why he has not made much advancement in the Church. His father, now Sir Robert Lauder, is the son of the eminent Baron Lauder who was Chancellor of Scotland and close friend of his grace King James. Sir Robert, Thomas's father, is a renowned philanderer and has left a number of children who are misbegotten.

'Thomas has held lowly clerical posts at the Council of Basel and in the see of St Andrews. You may be right, Peter. He is very young – younger than most of us – and with no history of leadership. Should we meet him, a small number of us, and try to engage him in confidences?'

Fergus requested permission to speak. 'I do not think this is a job for a committee. I have certainly antagonised him already and he won't open up to me. Might I suggest that Peter sees him on his own? Brother Peter, you have a gentle manner that invites people to confide. I think you are the best one of us to tackle him.'

So it was agreed that they would leave Thomas alone for the first day, although Richard would go with the chief clerk, Andrew, and lock away all the papers pertaining to Soltre to prevent any secret interference. Peter would make an appointment to see Thomas the following morning.

Chapter 34

Peter reflected that never in his life had he been tasked with a diplomatic mission. Yet he was not anxious; he was very accustomed to being the repository of people's confidences. He made no advance plans; he would let instinct take the lead.

On being shown into the residence parlour, he found Thomas standing rigidly behind the circular conference table, keeping his distance with a barrier between them. Thomas was silent, offering no greetings or openings, and with a fixed expression on his face that was hard to decipher. Peter walked to the table and placed his fingertips on it, leaning forward and trying to make eye contact. It was difficult to smile at such an empty visage, but he did.

'Good day to you, brother. I hope you slept well and have been well supplied by our kitchen?'

'Good day, brother. Yes, thank you. Now I cannot give you much time, as I wish to pray with my chaplain.'

Peter registered that this was a similar artifice to the one Thomas had reportedly adopted on the previous day – to appear occupied and so cut short the interview. Fergus was right, he thought, the poor man's terrified. Peter paused and stood upright, thinking it better not to acknowledge Thomas's wish. He would take charge.

'Thomas. May I sit?' Without waiting for permission, Peter moved around to a seat on Thomas's right, nearer but not too close. 'Please.' And he indicated that Thomas should also sit, which he did.

He is used to being given instructions and obeying them, Peter thought. Certainly not to giving them. 'We – the community of brothers at Soltre – met yesterday to discuss your coming, Thomas, and what it means for us. There is a need for us to find common ground. Am I right in thinking that you have no experience of an Augustinian establishment?'

'There is an Augustinian abbey at St Andrews. However, I have not had much to do with it, though I have seen the canons in the Church, of course.'

'Did you ask Bishop Wardlaw specifically for this post?'

Thomas gave a little laugh. 'People do not ask him for favours, or much else. He is the one who gives out jobs.'

'And he asked you – told you – that this was to be your job?'

'Yes.'

'Why do you think that was? When you had no connection with the Augustinian rule.'

'I suppose he thought I was suited to it.'

'And are you?'

There was a pause; after some time, it threatened to become a mulish silence.

'Thomas, I hope you will trust me. I am sorry to interrogate you like this. But we, the community here, need to understand you and your reason for being with us. At the moment, we are puzzled and feel as if we are lost at sea. It may be that you found my colleagues yesterday not very warm and friendly. If so, I apologise, as I am sure they will do later. You will sympathise with us when I tell you that we are still in great grief at losing our beloved Father John. He was literally like a father to us – a man who led the community and supervised the abbey in all its activities, central of which is the running of the hospital, as well as directing church routine, managing the farms and other related businesses, greeting visitors and pilgrims and making appointments.' He needed to go no further. Thomas was so pale he was on the point of fainting.

'Are you well, brother?' he asked with concern. He got up and fetched a flask from a side table, pouring some water from it into a drinking vessel and placing it on the table. Thomas tried to lift it, his hands shaking, needing both hands to get the cup to his lips. He drank, spilling some liquid. Then he sat, dejected, looking down at the puddle on the table.

Peter sat down again, turning towards Thomas. 'I think, brother, I should tell you what I believe. You can tell me if I am right. It may be that you have been pushed rather hard into accepting this post as master of Soltre. I need to know from your own lips, at some future date, just what tasks you have done in your life before now. I suspect that none of them have been in any senior or leadership capacities. Perhaps Bishop Wardlaw led you to believe that this would simply be a life spent in prayer on your knees, with no particular pressing duties. Am I right so far?' Peter's tone was gentle and coaxing, as if speaking to a child in the nursery. Thomas glanced up and nodded his head. He was still pale, and the trembling now affected his whole body.

'But still, this was a posting so far from your previous ones, and at such a distance, that it might have been a foreign country. I suspect you wished to discuss it further with the bishop but have been prevented by his illness?' He paused and again received a nod.

'I presume, from all we've heard, that the bishop's illness is serious? Possibly terminal?'

Thomas nodded more vigorously this time. 'He has had several crises – now he can hardly speak and is partly paralysed. He's bed-bound. That's why I delayed. But Bishop Kennedy told me I must come here, otherwise...'

After a lengthy pause, Peter gently prompted, 'Otherwise?'

Thomas made a despairing gesture. 'Otherwise, I'd be without a post at all. And never have a chance of... of... a bishopric.' Thomas began to shake again, and, losing control, put his elbows in the puddle of water on the table and began to sob, his hands over his face. Peter waited, hoping that the storm would pass.

After a few minutes, Thomas choked out, 'Sorry... not been well... myself.' The sobs continued noisily. Peter was aware of the chaplain hovering in the doorway. He put his arm gently across Thomas's shoulders, saying, 'Come, Thomas, dry your eyes and have another drink. No one is going to judge you here. No one is going to demand you do things you can't cope with.'

'I'd like to go and lie down now,' said Thomas petulantly, and Peter was aware of the chaplain moving across to take the man away. He stood up. He thought Thomas probably had a whole spectrum of childish behaviours designed to get him out of immediate difficulties. He kept his hand on Thomas's shoulder and put out a restraining hand towards the chaplain.

'No,' he said with authority. 'You will leave him with me. I am the infirmarer here and can deal with any immediate malaise. If Thomas is to do any work here he needs to face up to things.'

The chaplain stood his ground. 'Brother, I am glad to hear it. My name is Edgar, Edgar Grey. We have had great problems bringing Thomas here. He has been so anxious that he has made himself sick. We have been at our wits' end to know what to do. Thomas forbade us to talk to you. He copes by denying and avoiding. I should warn you that he has a terrible phobia about sickness, and a hospital hardly seems the best place for him to work. I'll be glad to give you any help I can.'

'Thank you,' said Peter. 'In spite of the phobia, we shall have to take him to the infirmary so that he is under my eye. It isn't too busy at the moment and I can't think of anyone who could cause him upset. Come, Thomas, come with me.' He put his hand under the man's elbow and guided him towards the door and across the garth to the infirmary. Thomas came like a lamb; clearly, thought Peter, comfortable to submit to authority. Peter also knew that his hands had a particular capacity to calm, as if they radiated comfort.

It was late evening before Peter had a chance to talk to Fergus, and he had already made his report to Richard.

'He is a complete wreck of a man, subject to phobias and anxieties. How even the arrogant Bishop Wardlaw thought he could fulfil the role of magister is beyond me. He has been working through the stresses of his breakdown most of the day. Storms of tears and terror, then a sleep lasting several hours. I have not given him any sedatives yet, and if we do that, we need to give him as little as possible. We can use this phase, of course, for getting information out of him. What is already clear is that he has always been a yes-man, told what to do and comfortable in performing regular, well-known rituals. I've picked up that he was taken on as tutor to the young Prince James, but could not cope even with a child of four.

'My instinct was right,' continued Peter. 'He has been promised a bishopric. He presumably thinks he could cope with the ceremonial part of it. What exactly he is supposed to do to win that prize is not yet clear. But we'll find out.

'I've had another thought, Fergus. Do you think you could talk to the chaplain? He seems a sensible young man – Edgar Grey is his name. He told me frankly about Thomas's current mental state. It's quite possible he may give us useful information.' His report finished, Peter let out a deep sigh of frustration.

'Well done, Peter,' said Fergus. 'Who would have thought this is how Thomas would turn out? Do you think he may milk his illness for all it's worth?'

'I'm sure he will – he's probably doing that already. We've got a job on our hands!'

Fergus went off to the residence to look for Edgar and found him sitting with Thomas's scribe, Hugh, drinking ale and looking bored. They both leapt to their feet as he entered.

'Brother Medicus, good evening. We were hoping to see you for some advice.'

'I'll do my best for you. How can I help you?'

'We do not wish to appear disloyal or unsympathetic, but... we have had such terrible toil getting Thomas here. Now he is sick and, we presume, unable to effectively take on the post of magister. We are very worried we might be called upon to take him back to St Andrews. Frankly, we've had enough. We would both of us like to go back to our old posts, and wish to leave here now – with your permission.'

Fergus nodded affably, seeing an opening to important confidences. He asked them to describe how Thomas had behaved on the journey.

Edgar said, 'He was reluctant to travel, did not help with the organisation, had to be pushed every inch of the way. And he got attacks of the tremors, as you've seen. He wouldn't eat anything and made himself disgustingly sick every night. He couldn't sleep, had nightmares, disturbed us and everybody else in the hostel. We had to nurse him and coax him all the way here.'

'I am surprised you got him here at all!' said Fergus. 'If you wish to return to St Andrews we shall help all we can, and give you testimonials to say you showed him every possible care. That should ensure you face no blame on your return.

'But perhaps you can help us, my friends. You may be aware that there has been disagreement over this role of magister, and our own man was not accepted. Thomas has been imposed on us by the bishop and the king. So far, it is clear that he was given some instructions – a task that probably does not bode well for Soltre. We wish to know what those instructions were. We shall, in time, extract it from Thomas, but if you are able to help us, that will speed things up and earn our gratitude.'

Edgar and Hugh glanced at each other; then Hugh spoke, with a brief hesitation. 'There were plans afoot, but all has been put on hold because of Bishop Wardlaw's illness. However, Bishop Kennedy of Dunkeld, who will probably take over at St Andrews when the time comes, has given me some idea of what they want. They want to know, essentially, how they can take control of the assets and landholdings here. Apparently you have a papal bull from two hundred years ago, giving you the right to the lands appertaining to the abbey. However, new lands have accrued since then. Thomas was told to look out this papal bull and other papers and, with my help, confiscate them, after which he would hand them over to the Bishop of St Andrews, who would hand them to the king.'

Fergus was stunned, both at the sheer audacity of the plot and the willingness of these two to reveal it.

'Friends, I thank you. You have done us a great service. I must share this with my colleagues. We shall do all we can to protect you both and enable you to enter suitable employment if you find yourselves in difficulties. Please do not admit you have told us about this plot. We can best combat it if the episcopal cabal does not know that we know. The fact of Thomas's collapse will help; you can say that we locked away all the papers and you could not get at them.'

Chapter 35

Fergus discovered from Jan, who was his best source of local gossip, that Soltre was, as ever, believed to be under sacred protection from malign forces. The new, unwanted magister, imposed by the 'high heid yins', had been struck down with incapacitating illness on his arrival at Soltre – so the story went among the peasants and villagers of the Borders.

The reality was, alas, much more complex. Thomas continued to show such mental instability that he was kept in the infirmary, and they had not extracted any more information nor had a chance to confront him about the plot to destabilise Soltre. His two attendants, chaplain and scribe, had left gratefully with their testimonials – and two of the three fine horses. Feeling there was some urgency to discover what scurrility had been planned, Fergus suggested to the others that they search Thomas's belongings. On arrival at Soltre he had been carefully nursing a leather satchel that had looked as if it contained papers.

'He is particularly terrified of you,' said Peter to Fergus, 'so you probably see him at his worst! But there is no doubt that he is playing to the galleries and that the worst of his illness is feigned. He is putting off the time when he will be challenged.'

Fergus said, 'I have little patience for such a spineless character. I know going through his papers is shocking, but we know he plots to ruin us and we must take every step we can to stop him.'

So Fergus, Richard and Andrew, the senior clerk, entered the residence. Richard looked out from the locked Soltre files the ancient papal bull concerning the rights of Soltre to their holdings while the others went to the bedchamber and found Thomas's satchel tucked away in a cupboard. It was stuffed with papers, some protected by folders of vellum, along with official documents and letters. They took it to the parlour and spread the contents on the table.

'Brother, look at this,' said Andrew, holding up a carefully covered document with the Great Seal of Scotland impressed on it. This stated explicitly that Thomas Lauder was to hold all lands, teinds, rents and profits belonging to the hospital of Soltre, for the whole of his life, for the purpose of supporting said hospital.

They looked at each other in horror. 'Confirmed by King James!' said Andrew. 'This Thomas is legally in control of all our assets.'

Fergus sat down to study the charter. 'It's very loosely worded,' he said. 'Note that it says, "for the whole of his life"! It's clear he doesn't want that, he wants to move on and be a bishop. And it doesn't say anything about him being appointed magister. Somehow, it's rather amateurish and incomplete. I wonder if the king, desperate for money, cobbled it together without the bishop's guiding hand and slapped his seal on it.'

Andrew was looking at more papers. 'Hah!' he said. 'This is interesting. Look here. A letter from the chief justice, warning that even a charter with the king's seal is not valid if the appointee is not qualified for the post of magister. And as Thomas has not been an Augustinian ever, never mind for ten years, the charter does not stand.'

'Well, praise be for the chief justice!' said Fergus. 'Let's see the dates on those papers. Look, this is dated from months back. What a pack of rogues! All this was going forward even as we were having our election. Now here is a copy of a letter that has been sent by Thomas himself to Pope Eugene. A supplication from Thomas Lauder, styling himself "Master of the Hospital at Soltre". Look at the date, again, sent months ago, when he had even less right to call himself master than he does now! He describes himself as "peacefully in possession and without adversary"! How dare he write such blatant lies to His Holiness!

'He goes on to request that he, Thomas, should rule the house and hospital of Soltre as a simple and secular benefice, suggesting that Soltre should be removed from the St Augustine Order. This is clearly in response to the objection made by the chief justice. And it seems to have been written without the guidance of Wardlaw himself, presumably because he had fallen ill by this time. Thomas gives his reasons for taking Soltre from Augustinian rule, all spurious and easily demolished. I don't suppose he knew about our ancient rights given by papal authority.'

Richard placed the delicate papal bull document on the table. 'The way it's worded is clever. It gives us the right to existing and all future landholdings.'

'I don't see any response from the pope to Thomas,' said Andrew. 'There's not been enough time, I suppose. I presume we shall write and make our own case.'

'Certainly we shall,' said Richard. 'And with almost complete hope of success. Not only do we have our ancient rights and the paper to prove it, but – and I'm sure Wardlaw would have known this, but Thomas clearly didn't – Pope Eugene is a member of our order! He's an Augustinian. And he won't let some upstart, writing with his own agenda, take that away from us!'

An emergency meeting in the chapter house was called, with all the canons present, in which Fergus, Richard and Peter updated everyone on the present state of the dilemma. Richard would write immediately to Pope Eugene, countermanding Thomas's letter and pointing out the falsehoods within it, as well as describing the documentation stored at Soltre proving its own legal position. They discussed how this vital letter should be sent and decided that it should be transported by a well-guarded and carefully selected messenger from among themselves.

'Do you think, friends and brothers,' asked Fergus, 'that we should ask our excellent friend Prior Graham to return and take up the post of temporary magister with us, while Thomas is sick? It is a lot to ask, I know. He will be involving himself in our political disputes and there is always danger in that.'

This was approved, and Fergus given leave of two days to ride to Jedburgh and discuss matters with their friends there. However, Thomas needed attention first.

'I think the time has come to face Thomas regarding his nefarious conduct,' said Robert. This also had the meeting's consent, and so a group consisting of Brothers Richard, Fergus, Robert and Peter rose and went over to the infirmary, carrying the incriminating papers. Fergus was to be spokesman and Peter to take a back seat, as the time for gentleness was past. They found Thomas sitting by the fire, reading his prayer book. He looked up in great alarm as they approached, casting looks around for help, clutching at his throat and beginning to gasp.

Fergus strode forward, waving the papers at him. 'Now you can stop all the play-acting, Thomas. We've been through your effects and we know exactly what you have been doing. Look at all this evidence of your plotting and duplicity. How dare you call yourself master of this place and allow it to be put on legal documents? How dare you write to His Holiness with a screed of falsehoods? You deserve to be excommunicated. What have you to say for yourself? Come, speak up! I'm not taken in by all this pretence of sickness; I've seen enough of the real thing.' He stood over the cowering priest, a commanding presence with justifiable anger radiating from him.

Thomas, pale and breaking out in a sweat, gulped. 'I was told to do it. Believe me, I didn't want to. Bishop Wardlaw instructed me; he said it was my duty to the king.'

Fergus hastily moved a step back, and his colleagues immediately saw why he had done so. Thomas was so terrified that he had lost control of his bladder and a pool of urine had appeared at his feet while his cassock quickly soaked through. Fergus held up his hand to stop James, the infirmary assistant, coming forward to mop up.

'We are unfortunately going to have to deal with you, Thomas,' he said, wrinkling his nose in disgust. 'Not many people are unwelcome in our midst, but people who betray us most certainly are. Do you realise if you left this place, you would be torn apart by the mob outside? Have you heard of the ferocity of the Borderer? Second only to that of the Highlander? And they know about you. Everything that happens in this place is known, because Soltre belongs to the people, and they care about it. They are loyal and faithful and prepared to defend Soltre to the death. They loathe its enemies. If I were you, I would not sleep easily at night.

'But you are here, and otherwise friendless. We shall lodge you somewhere humble, feed you and clothe you until we decide what to do with you. You may only move around the abbey with supervision. You may not have access to your belongings except with supervision. Above all, you may not write letters or have contact with anyone outside. If you receive letters, we shall confiscate them. I'd advise you not to give us any trouble.'

As they left the infirmary, Richard murmured, 'Wasn't that a little harsh, Brother? The man is weak and his sin is over-compliance.'

Fergus looked down at Richard in amazement. 'Weakness and a self-serving nature are a dangerous combination. I'd have no mercy on this man. He would stab us in the back if he had a chance. And I should say that my warning about the ordinary people was no empty threat. My outside contacts make it clear that he is infamous and hated out there. We could feed him to the lions simply by sending him out through the gate.'

The brothers spent many hours discussing how to manage Thomas Lauder. He was caught in a cleft stick. The post of magister was closed to him, yet the episcopal circle at St Andrews believed him to be in possession of it. And maybe it was in the interests of the Soltre community that Bishop Wardlaw's circle continued to think so. Thomas would be retained at Soltre for the present as a virtual prisoner, one that they were bound by their humanity to treat more kindly than he deserved. He could not join in the life of an Augustinian canon and it was distasteful to lodge him in the residence or the common dormitory, or in relative luxury in the guest house. He should do some kind of work to earn his keep, but not in a ministering capacity; it would have to be menial or repetitive.

In the end, he was lodged in a small servant's room in the residence. He could be observed there in his goings and comings, though the essential papers and documents lodged in the office would be locked away. They needed all to be aware he was not to be trusted.

'It won't be comfortable having someone like this in our midst,' observed Robert.

'Events have a habit of taking their own course,' mused Peter. 'When things are clarified with the pope, maybe we shall be able to send him away. Meantime, he's going to feel like a powder keg.'

Antagonistic feelings were running so powerfully against Thomas, especially among the secular staff of Soltre, that he could not easily be deployed in any task needing supervision. He was tried in the kitchen and the garden but he was shunned and insulted. In the end it was decided that they could make use of his literary capabilities and he was sent each morning to the scriptorium, a small room off the cloister, to copy documents and books, supervised by the sacrist. Strictness and discipline seemed to contain his histrionic tendencies and he behaved docilely, seemingly glad to be protected by the brothers against the hostility of the lay people.

Fergus visited Jedburgh and explained in detail the events surrounding Thomas Lauder. Father Patrick and Prior Graham listened, open-mouthed.

'Well, I thought nothing could surprise me in the world of men!' said Patrick. After some thought, prayers and discussion, they agreed that Graham could return with Fergus as acting temporary magister on the grounds of Thomas's sickness and incapacity. This formulation seemed wise, as it indicated they were not taking any action that could be construed as illegal in the future. They put this arrangement down in writing and all signed it, in case of future repercussions.

Chapter 36

While the new members of the Soltre community were still finding their feet, the relative harmony was shattered by news from the outside. King James I of Scotland had been assassinated by his own countrymen, while his wife and six-year-old son, Prince James, had barely escaped with their lives.

This was news of such importance that it was delivered by none other than Donald Dampierre. With the senior brothers solemnly gathered, he described events as far as he knew them.

The king, with his family, had been lodging at Perth, in a friary, when two ringleaders heading a band of around thirty men had broken in at night. His own chamberlain was privy to the plot. Someone had raised the alarm, and Queen Joan had been injured trying to stop the cabal entering the royal bedchamber while James had tried to hide in a sewer below the floorboards. He was discovered and put up a fight, but Sir Robert Graham set upon him with a sword and dealt several mortal blows. The queen and prince had managed to escape in the melee. The Earl of Atholl, who was next in line to the throne after Prince James, was behind the regicide plot and for the moment was still at large, although his grandson had been arrested. The country was in a most unstable state, and would remain so until and beyond the time when the young prince could be crowned.

'At times like these, anything could happen,' said Donald. 'I thought you should be on your guard. As you know, there have been attempted sieges on the English-held fortresses nearby, so incursions by the English are more than possible. Have your volunteers alerted and ready, and perhaps you should move some into the abbey and allow them arms. It would be as well to curtail any plans to travel for the time being. David Gordon or I will keep you informed of events.'

'Once again we have a child monarch,' said Father Graham. 'Skirmishing for the crown will no doubt continue for another ten years at least. Who will be regent, do you suppose, Sir Donald?'

'Impossible to say right now. It depends who gets the upper hand. It could be the queen, or any of her supporters – Douglas, Crichton, Angus. Or it could be Atholl, who instigated the plot, if he rallies enough supporters. His late grace the king caused much anguish by his harsh rule and greed for territory, as well as failing to pay for his hostages, many of whom died in captivity. I'm afraid royal support is thinly spread.'

The brothers nodded agreement at the mention of the king's greed for territory, and exchanged meaningful looks. After Donald had departed, they sat down to discuss the significance of the event for Soltre. It seemed probable that they may have a reprieve from the royal-episcopal endeavours to dispossess them, especially with Wardlaw also incapacitated.

'Perhaps we should encourage Thomas to leave here?' said Peter. 'What do you think, Brother Sacrist?'

'He's not shown any signs of restlessness,' said Jonathan the sacrist. 'From what he's said, he seems to still hope he'll earn his right to a bishopric by being here. Hard to see it happening. But he doesn't yet know of the king's murder.'

'We should hold him here until we get the pope's response,' said Fergus. 'Then we can send him packing with every justification. Mercifully, of his two sponsors, one is now dead and the other is sick unto death. He'll do what he's told – by us! Besides, you heard what Donald said. No one's going anywhere furth of here until things settle down outside. And our message to Pope Eugene or its response may be delayed.'

As time went on, the community at Soltre became accustomed to seeing glimpses of the short, slight figure of Thomas going furtively about his legitimate business, mainly from his bolthole in the residence to the scriptorium, and to the kitchen for his food. It had been decided that he was not to be favoured, or treated in any way as a respected member of the community, although bullying was actively discouraged. He was allowed into certain church services, where he sat on a stool at the back. Most of the canons ignored him, except for Peter. The sacrist reported he was attentive and careful, and did what he was asked, only speaking when it was necessary. Peter occasionally tried to speak kindly to him, enquiring about his health and welfare, finding that he responded politely but briefly, nervous as a kitten.

Brother Jonathan, the sacrist, told Thomas about the king's murder, and the priest sat digesting this for some minutes. Then he said, 'Brother, I am grateful to you for telling me this. I am very cut off from the outside world. I am not allowed even my own letters.'

Jonathan answered, 'There have been no letters for you, as far as I am aware. I think that Brother Richard intends simply to read them first and let you have them, as long as they do not contain subversive messages.'

'I should like to know how my friend and sponsor fares,' said Thomas. 'I mean Bishop Henry Wardlaw. He was seriously ill when I last saw him. I have some particular interest – other than personal. If Bishop Kennedy vacates Dunkeld and is appointed to St Andrews on the passing of Bishop Wardlaw, then I might be considered for Dunkeld.' Jonathan replied that, as far as he knew, the bishop was still alive, but that he would make enquiries. He duly reported this to his fellow brothers at chapter meeting, where the idea that Thomas might be appointed bishop anywhere raised eyebrows and a few wry smiles.

The brothers learned from their contacts, over the days and weeks, that the young Prince James had been hastily crowned King James II, and that Archibald, fifth Earl of Douglas and cousin to James, was head of the government as well as sharing the regency with Queen Joan. It was probably too much to hope that this arrangement would be stable for long, but the Douglas name and might was probably as good a deterrent as any to would-be troublemakers. At Soltre, life continued its cyclical pattern. The brothers waited anxiously for a reply from the pope, but knew that troubles and strife both at home and on the mainland of Europe would make travel and message carrying hazardous and slow.

Fergus thought about his friend Callum, and what he would do now that the king was dead. He wrote to him, hoping that the letter would reach him; a pious hope perhaps, given the chaos in the country and the doubt about the whereabouts of the late king's supporters. He hoped his friend was safe. He would probably find employment easily enough with his new skills and useful contacts in the royal court. It would be a grand turn of events if Callum could return to Soltre.

Chapter 37

After many months of waiting, and as autumn rolled into winter, a response arrived from Pope Eugene, the returning travellers being greeted with great excitement and celebration. They had, on the whole, had good luck in finding safe havens along the way at monasteries and abbeys, and were courteously received by Pope Eugene, who was glad to see some fellow Augustinians. They had located him at Florence, and were fortunate to do so, for he had his own political problems to deal with. A chance to give their grievances an airing in direct conversation with His Holiness was a clear advantage, and they knew the message they carried back from him was warmly in Soltre's favour; confirming that Soltre had been established, and would continue, as an Augustinian abbey and hospital, and would retain for its own use and purpose the lands it had legitimately inherited. With this ancient decree, he explicitly stated, the royal charter regarding Thomas Lauder was doubly invalid.

At chapter meeting the following morning, Thomas was brought before the assembled company and the papal decree read out to him. Thomas had not received any response to his own letter, but the pope's message included a reference to it, referring to his 'shameful and false' claim; it seemed he would bear the full brunt of the papal wrath, even though he claimed he was following episcopal directions.

'We shall of course make this outcome known to Bishop Wardlaw, or those acting on his behalf,' said Father Graham.

'And we shall be pleased to assist you in placing yourself as seems most appropriate to you and your own advisers.'

Mary and David had followed the highs and lows of Soltre's time as political pawn, and David had made it his business to pass on details of national events, so the excellent news from Pope Eugene ought to be shared with them, thought Fergus. He made time to ride to Lauder, where he found David and a group of burgesses deep in discussion.

David was jubilant to hear his news. 'It really looks as if Soltre is destined to be blessed and preserved,' he said. 'All those who work against you seem to get divine justice. It's very good for you that Earl Douglas is regent and head of government. I know him well and he is one of your staunchest supporters, as his father was before him. I've heard him say that he himself would lead an armed group of Borderers against anyone who threatened Soltre.'

'We hope we have weathered the storm,' said Fergus. At that moment, Mary quietly entered the room with refreshments, helped by Annie, who was staying the night between school-days. Male political discussion being strictly closed to women, they performed their duties unobtrusively. Fergus's eyes lingered on both, but especially Annie, now on the brink of woman-hood and a delight for his eyes, with her cheeks rosy, hair pret-tily arranged and her dress becoming. She caught his eye and smiled. He lost track of the conversation for a few minutes while he balanced her well-groomed prettiness against her previous gypsyish dishevelment. He thought she combined both aspects appealingly and wondered what the future held for her. His companions talked on, not noticing his abstraction.

Chapter 38

Thomas Lauder had wanted to be a bishop for as long as he could remember. He came from a large and influential family whose adult males seemed all to be either knights or bishops. The one thing the bishops had in common was that they were treated with unfailing respect, verging on adulation, and their every word was law. As far as Thomas could see, that privilege was only conferred by their episcopal status, because in other ways they seemed unexceptional men.

It was for this reason alone that he aspired to join them. He had been brought up in a large family of legitimate siblings, himself the odd one out, and he had been made to feel a nonentity. He had never known his mother, and his father, Sir Robert Lauder, ignored him; though he did enable him to attend the University of Paris, after which, he had been told, he must make his own way in the world.

Still, the name Lauder counted for a lot and after ordination he had managed to obtain clerical posts, usually with help from his many episcopal half-siblings. When Bishop Wardlaw had singled Thomas out for his devious task at Soltre, he was presumably so used to people trembling in their shoes in front of him that he had not appreciated how singularly inept Thomas was for the job.

Thomas meanwhile had braced himself, thinking the prize of a bishopric was in his grasp and all he had to do was sit out a few years of austerity on a windy southern moor. He had a particular phobia of Highlanders, and at least in the Borders he would not meet any of those violent mountain men. But then the details of his mission were explained… He was to persuade the pope, no less, to give him charge of all the worldly goods that belonged to Soltre, and he would then be required to hand them to the king. And do this in the face of righteous and indignant opposition.

Well, he had failed. But he felt he had failed honourably. Wardlaw had not investigated the case adequately. As he received his ignominious dismissal from Soltre, he felt he could go and face the music at St Andrews, hoping that he would see Bishop Kennedy rather than Wardlaw. And he presumed the pressure was off to some extent in that King James I was now dead. Maybe they would give him the see of Dunkeld for his brave efforts, when Wardlaw eventually passed away. Spurred on by these thoughts, he thought about preparing for his departure. He would have to beg for a mounted man of arms to give him protection. His own horse had been exercised regularly by the stable men, but he himself had not been on horseback for the year he had been at Soltre, although he had taken exercise by walking in the garden each week. He was anxious to depart from this degrading phase of his life and hoped to do so without meeting that terrifying medicus, typical of the worst of his breed.

Yet he would have to cope with a journey and, at the end of it, an encounter with an equally terrifying bishop. He put off the preparations and soon the winter weather closed in, making travel impossible.

Chapter 39

1438

The community at Soltre breathed a collective sigh of relief at the advent of the thaw, when Brother Robert, the bursar, took matters in hand and finally coerced Thomas into getting on his way. He had been an unwelcome presence in their midst for a year and a half. The countryside was quiescent compared to the upheavals after the assassination of James I, and Thomas arrived at St Andrews without incident. He soon found himself in the presence of Bishop Kennedy, who was astonished to see him and not very welcoming. Thomas enquired about Wardlaw's health and was told his demise was only a matter of time. The man had been on his deathbed for months, but things were drawing to an end.

Thomas congratulated himself; maybe the timing was in his favour! But he must not seem too eager, and he had some explaining to do. When Kennedy heard that Thomas had spent a year and a half at Soltre without being magister, he was enraged, and it was some time before Thomas could make himself heard. He had all his papers with him, carefully packed into his satchel, and spread these out on the table, showing how he had taken the matter up with the pope, and how the pope had responded to the Soltre letter.

'But you had the charter with the king's seal saying you were the master!' said Kennedy. 'Who can gainsay that?'

'As you see, my lord, the charter says nothing about me being master. It simply calls me the king's chaplain and talks about granting me the right, essentially, to administer the lands and effects. But it seems the chancellor at the time said I did not qualify for magister because I was not an Augustinian. Here's his letter, see? Nor could the charter countermand the ancient papal document about the holdings of Soltre, which was eventually confirmed by the present Pope Eugene; here's the copy, the brothers let me have this. And it is not very complimentary to me, even though I was acting as Bishop Wardlaw's agent – and the late king's, of course.

'And so, my lord, I was kept as a virtual prisoner while the brothers were getting their message to the pope and waiting for an answer. And then I was sent away, but the winter – which is as fierce there as in the north – closed in. I believe I kept my part of the bargain to Bishop Wardlaw and now I should be given my reward. I should be next in line for the see of Dunkeld, my lord, when, as seems probable, you vacate it and go to St Andrews.'

Kennedy had been browsing through the papers, cooling down a little as he saw that Wardlaw and the king had acted impulsively and without proper consideration. Probably because one was already infirm and the other desperate. And this craven nonentity had suffered as a result.

'Why did you not leave if you were not accepted as magister? You say you were a prisoner, but they didn't lock you up or keep you in chains, I presume?'

Thomas shook his head. 'They threatened me that I would be torn in pieces if I went out the gate; that the common people believed I was a usurper...'

'And who is acting as magister now?'

'The choice of the Soltre community, Father Graham, previously prior of Jedburgh.'

'Who is acting without a licence!' Kennedy tapped his fingers on the desk and gazed at Thomas, assessing him. 'You were a bit gullible, weren't you? Well, I can't give you Dunkeld, as there are other people in line ahead of you. In any case, you haven't exactly fulfilled your brief, have you? Even with the difficulties you encountered, it seems to me that you could have been more resourceful. And finally, the pope certainly would not allow you Dunkeld after those remarks he has made about you in his letter.'

Thomas was very downcast. 'My lord, I have put up with a great deal in trying to do the late King James 's bidding. I have suffered and my reputation has been trampled on. And, for the moment, I am left without employment and a source of income.'

'We can find you a clerical position, I am sure. They require a priest or two in the chapter of Aberdeen cathedral; we can give you the title of canon. You could live in the communal quarters, which are very comfortable. If you practise the rule – you know, poverty, chastity, obedience – you would qualify for an Augustinian. We could send you back to Soltre after ten years!'

Thomas blanched and shuddered, but understood that this was a piece of typical episcopal teasing. 'Aberdeen will be fine, thank you, my lord.'

Kennedy was still thinking. 'There may be a way that you could help us out with the Soltre matter. I need to think and maybe confer with Archibald Douglas, who leads the government in the young king's minority, as I expect you know. You appreciate, of course, that the amount of land held by Soltre seems, in this day and age, disproportionately large, and that the Crown could make better use of it. But the problem of how to retrieve it needs careful planning. Don't worry,' he added, for Thomas had begun to show signs of anxiety, 'we won't require you to go back to Soltre. But you must have useful information about the place that we could use. Stay here in the abbey for a day or two and I'll talk to you again.'

Chapter 40

Bishop Kennedy thought the matter of sufficient importance to travel to Restalrig estate, east of Edinburgh, to see Earl Archibald Douglas. He knew the earl was not in good health, but was still compos mentis, unlike poor Bishop Wardlaw.

In the gardens of the estate he found the earl ambling with a stick and a favourite hound. Kennedy explained the bizarre situation of Thomas Lauder and Soltre Abbey.

'It's not possible to know exactly what plot the late king and Bishop Wardlaw were hatching up between them,' he said. 'Wardlaw is nearer the next world than this, and I cannot communicate with him. They seemed to think that once Lauder was magister, he would be in a position to hand over the estates to the Crown.'

Douglas glowered and looked bull-like, in the way heads of his family had always been able to do. 'His late grace the king helped himself to many estates, by fair means or foul, but with Soltre he would have taken on more than he knew. The Borders folk would take up arms to defend it, you know. It is the holy of holies to them, and rightly so. Furthermore, it's not just the common folk who would leap to its defence. The reason why Soltre is so well endowed is that families like mine – mine – have bequeathed land to the abbey in exchange for Masses to be said in perpetuity for our eternal souls. Believe me, none of the Douglases or other big Border families would see any part of Soltre slip into hands that squander money as trivially as our late king did, Lord have mercy on his soul.'

Kennedy was taken back by this response, completely at odds with what he had expected.

'I could map out for you which of Soltre's estates came from the Douglas family over the centuries,' the earl continued, glaring at Kennedy. 'And you will no doubt know of the famous Thomas the Rhymer of Erceldoune? The mystic that accurately prophesied the death of Alexander III, riding through a storm to be with his new wife? Thomas Rhymer's estate was bequeathed to Soltre. It's all hallowed ground, my good lord bishop. Sacrosanct.

'And I believe that the abbey is guarded by special forces – though whether Christian or white magic I know not. King James, bless his soul, met an untimely end as he was trying to interfere with Soltre. Bishop Wardlaw was struck down by a lingering illness that has deprived him of his wits and the capacity to intrigue. There are many stories about the place that suggest it is specially blessed. And a good thing too. It is a haven of holiness in a very wicked world, bishop. My advice to you is to leave well alone.'

'Well, my lord, I am grateful for your advice. But it may be that I am called, acting on behalf of Bishop Wardlaw, to intervene to the extent of finding a suitable candidate for magister. We have an irregular situation at present, in which the acting magister, Father Graham, has been voted in by the brotherhood but has not been licensed. He seems in all respects a most suitable man and I am left wondering what was the purpose of trying to shoehorn in Thomas Lauder.'

Douglas was already heading purposefully towards the house. 'The solution is easy,' he said. 'Give this man, Graham, the licence. I think, bishop, the plot was rather more devious than you, in your decorous clerical world, have recognised. If Lauder is as weak and clueless as you suggest, he could easily have been ensnared in some heretical mishap or other. That is the only way the king could legitimately seize the holdings. Lauder is not the same calibre of man as are those at Soltre. He was to be a sacrificial lamb. But the fates have prevented all that.'

They entered the room Douglas was using as his study and he briskly scribbled some words on a piece of parchment, then removed the Great Seal from a locked drawer, inked it and applied it to the document. He enclosed it in another sheet and rolled it carefully before handing it to Kennedy.

'There's the licence for Father Graham,' he said. 'You'll find a way of giving it safe passage to Soltre, I'm sure.'

Bishop Kennedy was deep in thought as he travelled back to St Andrews with his entourage. He was intrigued by Douglas's observations and the extreme reverence shown by this powerful man towards Soltre and its inhabitants, in addition to the overlay of superstition and the interpretation of historic events that seemed to favour the abbey. The bishop was a man who liked a challenge, and was not altogether disposed to accept Douglas's instruction to leave well alone.

For that reason, he recalled Thomas and questioned him closely about the people at Soltre, their characters and habits.

'I was not allowed much access, my lord, as I told you. But I noticed no irregularities. They expend considerable workforce and energy on attending to the sick, as I witnessed. They extend hospitality to travellers. Judging by the sound of bells, they kept the services regularly. There was nothing lavish about their food or clothing. I saw or heard no feasts or entertaining in the time I was there. The country has been going through a time of austerity, of course.'

'Who seemed to have most leadership qualities?'

'That was undoubtedly the medicus, Brother Fergus. A fiery redhead, who treated me badly. Near enough threatened to throw me to the hordes of peasants outside.'

'And did you see or hear any sign of sexual irregularities? In my experience, men in positions of leadership are nearly always sexually active.'

'No. I'm not sure I had the opportunity. There were choirboys who visited for Mass at times. No women, of course. Oh, but...' He paused, struck by a thought, and Kennedy looked expectant.

'It's probably not relevant, but the guard who travelled back with me, who was mostly silent and surly, did give me a lecture on how hard-working and virtuous the brothers were, and how the country folk loved them for the good work they do. He mentioned that there was a service for women that the medicus had begun and fostered in the community. Then he clammed up, as if he'd said too much.'

Kennedy let Thomas Lauder go, off for his new life in Aberdeen, with all recommendations and instructions to the cathedral community there. He thought there was no immediate need to send off the licence to Soltre; that could wait until he could spare a suitably guarded envoy.

Chapter 41

One year after his visit to Restalrig, Bishop Kennedy received the news by urgent despatch that the Earl of Douglas, the regent, had died of a fever.

He took the licence out of its wrapper and inspected it closely. It was convenient that the earl should die now. No one else knew of the licence. He decided not to send it.

Not long after these events, when Kennedy was visiting Florence at the pope's behest, Bishop Wardlaw was finally gathered to his fathers. He was buried in state in the cathedral, and Kennedy succeeded to the prestigious see of St Andrews; he was now the senior bishop in Scotland.

After the death of the regent of Scotland, Earl Douglas, the country was again stricken by turmoil and bloodshed. With King James II still a minor, fights over power-sharing between Livingston, the governor of Stirling Castle and Crichton, Chancellor of Scotland, caused extreme stress for the dowager Queen Joan as she struggled to shield and protect her son. She and her new husband, James Stewart the Black Knight of Lorne, allied themselves with the Douglases, provoking savage jealousy and leading to the so-called 'Black Dinner', where the sixteen year-old Earl of Douglas and his brother were murdered at Edinburgh Castle.

The immediate effect of these events on the Soltre community was beneficial. Everyday life went on much as usual, and so the years passed. Father Graham had stayed on, and all assumed that no one in exalted circles would remember that he was not actually licensed as their magister. The more the country's leaders were distracted by internecine fighting, the less chance there was that they would interfere with Soltre's calm orderliness. David Gordon's pronouncements were proving to be correct. For the years of the king's minority, abbey life followed the well-worn ruts of duty, work and worship, immune from the savagery without. And savagery there was among the warring factions, sufficient to test the diplomatic skills of the influential Bishop Kennedy to the limit, and to prevent him from worrying about Soltre's affairs.

Fergus had received a letter from Callum, who had been in the employ of Queen Joan since her widowhood. Then for a while the brothers heard no more of him, and all they could do was pray for his deliverance from the troubled times. Fergus felt strangely confident that Callum would survive and reappear in their lives. He felt an optimism born of the success of past challenges to the Soltre community, and enjoyed the prevailing peace of their enclosed world.

During this calm interlude, Fergus's happiest moments in his busy life were those he spent among the women in the countryside, and he thought wryly of how he had chosen to live in a community of celibate men. Life had been kind to him, letting him work at what he loved and was good at, and in mostly congenial company. He was making a difference within his world. Now in his early thirties, he carried his years well; still striking in appearance, lean, muscular and agile, he wore an air of confidence and authority born of a life well lived.

Since he had first engaged her to work with him, Jan had spread her influence to huge effect. She had connected with a number of country women who had skills of midwifery that could be polished and employed on a routine basis. Mary Gordon was an established partner in her team, occupied more in the social aspects of childbearing but competent in a bedside emergency also. Under Mary's influence as a teacher, Jan and Annie had flowered in literacy, and she was guiding their hands in record-keeping with regard to patients and treatments. One of Mary's friends, the wife of a local schoolteacher, had joined in the enterprise. What a long way they had all come since those early days, he recalled, when he had rescued Jan and her daughter from the direst poverty.

He thought with satisfaction of the improvement they had all made simply in the nutrition of expectant mothers, by diverting to them some of the plentiful supplies of milk, eggs and even meat – in the shape of poultry, pigeons and rabbit – from Soltre's farms. They had worked out a system of supplying mothers directly from farms nearby, all overseen by Soltre's agents. The mothers were supplied with goats if they had milking skills, so their milk was readily available. The network had not yet extended to the whole of Soltre's domains, but reports of the welfare system spread widely and it was very popular. And the benefits to the mothers extended naturally to the children.

Fergus had managed to get Jan and her daughter rehoused in a slightly more substantial cottage, one that lay between Soltre and Lauder, a more practical placement. Since the troubles over the magister had been resolved, his work with women was no longer opposed by the community – certainly not by Father Graham. However, he remembered Father John's advice to him to be an enabler and let the women do it themselves. The protective canopy of Soltre's sponsorship, in the shape of himself, was critical, but it was the women who worked and organised. He had only once had to assist at a case of the toxic syndrome of late pregnancy he had learned about from Malcolm; he had received an urgent message, in the middle of the night as usual, and arrived just as Jan and Mary were completing the induced delivery. The child was barely alive and died within minutes, but they saved a very sick mother. Then there was another tiny baby to bury in the cemetery beside his own half-sister, and the parents were comforted in their grief, knowing their baby would be buried in such hallowed ground.

His visits to Jan nowadays were infrequent, partly owing to his other duties but partly also because the ladies needed so little of his direct help. So it was in the spirit of a treat and a holiday that, one autumn morning in 1442, Fergus dismounted outside the cottage beside the burn and tied up Percy with a pat and a carrot; taking pleasure in the autumn colours, the weak sunlight and the playful breeze wafting a good scent of earth and smoke. Jan greeted him at the door and he entered the cottage.

'See who's here, Fergus – someone you haven't seen for a while!'

Seated at the table, surrounded by writing materials, was Annie. Fergus had indeed not seen her for... was it a year? No, it was more, two at least, maybe more. Goodness, he thought, she had been a child when they last met, and now... she was most definitely a woman. She smiled at him, the sunny smile he remembered so well, and said, 'Greetings, Brother Fergus. Such an age since we met. Maybe you don't recognise me.'

There must have been a long pause while he took in the vision of her. At last he found his voice. 'Annie! I can't believe it. You look so... wonderful!' He had been about to say beautiful, but that sounded too smitten. They began to discuss the occasion they had last met together, which was indeed longer ago even than Fergus had thought. Annie was often away at Mary's when Fergus visited the cottage; he was completely nonplussed by this unexpected vision of her. Jan had often talked about her, but the image he had conjured up was of Annie the rustic child.

Somewhat bashful under his admiring gaze, she scrambled up from her seat. 'I must say hello to Percy – or have you got a new horse?'

'No,' said Fergus. 'I mean, yes, do go and see him. It's still Percy, not a new horse.'

Outside, fondling Percy and looking him over with a practised eye, Annie gave Fergus a chance to see her in her full grace and charm, glossy light brown hair falling in curls round her shoulders, her slender figure, clear complexion, shapely limbs and overall appearance of well-being.

'May I ride him, brother? Much more exciting than a mule!' Her enthusiasm was still the gypsy child part of her, and he watched, mesmerised, as she sprang gracefully into the saddle, gathering her skirt and sitting astride. He and Jan followed the pair of them along the burn.

Fergus was dealing with some strange sensations in his abdomen, and greedily followed Annie with his eyes. He knew he was acting oddly, but could hardly help himself.

At last he said, 'Even though you know people grow up, it's always a shock! She's looking bonny, isn't she? A credit to you, Jan.'

'She's thrived on the blessings from Soltre, and from Mary. Aye, I'm pleased with her. And she's a good help too. My women love her!'

After another pause, she said, 'Was there anything special you wanted with me today?' Fergus took a moment to think what he'd had in mind when he set out that morning. 'Mainly I wanted to check on how things were with you. I haven't come to see you for a long time, and the country is always disturbed. I wondered if you were still able to get about to do your visits and if Annie could get to Mary's safely.'

'We've not had too much upset. Mary keeps Annie over at their place when there are rumours of trouble. But it's quiet just now.'

'How about you, though?' said Fergus looking down at her with a frown. 'When Annie's away and you're here on your own?'

'It's better here than where we were before,' she said. 'Neighbours are closer. Their dogs bark if they hear someone a mile off.'

Annie had ridden some distance along the path, then turned Percy and urged him to a canter as she returned.

'She sits him well!' said Fergus. 'Jan, do you want to do any collecting while I'm here? It makes it safer for you both, and there's Percy to carry the plants.' He knew his reason for wanting to prolong his visit was transparent to Jan. He looked at her, wondering if she was jealous; she met his eyes and smiled. 'Aye, we could do with restocking some herbs, and it's a braw day for it.'

Fergus was musing on all the things he should have been doing that day as he accompanied Jan back to the house after their outing. Annie rode Percy again, exploring side paths and falling behind them. He thought of owning up to his shortcomings in the confessional, aware that he would not admit to the real reason for today's lapse of duty.

Breaking into his distracted silence, Jan said, 'I can see she's made a big impression on you, Fergus. And believe me, she's already used to doing that with men.'

Fergus felt pangs of jealousy, thinking of all the other nameless men who had met and admired her. 'Has she got a laddie?' he asked.

'Not as far as I know. And I think I would know. She's not gone through that cankry phase that some girls get at her age.'

'She's old enough to be married, I suppose.'

'Aye, but not ready in other ways, I hope. She's enjoying life right now and who knows how long that will last? It's a great pity you're celibate, Fergus.'

Fergus received another jolt in the midriff. 'You're always one for straight talking, Jan. And believe me, at this moment I feel it's a pity too.'

She looked up and smiled at him, a big beaming smile. 'There have been times when I have felt that pity for my own sake,

Fergus,' she said, looking impishly up at him, eyes bright with just a hint of tears. 'But you always behaved so properly.'

Fergus was overwhelmed and stopped in his tracks, his hand on her arm. 'Believe me, Jan, I have been sore tempted, almost to the point of giving way. You are beautiful, as you ever were. But I always felt it would be wrong – not just a sin in the Church's terms. It would have got in the way of a working relationship. And I remembered how you had been treated in the past.' Jan laughed, but clearly could not trust herself to speak.

'You said to me, more than once,' said Fergus, looking down at her averted face, 'that you would be glad never to service any man ever again.'

'Aye, I did, brother. But there's a difference between servicing and loving. And I've never had a chance to do it for love. I'll settle for having brought you to the brink, though. I give you leave to love Annie.'

He looked at her, not sure of the depth and breadth of her meaning. But she was not looking at him, quickly brushing away a tear. Just then, Annie rode up behind them.

'What are you talking about so seriously, you two, with your heads together?' she asked pertly. Jan looked up, putting on a cheerful face.

'We were talking about you, my lady. Who else?'

Fergus had the delicious experience of seeing Annie blush, pink rose petals settling on her cheeks, her lashes lowered for a second before she tossed her tangled locks over her shoulder then turned again to look at him. He would remember that look as long as he lived: as fresh and innocent as a fawn, yet full of meaning and awareness, hope and awakening. His midriff was behaving very oddly again. Suddenly he felt a terrible panic – here they were at the cottage door and he had no further excuse to prolong his stay. Fergus, the strong, confident, coping physician, was helpless and did not know what to do. Annie was busy handing the bundles of plants and herbs down to Jan, who carried them in her pinny into the cottage. Fergus turned to help Annie down from Percy and said softly, pleadingly, 'Walk a little way back with me, Annie. Otherwise...'

And so, after a hasty farewell to Jan, he found himself leading Percy and walking beside Annie, whose hand had found its way into his, almost as if by accident. He held hers warmly, as if this precious connection must never be broken. Nothing was said, but as soon as they were out of sight, they turned to each other, eyes looking deep into eyes, bodies pressed, arms around, mouths gently touching. The sensation of contact was so new, so delectable; exploration followed slowly, gently, almost reverently.

Annie was the first to speak, pulling away and murmuring, 'I have loved you since I first met you, Fergus. Was that very wicked of me?'

He looked down tenderly at this sprite in his arms. 'No, it was right, Annie. I loved you too, but did not realise it till now. You were a tiny rosebud and now you are a rose in full bloom.'

Fergus slipped off his cowl and spread it on the ground. Neither of them felt the need to hold back. Gently he asked, 'Annie, have you seen a man's body before?' She shook her head. 'It's a bit frightening, maybe,' he said looking at her. But without hesitation, Annie helped him remove his tunic and underclothes, and lovingly put her hands on him, face, chest, belly, and his erect member. Then he gently helped her take off her dress. After which, all that followed felt like something they had known and exulted in for all eternity.

Fergus hardly knew how he – or rather Percy – got back to Soltre, so intoxicated was he by his surging emotions. It had been hard to finally part from Annie. He could only think over those precious moments with her, bringing back the dizzying delight. Then at last he was in the abbey garth, and there was Peter coming towards him with an anxious air and a face of huge relief.

'Fergus! Brother! My son! I've been in such a state wondering where you were, I've twice sent out someone looking for you.' Fergus dismounted, patting Percy and stroking him while thinking of Annie's beautiful hands caressing his nose and flank. Someone took Percy off to the stable, and Fergus turned to Peter, the prosaic world beginning to break through to his distracted mind.

'Are you well, my son?'

Fergus stood looking at Peter's beloved, troubled, puzzled face, and suddenly the emotions coalesced and collided with reality; he found he could not speak. He gasped, on the brink of tears, holding out his arms. He found himself supported by Peter and led hastily towards the infirmary and the privacy of the pharmacy.

'Come, have a seat,' said Peter, busying himself to give Fergus time to collect himself. 'You're probably starving. I've got some food and ale here, the kitchen staff always assume I neglect myself.' He handed Fergus a flagon and drew up a seat beside him, reminded of the first time he had ministered to the young man's distress and need. 'What happened? Are you hurt? My dear Fergus, please tell me.'

With a great effort, Fergus gathered himself and began to think of his neglected duties and the worry he had caused. 'Peter, I am sorry. There was so much work today and I left you to do it. I have been much at fault.'

'But never mind that, my son. I am full of relief you are safe. I really thought you had met with some grief out in the wilds. Something's happened, Fergus. I have never seen you like this before.'

'Peter... I hardly know. I am bewitched. I am crazy. I have fallen off a precipice; I have learned how to fly. I never knew one could feel like this. Is it seriously possible to fall in love in an instant? Am I possessed? All I can think of is her – and being with her, looking at her. There is no other meaning in the world. I would go through fire and flood, I would die for her. I want to rush away right now...' And he half rose as Peter put out a hand to restrain him.

Peter patiently and gently elicited the story. Fergus found, as lovers always do, that second best to being with his love was talking about her to a sympathetic ear; and none was more tenderly tuned than Peter's.

Peter had far too much wisdom to attempt to pull Fergus back to earth, to urge him to consider the consequences or even think about the moral aspects of his situation. Fergus would have to ride out the storm in his own way, and Peter would be there for him and give him every ounce of support he needed. Peter was reminded again and again, as Fergus talked, of his own obsessive love for this young man all those years ago, a love that had stood the test of time and absence and had matured into an abiding, all-forgiving father-son relationship. But Fergus's love for Annie had an extra dimension, as Peter well knew, and Peter had no basis whatever for imagining what ought to be done. Fergus's joy knew no bounds, but Peter knew that the agony that might follow could also be without limit.

Chapter 42

Bishop Kennedy was an ambitious man, and set out to make his mark in matters of state as well as the Church. It was unfortunate that Scotland was in such a turbulent state, with factions of recalcitrant nobility that were impossible to reconcile. He befriended Queen Joan; she was now marginalised from matters of state, but through her he had access to King James II, still in his minority.

On one occasion, meeting the dowager queen and her son, the topic of Soltre arose in conversation. Kennedy found that the queen had been privy to the discussions between Bishop Wardlaw and her late husband, the king, shortly before his assassination. She knew that the plan to dispossess the abbey was unfulfilled, having been overtaken by events, and urged both Kennedy and her son to pursue the matter. And so, when Chancellor William Crichton, leader of one of the anti-Douglas factions, fell from favour, Kennedy submitted to being made chancellor.

To general surprise among those who knew of his vaulting ambition, Kennedy resigned from this office after a matter of weeks. He protested that his episcopal duties were onerous and should come first – this was partly true, as he had been drawn more deeply into the Douglas-Crichton-Livingston warfare than was prudent. What he did not admit to a soul was that fiscal responsibility for Scotland was a poisoned chalice indeed, so dire was the economic position, and taking it on invited certain failure. He refused to be even a heroic failure, but he did feel obliged to do anything in his power to restore the economic health of the realm.

He delved in his files for the licence given him by the Earl of Douglas some years before to make Father Graham the legitimate master of Soltre. He scrutinised it carefully. The name, signature and date could, with the help of a competent scribe, be changed without trace. Who could he engage to become master of Soltre? He would need to lay his plans considerably more subtly and carefully than his predecessor had done. He thought of all that Thomas Lauder had told him about the canons, their virtue and good works, and all that the Earl of Douglas had said about the worshipful attitude of the community. Soltre could not be dispossessed without a mighty upsurge of wrath, protest, passion and violence; perhaps even local war.

Unless… unless, what was being charged against them was so dreadful that the very thought of it struck terror into all hearts. Some circumstance following which the lands could be confiscated and the church removed, all under a terrible slur of unnameable disgrace. And the whole matter hushed up. Expunged from the record. Though perhaps the centre of benevolence, the hospital, might be allowed to continue, mused the bishop.

He thought of this young medicus, who could well be a freethinker, a non-conformist. He remembered Thomas Lauder's mention of services for women. There was scope there for heretical accusation. On the flimsiest evidence, his inner conscience whispered, but he drowned that thought. Where women were concerned there was also the possibility of witchcraft. His own reputation must not be besmirched, whatever happened. He would stand above it all, a figure of authority who would condemn, punish and purify. To do that, he would need a factotum to get down and dirty. Who but Thomas Lauder? He would do anything for the promise of a bishopric.

Thomas was summoned from Aberdeen, where he had settled into the work of the cathedral chapter. Kennedy explained that he was tasked with the retrieval of the Soltre property and needed help. Thomas must be totally discreet, but if successful, he would be next in line for whatever bishopric became available. 'We may need to resort to unconventional methods,' said Kennedy. 'And my name must be kept out of it. If there is any blame or accusation, it will fall at your door. But I shall protect you – as long as we get results.

'First, we need a new magister. Here are his qualifications: he must be Augustinian, have been a member of the order for ten years and be of sound reputation. He must be totally acceptable to the Soltre community, but at the same time, it would be preferable that they do not know him. He may need to disappear after the denouement. He must be prepared to spy and report – that is, he must be our man. He will have a price and we shall pay it.'

Thomas laughed hollowly. 'My lord, it sounds like you need a low-life, an actor, a reformed offender.' Kennedy looked at him, his hopes and esteem rising. 'Yes, Thomas, all those might be considered. I agree, the ready-made article won't be available. This is your first task: to find a candidate for magister. And once we have him, you must find me a competent but discreet clerk to doctor this document so that it looks genuine.' He lifted the charter prepared by Douglas for Father Graham. 'We shall find ways of ensuring the clerk's silence.'

Thomas looked quite animated at the task presented to him. 'My lord, may I speak? The Soltre brothers will be deeply suspicious of an imposed magister after their experience with me. He will have to be as near the genuine article as possible. They are so guileless, they can see straight through duplicity and cant. What exactly will you ask of the magister?'

'He must find some pretext of errant or heretical behaviour of sufficient egregiousness that it forms grounds for confiscating the lands and holdings. And if he does not find it, he must engineer it.'

Thomas sat back, deep in thought. 'If heresy is the key, why not engage one of the pope's commissioned officers who are expert and zealous in sniffing it out? I recall meeting some of them at the Council of Basel a few years ago.'

Kennedy slapped his hand on the table in excitement. 'Good gracious, Thomas, you may have struck gold! That is an idea with much potential in it. I have met some of these men too, at the Council of Florence. They are zealots all, and have great bearing, authority and presence. We should need to manipulate the identity somewhat. Inspirational, my good man!'

Thomas had never in his life received such enthusiastic praise. Kennedy's thoughts were galloping ahead. 'It will be better, at least at first, to keep this matter unknown to Pope Eugene himself. However, once accusations of heresy are substantiated, he is bound to support us. He has been rigorously active against heresy. Now, I remember one man in particular who would answer our needs. What was his name? I have files of documents containing details of the Council of Florence deliberations and the people who attended.' Kennedy was now talking to himself as much as Thomas. He called his secretary in and gave him instructions.

In next to no time, Kennedy had unearthed the name of the man he had in mind: Dominic Bruce. He had been a Dominican monk, an order that was sufficiently close to that of Augustine for the purpose. He had been a striking presence at the council: a large man with noble mien, a slick tongue and compelling eyes – every inch a preacher. Kennedy was impressed at the time and had had some conversation with him. Now he remembered some of his history: the surname was that of his mother, a Scottish lady of high birth; his father was reputed to be a member of the French royal family. This irregular origin followed a pattern that was common enough among high-ranking churchmen.

The papers in the file recorded that Bruce's home monastery was Notre-Dame-de-Prouille in the Languedoc region of France; an area that had fostered some ruthless heretic hunting in a past era. How appropriate, thought Kennedy. But was entirely possible that Bruce would be elsewhere at present – in Rome perhaps, where the pope now resided, or travelling on his duties.

Kennedy knew that once he had put his hand to this particular plough, there would be no going back. These heretic investigations took on a life of their own. Needing some time to reflect in solitude and quiet, he took himself off to a forested area just north of St Andrews, overlooking the coast, where the wind usually whipped off the North Sea. A contingent of his guardsmen came and waited at the entrance of the forest, and he knew that one of them would discreetly dog his footsteps. But it was as near solitude as he could get.

He strode along the clifftops, his garments flapping, enjoying the wildness of the surging waves, the winds rushing through the tree canopy. Kennedy had recently experienced a great boost to his belief in his own godliness. In recent disputes with the nobles, he had opposed the Earl of Crawford, who retaliated with a raiding army over Kennedy's own estates in Fife, dealing out destruction and death. Armed with his full episcopal paraphernalia, Kennedy had ceremonially and repeatedly cursed Crawford; and exactly a year after the first anathema, Crawford was killed in battle. Such was the fear of the bishop's powers that no one dared to bury the body until his sanction was given.

So Kennedy had implicit faith in his own judgement as he examined his conscience. Did he approve of this forcible removal of Soltre's lands and goods under a trumped-up charge? The land and riches had all been gifted, as Douglas had indicated, so that Masses could ensure eternity for the souls of the wealthy and powerful. This was a form of simony, in his opinion – sacred privileges were being bought and churchmen were being enriched from the transaction. He wondered how dutifully those Masses were said. He thought it probable that the families were not getting their money's worth, that there would exist some catch-all form of words to cover members of the great families, going back in time.

This worldly wealth was improperly earned, and should therefore belong to the state, his conscience affirmed. The practice, once exposed, could be used to good effect to deprive other rich monasteries and abbeys of their land. However, he did not know how his inquisitor, Dominic Bruce, would react to that.

Next, he turned his mind to the question of the women's services at Soltre. These needed to be examined. If they should be found to include anything related to childbearing, condemnation would be immediate and undisputed. Men of the Church were expressly forbidden to meddle in this area. The Church's view was that breeding women should submit to whatever God required of them, and if that was suffering and death, so be it. There was a not dissimilar attitude to sickness in general, considered to be the result of sin and error. He knew that his late colleague Henry Wardlaw had taken this view, which was central to medical teaching at St Andrews. However, this was less strictly enforced than the women's issue because eminent men of Church and state fell ill, of course, and the relationship between sin and disease in them was not always apparent as it usually was with the peasantry. He knew that Soltre's reputation had initially been made in the treatment of battle wounds, and no one could deny that this was perfectly proper; otherwise, no man would fight when required.

Back at his palace, he dictated letters to Dominic Bruce, using flowery and complimentary language, but essentially requesting his help in uncovering heresy at Soltre Abbey on Fala Moor. He knew that the inquisitors of the Church usually carried out these investigations with a strong armed support, and he indicated that this could be necessary here; the abbey and the community had a great deal to lose. He had also heard Dominic boast of the various methods he had employed to entrap heretics; the end justified the means.

Kennedy thought that Thomas Lauder might be too timid to seek out Dominic Bruce, but found him full of enthusiasm for a task that did not require him to dissimulate. Kennedy perceived that there was an element of revenge for past humiliations in Thomas's willingness to help. Thomas was strictly instructed not to come back empty-handed; if Bruce was unavailable, he was to find another inquisitor. So the canon was despatched, well supported with a contingent suitable for a bishop's legate, knowing that the trials of travel would be mitigated by the comforts of welcoming monasterial and abbey houses on the way.

Chapter 43

1443

A few months after his departure, Thomas returned in triumph with Dominic Bruce and a large contingent of armed men, officials, scribes and chaplains. Bruce and Kennedy greeted each other like soulmates and settled down to talk business. Kennedy quickly realised that he need not have worried about trying to conceal the territorial motive – Bruce was accustomed to heresy trials being conducted for a variety of self-serving reasons for men in high places.

'As you will be paying for me and my attendants, I am sure you will be as keen as I am to complete the business quickly,' said Bruce. 'Maybe a month or two?'

This startled even the driven Kennedy. He explained about the subterfuge he felt was necessary, to present Bruce in the shape of a new magister. It would give him a chance to investigate from the inside, as well as preparing for the possible explosion that might take place among the peasantry.

'You realise, I am sure,' said Bruce, 'that the military troop with me is for my personal protection only. If a force is needed for other purposes, you will have to provide that.'

Kennedy, who had used the network of spies created by his predecessor to inform himself of conditions in the Borders, and had consulted Wardlaw's detailed files, explained the nature of the abbey and how the locals had made a saint of the medicus, Brother Fergus. Bruce's receptors were alerted; he wanted to know the origin of this myth.

'He does not lay claim to saintliness,' said Kennedy. 'He is not a mystic or a visionary. There is a story that he had been one of Douglas's band of soldiers but thought better of it. He was hunted down at Soltre, where he stood up to the militia and apparently brought down a thunderstorm that terrified them all. So he became a canon, then studied medicine and returned as medicus. He is a Highlander from the Western Isles and closely related to the MacDonalds.'

'So which particular Douglas did he defy?' asked Bruce.

'It was the heir apparent, Colin Douglas. He was killed soon after, fighting with his father, the fourth earl, at Verneuil. That was near the beginning of King James I's reign. And the local people had cause to be grateful, which added to Fergus's reputation.'

'Now that's interesting,' said Bruce. 'This Colin Douglas was the one who was condemned to death, but was reprieved and banished instead?'

'That is correct, as far as I understand.'

'Well, I have news, Bishop, that may surprise you. This Colin – who, by the by, was not in truth the heir, he was the natural but legitimated eldest son – was not killed in battle. He is alive and well. He has spent his life as a mercenary on the continent, lived a wild life in all respects, and is now at the head of my troop.'

'He is here with you?'

'Indeed he is. He has not told me of this contretemps with the medicus. He usually goes by a pseudonym in this country, since he is still under banishment. But I doubt if anyone significant remembers the charge. He calls himself Sir Roger de Vere – a Scottish knight with whom he had some quarrel, fought a duel many years ago and killed.'

'You could produce him at Soltre as proof that Fergus's trickery was false,' said Kennedy with a smirk. 'However, there will be need to handle the situation, and you are right, a strong militia to enforce our seizure of the lands will be engaged. Now, let us discuss your new persona. I suggest we keep it as near your own identity as we possibly can. That will make it seem more genuine. Once we have your new character I will write post-haste to Soltre and prepare the way for your arrival.'

They decided to keep Bruce's half-Scottish identity and find a suitable Scottish name to indicate membership of obscure aristocracy, the name illustrious but not too well known. The other parent would be a member of French royalty whose identity must be kept secret. They constructed his identity with relish, as actors and theatrical directors did, both taking notes.

Rather as an afterthought, Bruce asked, 'What are the particular items of heresy to be examined?'

'The basis for the donations of land and gifts; and the premises on which medical treatment is given. The services for women, in detail. And perchance we shall find evidence of sorcery,' said Kennedy.

Chapter 44

One morning at Soltre, three letters arrived. The first, addressed to Fergus, caused general rejoicing: Callum had found himself idle following the untimely death of Queen Joan and he was proposing to visit them all and perhaps even find some occupation at the abbey, if they would have him. Fortunately, there was need for an extra scribe, Richard said, with the ever-increasing holdings and activities, so Callum's skills would be welcomed. The second letter Fergus saw came from his family in Islay and he put it away to read in private.

The third letter, addressed to Prior Richard, came from Bishop Kennedy, and quickly caused gloom, anxiety and despondency. Couched in dictatorial language, it stated that Father Graham, acting magister, had never been licensed. Kennedy wished to set matters in order, and to that end, Father Graham must immediately demit office. Depending on his wishes, he could return to his previous abbey of Jedburgh or stay at Soltre as an ordinary canon; there would be no punishment for his lengthy holding of an unlicensed position. Bishop Kennedy was thoroughly conversant with the qualifications needed for the magister of an Augustinian establishment and he had appointed the best possible candidate, who had the licence under the Great Seal of Scotland and who also had the pope's approval. He would be with them in three days following the receipt of the letter.

His name was Stephen Fleming.

*

In the days following Fergus's love crisis, towards the end of the previous year, Peter had been quite as destabilised as Fergus himself; possibly more so, since he did not know how things stood. He could not sleep; he lost his appetite. Because Fergus did not offer any more confidences, Peter was sure that the love story was unfolding. The brothers met with affection, as always, but Peter would not ask questions, knowing that Fergus was too honest to lead a double life for any length of time. His friend was distracted and dreamy, withdrawn and buoyant by turns – as one might expect.

He was aware that the young man slipped secretly away from the abbey every few days, on foot, usually towards the evening. Since the medicus had many reasons to be abroad, probably no one but himself observed anything unusual. With life in the abbey free from political disturbance, Peter had hoped that matters would resolve without any scandal or exposure erupting first. But now, with the new magister arriving within days, Peter felt very uneasy indeed.

Fergus and Peter met as usual in the cloister, and discussed the impending arrival.

'I knew there was something going on, Peter. Not just nebulous feelings of fate! There have been strange visitors to the area with no proper business, making enquiries and nosing about. These are not just my own observations; the local folk have mentioned it too.'

'It bodes no good, Fergus. But you know we have weathered many storms before. We must continue to do what we do best – just get on with our work.'

'No one has ever heard of this Stephen Fleming. The bishop's letter told us very little. I suspect he will be a very different man from Thomas Lauder, and we shall not be able to demote or ignore him!'

'Yet again, poor Father Graham is being treated shamefully, and he has been such a good friend to us,' said Peter. 'That bit in the letter about him "not being punished" made me angry! Very gracious of the bishop, I'm sure.'

'I do believe Graham has been looking forward to retirement, maybe at one of the daughter houses of Jedburgh,' said Fergus.

His greatest concern however was for Annie, knowing that he would be more restricted in his movements under a new Magister; but also accepting that he had decisions to make and to act upon. Peter was right. Leading a double life sat ill with him. He soon found time to slip away, going on horseback as Annie was with Mary at Lauder.

He walked out with Annie into the woods, holding hands and not needing to hide their love in this secluded place. Even after many months of adoration and snatched hours spent gazing into each others' eyes they were still intoxicated with each other.

After the first joys of meeting, he told her of the new developments at Soltre, and how that increased the urgency of divesting himself of his current duties. He had received good news that morning in a letter from his family in Islay that there was a physician's post waiting for him there. He would take Annie with him to where a new life beckoned. 'Oh let's go now!' she exclaimed in delight. 'We'll just ride off into the sunset together. Every time we part, Fergus, I'm afraid I'll never see you again. Life can be so uncertain. Why do we need to wait?'

Fergus knew he could, if he chose, leave office and make his departure from Soltre with no formalities. He was not a priest, and canons were allowed to leave the order at will. His loyalty to Soltre caused him some restraint, however, and his strong wish to see Callum again. Yet he shared Annie's anxiety.

'Beloved Annie, I would go through all possible trials and tribulations to be with you. I promise you, we shall be on our way inside a month!'

*

The community at Soltre were not left speculating for long about the new magister because, right on the appointed day, Father Stephen Fleming arrived in state with his retinue. He made a hustle and bustle, talking to all in a friendly but self-confident way. The canons all rushed to greet him in the garth, observing a large man in middle life, clad in Augustinian garb, rather florid and overweight. He had just one armed guard and three attendants, all well mounted. And there was another figure with him.

'Behold!' said Father Stephen, making a sweeping gesture with his arm. 'Like the Magi, I come bearing gifts. See whom I have brought with me.' Fergus had already recognised Callum, and the greetings they all showered on him almost left Father Stephen neglected. But he took it in good part. Amid all the ceremonies of greeting and introducing, taking care of baggage and horses and escorting into the residence, Stephen kept up a merry stream of banter and boisterous laughter.

He was asked if he wished to dine as they ordinarily did, on humble fare, or if he wished to make it a celebratory meal. This had been discussed; it was rather a delicate issue, as the brothers wanted to make the right impression. He looked around as if gauging their wishes, then said, 'You will want to greet your friend Callum in style, so I suggest a feast tonight. Then we shall go back to parsimonious habits tomorrow!'

So the office-holders, with Father Stephen and Callum, ate together in the residence, while the same good fare was served to all the rest of the company in the refectory. During the meal, Father Stephen dominated the talk, giving them his life story as if establishing his credentials. Although his diction was good, he had an unmistakable French accent. He was astoundingly frank about his parentage; his mother was a noble Scottish lady who had had a dalliance with a member of the French royal family, whose identity he was forbidden to reveal. He had been brought up to wealth and luxury. A fall from his horse when out hunting had led to a near-death experience, after which he had had a revelation, a calling. He had taken holy orders and become an Augustinian at a house in Toulouse, from where he had done preaching and pastoral work, also being nominated as a delegate to various ecumenical Councils. Lately he had taken on the role of deputy to the abbot at Toulouse, who had heard of Bishop Kennedy's need for a magister for Soltre, and since he, Stephen, was half Scottish, he seemed a happy choice. 'It takes at least half a Scot to thole these wild climes,' he said.

Fergus wanted to talk to Callum, but it was difficult to find a private moment. He picked up that Callum had fallen in with the father's company in Edinburgh. 'Was he like this all the way?' asked Fergus. 'You must be exhausted!'

'No, he was quiet and brooding,' said Callum. 'Quite different. Perhaps he is nervous.'

But Father Stephen was very much in charge, thought Fergus. He was paving the way for something. He wanted to shape events to his own liking, and he was sugaring the pill with all the bonhomie. Perhaps he was getting them to relax, reveal an error or two so that he could pounce and assert authority. Fergus was wearied with the incessant flow of rhetoric and did not like him one bit.

After the meal, the table was cleared and Stephen sat on, contemplating. He looked round at each canon sitting in silence. Then, starting at his left, he repeated the name of each person and his official role. They were used to memorising things by rote, but this was impressive; he had hardly seemed to take notice during introductions and had held the floor with talk ever since.

When the round was complete, he returned his gaze to Fergus. 'My friend, medicus, Brother Fergus MacBeath. You and I have a similar story in regard to our parentage. I understand that your mother is a member of a revered medical family in Islay. Your father is almost royal – brother to Lord Alexander MacDonald. We have much in common, you and I. I look forward to a productive friendship.'

Fergus was nonplussed. How did this man know so much about his background? He had certainly prepared himself very thoroughly.

'Now,' said Stephen, 'here's how we shall proceed, my friends and brothers. Tomorrow I wish you all to go about your normal routine – please take no notice of me! I come not to interfere, but to fit in seamlessly with your ways. Keep to your services, your hours of working, your chapter meeting, your meals and hours of rest. I shall not take the lead in any activity until I am conversant with the daily round. I shall hover and wander at will, asking a question here, making a query there. Maybe some of your ways will be very mysterious to me. I am not at all familiar with medical practice. I have no experience there – except from when I was injured, of course. Therefore, I shall familiarise myself with other aspects first, because the infirmary and your clinics and physic will require much harder work on my part. I fear you will find me sadly ignorant.' He smiled self-deprecatingly and they dutifully laughed.

'But my friends and brothers, I am very aware of the reputation of your hospital here; your fame is international. And so I am honoured to be your father and will serve you to the best of my ability. Those healing skills, of which you have reason to be proud, were honed at a time of bitter and incessant warfare. They are now adapting to a different world, a more connected world, where we should resolve disputes by other means than battles.'

There was more nebulous talk, a kind of stream-of-consciousness flow without obvious meaning, during which they began to wonder if he was drifting into trance. Fergus observed him closely, feeling that this was put on and that in reality Stephen was as alert as anyone. At last he dismissed them with a benign blessing.

*

In the pharmacy of the infirmary, Peter, Fergus and Callum gathered to discuss the new arrival. Callum had been talking with Andrew Sinclair, the senior magister's clerk, whom he was going to assist.

'Andrew has been given the licence for Father Stephen,' he said. 'And he showed it to me. He says it has been altered. There have been changes made to the date, the signature and the name. The seal is quite obviously old – probably a few years.'

Peter and Fergus looked at each other. 'Does that invalidate it?' asked Peter.

'It adds to the feeling that there is something going on that does not bode well for us,' said Fergus. 'Why did we have to import someone from France? And by the way, the name Toulouse sends a shiver down my spine. It suggests this man has had to do with heretic hunters.' He turned to Peter. 'Do you remember Father John's warnings? When we thought he was wandering in his mind? He foresaw the contagion of paranoia.'

'I think this man is an impostor,' said Callum. 'He's not what he seems. He's like a cat that pretends to be soft and friendly – but wait for the pounce!'

'I agree,' said Fergus. 'I found it very scary that he knew so much about me.'

Chapter 45

True to his word, Father Stephen was not obtrusive, but they were aware of his presence. He attended all of the services and prayed loudly and ostentatiously. He appeared in the refectory at their midday meal, and as all hastened to rise, waved them back to their seats and asked for the reading to continue. He sat quietly on a stool near the reader. After taking in the general picture for a couple of days, he began going round the various departments – the stables, gardens, kitchens, cellars, storerooms and the guest house. The church, dormitory, chapter house and parlour he scrutinised with great care, first on his own, then with Brother Richard. They were all reminded, of course, of Bishop Wardlaw's inspection with his 'sniffer dogs', and even though Father Stephen was mildness itself, this process felt sinister. One thing he showed no interest in was the locked file of documents in the residence.

After ten days or so, they were all beginning to relax – except Fergus. It was his turn to be inspected. Again, Stephen merely stood by and watched, yet his presence was strongly felt. In the garth at the morning clinic, the patients were curious, staring and asking who he was. Fleming showed more interest in the contents of the pharmacy, requiring a detailed explanation of the plants they used and stored, how they were prepared and what they were used for. The concoctions used for pain relief – black henbane, opium poppy and hemlock – particularly caught his attention. He seemed genuinely interested and even asked if he could try a small dose.

Fergus caught Peter's eye. 'No, father, I regret to say – unless of course you have some medical need for it. The dose is tapered according to the condition and the amount for good health equals zero!' Stephen made an accepting gesture and Fergus hastened to change the subject. 'Here, father, are items used for centuries – nettles, lavender and bitter vetch. Nettles were used by armies on the march, to whip tired feet and legs to alleviate aches. Lavender they used on sword wounds to prevent gangrene setting in. And the vetch tubers are grown in one of our fields; we chew them in winter if the bad weather closes in and we have to go on short supplies. They prevent hunger pangs.'

The fields and their medical crops were visited; the Lindean Gorge occupied an entire morning. Stephen had discovered the tiny graves in the cemetery on his walkabouts. He wanted to know in detail how infants came to be buried there. Fergus repeated the story about his half-sister, which was accepted. The newer grave, however, needed more explanation. Stephen listened intently to his description of the women's network in the countryside and of how the midwives trained others, and, on rare occasions, had to perform an induced delivery to save the mother's life. This little grave was filled after one such occasion.

'What is your role in this network, brother?'

'I provide overarching protection. Without that, the local priests would interfere, thinking there is sorcery going on. I have brought certain expertise from my home, Islay, mostly in the form of herbs and how to use them. However, the ladies do the work themselves. Soltre does provide much produce, which is directed to expectant and nursing mothers and infants. It is a community welfare system.'

Stephen mused over this. 'And have you been involved directly with any of these induced deliveries, as you call them?'

'Yes. I was involved with my half-sister. Although it was my own mother, it was an emergency and I was needed to assist.'

Fergus was well aware he was in dangerous waters. But there was no point in dissembling. He did his best to keep Jan's name out of the discussion, but Stephen's probing got to her at last.

'I should like to visit this lady,' said Stephen, to Fergus's dismay.

Fergus managed to send a message to Jan to give her warning of their visit. He hoped with all his heart that Annie would not be there, as he knew his feelings for her would be transparent. As he and Stephen rode to the cottage, he was required to give a detailed explanation of how the welfare system worked.

'The farmers don't object to distributing their goods in this way?'

'No, why should they? They are our tenants and they have wives, daughters and grandchildren who benefit in their turn.'

Fergus did not know how he got through the meeting between Jan and Stephen, but she helped by being her usual charming, down-to-earth self. Stephen was again deeply taken with the pharmaceuticals, mainly the dried plants hanging on the walls, including those for bringing on labour and for contraception. Fergus had hoped those would not be mentioned, but Stephen was an unparalleled expert in extracting information. He admitted he was impressed by the, admittedly limited, system for patient records.

Relieved when at last a move was made to leave, Fergus murmured in Jan's ear, 'Is Annie with Mary?' Jan nodded. Stephen was outside and just out of earshot. Almost inaudibly, she added, 'Fergus, she is with child!'

His heart thudded and he was unable to speak, such was his delight. They locked eyes and each knew the other's euphoria. 'I'll come and see you both as soon as I can. It's not easy just now – give her my love!' He knew he had to hold himself together and pretend to be normal as they mounted up and made their farewells, Stephen giving Jan a gallant bow.

Suddenly the infirmary was busy. The rhythm of overwhelming demands alternating with periods of quiet was one to which they were all accustomed. Fergus welcomed the stressed period as it stopped his own mood swings between delirious delight and terrible anxiety, and helped disguise them too.

They had admitted a young man to the hospital who had been gored by a bull. Besides the injury itself there had been serious loss of blood and his life hung in the balance. An older man, a farmer, had a swollen foot after an injury with a steel-tipped plough. They knew they would certainly have to amputate, but timing was everything, and while they did not want gangrene to set in, they wished to wait for the swelling to settle so they could remove the leg below the knee. There were two other men causing concern: one a case of near drowning; the other with convulsions, over which they were trying to gain some measure of control with herbal mixtures. There were others too, not yet ready to be sent back to work.

Stephen seemed to have gone to ground, staying in the residence and seldom appearing even at services. But there was activity, his own clerks speeding off with messages and returning with others. The watchmen at the gate reported to the brothers that the timings of these messages suggested trips as far as Edinburgh and back. Callum told Fergus that Stephen only communicated with his own clerks and that Andrew and he had been excluded.

Peter and Fergus planned to operate on the farmer the following day. Preparations went ahead, with adequate supplies of potent painkillers being laid ready. Speed would be essential in the operation in order to minimise the pain that not even opium could completely prevent, and James and Thomas honed the surgical knives to razor-sharpness. They were careful to do this well out of sight and hearing.

That evening brought unwelcome activity when a group of soldiers appeared at the gate. Father Stephen gave instructions that they were to be allowed in, with their weapons, and to be provided with accommodation. They were admitted to the guest house and all went quiet. Now all the company of Soltre was alarmed. No such thing would have happened in the past without everybody being aware of the reason for it. Callum came to find Fergus in the infirmary, near to the hour at which the abbey retired.

'I've just seen a ghost,' he said, looking pale and shaken. 'Come with me.' They went out into the garth, where nothing stirred in the dark, clear night. Their eyes adjusted in the starlight. Then they heard the sound of the residence door opening and Callum put his hand on Fergus's arm. Fergus flipped up his hood and the two stood motionless in the shadows, covertly watching the soldierly figure stride across to the guest house, spurs and arms clanking.

It was unmistakably Colin Douglas.

Chapter 46

'That was no ghost,' said Fergus grimly. 'That was the real, indestructible Devil himself.'

'I thought he was killed in battle, after he was banished,' said Callum looking bewildered.

'Our new master needs to tell us what is going on,' said Fergus. 'It's late, but I'm going to ask him. Come with me.' They moved across to the residence, where they found the door locked.

'This never happened in the good father's day,' said Fergus as he hammered on the door. It was opened a small crack by one of Father Stephen's own clerks.

'Father Stephen has retired,' he said.

Fergus said testily, 'We need to know what is happening. Why all the soldiers, armed to the teeth and staying in the guest house? We are accustomed to being fully conversant with all that goes on here. No, don't close the door.' He stuck his foot across the threshold. 'I insist that you go and ask Father Stephen.'

The clerk said, 'I'll go and ask. But I'm locking the door while I go.'

They waited some minutes before he returned and said, 'Father Stephen will see you tomorrow after breakfast, Brother Fergus.' He slammed the door before there was any argument.

'I shan't be here after breakfast,' Fergus said to the closed door. 'We're starting the amputation at first light. Callum, let's go talk to the watch and find out if there are soldiers around in the countryside.'

At the gate they spoke to the guards, who said no military movements had been reported other than the contingent lodged at the abbey.

'Why do I not feel reassured, Callum? Listen, my dear friend, can I ask you to do something for me? I am worried for Mistress Jan and her daughter, Annie, if there are military men about. Would you, at first light, ride out and keep her company? In fact, you should escort them to Lady Mary's home in Lauder. Though hopefully Annie is there already. I'll get one of the stable lads to go with you and show the way. It's not far. Don't return until you are sure things are settled out there.'

Callum was looking thoughtfully at Fergus, in a way that he knew so well. 'This Mistress Jan, she is very dear to you, Fergus?'

'Yes, though not in the way you mean. But her daughter is. And her grandchild will be.'

Callum put his arm around Fergus's shoulders and squeezed. 'This does not surprise me, friend. I shall do as you ask, with pleasure. But you must do something for me. I am not happy to leave you where that foul fiend is dwelling. I shall leave you my pilgrim's staff and you must promise me to keep it by you all the time – *all the time*! It has protected me in many a tight situation and will do the same for you. I would never lend it to any other than you.'

Fergus's sense of foreboding propelled him to Peter's side. The infirmarer was talking to the man being prepared for amputation and arranging his pre-operative medicine. As soon as they could, the two brothers walked out into the cloister, where Fergus shared the grim news about Colin Douglas.

'Peter, I haven't talked to you about my personal affairs, and you have been so tactful in not pressing me. But now I must tell you all. It's by way of an informal confession, I suppose. Though I am not sorry and shan't do penance! I feel that trouble is here, maybe dire trouble, for all of us. I have a bad feeling... But if we do all come through whatever fate has waiting for us, I am going to quit Soltre. I cannot go on pretending to be a canon. I shall take Annie, and her coming child, and we shall return to Islay where I can find employment as a secular doctor and be a family man. Falling in love was my moment of revelation, Peter. My road to Damascus, my transfiguration. To love with such intensity, Peter, it feels so good, the very best, nothing else comes close. That is what it means to live.'

Peter could only nod and press Fergus's two hands in his, bowing his head to hide the tears. He knew exactly what his friend meant.

Fergus stood up. 'But I have a bad feeling. We should have left earlier...'

Chapter 47

1443

The following morning at first light, Callum and his attendant were dispatched southwards on the Lauder road. The watch reported that there were more military men arriving, less than an hour's ride away and coming from the north, probably Edinburgh, so Fergus bade Callum to make all haste. He and Peter repaired to the infirmary, where, with the daylight giving better vision, they would do their best for the farmer with the injured foot.

Even as they worked, operating in a room adjacent to the infirmary, absorbed, concentrating and moving at speed, the sounds coming from the garth were distracting; sounds indicating the arrival of mounted and armed reinforcements. At completion, the patient's condition was poor. Fergus and Peter both knew that he would not survive. Fergus washed his hands and put on a clean tunic feeling depressed as he walked over to the residence. In the garth a number of horses were tethered, suggesting that the stables were struggling to cope with the influx. Then Fergus remembered Callum's staff. He was on the point of going on, but just in time remembered his solemn promise. He returned to where he had left it, just inside the door of the infirmary.

He was admitted to the residence, carrying the staff, and found Father Stephen in the parlour.

'Well, Brother Fergus MacBeath! You don't follow the rule of obedience to the letter, I note.'

'Father, it has always been the principle here at Soltre that our first duty is to the sick. We needed to perform the amputation at first light.'

'Successful?'

'The operation, yes; but I doubt we have saved his life.' There was a pause as both men eyed each other sternly. They stood at opposite ends of the room.

'It is time to stop play-acting, brother. I am not Father Stephen Fleming, I am Canon Dominic Bruce, one of His Holiness's inquisitors. My story as you heard it was not too far from the truth, but I am a Dominican from Notre-Dame-de-Prouille in Languedoc, not an Augustinian. My purpose here was to hunt out suspected heresy, and I now charge you, Fergus MacBeath, with multiple charges of heresy. It is my duty to detail these and to persuade you to recant. Nevertheless, there are penalties and these will be exacted whether or not you confess.'

Fergus did not flinch, drop his gaze or change his expression. 'And what are these penalties?'

'Confiscation of property.'

'Being an Augustinian, I have no property,' said Fergus, although he knew what was coming.

'The property that will be confiscated consists of all the lands, holdings and portable wealth of Soltre Abbey. This will be transferred to the Crown, with appropriate portions to the Church in Scotland. Your Church of the Holy Trinity will be closed down and transferred elsewhere.'

'These are heavy penalties indeed, and will adversely affect many others besides myself.'

Dominic made an expansive gesture that might have been construed as apologetic. 'You are a man who knows the world, brother. You are no doubt as aware as I am that heresy accusations are motivated by many factors far removed from the sacred. You know that there has been a strong feeling among the leaders of Church and state that Soltre is grossly over-endowed. And there should be thought given to how Soltre has repaid those endowments. The agreements in most cases involved Masses to be said in perpetuity for certain souls. Now, I have been present at all the ceremonies in the church here, and such prayers and Masses are certainly said, but not in such regularity or individuality as the original donor anticipated. There is a tokenism and a ritualistic approach that is scarcely what the donors had in mind. One would certainly feel they are not getting what they paid for. Soltre is cheating them! Do you not agree?'

'If prayers for the dead itemised everyone for whom the land was given, then all the priests here would do nothing else!' said Fergus. 'But I agree that it is a false transaction. In my view, our God the father does not look more favourably on a Douglas or a Kerr simply because of endowments, whether or not Masses are said. I doubt whether heaven is full of the souls of the rich.'

'Should you not then have voiced your views and shown yourself more ready to give up these lands?'

'I suspect my heresy accusations are nothing to do with the land, canon. You know as well as I do that the Crown has been trying to find a way to grab our holdings for years past. This is a travesty of justice. Tell me what the accusations against *me* are, if you please. And if the rest of the people at Soltre will be exonerated.'

For the first time, Fergus felt a stab of fear in his belly. Despite Dominic's mild and formal ways of speaking, this man was made of the hardest granite.

'Your medical work contravenes the Church's teaching in almost every way. Sickness is a consequence of sin and bad living and should be corrected accordingly.'

'What of this farmer with his injured foot? Should we have let him suffer the agonies of gangrene while we preached at his bedside?'

'You see, your error is to let your compassion run away with you. Suffering is our lot on earth. We should accept it and hold to the prospect of joy in eternity.'

'As I recall, the founder of Christianity was known for his compassion, for healing the sick and for forgiving sinners without extorting terrible penalties.'

'This is a naive interpretation of Christian teaching, brother. The Church has moved on from that. The concept of forgiveness has been used to tolerate egregious, wanton, indulgent straying from the true path. Forgiveness must be earned by suffering. The teaching of the true Church is ascetic, hard, demanding.' Dominic's eyes took on that staring, almost fanatical look that he had shown on that first evening. Fergus hastened to interrupt, trying to recall the canon from his incipient trance-like state.

'I believe Christ would look with favour on the work we do here for the sick and the poor. I admire the Muslim concept that where God has imposed a sickness he has also provided a remedy. It is up to us to find it.'

'You must hold that straying tongue of yours, which will lead you into worse heresies even while I try to reclaim you. Your use of plants and herbs will be viewed as suspect, as akin to the Devil's work, but your links with childbirth practice are what condemn you beyond recall. This is absolutely forbidden by the Church, without exemption. Those children's graves in the cemetery – *female* infants' graves...' Dominic was momentarily lost for words and he hastily made the sign of the cross.

'Canon Dominic, it is you who are misled. If we are not to follow the teaching of Christ, how can we call ourselves Christians? Are there better men who have followed on? If so, they should give their own name to their new brand of religion so that we can recognise it and eschew it. I have always been motivated by compassion and I shall not deny that, or my life's work. You may as well give up on your rhetoric and tell me what you plan to do with me.'

Dominic groaned theatrically at Fergus's words and tore violently at his clothing in biblical style. 'This grieves me sorely, brother. I would wish to save you. Bishop Kennedy did not wish to see you consigned to the flames. If he has any hand in your trial, he will try to save you from that fate.'

Fergus thought of all his friends and brothers at Soltre, and those in the community too. His thoughts settled on Jan, on his dearest Annie and the little one she carried. They were his family. Life was going to change for them all, catastrophically, seismically, and he could not help them. He wondered if he would make things worse or better by bargaining for clemency.

'Dominic, come down to earth for a moment and listen to me with an honest ear. You have admitted that this is about forces beyond our control wanting this land and wealth. There must be somebody held as scapegoat, to carry the supposed weight of responsibility; I shall not call it wrongdoing. I offer myself as that scapegoat. Do with me what you will, even if it is burning or worse. But let me beg of you not to punish anyone else. No one else – at Soltre or outside it.' He lost his cool demeanour and choked with emotion as he thought of all the people those last words included.

Dominic gave him an inscrutable look, then strode to the door and hollered, 'Guard!'

Dominic moved back to the furthest side of the room. In strode a soldier, his sword buckled to his side. It was Colin Douglas, who, also with a touch of the theatrical, took three steps into the middle of the room and bowed to the canon. For a moment, Fergus thought Colin had not seen him.

'Best of the morning to you, canon. There is good sport to be had here among these... *heretics*!' He spoke half mockingly, drawing his sword and holding it aloft. The canon looked aside and it was only then that Fergus realised the sword was stained with fresh blood.

Colin swivelled on his heels, and with mock surprise appeared to discover Fergus standing there. 'Why, here is my old friend and adversary, Fergus MacBeath! And, I do believe, armed with that pilgrim's staff from days of yore.' He put his head back and roared with laughter, a sound Fergus remembered so well.

'But no pilgrim to carry it, I fear. And I hear no thunder!' He cupped his hand to his ear, looking upwards with a sneer on his face.

'You are getting your just rewards, MacBeath! I have visited your light o' love this morning. I had her, of course. She's a bit long in the tooth, isn't she, Fergus? Still, a good enough lay. Oh, I regret I had to deal with the man there with her – your old friend, the pilgrim!' He lifted the sword again, indicating the blood stains.

Fergus instinctively let out a gargantuan roar, as if from the bowels of his Highland ancestry, levelled his staff and charged with lightning speed at Colin, aiming the head of the staff for his groin. Such was the momentum that Colin staggered backwards in agony, arms thrown up, releasing the sword. He fell on his back as Fergus swiftly kicked the sword out of reach, dropped the staff and whipped out a surgical knife that he had concealed on his person that morning. He plunged the knife into Colin's chest where he knew the heart to be. The newly sharpened knife slid in like butter, and, still in the intoxication of fury, he pulled it out and plunged it in repeatedly.

Fergus stood up as the body at his feet bubbled from the mouth, spewing blood and seeping gore at the chest, twitching and jerking, until at last it was still. All Fergus could hear then was the sound of Dominic vomiting violently in the corner.

Chapter 48

1455

Annie, wrapped in the story of those terrible events of twelve years previously, stared at Peter, open-mouthed and wide-eyed. 'He actually killed the man who raped my mother and killed Callum?' she asked. Peter nodded and Annie thought about this, pink-cheeked and wondering. 'I do wish mother had known that. I think she would have liked to know he did that.'

The Grey Friar, Peter – for it was he – had continued his journey with Annie and her son Euan for a further few days, relating Fergus's story to them each evening. On this night they had reached a small monastic house near the west coast that Peter knew was safe. They were warm and well fed and the story had continued apace.

Peter said, 'They came looking for you and Jan then – the inquisitor's men. They had wanted you both, but especially Jan, since Soltre fell. It is surprising it took them so long. Mary and David managed to keep you safely concealed and out of sight, and I believe it was Father Leonard who betrayed you at last.

'At the time of the seizure of Soltre there was enough to keep the military occupied, for the countryside was in ferment, as I am sure you remember. The king's troops were called in to suppress the revolt of the common folk. The priests in the village churches were told at sword point to preach that protesters and heretics would be consigned to the flames. At first, they tried to accuse Fergus of heresy, but this caused such uncontrollable fury among the people, who regarded him as a saint, that they had to change the message. The official line then said it was Stephen Fleming, the master, who was the cause of the wickedness and the downfall of Soltre. They were on safe ground there, since there was no such person as Stephen Fleming.'

'What became of Fergus?' asked Annie. 'We heard nothing. It was unbearable, not knowing. Mary said that even they could not make enquiries, for fear of being accused of being heretics.'

'He was put to death, Annie.'

Peter paused in sympathy as Annie'e eyes filled and tears rolled down her cheeks. Euan put his arm round her.

'We all hoped at first that maybe he had escaped and was still alive,' she said with streaming eyes. 'Perhaps the country folk had rescued him. But after Euan here was a year old, mother said she knew he was dead, because of a family myth that he would not live to see his child reach the age of one year. Mother believed that. It helped her, to be able to drop the uncertainty. I went on hoping all these years.'

'I do believe,' said Peter, 'that Bishop Kennedy did not mean Fergus to die on heretical charges. All he wanted was the land and property. And it was hardly a criminal act to dispose of Colin Douglas; it was time for his debts to be paid.'

'Continue the story, Peter, please. Tell us what you remember.'

Peter grimaced at the memories, but felt they should know it all.

'We all heard this terrible, hysterical screaming coming from the residence. That was Dominic, terrified for his own life. He could commit folk to death and watch them burn, but could not stand the sight of blood. Probably Colin knew this when he waved his bloody sword around. And by the way, Dominic had assumed Fergus and Jan were lovers and told Colin that, so the rape was done out of pure spite.

'By the time the rest of the guard arrived, Fergus had dropped his knife and was not threatening anyone. He was dragged off, tied up in chains and locked in a storeroom. The soldiers were very aggressive with us canons, they herded everyone into the church at sword point and locked us in. We were bewildered and fearful of what had become of Fergus. Brother Jonathan tried to get out by the night stair. He was intercepted and killed without ceremony.

'We could hear activity outside, chains clanking and horses being moved. We were desperate to get out and find out what was happening. The patients in the infirmary, many severely sick and in need of care, what was happening to them?

'So we rang the church bell. We hoped to alert the countryside and perhaps get some help. That brought soldiers to us quickly enough. There was more violent manhandling, and a soldier was left to keep us under submission. We got no food or water that day, and no questioning was tolerated. Our single guard was very twitchy, and we quickly learned not to give trouble. We could hear shouts and yells in the distance, outside the walls, as if a crowd was gathering. The atmosphere in the church quickly turned foul, as you can imagine. The noise from outside took on a new dimension; we heard sounds of uproar and fighting, clashing arms and screams of the wounded.

'When we were finally released, after nearly two days, the place looked like a military camp. These were now the king's men in charge. And outside the gates, where they had come upon the crowds of protesting folk, there had been a massacre, before the rest were put to flight. All our secular staff had gone. In the infirmary, some patients had died while others had escaped. There was no sign of Fergus or Dominic, or Dominic's soldiers.

'You can imagine how disorientated, distraught and bewildered we were. As people do, we set about finding the nearest useful thing to do, and that was burying bodies. We buried Colin Douglas too – outside Soltre's grounds. I found Callum's staff near Colin's body. We cleaned the church of our own filth.

'After some days, the bishop's acolytes came and began stripping Soltre's valuables, including those from the church. The pharmacy was stripped of all our stocks and preparations, which were thrown on a huge bonfire they built in the garth. They gathered us together, still treating us like criminals or serfs. The senior canons, the office bearers, were instructed on pain of dire penalties not to talk about events, and we were dispersed to various other houses, all at a distance. We were supposed to find our own way. Others were told they might stay if they chose. They told me to get moving fast, or I might be a target for heretical accusations too.

'They brought in various men, lordlings and agents, friends of those in high places, to take over the farms and the businesses belonging to Soltre. People were evicted from their cottages and livelihoods and there was terrible hardship. Village priests were instructed to preach about the wages of sin and to invoke an atmosphere of fear. They were told that informing on heresy in others would be rewarded.

'I was directed to a monastery in the north of England, so started walking south, not having any plans, sleeping rough and living off berries and nuts.

'Then one day I was accosted by a pair of soldiers, who thought they'd get a great reward for catching me. I had an idea I was near Galagate and suggested they take me there and hand me over to the King's Councillor. I pretended I was sick and weary of being on the run. So they did indeed take me to Galagate. Both Sir Donald and his wife were at home and Donald recognised me. He praised the soldiers and gave them a reward, then sent them on their way. He may have saved my life.

'They gave me news of you and Jan, which heartened me. They told me that David had rescued Callum's body and given him a decent burial. He had found Callum's scallop shell in a pouch among his clothes and put it in his mouth for the burial.

They helped me disguise myself as a Grey Friar, finding these garments and keeping me while I grew a full beard. Since then I have been a mendicant friar, living off charity in the main, but also using my medical skills where possible. In my disguise I retraced my steps back northwards, to try and hear what was happening, and it became part of my life's work to establish the story of Soltre as far as I could. Periodically I called back at Galagate to get news of you. I rejoiced when Euan was born, and for me, then, life regained some meaning. I did not come near you though; I feared ensnaring you in suspicions and accusations. The Church's obsession with heresy was growing and your mother was at risk, as events have shown.

'My chief wish was to know what became of Fergus. And no one knew. No one had any inkling. So finally I took myself to St Andrews. There was one person who knew, and that was Bishop Kennedy.'

Peter paused. 'Shall I continue, Annie? Can you bear it?'

She nodded, holding tight to Euan's hand.

'To my surprise, he agreed to see me as soon as I announced myself, treating me courteously even though I looked like a tramp. It soon became apparent that he was consumed by guilt at the mass violence, the slaughter of the protesting people, the wanton, mindless destruction of the hospital. He knew he had released devils that could not be recalled. And he was willing to tell me about Fergus.

'Dominic had been warned about the strength of local affection for Soltre, but he was still taken unawares by the protest. He wanted military back-up before he fled, fearing for his own skin. Although the plan had been to abduct and take Fergus for trial, probably in France, he feared the violence of the peasants. And he was terrified of Fergus. So he ordered that he should be killed by the sword right there, at Soltre. And it was done, in a hole-and-corner way, while he was helpless and chained to the wall.' Now Peter too was weeping. 'They wanted no one to know. Hide everything, cover it all up, deny it all. He was buried in the cemetery. The soldiers, having heard all the myths, made a thorough job of it, and concealed the grave so that it did not look new.'

Annie moved over and hugged Peter as they wept together. 'So he is buried at Soltre! Peter, I want to go and see his grave!'

'My darling Annie, that you must not do. Maybe, some day in the future, it will be safe.' Peter composed himself. 'My dearest children, let us finish this tale tonight. Kennedy had travelled to Soltre. He wanted to do penance and also see that Fergus was buried properly. Some day, he told me, the grave would be marked with due acknowledgement of his good deeds. But I fear Fergus will rest unknown, except to ourselves. The story has been thoroughly suppressed through fear and shame. Kennedy propagated the myth that Stephen Fleming was the rogue who caused the downfall, and in a way that is true. Stephen's name will be remembered in history, but Fergus's will not.

'Kennedy said a tiny community remained at Soltre still, living very poorly, hand to mouth. They can grow very little on that hillside except the old vetch tubers, the starvation diet. They rely on charity from people who have been grateful in the past. The glory days are gone. No medical work remains and few travellers stay over – only a few pilgrims who are as destitute as themselves. The church has been demolished.

'One person who did well out of the wreckage was Thomas Lauder. He achieved his life's ambition to be made a bishop, and now has the see of Dunkeld. He made a great show of being one of the first donors to the new Church of the Holy Trinity. That is, *our* Church of Soltre which has been re-established in Edinburgh. Kennedy spoke of him with ill-concealed contempt, but then recalled with anguish his own part in this tale of depredation. He feared the heresy hunt was gaining momentum, in spite of his own warnings of the terrible collateral damage that could follow. He warned me to be careful.'

Euan, who had absorbed all the talk, asked, 'Where are we heading for, Peter?'

'We are going to Islay, where your father came from. We are only a day or so from the coast, and one of the monks from among our hosts here is travelling there and will take us in his cart. Lady Catriona suggested Islay as a refuge to me long ago. She knew if we could get there we would be safe from the Church's accusers on the mainland. I waited too long, fearing to take you out of hiding. I hope your mother will forgive me.'

'She will, Peter. I feel her presence often, as we travel or sit talking. Sadly, I have never felt Fergus's presence like that. Maybe he will come now I know his story.'

'You have Fergus near you all the time, Annie. Here he is in Euan's form. Almost as if he was reincarnated!'

'Will you stay on Islay too, Peter?' asked Euan.

'No, I shall fulfil my own pilgrimage, back to Soltre and Fergus's grave, and lay down this staff beside him. It is Callum's staff.'

Annie said, 'I shall cover it with kisses for you to take to him. And one day, however far in the future, Euan and I shall visit him there.'

About The Author

Margaret Cook was born in South Africa, brought up in Somerset, and studied medicine at Edinburgh University where she met and later married fellow student, Robin Cook. While bringing up their two sons, she continued to work full-time in NHS hospitals, taking a consultant haematology post at St John's Hospital Livingston.

When Robin was UK Foreign Secretary, the couple famously split as a result of the press "outing" his affair with his secretary. Margaret wrote her memoir, "A Slight and Delicate Creature", and followed this with a study of the effect of power on personality, "Lords of Creation". She also combined a number of years of freelance journalism with her day job.

Her first novel, "A Bit on the Side", was published in 2014, and was her first self-published work. She lives in active retirement in Edinburgh, with her second husband and fellow author, Robin Howie.

Lightning Source UK Ltd.
Milton Keynes UK
UKOW01f1431200617
303763UK00001B/14/P